THE OFFICE OF THE DEAD

ALSO BY ANDREW TAYLOR

Caroline Minuscule
Waiting for the End of the World
Our Fathers' Lies
An Old School Tie
Freelance Death
The Second Midnight
Blacklist
Blood Relation
Toyshop
The Raven on the Water
The Sleeping Policeman
The Barred Window
Odd Man Out
An Air That Kills
The Mortal Sickness
The Lover of the Grave
The Suffocating Night
The Four Last Things
The Judgement of Strangers

THE OFFICE OF THE DEAD

Andrew Taylor

St. Martin's Minotaur
New York

THE OFFICE OF THE DEAD. Copyright © 2000 by Andrew Taylor. All rights reserved. Printed in the United States of America. No part of this book may be used or reproduced in any manner whatsoever without written permission except in the case of brief quotations embodied in critical articles or reviews. For information, address St. Martin's Press, 175 Fifth Avenue, New York, N.Y. 10010.

www.minotaurbooks.com

ISBN 0-312-20348-9

First published in Great Britain by Collins Crime, an imprint of HarperCollins*Publishers*

First U.S. Edition: August 2000

10 9 8 7 6 5 4 3 2 1

For Vivien, with love and thanks

AUTHOR'S NOTE

The Office of the Dead is the third novel in the Roth Trilogy, which deals layer by layer with the linked histories of the Appleyards and the Byfields. Each book may be read on its own as a self-contained story. The three novels are also designed to work together, though they may be read in any order.

The first novel, *The Four Last Things*, is set in London during the middle of the 1990s. The second, *The Judgement of Strangers*, is set in Roth, a remote suburb of London, in 1970.

PART I

The Door in the Wall

1

'I'm nobody,' Rosie said.

It was the first thing she said to me. I'd just pushed open the door in the wall and there she was. She wore red sandals and a cotton dress, cream-coloured with tiny blue flowers embroidered on the bodice, and there were blue ribbons in her blonde hair. The ribbons and flowers matched her eyes. She was very tidy, like the garden, like everything that was Janet's.

I knew she was Rosie because of the snapshots Janet had sent. But I asked her name because that's what you do when you meet a child, to break the ice. Names matter. Names are hard to forget.

'Nobody? I'm sure that's not right.' I put down the suitcase on the path and crouched to bring my head down to her level. 'I bet you're really somebody. Somebody in disguise.'

'I'm nobody.' Her face wasn't impatient, just firm. 'That's my name.'

'Nobody's called nobody.'

She folded her arms across her chest, making a cross of flesh and bone. 'I am.'

'Why?'

'Because nobody's perfect.'

She turned and hopped up the path. I straightened up and watched her. Rosie was playing hopscotch but without a stone and with an invisible pattern of her own making. Hop, both legs, hop, both legs. Instead of turning to face me, though, she carried on to the half-glazed door set in the wall of the house. The soles of her sandals slapped on the

3

flagstones like slow applause. Each time she landed, on one foot or two, the jolt ran through her body and sent ripples through her hair.

I felt the stab of envy, almost anger, sharp as John Treevor's knife. Nobody was beautiful. Oh yes, I thought, nobody's perfect. Nobody's the child I always wanted, the child Henry never gave me.

I'd been trying not to think about Henry for days, for weeks. For a moment his face was more vivid than Rosie and the house. I wished I could kill him. I wished I could roll up Henry and everything else that had ever happened to me into a small, dark, hard ball and throw it into the deepest, darkest corner of the Pacific Ocean.

Later, in one of those fragmentary but intense conversations we had when Janet was ill, I tried to explain this to David.

'Wendy, you can't hide away from the past,' he said. 'You can't pretend it isn't there, that it doesn't matter.'

'Why not?' I was a little drunk at the time and I spoke more loudly than I'd planned. 'If you ask me, there's something pathetic about people who live in the past. It's over and done with.'

'It's never that. Not until you are. It *is* you.'

'Don't lecture me, David.' I smiled sweetly at him and blew cigarette smoke into his face. 'I'm not one of your bloody students.'

But of course he was right. That was one thing that really irritated me about David, that so often he was right. He was such an arrogant bastard that you wanted him to be wrong. And in the end, when he was so terribly wrong, I couldn't even gloat. I just felt sorry for him. I suppose he wasn't very good at being right about himself.

2

When I was young, the people around me were proud of their pasts, and proud of the places where they lived.

My parents were born and bred in Bradford. Bradford was superior to all other towns in almost every possible way, from its town hall to its department stores, from its philanthropists to its rain. Similarly, my parents were quietly confident that Yorkshire, God's Own County, outshone all other counties. We lived in a tree-lined suburb at 93, Harewood Drive, in a semi-detached house with four bedrooms, a Tudor garage and a grandfather clock in the hall.

My father owned a jeweller's shop in York Street. The business had been established by his father, and he carried it on without enthusiasm. He had two interests in life and both of them were at home – his vegetable garden and my brothers.

Howard and Peter were twins, ten years older than me. They were always huge, semi-divine beings who took very little notice of me, and they always will be. I find it very hard to recall what they looked like.

'You must remember something about them,' Janet said in one of our heart-to-hearts at school.

'They played cricket. When I think about them, I always smell linseed oil.'

'Didn't they ever talk to you? Do things with you?'

'I remember Peter laughing at me because I thought Hitler was the name of the greengrocer's near the station. And one of them told me to shut up when I fell over on the path by the back door and started crying.'

5

Janet said wistfully, 'You make it sound as if you're better off without them.'

That's something I'll never know. When I was ten, they were both killed, Peter when his ship went down in the Atlantic, and Howard in North Africa. The news reached my parents in the same week. After that, in memory, the house was always dark as though the blinds were down, the curtains drawn. The big sitting room at the back of the house became a shrine to the dear departed. Everywhere you looked there were photographs of Peter and Howard. There were one or two of me as well but they were in the darkest corner of the room, standing on a bookcase containing books that nobody read and china that nobody used.

Even as a child, I noticed my father changed after their deaths. He shrank inside his skin. His stoop became more pronounced. He spent more and more time in the garden, digging furiously. I realized later that at this time he lost interest in the business. Before it had been his duty to nurse it along for Peter and Howard. Without them the shop's importance was reduced. He still went into town every day, still earned enough to pay the bills. But the shop no longer mattered to him. He no longer had any pride in it. I don't think he even had much pride in Bradford any more.

In my father's world girls weren't important. We were needed to bear sons and look after the house. We were also needed as other men's objects of desire so the men in question would buy us jewellery at the shop in York Street. We even had our uses as sales assistants and cleaners in the shop because my father could pay us less than he paid our male equivalents. But he hadn't any use for a daughter.

My mother was different. My birth was an accident, I think, perhaps the result of an uncharacteristically unguarded moment after a Christmas party. She was forty when I was born so she might have thought she was past it. But she wanted a daughter. The problem was, she didn't want the sort of daughter I was. She wanted a daughter like Janet.

My mother's daughter should have looked at knitting patterns with her and liked pretty clothes. Instead she had one who acquired rude words like cats acquire fleas and who wanted to build streams at the bottom of the garden.

It was a pity we had so little in common. She needed me, and I needed her, but the needs weren't compatible. The older I got, the more obvious this became to us both. And that's how I came to meet Janet.

I suspect my father wanted me out of the house because I was an unwelcome distraction. My mother wanted me to learn how to be a lady so we could talk together about dressmaking and menus, so that I would attract and marry a nice young man, so that I would present her with a second family of perfect grandchildren.

My mother cried when she said goodbye to me at the station. I can still see the tears glittering like snail trails through the powder on her cheeks and clogging the dry ravines of her wrinkles. She loved me, you see, and I loved her. But we never found out how to be comfortable with one another.

So off I went to boarding school. It was wartime, remember, and I'd never been away from my parents before, except for three months at the beginning of the war when everyone thought the Germans would bomb our cities to smithereens.

This was different. The train hissed and clanked through a darkened world for what seemed like weeks. I was nominally in the charge of an older girl, one of the monitors at Hillgard House, whose grandmother lived a few miles north of Bradford. She spent the entire journey flirting with a succession of soldiers. The first time she accepted one of their cigarettes, she bent down to me and said, 'If you tell a soul about this, I'll make you wish you'd never been born.'

It was January, and the cold and the darkness made everything worse. We changed trains four times. Each train seemed smaller and more crowded than its predecessor. At last the monitor went to the lavatory, and when she came back she'd washed the make-up off her face. She was a pink, shiny-faced schoolgirl now. We left the train at the next stop, a country station shrouded in the blackout and full of harsh sounds I did not understand. It was as if I'd stepped out of

7

the steamy, smoky carriage into the darkness of a world that hadn't been born.

Someone, a man, said, 'There's three more of you in the waiting room. Enough for a taxi now.'

The monitor seized her suitcase in one hand and me with the other and dragged me into the waiting room. That was where I first saw Janet Treevor. Sandwiched between two larger girls, she was crying quietly into a lace-edged handkerchief. As we came in, she looked up and for an instant our eyes met. She was the most beautiful person I'd ever seen.

'Is that a new bug too?' the monitor demanded.

One of the other girls nodded. 'Hasn't turned off the waterworks since we left London,' she said. 'But apart from the blubbing, she seems quite harmless.'

The monitor pushed me towards the bench. 'Go on, Wendy,' she said. 'You might as well sit by her.' She watched me as I walked across the room, dragging my suitcase after me. 'At least this one's not a bloody blubber.'

I have always loathed my name. 'Wendy' sums up everything my mother wanted and everything I'm not. My mother loved *Peter Pan*. When I was eight, it was that year's Christmas pantomime. I sat hugely embarrassed through the performance while my mother wept happy tears beside me, the salty water falling into the box of chocolates open on her lap. They say that James Barrie invented the name for the daughter of a friend. First he called her 'Friendy'. Then with gruesome inevitability this became 'Friendy-Wendy'. Finally it mutated into 'Wendy', and the dreadful old man left it as part of his legacy to posterity in general and me in particular. The only character I liked in his beastly story was Captain Hook.

'Wendy,' Janet whispered as we huddled together in the back of the taxi on the way to school, squashed into a corner by a girl mountain smelling of sweat and peppermints. 'Such a pretty name.'

'What's yours?'

'Janet. Janet Treevor.'

'I like Janet,' I said, not wanting to be outdone in politeness.

8

'I hate it. It's so plain.'

'Shame we can't swap.'

I felt her breath on my cheek, felt her body shaking. I couldn't hear anything, because of the noise the other girls were making and the sound of the engine. But I knew what Janet was doing. She was giggling.

So that's how it started, Janet and me. It was January, the Lent Term, and we were the only new children in our year. All the other new children had come in September and had already made friends. It was natural that Janet and I should have been thrown together. But I don't know why we became friends. Janet was no more like me than my mother was. But in her case – our case – the differences brought us together rather than drove us apart.

Hillgard House was a late-eighteenth-century house in the depths of the Herefordshire countryside. The nearest village was two miles away. The teaching was appalling, the food was often barely edible. When it rained heavily they put half a dozen buckets to catch the drips in the dormitories on the top floor where the servants' bedrooms had been, and you would go to sleep hearing the gentle *plop-plip-plop* as the water fell.

The headmistress was called Miss Esk, and she and her brother, the Captain, lived in the south wing of the house. There were carpets there, and fires, and sometimes when the windows were open you could hear the sound of music. The Esks had their own housekeeper who kept herself apart from and superior to the school's domestic staff. The Captain was rarely seen. We understood that he had suffered from a mysterious wound in the Great War and had never fully recovered. The senior girls used to speculate about the nature of this wound. When I was older, I gained considerable respect by suggesting he had been castrated.

We were always hungry at Hillgard House. It was wartime, as Miss Esk reminded us so often. This meant that we could not expect the luxuries of peace, though we could not help but notice that Miss Esk seemed to have most of them. I think now that the Esks made a fortune during the war. The school was considered to be in a relatively safe area, remote from the risks of both bombing raids and a possible invasion. Many of the girls' fathers were in the services. Few parents had the time and inclination to check the pastoral and educational standards of the school. They wanted their daughters to be safe, and so in a sense we were.

Janet and I never liked the place but we grew used to it. As far as I was concerned, it had three points in its favour. No one could have a more loyal friend than Janet. Because of the war, and because of the Esks' incompetence, we were left alone a great deal of the time. And finally there was the library.

It was a tall, thin room which overlooked a lank shrubbery at the northern end of the house. Shelves ran round all the walls. There was a marble fireplace, its grate concealed beneath a deep mound of soot. The shelves were only half full, but you never quite knew what you would find there. In that respect it was like the Cathedral Library in Rosington.

During the five years that we were there, Janet must have read, or at least looked at, every volume there. She read *Ivanhoe* and *The Origin of Species*. She picked her way through the collected works of Pope and bound copies of *Punch*. I had my education at second hand, through Janet.

In our final year, she found a copy of *Justine* by the Marquis de Sade – in French, bound in calf leather, the pages spotted with damp like an old man's hand – concealed in a large brown envelope behind the collected sermons of Bishop Berkeley. Janet read French easily – it was the sort of accomplishment you seemed to acquire almost by osmosis in her family – and we spent a week in the summer term picking our way through the book, which was boring but sometimes made us laugh.

In our first few terms, people used to laugh at us. Janet was small and delicate like one of those china figures in the glass-fronted cabinet in Miss Esk's sitting room. I was always clumsy. In those days I wore glasses, and my feet and hands seemed too large for me. Janet could wear the same blouse for days and it would seem white and crisp from beginning to end, from the moment she took it from her drawer to the moment she put it in the laundry basket. As for me, every time I picked up a cup of tea I seemed to spill half of it over me.

My mother thought Hillgard House would make me a lady. My father thought it would get me out of the way for most of the year. He was right and she was wrong. We didn't learn to be young ladies at Hillgard House – we learnt to be little savages in a jungle presided over by the Esks, remote predators.

3

I had never known a family like Janet's. Perhaps they didn't breed people like the Treevors in Bradford.

For a long time our friendship was something that belonged to school alone. Our lives at home were something separate. I know that I was ashamed of mine. I imagined Janet's family to be lordly, beautiful, refined. I knew they would be startlingly intelligent, just as Janet was. Her father was serving in the army, but before the war he had lectured about literature and written for newspapers. Janet's mother had a high-powered job in a government department. I never found out exactly what she did but it must have been something to do with translating – she was fluent in French, German and Russian and had a working knowledge of several other languages.

In the summer of 1944 the Treevors rented a cottage near Stratford for a fortnight. Janet asked if I would like to join them. My mother was very excited because I was mixing with 'nice' people.

I was almost ill with apprehension. In fact I needn't have worried. Mr and Mrs Treevor spent most of the holiday working in a bedroom which they appropriated as a study, or visiting friends in the area. John Treevor was a thin man with a large nose and a bulging forehead. At the time I assumed the bulge was needed to contain the extra brain cells. Occasionally he patted Janet on the head and once he asked me if I was enjoying myself but did not wait to hear my answer.

I remember Mrs Treevor better because she explained

the facts of life to us. Janet and I had watched a litter of kittens being born at the farm next door. Janet asked her mother whether humans ever had four at a time. This led to a concise lecture on sex, pregnancy and childbirth. Mrs Treevor talked to us as if we were students and the subject were mathematics. I dared not look at her face while she was talking, and I felt myself blushing.

Later, in the darkness of our shared bedroom, Janet said, 'Can you imagine how they . . . ?'

'No. I can't imagine mine, either.'

'It's *horrible*.'

'Do you think they did it with the light on?'

'They'd need to see what they were doing, wouldn't they?'

'Yes, but just think what they'd have looked like.'

A moment afterwards Mrs Treevor banged on the partition wall to stop us laughing so loudly.

After Christmas that year, Janet came to stay with me at Harewood Drive for a whole week. She and my mother liked each other on sight. She thought my father was sad and kind. She even liked my dead brothers. She would stare at the photographs of Howard and Peter, one by one, lingering especially at the ones of them looking heroic in their uniforms.

'They're so handsome,' she said, 'so beautiful.'

'And so dead,' I pointed out.

In those days, the possibility of death was on everyone's minds. At school, fathers and brothers died. Their sisters and daughters were sent to see matron and given cups of cocoa and scrambled eggs on toast. The deaths of Howard and Peter, even though they had happened before my arrival at Hillgard House, gave me something of a cachet because they had been twins and had died so close together.

To tell the truth, I was jealous when Janet admired my doomed brothers, but I was never jealous of the friendship between Janet and my mother. It was not something that excluded me. In a sense it got me off the hook. When Janet was staying with us, I didn't have to feel guilty.

During that first visit, my mother made Janet a dress, using precious pre-war material she'd been hoarding since 1939. I

13

remember the three of us in the little sewing room on the first floor. I was sitting on the floor reading a book. Every now and then I glanced up at them. I can still see my mother with pins in her mouth kneeling by Janet, and Janet stretching her arms above her head like a ballet dancer and revolving slowly. Their faces were rapt and solemn as though they were in church.

Janet and I shared dreams. In winter we sometimes slept together, huddled close to conserve every scrap of warmth. We pooled information about proscribed subjects, such as periods and male genitalia. We practised being in love. We took it in turns at being the man. We waltzed across the floor of the library, humming the Blue Danube. We exchanged lingering kisses with lips clamped shut, mimicking what we had observed in the cinema. We made up conversations.

'Has anyone ever told you what beautiful eyes you have?'

'You're very kind – but really you shouldn't say such things.'

'I've never felt like this with anyone else.'

'Nor have I. Isn't the moon lovely tonight?'

'Not as lovely as you.'

And so on. Nowadays people would suggest there was a lesbian component to our relationship. But there wasn't. We were playing at being grown up.

Somewhere in the background of our lives, the war dragged on and finally ended. I don't remember being frightened, only bored by it. I suppose peace came as a relief. In memory, though, everything at Hillgard House went on much as before. The school was its own dreary little world. Rationing continued, and if anything was worse than it had been during the war. One winter the snow and ice were so bad the school was cut off for days.

Our last term was the summer of 1948. We exchanged presents – a ring I had found in a dusty box on top of my mother's wardrobe, and a brooch Janet's godmother had given her as a christening present. We swore we would always be friends. A few days later, term ended. Everything changed.

14

Janet went to a crammer in London because the Treevors had finally woken up to the fact that Hillgard House was not an ideal academic preparation for university. I went home to Harewood Drive, helped my mother about the house and worked a few hours a week in my father's shop. There are times in my life when I have been more unhappy and more afraid than I was then, but I've never tasted such dreariness.

The only part I enjoyed was helping in the shop. At least I was doing something useful and met other people. Sometimes I dealt with customers but usually my father kept me in the back, working on the accounts or tidying the stock. I learned how to smoke in the yard behind the shop.

I got drunk for the first time at a tennis club dance. On the same evening a boy named Angus tried to seduce me in the groundsman's shed. It was the sort of seduction that's the next best thing to rape. I punched him and made his nose bleed. He dropped his hip flask, which had lured me into the shed with him. I ran back to the lights and the music. I saw him a little later. His upper lip was swollen and there was blood on his white shirtfront.

'Went out to the gents,' I heard him telling the club secretary. 'Managed to walk into the door.'

The club secretary laughed and glanced in my direction. I wondered if I was meant to hear, I wondered if the secretary knew, if all this had been planned.

It was a way of life that seemed to have no end. Janet wrote to me regularly and we saw each other once or twice a year. But the old intimacy was gone. She was at university now and had other friends and other interests.

'Why don't you go to university?' she asked as we were having tea at a café in the High on one of my visits to Oxford.

I shrugged and lit a cigarette. 'I don't want to. Anyway, my father wouldn't let me. He thinks it's unnatural for women to have an education.'

'Surely he'd let you do something?'

'Such as?'

'Well, what do you want to do?'

15

I watched myself blowing smoke out of my nostrils in the mirror behind Janet's head and hoped I looked sophisticated. I said, 'I don't know what I want.'

That was the real trouble. Boredom saps the will. It makes you feel you no longer have the power to choose. All I could see was the present stretching indefinitely into the future.

But two months later everything changed. My father died. And three weeks after that, on the 19th July 1952, I met Henry Appleyard.

4

Memory bathes the past in a glow of inevitability. It's tempting to assume that the past could only have happened in the way it did, that this event could only have been followed by that event and in the order they happened. If that were true, of course, nothing would be our fault.

But of course it isn't true. I didn't have to marry Henry. I didn't have to leave him. And I didn't have to go and stay with Janet at the Dark Hostelry.

During her last year at Oxford, Janet decided that after she had taken her degree she would go to London and try to find work as a translator. Her mother's contacts might be able to help her. She told me about it over another cup of tea, this time in her cell-like room at St Hilda's.

'Is it what you want to do?'

'It's all I can do.'

'Couldn't you stay here and do research?'

'I'll be lucky if I scrape a third. I'm not academic, Wendy. I feel I don't really belong here. As if I got in by false pretences.'

I shrugged, envious of what she had been offered and refused. 'I suppose there are lots of lovely young men in London as well as Oxford.'

'Yes. I suppose so.'

Men liked Janet because she was beautiful. She didn't say much to them either so they could talk to their hearts' content and show off to her. But she went out of her way to avoid them. Janet wanted Sir Galahad, not a spotty undergraduate from Christchurch with an MG. In the end, she compromised as we all do. She didn't get Sir Galahad and she didn't get the spotty undergraduate with the MG. Instead she got the Reverend David Byfield.

Early in 1952 he came over to Oxford for a couple of days to do some work in the Bodleian. He was writing a book reinterpreting the work of St Thomas Aquinas in terms of modern theology. That's where he and Janet saw each other, in the library. It was, Janet said, love at first sight. 'He looked at me and I simply *knew*.'

Even now, I find it very hard to think objectively about David. The thing you have to remember is that in those days he was very, very good-looking. He turned heads in the street, just as Janet did. Like Henry, he had charm, but unlike Henry he wasn't aware of it and rarely used it. He had a first-class degree in theology from Cambridge. Afterwards he went to a theological college called Mirfield.

'Lots of smells and bells,' Janet told me, 'and terrifyingly brainy men who don't like women.'

'But David's not like that,' I said.

'No,' she said, and changed the subject.

After Mirfield, David was the curate of a parish near Cambridge for a couple of years. But at the time he met Janet he was lecturing at Rosington Theological College. They didn't waste time – they were engaged within a month. A few weeks later, David landed the job of vice-principal at the Theological College. They were delighted, Janet wrote, and the prospects were good. The principal was old and would leave a good deal of responsibility to David. David had also been asked to be a minor canon of the Cathedral, which would help financially. The bishop, who was chairman of the Theological College's trustees, had taken quite a shine to him. Best of all, Janet said, was the house that came with the job. It was in the Cathedral Close, and it was called the Dark Hostelry. Parts of it were medieval. Such a romantic name, she said, like something out of *Ivanhoe*. It was rather large for them, but they planned to take a lodger.

The wedding was in the chapel of Jerusalem, David's old college. Janet and David made a lovely couple, something from a fairy tale. If I was in a fairy tale, I told myself, I'd be the

18

Ugly Duckling. What made everything worse was my father's death – not so much because I'd loved him but because there was now no longer any possibility of his loving me.

Then I saw Henry standing on the other side of the chapel. In those days he was thickset rather than plump. He was wearing a morning suit that was too small for him. We were singing a hymn and he glanced at me. He had wiry hair in need of a cut and straight, strongly marked eyebrows that went up at a sharp angle from the bridge of his nose. He grinned at me and I looked away.

I've still got a photograph of Janet's wedding. It was taken in the front court of Jerusalem. In the centre, with the Wren chapel behind them, are David and Janet looking as if they've strayed from the closing scene of a romantic film. David looks like a young Laurence Olivier – all chiselled features and flaring nostrils, a blend of sensitivity and arrogance. He has Janet on one arm and is smiling down at her. Old Granny Byfield hangs grimly on to his other arm.

Henry and I are away to the left, separated from the happy couple by a clump of dour relations, including Mr and Mrs Treevor. Henry is trying half-heartedly to conceal the cigarette in his hand. His belly strains against the buttons of his waistcoat. The hem of my dress is uneven and I am wearing a silly little hat with a half-veil. I remember paying a small fortune for it in the belief that it would make me look sophisticated. That was before I learned that sophistication wasn't for sale in Bradford.

John Treevor looks very odd. It must have been a trick of the light – perhaps he was standing in a shaft of sunshine. Anyway, in the photograph his face is bleached white, a tall narrow mask with two black holes for eyes and a black slit for the mouth. It's as if they had taken a dummy from a shop window and draped it in a morning coat and striped trousers.

A moment later, just after the last photograph had been taken, Henry spoke to me for the first time. 'I like the hat.'

'Thanks,' I said, once I'd glanced over my shoulder to make sure he was talking to me and not someone else.

'I'm Henry Appleyard, by the way.' He held out his hand. 'A friend of David's from Rosington.'

'How do you do. I'm Wendy Fleetwood. Janet and I were at school together.'

'I know. She asked me to keep an eye out for you.' He gave me a swift but unmistakable wink. 'But I'd have noticed you anywhere.'

I didn't know what to say to this, so I said nothing.

'Come on.' He took my elbow and guided me towards a doorway. 'There's no time to lose.'

'Why?'

The photographer was packing up his tripod. The wedding party was beginning to disintegrate.

'Because I happen to know there's only four bottles of champagne. First come first served.'

The reception was austere and dull. For most of the time I stood by the wall and pretended I didn't mind not having anyone to talk to. Instead, I nibbled a sandwich and looked at the paintings. After Janet and David left for their honeymoon, Henry appeared at my side again, rather to my relief.

'What you need,' he said, 'is a dry martini.'

'Do I?'

'Yes. Nothing like it.'

I later learned that Henry was something of an expert on dry martinis – how to make them, how to drink them, how to recover as soon as possible from the aftereffects the following morning.

'Are you sure no one will mind?'

'Why should they? Anyway, Janet asked me to look after you. Let's go down to the University Arms.'

As we were leaving the college I said, 'Are you at the Theological College too?'

He burst out laughing. 'God, no. I teach at the Choir School in the Close. David's my landlord.'

'So you're the lodger?'

He nodded. 'And resident jester. I stop David taking himself too seriously.'

For the next two hours, he made me feel protected, as I had made Janet feel protected all those years ago. I wanted to believe I was normal – and also unobtrusively intelligent, witty and beautiful. So Henry hinted that I was all these things. It was wonderful. It was also some compensation for a) Janet getting married, b) managing to do it before I did, and c) to someone as dashing as David (even though he was a clergyman).

While Henry was being nice to me, he found out a great deal. He learned about my family, my father's death, the shop, and what I did. Meanwhile, I felt the alcohol pushing me up and up as if in a lift. I liked the idea of myself drinking dry martinis in the bar of a smart hotel. I liked catching sight of my reflection in the big mirror on the wall. I looked slimmer than usual, more mysterious, more chic. I liked the fact I wasn't feeling nervous any more. Above all I liked being with Henry.

He took his time. After two martinis he bought me dinner at the hotel. Then he insisted on taking me back in a taxi to my hotel, a small place Janet had found for me on the Huntingdon Road. On the way the closest he came to intimacy was when we stopped outside the hotel. He touched my hand and asked if he might possibly see me again.

I said yes. Then I tried to stop him paying for the taxi.

'No need.' He waved away the change and smiled at me. 'Janet gave me the money for everything.'

5

In those days, in the 1950s, people still wrote letters. Janet and I had settled into a rhythm of writing to each other perhaps once a month, and this continued after her marriage. That's how I learned she was pregnant, and that Henry had been sacked.

Janet and David went to a hotel in the Lake District for their honeymoon. He must have made her pregnant there, or soon after their return to Rosington. It was a tricky pregnancy, with a lot of bleeding in the early months. But she had a good doctor, a young man named Flaxman, who made her rest as much as possible. As soon as things had settled down, Janet wrote, I must come and visit them.

I envied her the pregnancy just as I envied her having David. I wanted a baby very badly. I told myself it was because I wanted to correct all the mistakes my parents had made with me. With hindsight I think I wanted someone to love. I needed someone to look after and most of all someone to give me a reason for living.

Henry was sacked in October. Not exactly sacked, Janet said in her letter. The official story was that he had resigned for family reasons. She was furious with him, and I knew her well enough to suspect that this was because she had become fond of him. Apparently one of Henry's responsibilities was administering the Choir School 'bank' – the money the boys were given as pocket money at the start of every term. He had to dole it out on Friday afternoon. It seemed he had borrowed five pounds from the cash box that housed the bank and put it on a horse. Unfortunately he was ill the following Friday.

The headmaster had taken his place and had discovered that money was missing.

At this time I was very busy. My mother and her solicitor had decided to sell the business. I was helping to make an inventory of the stock, and also chasing up creditors. To my surprise I rather enjoyed the work and I looked forward to going to the shop because it got me away from the house.

When there was a phone call for me one morning I thought it was someone who owed us money.

'Wendy – it's Henry.'

'Who?'

'Henry Appleyard. You remember? At Cambridge.'

'Yes,' I said faintly. 'How are you?'

'Wonderful, thanks. Now, what about lunch?'

'What?'

'Lunch.'

'But where are you?'

'Here.'

'In *Bradford*?'

'Why not? Hundreds of thousands of people are in Bradford. Including you, which is why I'm here. You can manage today, can't you?'

'I suppose so.' Usually I went out for a sandwich.

'I thought the Metropole, perhaps? Is that OK?'

'Yes, but –'

Yes, but isn't it rather expensive? And what shall I wear?

'Good. How about twelve-forty-five in the lounge?'

There was just time for me to go home, deal with my mother's curiosity ('A friend of Janet's, Mother, no one you know'), change into clothes more suitable for the Metropole and reach the hotel five minutes early. It was a large, shabby place, built to impress at the end of the century. I had never been inside it before. Only the prospect of Henry gave me the courage to do so now. I sat, marooned by my own embarrassment, among the potted palms and the leather armchairs, trying to avoid meeting the eyes of hotel staff. Time moved painfully onwards. After five minutes I was convinced that everyone was looking at me, and convinced that he would not come. Then suddenly Henry

23

was leaning over me, his lips brushing my cheek and making me blush.

'I'm so sorry I'm late.' He wasn't – I'd been early. 'Let's have a drink before we order.'

Henry wasn't good-looking in a conventional way or in any way at all. At that time he was in his late twenties but he looked older. He was wearing a grey double-breasted suit. I didn't know much about men's tailoring but I persuaded myself that it was what my mother used to call a 'good' suit. His collar was faintly grubby, but in this city collars grew dirty very quickly.

Once the dry martinis had been ordered he didn't beat about the bush. 'I expect you've heard my news from Janet?'

'That you've – you've left the Choir School?'

'They gave me the push, Wendy. Without a reference. You heard why?'

I nodded and stared at my hands, not wanting to see the shame in his eyes.

'The irony was, the damn horse won.' He threw back his head and laughed. 'I knew it would. I could have repaid them five times over. Still, I shouldn't have done it. You live and learn, eh?'

'But what will you do now?'

'Well, teaching's out. No references, you see, the head-master made that very clear. It's a shame, actually – I *like* teaching. The Choir School was a bit stuffy, of course. But I used to teach at a place in Hampshire that was great fun – a prep school called Veedon Hall. It's owned by a couple called Cuthbertson who actually *like* little boys.' For an instant the laughter vanished and wistfulness passed like a shadow over his face. Then he grinned across the table. 'Still, one must look at this as an opportunity. I think I might go into business.'

'What sort?'

'Investments, perhaps. Stockbroking. There's a lot of openings. But don't let's talk about that now. It's too boring. I want to talk about you.'

So that's what we did, on and off, for the next four months. Not just about me. Henry wooed my mother as well and persuaded her to talk to him. We both received the

24

flowers and the boxes of chocolates. I don't know whether my mother had loved my father, but certainly she missed him when he was no longer there. She also missed what he had done around the house and garden. Here was an opportunity for Henry.

He had the knack of giving the impression he was helping without in fact doing very much. 'Let me,' he'd say, but in fact you'd end up doing the job yourself or else it wouldn't get done at all. Not that you minded, because you somehow felt that Henry had taken the burden from your shoulders. I think he genuinely felt he was helping.

Even now it makes me feel slightly queasy to remember the details of our courtship. I wanted romance and Henry gave it to me. Meanwhile he must have discovered – while helping my mother with her papers – that my father's estate, including the house and the shop, was worth almost fifty thousand pounds. It was left in trust to my mother for her lifetime and would afterwards come to me.

All this makes me sound naive and stupid, and Henry calculating and mercenary. Both are true. But they are not the whole truth or anything like it. I don't think you can pin down a person with a handful of adjectives.

Why bother with the details? My father's executor distrusted Henry but he couldn't stop us marrying. All he could do was prevent Henry from getting his hands on the capital my father left until after my mother's death when it became mine absolutely.

We were married in a registry office on Wednesday the 4th of May, 1953. Janet and David sent us a coffee set of white bone china but were unable to come in person because Janet was heavily pregnant with Rosie.

At first we lived in Bradford, which was not a success. After my mother died we sold the house and went briefly to London and then to South Africa in pursuit of the good life. We found it for a while. Henry formed a sort of partnership with a persuasive businessman named Grady. But Grady went bankrupt and we returned to England poorer and perhaps wiser. Nevertheless, it would be easy to forget that

25

Henry and I had good times. When he was enjoying life then so did you.

All things considered, the money lasted surprisingly well. Henry worked as a sort of stockbroker, sometimes by himself, sometimes with partners. If it hadn't been for Grady he might still be doing it. He once told me it was like going to the races with other people's money. He was in fact rather good at persuading people to give him their money to invest. Occasionally he even made them a decent profit.

'Swings and roundabouts, I'm afraid,' I heard him say dozens of times to disappointed clients. 'What goes up, must come down.'

So why did his clients trust him? Because he made them laugh, I think, and because he so evidently believed he was going to make their fortunes.

So why did I stay with him for so long?

It was partly because I came to like many of the things he did. Still do, actually. You soon get a taste for big hotels, fast cars and parties. I liked the touch of fur against my skin and the way diamonds sparkled by candlelight. I liked dancing and flirting and taking one or two risks. I occasionally helped Henry attract potential clients, and even that could be fun. 'Let's have some old widow,' he'd say when things were going well for us, and suddenly there would be another bottle of Veuve Clicquot and another toast to us, to the future.

When Henry met me I was a shy, gawky girl. He rescued me from Harewood Drive and gave me confidence in myself. I think I stayed with him partly because I was afraid that without him I would lose all I had gained.

Most of all, though, I stayed because I liked Henry. I suppose I loved him, though I'm not sure what that means. But when things were going well between us, it was the most wonderful thing in the world. Even better than dry martinis and the old widow.

Letters continued to travel between Janet and me. They were proper ones – long and chatty. I didn't say much about Henry and she didn't say much about David. A common theme was our plans to meet. Once or twice we managed to snatch a day in London together. But we never went to stay with each other. Somehow there were always reasons why visits had to be delayed.

We were always on the move. Henry never liked settling in one place for any length of time. When he was feeling wealthy we rented flats or stayed in hotels. When money was tight, we went into furnished rooms.

But I was going to spend a few days with Janet and David in Rosington after Easter 1957. Just me, of course – Henry had to go away on what he called a business trip, and in any case he didn't want to go back to Rosington. Too many people knew why he'd left.

I'd even done my packing. Then the day before I was due to go, a telegram arrived. Mrs Treevor had had a massive heart attack. Once again the visit was postponed. She died three days later. Then there was the funeral, and then the business of settling Mr Treevor into a flat in Cambridge. Janet wrote that her father was finding it hard to cope since her mother's death.

So we continued to write letters instead. Despite her mother's death, it seemed to me that Janet had found her fairy tale. She sent me photographs of Rosie, as a baby and then as a little girl. Rosie had her mother's colouring and her father's features. It was obvious that she too was perfect, just like David and the Dark Hostelry.

Life's so bloody unsubtle sometimes. It was all too easy to contrast Janet's existence with mine. But you carry on, don't you, even when your life is more like one long hang-over than one long party. You think, what else is there to do?

But there was something else. There had to be, as I found out on a beach one sunny day early in October 1957. Henry and I were staying at a hotel in the West Country. We weren't on holiday – a potential client lived in the neighbourhood, a wealthy widow.

It was a fine afternoon, warm as summer, and I went out after lunch while Henry went off to a meeting. I wandered aimlessly along the beach, a Box Brownie swinging from my hand, trying to walk off an incipient hangover. I rounded the corner of a little rocky headland and there they were, Henry and the widow, lying on a rug.

She was an ugly woman with a moustache and fat legs. I had a very good view of the legs because her dress was up around her thighs and Henry was bouncing around on top of her. His bottom was bare and for a moment I watched the fatty pear-shaped cheeks trembling. The widow was still wearing her shoes, which were navy-blue and high-heeled, surprisingly dainty. I wouldn't have minded a pair of shoes like that. I remember wondering how she could have walked across the sand in such high heels, and whether she realized that sea water would ruin the leather.

I had never seen Henry from this point of view before. I knew he was vain, and hated the fact that he was growing older. (He secretly touched up his grey hairs with black dye.) The wobbling flesh was wrinkled and flabby. Henry was getting old, and so was I. It was the first moment in my life when I realized that time was running out for me personally as well as for other people and the planet.

Maybe it was the alcohol but I felt removed from the situation, capable of considering it as an abstract problem. I walked towards them, my bare feet soundless on the sand. I crouched a few yards away from the shuddering bodies. Suddenly they realized they were not alone. Simultaneously they turned their heads to look at me, the widow with her legs raised and those pretty shoes in the air.

Still in that state of alcoholic transcendence, I had the sense to raise the Box Brownie and press the shutter.

6

I don't keep many photographs. I am afraid of nostalgia. You can drown in dead emotions.

Among the photographs I have thrown away is the shot of Henry bouncing on his widow on the beach. I knew at once that it could be valuable, that it meant I could divorce Henry without any trouble. At the time, the remarkable thing was how little the end of the marriage seemed to matter. Perhaps, I thought as I took the film out of the camera, perhaps it was never really a marriage at all, just a mutually convenient arrangement which had now reached a mutually convenient end.

I still have a snap of us by the pool in somebody's back garden in Durban with Henry sucking in his tummy and me showing what at the time seemed a daring amount of naked flesh. There's just the two of us in the photograph, but it's obvious from the body language that Henry and I aren't a couple in any meaningful sense of the word. Obvious with twenty-twenty hindsight, anyway.

In my letters to Janet I had been honest about everything except Henry. I didn't conceal the fact that money was sometimes tight, or even that I was drinking too much. But I referred to Henry with wifely affection. 'Must close now – His Nibs has just come in, and he wants his tea. He sends his love, as do I.'

It was pride. Janet had her Mr Perfect and I wanted mine, or at least the illusion of him. But I think I'd known the marriage was in trouble before the episode with the widow. What I saw on the beach merely confirmed it.

'I want a divorce,' I said to Henry when he came back to our room in the hotel. By the smell of him he'd fortified himself in the bar downstairs.

'Wendy – *please*. Can't we –?'

'No, we can't.'

'Darling. Listen to me. I –'

'I mean it.'

'All right,' he said, his opposition crumbling with humiliating speed. 'As soon as you like.'

I felt sober now and I had a headache. I had found the bottle of black hair dye hidden as usual in one of the pockets of his suitcase. It was empty now. I'd poured the contents over his suits and shirts.

'No hard feelings,' I lied. 'I'll let you have some money.'

He looked across the room at me and smiled rather sadly. 'What money?'

'You know something?' I said. 'When I saw you on top of that cow, your bum was wobbling around all over the place. It was like an old man's. The skin looked as if it needed ironing.'

In the four months after I found Henry doing physical jerks on top of his widow, I wrote to Janet less often than usual. I sent her a lot of postcards. Henry and I were moving around, I said, which was true. Except, of course, we weren't moving around together. In a sense I spent those four months pretending to myself and everyone else that everything was normal. I didn't want to leave my rut even if Henry was no longer in there with me.

Eventually the money ran low and I made up my mind I had to do something. I came back to London. It was February now, and the city was grey and dank. I found a solicitor in the phone book. His name was Fielder, and the thing I remember most about him was the ill-fitting toupee whose colour did not quite match his natural hair. He had an office in Praed Street above a hardware shop near the junction with Edgware Road.

I went to see him, explained the situation and gave him the address of Henry's solicitor. I told him about the photograph but didn't show it to him, and I mentioned my mother's money too. He said he'd see what he could do and made an appointment for me the following week.

Time crawled while I waited. I had too much to think about and not enough to do. When the day came round, I went back to Fielder's office.

'Well, Mrs Appleyard, things are moving now.' He slid a sheet of paper across the desk towards me. 'The wheels are turning. Time for a fresh start, eh?'

I opened the sheet of paper. It was a bill.

'Just for interim expenses, Mrs Appleyard. No point in letting them mount up.'

'What does my husband's solicitor say?'

'I'm afraid there's a bit of a problem there.' Mr Fielder patted his face with a grubby handkerchief. He wore a brown double-breasted pinstripe suit which encased him like a suit of armour and looked thick enough for an Arctic winter. There were drops of moisture on his forehead, and his neck bulged over his tight, hard collar. 'Yes, a bit of a problem.'

'Do you mean there isn't any money?'

'I did have a reply from Mr Appleyard's solicitor.' Fielder scrabbled among the papers on his desk for a few seconds and then gave up the search. 'The long and the short of it is that Mr Appleyard told him your joint assets no longer seem to exist.'

'But there must be something left. Can't we take him to court?'

'We could, Mrs Appleyard, we could. But we'd have to find him first. Unfortunately Mr Appleyard seems to have left the country. In confidence I may tell you he hasn't even settled his own solicitor's bill.' He shook his head sadly. 'Not a desirable state of affairs at all. Not at all. Which reminds me . . . ?'

'Don't worry.' I opened my handbag and dropped the bill into it.

'Of course. And then we'll carry on in Mr Appleyard's absence. It should be quite straightforward.' He glanced at his watch. 'By the way, your husband left a letter for you care of his solicitor. I have it here.'

31

'I don't want to see it.'

'Then what would you like me to do with it?'

'I don't care. Put it in the wastepaper basket.' My voice sounded harsh, more Bradford than Hillgard House. 'I don't mean to seem rude, Mr Fielder, but I don't think he has anything to say that I want to hear.'

Walking back to my room along the crowded pavement I wanted to blame Fielder. He had been inefficient, he had been corrupt, but even then I knew neither of these things were true. I just wanted to blame somebody for the mess my life was in. Henry was my preferred candidate but he wasn't available. So I had to focus my anger on poor Fielder. Before I reached my room, I'd invented at least three cutting curtain lines I might have used, and also constructed a satisfying fantasy which ended with him in the dock at the Old Bailey with myself as the chief prosecution witness. Fantasies reveal the infant that lives within us all. Which is why they're dangerous because the usual social constraints don't operate on infants.

When I went into the house, Mrs Hyson, the landlady, opened the kitchen door a crack and peered at me, but said nothing. I ate dry bread and elderly cheese in my room for lunch to save money. I kept on my overcoat to postpone putting a shilling in the gas meter. Since leaving Henry I had lived on the contents of my current account at the bank and my Post Office Savings Account, a total of about two hundred pounds, and by selling a fur coat and one or two pieces of jewellery.

I wasn't even sure I could afford to divorce Henry. First I needed to find a job but I was not trained to do anything. I was twenty-six years old and completely unemployable. There were relations in Leeds – a couple of aunts I hadn't seen for years and cousins I'd never met. Even if I could track them down there was no reason why they should help me. That's when I opened my writing case and began the letter to Janet.

Looking back, I think I must have been very near a nervous breakdown when I wrote that letter. It's more than forty years ago now, but I can still remember how the panic welled

32

up. The certainties were gone. In the past I'd always known what to do next. I often didn't want to do it but that was not the point. What had counted was the fact the future was mapped out. I'd also taken for granted there would be a roof over my head, clothes on my back and food on the table. But now I had nothing.

I looked for the letter after Janet's death and was glad I could not find it. I hope she destroyed it. I cannot remember exactly what I told her, though I would have kept nothing back except perhaps my envy of her. What I do remember is how I felt while I was writing that letter in the chilly little room in Paddington. I felt I was trying to swim in a black sea. The waves were so rough and my waterlogged clothes weighed me down. I was drowning.

Early in the evening I went out to post the letter. On the way back I passed a pub. A few yards down the pavement I stopped, turned back and went into the saloon bar. It was a high-ceilinged room with mirrors on the walls and chairs upholstered in faded purple velvet. Apart from two old ladies drinking port, it was almost empty, which gave me courage. I marched up to the counter and ordered a large gin and bitter lemon, not caring what they thought of me.

'Waiting for someone then?' the barmaid asked.

'No.' I watched the gin sliding into the glass and moistened my lips. 'You're not very busy tonight.'

I doubt if the place was ever busy. It smelled of failure. That suited me. I sat in the corner and drank first one drink, then another and then a third. A man tried to pick me up and I almost said yes, just for the hell of it.

There were women around here who made a living from men. You saw them hanging round the station and on street corners, huddled in doorways or bending down to a car window to talk to the man inside. Could I do that? Would you ever get used to having strange men pawing at you? How much would you charge them? And what happened when you grew old and they stopped wanting you?

To escape the questions I couldn't answer, I had another drink, and then another. In the end I lost count. I knew I was drinking tomorrow's lunch and tomorrow's supper, and then the day after's meals as well, and in a way that added to the despairing pleasure the process gave me. The barmaid and her mother persuaded me to leave when I ran out of money and started crying.

I dragged myself back to the bed and breakfast. On my way in I met Mrs Hyson. She knew what I'd been doing, I could see it in her face. She could hardly have avoided knowing. I must have smelt like a distillery and it was a miracle I got up those stairs without falling over. It was too much trouble to take off my clothes. The room was swaying so I lay down on top of the eiderdown. Slowly the walls began to revolve round the bed. The whole world had tugged itself free from its moorings. The last thing I remember thinking was that Mrs Hyson would probably want me out of her house by tomorrow.

7

I began the slow hard climb towards consciousness around dawn. For hours I lay there and tried to cling to sleep. My mouth was dry and my head felt as though there were a couple of skewers running through it. I was aware of movement in the house around me. The doorbell rang and the skewers twisted inside my skull. A few moments later there was a knock on the door.

Trying not to groan, I stood up slowly and padded across the floor in my stockinged feet. I opened the door a crack. Her nose wrinkling, Mrs Hyson stared up at me. I had slept in my clothes. I hadn't removed my make-up either.

'There's a gentleman to see you, Mrs Appleyard.'

'A gentleman?'

Mrs Hyson frowned and walked away. My stomach lurched at the thought it might be Henry. But I had nothing left for him to take. Maybe it was that solicitor, anxious about his cheque.

A few minutes later I went downstairs as if down to my execution and into Mrs Hyson's front room. I found David Byfield examining a menacing photograph of the dear departed Mr Hyson. He turned towards me, holding out his hand and offering me a small, cool smile. He didn't seem to have changed since his wedding day. Unlike me.

'I hope you don't mind my calling. I was up in town anyway, and Janet phoned me this morning with the news.'

'She's had my letter, then?'

He nodded. 'We're so sorry.'

How I hated that *we*. 'No need. It had been coming to an

end for a long time.' I glared at him and winced at the stabs of pain behind my eyes. 'You should be glad, not sad.'

'It's always sad when a marriage breaks down.'

'Yes, well.' I realized I must sound ungracious, and added brightly, 'And how are you? How are Janet and Rosie?'

'Very well, thank you. Janet's hoping – we're hoping that you'll come and stay with us.'

'I can manage quite well by myself, thank you.'

'I'm sure you can.'

The Olivier nostrils flared a little further than usual. 'It would give us all a great deal of pleasure.'

'All right.'

'Good.'

He smiled at me now, showing me his approval. That's what really irritated me, the way I felt myself warming in the glow of his attention. Sex appeal can be such a depressingly impersonal thing.

David swiftly arranged the next stage of my life, barely bothering to consult me. His charity was as impersonal as his sex appeal. He was helping me because he felt he ought to or because Janet had asked him to. He was earning good marks in heaven or with Janet, possibly both.

A few hours later I was in a second-class smoking compartment and the train was pulling out of the echoing cavern of Liverpool Street Station. I still had the hangover but time, tea and aspirins had dulled the skewers of pain and made them irritating but bearable, like a certain sort of old friend. My suitcase was above my head and the two trunks would be following by road. I had bathed and changed. I'd even managed to eat and keep down a meal that wasn't quite breakfast and wasn't quite lunch. David wasn't with me – his conference ended at lunchtime tomorrow.

The train lumbered north between soot-streaked houses beneath a smoky sky.

'Let's face it,' I told myself as the train began to gather speed and I fumbled for my cigarettes, 'he doesn't give a damn about me. And why the hell should he?'

It occurred to me that I wasn't quite sure which *he* I meant.

After Cambridge the countryside became flat. The train puffed on a straight line with black fields on either side. It was already getting dark. The horizon was a border zone, neither earth nor sky. I was alone in my compartment. I felt safe and warm and a little sleepy. If the journey went on for ever, that would have been quite all right by me.

The train began to slow. I looked out of the window and saw in the distance the spire of Rosington Cathedral. The closer we got to it, the more it looked like a stone animal preparing to spring. I went to the lavatory, washed a smut off my cheek and powdered my nose. David had telephoned Janet and asked her to meet me.

By the time I got back to the compartment, the platform was sliding along the window. I pulled down my suitcase and left the train. The first thing I noticed was the wind that cut at my throat like a razor blade. The wind in Rosington isn't like other winds, Janet had written in one of her letters, it comes all the way from Siberia and over the North Sea, it's not like an English wind at all.

Janet wasn't on the platform. She wasn't at the barrier. She wasn't outside, either.

I dragged my suitcase through the ticket hall and into the forecourt beyond. The station was at the bottom of the hill. At the top was the stone mountain. The wind brought tears to my eyes. A tall clergyman was climbing into a tall, old-fashioned car. He glanced at me with flat, incurious eyes.

Before I went to Rosington I didn't know any priests. They were there to be laughed at on stage and screen, avoided like the plague at parties, and endured at weddings and funerals of the more traditional sort. After Rosington, all that changed. Priests became people. I could believe in them.

I wasn't any nearer believing in God, mind you. A girl has her pride. Sometimes, though, I wish I could think that it was all for the best in the long run. That God had a plan we could follow or not follow, as we chose. That when bad things happened they were due to evil, and that even evil had a place in God's inscrutable but essentially benevolent plan.

It's nonsense. Why should we matter to anyone, least

37

of all to an omnipotent god whose existence is entirely hypothetical? I still think that Henry got it right. It was one evening in Durban, and we were having a philosophical discussion over our second or third nightcaps.

'Let's face it, old girl,' he said, 'it's as if we're adrift on the ocean in a boat without oars. Not much we can do except drink the rum ration.'

At Rosington station, I watched the clergyman's car driving up the hill into the darkening February afternoon. I waited a few more minutes for Janet. I went back into the station and phoned the house. Nobody answered.

So there was nothing for it but one of the station taxis. I told the driver to take me to the Dark Hostelry in the Close. In one of her letters, Janet said someone told her that in the Middle Ages, when Rosington was a monastery, the Dark Hostelry was where visiting Benedictine monks would stay. The 'Dark' came from the black habits of the order.

The taxi took me up the hill and through the great gateway, the Porta, and into the Close. I saw small boys in caps and shorts and grey mackintoshes. Perhaps they were at the Choir School. None of the boys would remember Henry. Six years is a long time in the life of a school.

We followed the road round the east end of the Cathedral and stopped outside a small gate in a high wall. I didn't ask the driver to carry in my suitcase – it would have meant a larger tip. I pushed open the gate in the wall, and that's when I saw Rosie playing hopscotch.

'And what's your name?' I asked.

'I'm nobody.'

Rosie wasn't wearing a coat. There she was in February playing outside and wearing sandals and a dress, not even a cardigan. The light was beginning to go. Some children don't feel the cold.

'Nobody?' I said. 'I'm sure that's not right. I bet you're really somebody. Somebody in disguise.'

'I'm nobody. That's my name.'

'Nobody's called nobody.'

'I am.'

'Why?'

'Because nobody's perfect.'

And so she was. Perfect. I thought, *Henry, you bastard, we could have had this.*

I called after Rosie as she skipped down the path towards the house. 'Rosie! I'm Auntie Wendy.'

I felt a fool saying that. Auntie Wendy sounded like a character in a children's story, the sort my mother would have liked.

'Can you tell Mummy I'm here?'

Rosie opened the door and skipped into the house. I picked up my case and followed. I was relieved because Janet must have come back. She wouldn't have left a child that age alone.

The house was part of a terrace. I had a confused impression of buttresses, the irregular line of high-pitched roofs against a grey velvet skyline, and small deeply recessed windows. At the door I put down my case and looked for the bell. There were panes of glass set in the upper panels and I could see the hall stretching into the depths of the building. Rosie had vanished. Irregularities in the glass gave the interior a green tinge and made it ripple like Rosie's hair.

A brass bell pull was recessed into the jamb of the door. I tugged it and hoped that a bell was jangling at the far end of the invisible wire. There was no way of knowing. You just had to have faith, not a state of mind that came easily to me at any time. I tried again, wondering if I should have used another door. The skin prickled on the back of my neck at the possibility of embarrassment. I waited a little longer. Someone must be there with the child. I opened the door and a smell of damp rose to meet me. The level of the floor was a foot below the garden.

'Hello?' I called. 'Hello? Anyone home?'

My voice had an unfamiliar echo to it, as though I had spoken in a church. I stepped down into the hall. It felt colder inside than out. A clock ticked. I heard light footsteps running above my head. There was a click as a door opened, then another silence, somehow different in quality from the one before.

Then the screaming began.

There's something about a child's screams that makes the heart turn over. I dropped the suitcase. Some part of my mind registered the fact that the lock had burst open in the impact of the fall, that my hastily packed belongings, the debris of my life with Henry, were spilling over the floor of the hall. I ran up a flight of shallow stairs and found myself on a long landing.

The door at the end was open. I saw Rosie's back, framed in the doorway. She wasn't screaming any more. She was standing completely still. Her arms hung stiffly by her sides as though they were no longer jointed at the elbows.

'Rosie! Rosie!'

I walked quickly down the landing and seized her by the shoulders. I spun her round and hugged her face into my belly. Her body was hard and unyielding. She felt like a doll, not a child. There was another scream. This one was mine.

The room was furnished as a bedroom. It smelled of Brylcreem and peppermints. There were two mullioned windows. One of them must have been open a crack because I heard the sound of traffic passing and people talking in the street below. At times like that, the mind soaks up memories like a sponge. Often you don't know what's there until afterwards, when you give the sponge a squeeze and you see what trickles out.

At the time I was aware only of the man on the floor. He lay on his back between the bed and the doorway. He wore charcoal-grey flannel trousers, brown brogues and an olive-green, knitted waistcoat over a white shirt with a soft collar. A tweed jacket and a striped tie were draped over a chair beside the bed. His left hand was resting on his belly. His right hand was lying palm upwards on the floor, the fingers loosely curled round the dark bone handle of a carving knife. There was blood on the blade, blood on his neck and blood on his shirt and waistcoat. His horn-rimmed glasses had fallen off. Blue eyes stared up at the ceiling. His hair was greyer and scantier than when I'd seen it last, and his face was thinner, but I recognized him right away. It was Janet's father.

'Come away, Rosie,' I muttered, 'come away. Grandpa's sleeping. We'll go downstairs and wait for Mummy.'

As if my words were a signal, Mr Treevor blinked. His eyes focused on the two of us in the doorway.

'Fooled you,' he said, and then he began to laugh.

PART II

The Close

8

'I'm so sorry.' Janet was brushing Rosie's hair. The bristles caught in a tangle, and Janet began carefully to tease it out. 'He just *arrived*.'

'It doesn't matter,' I said.

'Oh, but it does.' Her eyes met mine, then returned to the shining hair. 'The doorbell rang at half past three and there he was. He'd come all the way from Cambridge in a taxi.'

Rosie was sitting on a stool on the hearthrug, her back straight, not leaning against her mother's knees. In her place I would have been fidgeting, or playing with a toy, or looking at a book. But Rosie seemed hypnotized by the gentle scratching of the brush.

'It didn't occur to him to telephone. He just came as he was. No luggage, no overcoat. He even forgot his wallet. I had to use the housekeeping.' Janet smiled but I knew her too well to be fooled. 'He was still in his slippers.'

We were in a narrow, panelled sitting room. The three of us were huddled round the hearthrug in front of the fire. Rosie was in her nightclothes. Janet had given me a gin and orange, with rather too much orange for my taste, and I was nursing it between my hands, trying to make it last.

'He'd forgotten his medicine too. Actually they're laxatives. He gets terribly concerned about them. That's why I had to pop out to the chemist's before it closed. And then the dean's wife swooped and I couldn't get away.' The brush faltered. Janet rested her hands on Rosie's shoulders. 'Poor Grandpa will forget his own name next, won't he, poppet? Now, say good night to Auntie Wendy and we'll put you into bed.'

45

When they went upstairs, I wandered over to the drinks tray and freshened my glass with a little gin. All three of us had tiptoed round what Mr Treevor had done upstairs. I wondered what Janet was saying to Rosie about it now. If anything. How *do* you explain to a child that Grandpa found a bottle of tomato ketchup in the kitchen, took it upstairs to his room and splashed it over him to make it look as if he'd stabbed himself to death? What on earth had he been thinking about? He had ruined his clothes and the bedroom rug. God knew what effect he had had on Rosie. The only consolation was that all the excitement had tired him out. He was resting on his bed before supper.

Glass in hand, I wandered round the room, picking up ornaments and looking at the books and pictures. I had grown sensitive to poverty in others as you do when your own money runs low. I thought I saw hints of it here, a cushion placed to cover a stain on a chair's upholstery, a fire too small for the grate, curtains that needed relining. David couldn't earn much.

There was a wedding photograph in a silver frame on the pier table between the windows, just the two of them in front of Jerusalem Chapel, David's clerical bands snapping in the breeze. I didn't have any photographs of my wedding, a hole-in-the-corner affair compared with theirs. My mother had thought we should have a white wedding with all the trimmings but Henry persuaded her to let us have the money instead for the honeymoon.

Janet came downstairs.

'Supper will have to be very simple, I'm afraid. Would cheese on toast be all right? There's some apple crumble in the larder.'

'That's fine.' I noticed her shiver. 'What's wrong?'

'I wanted it to be nice for you on your first evening especially. We haven't seen each other in such ages.'

'It's all right. It's lovely to be here. Will your father be coming down?'

'He's dozed off.' She went over to the fire and began to add coal. 'I didn't like to wake him.'

I sat on the sofa. 'Janet – does he often do things like that?'

'The tomato ketchup?'

I said nothing.

'He's always had a sense of humour,' she said, and threw a shovelful of coals on the fire.

'He kept it well concealed when I came to stay with you.'

Janet glanced at me. Tears made her eyes look larger than ever. 'Yes. Well. People change.'

'Come on.' I patted the seat of the sofa. 'Come and tell me about it.'

'But supper –'

'Damn supper.'

'I wish I could.' Suddenly she was almost shouting. 'You've no idea how much I hate cooking. In the morning the sight of a fried egg makes my stomach turn over.'

'Me too. Anyway, I'm going to help with supper. But come and sit down first.'

She dabbed her eyes with a dainty little handkerchief. She was one of the few people I've ever known who don't make a spectacle of themselves when they cry. Janet managed everything gracefully, even tears. I brought her another drink. She made a half-hearted attempt to push the glass away.

'I shouldn't drink this. I've already had one tonight.'

'It's medicinal.' I watched her take a sip. 'Tell me, how long's he been like this?'

'I don't know. I think it must have started before Mummy died. It's been very gradual.'

'Have you thought about putting him in a home?'

'I couldn't do that. He's not old. He's not even seventy yet. And it's not as if he's ill. Just a bit forgetful at times.'

'Has he seen the doctor?'

'He doesn't like doctors. That business with the tomato sauce . . .'

'Yes?'

'I think he was just trying to be friendly. Just trying to play a game with Rosie, to make her laugh. But he didn't realize the effect he would have.'

She hesitated and added carefully, 'He was never very good with children.'

'And what does David say?'

'I haven't liked to bother him too much. He's very busy at present. There's a possibility of a new job . . .'

'But surely he must have noticed?'

'He hasn't seen Daddy for a while. Anyway, for most of the time he's all right.'

I felt like an inquisitor. 'And what did Rosie say?'

'Nothing really.' Janet ran her finger round the rim of her glass. 'I told her that Grandpa was just having a joke, and it was one of those grown-up jokes that children don't always understand. And she nodded, and that was that.'

It turned into quite a nice evening in the end. Rosie fell asleep, and so did that dreadful old man upstairs. Janet and I ended up making piles of toast over the sitting room fire and getting strawberry jam all over the hearthrug. Janet gave me a chance to talk about Henry but I didn't want to, not then. So we ignored him altogether (which he would have hated so much) and I was happy. There was I acting the tower of strength while inside I felt like a jelly, just as I had all those years ago at school. Between them, Janet and Mr Treevor made me feel useful again. We choose our own families, especially if our biological ones aren't very satisfactory.

9

Even now, when I am as old as John Treevor, I dream about the day I came to Rosington. Not about what happened in the house. About talking to Rosie outside. The odd thing, the disturbing thing, is what Rosie says. Or doesn't say.

When I see her in the dream I know she's going to tell her joke, that she's called Nobody because nobody's perfect. But the punchline is scrambled. That's what makes me anxious – the fact I don't know how the words will come out. Perfect but nobody. Nobody but perfect. A perfect nobody. Perfect no body. No perfect body. Maybe my sleeping mind worries about that because it's less painful than worrying about what was going on in the house.

But the dream came much later. On my first night in Rosington I slept better than I had for years. I was in a room on the second floor away from the rest of the house. When I woke I knew it was late because of the light filtering through the crack in the curtains. The air in the bedroom was icy. I stayed in the warm nest of the bedclothes for at least twenty minutes more.

Eventually a bursting bladder drove me out of bed. The bathroom was warmer than my room because it had a hot-water tank in it. I took my clothes in there and got dressed. I went downstairs and found Janet's father sitting in a Windsor chair at the kitchen table reading *The Times*.

We eyed each other warily. He had not come downstairs again the previous evening; Janet had taken him some soup. He stood up and smiled uncertainly.

'Hello, Mr Treevor.'

He looked blank.

'I'm Wendy Appleyard, remember – Janet's friend from school.'

'Yes, yes. There's some tea in the pot, I believe. Shall I –?' He made a half-hearted attempt to investigate the teapot on my behalf.

'I think I might make some fresh.'

'My wife always says that coffee never tastes the same if you let it stand.' He looked puzzled. 'Good idea. Yes, yes.'

I was aware of him watching me as I filled the kettle, put it on the stove and lit the gas. He had put on weight since I had seen him last, a great belt of fat. The rest of him still looked relatively slim, including the face with its nose like a beak and the bulging forehead, now even more prominent because the hairline had receded further. His hair was longer than it used to be and unbrushed. He wore a heavy jersey that was too large for his shoulders and too small for his stomach. I wondered if it belonged to David. He did not refer to the incident yesterday and nor did I.

'I hope you slept well?' he said at last.

'Yes, thank you.'

'The noises didn't keep you awake?'

'The noises?'

'Yes, yes. You tend to get them in these old houses.'

'I didn't hear any. I slept very well.'

He gathered up his newspaper. 'I must be going. It's getting quite late.'

'Where's Janet?'

'Taking Rosie to school. Will you be all right? Can you fend for yourself?'

Once he'd established my ability to do this, at least to his own satisfaction, he pottered out of the kitchen. I heard him in the hall. A door opened, then closed and a bolt smacked home. He had taken refuge in the downstairs lavatory.

He was still in there after I'd drunk two cups of tea, eaten a slice of toast and started the washing-up. A bell jangled – one of a row of bells above the kitchen door. I guessed it must be the garden door, so I dried my hands and went to answer it. There was a small, sturdy clergyman on the doorstep. He touched his hat.

'Good morning. Is David in?'

'I'm afraid he's up in town at a conference. Janet's out but she should be back soon. May I take a message?'

'Do you happen to know when he's coming back?'

'This evening, I think.'

'I'll ring him tomorrow or perhaps drop in. Would you tell him Peter Hudson called? Thank you so much. Goodbye.'

He touched his hat again and walked briskly down the path where Rosie had played hopscotch to the gate in the wall. The lawn on either side of the path was still white with frost. At the gate, he turned, glanced back and waved.

That was my first meeting with Canon Hudson. A meek and mild little man, I thought at the time, with one of those forgettable faces and a classless voice that could have come from anywhere. If I had to have dealings with a clergyman, I thought, I'd much prefer he looked and sounded like Laurence Olivier.

10

In the evening David came home from London. The mood of the house changed. He arrived in the lull between Rosie being put to bed and supper. I hadn't been looking forward to seeing him. Janet and I were in the kitchen, Mr Treevor was dozing in the sitting room.

David kissed Janet and shook hands with me.

'Did you have a good time?' Janet asked him.

'Most of it was hot air but some useful people were there. Any messages?'

'On the desk in the study. Rosie might still be awake if you want to say good night to her.'

'Just a few phone calls I should make first.'

'Oh, and Peter Hudson called.'

Already at the kitchen door, David turned. His face was sharper than it had been. 'And?'

'It was this morning – Wendy saw him. He said he'd phone or drop in tomorrow.'

'He'll want to talk about the library. I'll see if I can get hold of him now.'

He left the room. I avoided looking at Janet.

'He's concerned about this library business,' Janet said hastily, as if in apology. 'There's a proposal to merge the Theological College Library with the Cathedral one. Hardly anyone uses the Cathedral Library, you see, and it would be much better for everyone if it was housed in the Theo. Coll. Peter Hudson's the new Cathedral librarian so his opinion's very important.'

'The marriage of two libraries? Gosh.'

She winced. 'It's more than that. You know David's boss is getting on? It's an open secret he may retire at the end of the summer term.'

'And David wants the job?' I smiled at her and tried to make a joke of it. 'I thought the clergy weren't supposed to have worldly ambitions.'

'It's more that David feels he could do useful work there. Canon Osbaston likes him. He's the principal. So does the bishop. But the appointment needs the agreement of the Cathedral Chapter as well. It's a bit like a school, you see. The bishop and the others are like the college's board of governors.'

'So where's the problem?'

'Some of the canons aren't very enthusiastic about David getting the job. Including Peter Hudson.'

Janet began to lay the table. The Byfields usually ate in the kitchen because it was warmer and because the dining room was a day's march away up a flight of stairs and at the other end of the house.

'Hudson seemed quite a nice little man,' I said. 'Inoffensive.'

Janet snorted. 'That's a mistake a lot of people make.' She sat down suddenly and rubbed her eyes. 'God, I'm tired.'

I took the cutlery from her and continued laying the place settings. She fiddled with one of the napkin rings, rubbing at a dull spot on the silver.

'It's not really about this library,' she went on slowly. 'Or even about the job. It's about the college itself. They're talking about closing it down.'

'Why should they do that?'

'Because applications are down and money's tight. It's a problem all over the country. David says the Church of England needs between six and seven hundred ordinations a year at the minimum if it wants to keep its parishes going. But they haven't managed six hundred a year for nearly half a century. And meanwhile everything's more expensive. The Theo. Coll.'s a great barrack of a place. It simply eats up money.'

'Why does David want to be principal of it? Couldn't he

do something else? Why can't he have a parish like normal priests?'

'He feels his vocation is to be a teacher and a scholar – perhaps even an administrator.' She straightened one of the knives. 'And – and I think it's the sort of job that gets you noticed. David wouldn't look at it like that, of course, but that's what it amounts to.'

'Sounds more like Imperial Tobacco than the Church of England.'

'The Church is an organization, Wendy. They all work the same way. The C of E isn't there to make money but it's still an organization.'

I was tempted to make a joke about God being the chairman for life but decided that Janet might think it in bad taste.

'The salary would be much better, too,' she said in a voice barely louder than a whisper.

It was at that point that a handful of suspicions coalesced into a certainty. 'Money's tight for you, isn't it?'

Janet said nothing. I remembered how David had paid my bill at Mrs Hyson's and bought my train ticket. I thought about the cost of Mr Treevor's taxi from Cambridge, and how having two extra mouths to feed – and in my case water – would affect a household budget.

I drew out a chair and sat down beside her. 'You've been very good to me,' I said. 'Both of you, real friends in need. But I shan't stay long.'

Janet lifted her face. 'I don't want you to go. I like having you here. Anyway, where would you go? What would you do?'

'I'll find something.'

She shook her head. 'Not yet. God knows what would happen to you.'

'Other people manage,' I said airily.

'You're not other people. You're Wendy. Anyway, what about Henry?'

My heart twisted. 'What about him?'

'You don't think –?'

'I told you in the letter. It's over. I'm going to divorce him.

He can't contest it. He only married me for the bit of money I had.' I rubbed a patch of rough skin on my hand, trying to smooth away the hurt. 'I caught him making love to another woman and she was the ugliest bitch you've ever seen.'

'Oh, Wendy.'

She took my hand. I stared at them, her hand and mine lying on the scrubbed deal table.

Janet said, 'You must stay for a while.'

'Only if you let me pay something. And if you let me help you around the house.'

'You haven't got any money.'

'I've got one or two little bits of jewellery.'

'You're not to sell them.'

'Then I'll have to go.'

We glared at each other. She began to cry. So did I. While we finished laying the table we shared a brief companionable weep. By the time we'd dried our eyes, hugged each other and cleared the draining board we both knew that I would stay.

11

The first Saturday of my visit was cold but sunny. David took Janet and me up the west tower of the Cathedral. We climbed endless spiral staircases and edged along narrow galleries thick with stone dust. At last he pushed open a tiny door and we crawled out on to an unbearably bright platform of lead.

There was no wind. I swear it was colder and sunnier up there than it had been on the ground. I leaned against one of the walls, which were battlemented like a castle's. I was gasping for breath because of too many stairs and too many cigarettes.

I looked out. The tower went down like a lift in a horror film. The ground rushed away. I held on to the parapet, the roughness of the stone scouring my hands as I squeezed it more and more tightly.

Below me was the great encrusted hull of the Cathedral and the tiled and slated roofs of Rosington. Around them as far as the eye could see were the grey winter Fens. They stretched towards the invisible point where they became one with the grey winter sky.

For an instant I was more terrified than I had ever been in my life. I was adrift between the sky and the earth. All my significance had been stolen from me.

Then Janet put her hand on my arm and said, 'Look, there's Canon Osbaston coming out of the Theological College.' She lowered her voice. 'If tortoises waddled they'd look just like him.'

In those days Rosington was a small town – perhaps eight

56

or nine thousand people. Technically it was a city because it had a cathedral, so its sense of importance was out of proportion to its size. It was also an island set in the black sea of the Fens, a place apart, a place of refuge. It was certainly a place of refuge for me. Even if he wanted to, Henry would hardly follow me to the town where he had made such a fool of himself.

David told me that in the Middle Ages the Isle of Rosington was largely surrounded by water. It was a liberty, almost a County Palatine, in which the abbots who preceded the bishops wielded much of the authority usually reserved for the king. Here the Saxons made one of their last stands against the invading armies of the Normans.

The city still felt a place under siege. And the Cathedral Close, a city within a city, was doubly under siege because the town around it nibbled away at its rights and privileges. The Close was an ecclesiastical domain, older than the secular one surrounding it, and conducted according to different laws. Its gates were locked at night by an assistant verger named Gotobed who lived beside the Porta with his mother and her cats.

Rosington wasn't like Bradford or Hillgard House or Durban or any of the other places I'd lived in. The past was more obvious here. If you glanced up at the ceiling while you were sitting in Janet's kitchen you saw the clumsy barrel of a Norman vault. The Cathedral clock rang the hours and the quarters. The Close and its inhabitants were governed by the rhythm of the daily services, just as they had been for more than a thousand years. I had never lived among religious people before and this was unsettling too. It was as though I were the one person capable of seeing colours, as if everyone else lived in a monochrome world. Or possibly it was the other way round. Either way I was in a minority of one.

When we were at school Janet and I used to laugh at those who were religious. Now I knew she went to church regularly, though it was not something we had talked about in our letters.

On my first Sunday morning in Rosington I stayed at

home. Janet and Rosie were going to matins at ten-thirty. The pair of them looked so sweet dressed up for God in their Sunday finery.

'If you don't mind I won't come to church,' I said to David at breakfast. I'd already made this clear to Janet but I wanted to say it to him as well. I didn't want there to be any misunderstandings.

He smiled. 'It's entirely up to you.'

'I'm sorry, but I'm not particularly godly. I'd rather do the vegetables.'

'That's very kind of you. But are you sure it isn't too much trouble?'

I don't know how, but he made me feel like the prodigal daughter a long way from home.

'I suppose you have to go to church,' I said to Janet as we were washing up after lunch. 'Part of your wifely duties.'

She nodded but added, 'I like it too. No one makes any demands on you in church. You can just be quiet for once.'

I was stupid enough to ignore what she was really saying. 'Yes, but do you believe in God?'

I didn't want Janet to believe in God. It was as if by doing so she would believe a little less in me.

'I don't know.' She bent over the sink and began to scour the roasting tin. 'Anyway, it doesn't really matter what I believe, does it?'

During my first fortnight in Rosington the five of us settled into a routine. Given how different we were, you would have expected more friction than there was. But David was out most of the time – either at the Theological College or in the Cathedral. Rosie was at school during the week – she was in her second term at St Tumwulf's Infant School on the edge of the town. Old Mr Treevor – I thought of him as old, though he was younger than I am now – spent much time in his bedroom, either huddled over a small electric fire or in bed. As far as I could see his chief interests were food, the contents of *The Times* and the evacuation of his bowels.

The house itself made co-existence easier. The Dark Hostelry was not so much large as complicated. Most of the rooms were small and there were a great many of them. David said

58

the building had been in continuous occupation for seven or eight hundred years. Each generation seemed to have added its own eccentricity. It was a place of many staircases, some of which led nowhere in particular, small, crooked rooms with sloping floors and thick walls. The kitchen was in a semi-basement, and as you washed up you could watch the legs of the passers-by in the High Street, which followed the northern boundary of the Cathedral Close.

Although the Dark Hostelry was good for keeping people apart, it was not an easy house to run. A charwoman came in three mornings a week to 'do the rough'. Otherwise Janet had to do the work herself. And there was a lot of it – this was 1958, and the nearest thing Janet had to a labour-saving device was a twin-tub washing machine with a hand mangle attached. The last time the place had had a serious overhaul was at the turn of the century when the occupants could probably have afforded two or three servants.

In some ways I think Janet would have preferred to be a paid servant. She loathed the work but at least she would have been getting a wage for it. A simple commercial transaction has a beginning and end. It implies that both parties to it have freedom of choice.

Janet had the worst of both worlds. There was a dark irony in the fact that as well as running that ridiculous old house she also had to pretend to be its mistress, not its slave. Janet was expected to be a lady. When the Byfields came to Rosington she had visiting cards engraved. I've still got one of them – yellowing pasteboard, dog-eared at the corners, the typeface small and discreet.

> Mrs David Byfield
> The Dark Hostelry
> The Close
> Rosington
>
> Telephone: Rosington 2114

When the Byfields arrived at the Dark Hostelry, the ladies

of the Close and the ladies of the town called and left their cards. Janet called on them and left hers. It was a secular equivalent to what David was doing every day in that echoing stone mountain in the middle of the Close. A ritualistic procedure which might once have had a purpose.

I doubt if David knew what a burden he'd placed on her shoulders. Not then, at any rate. It's not that he wasn't a sensitive man. But his sensitivity was like a torch beam. It had to be directed at you before it became effective. But it wasn't just a question of him being sensitive or not being sensitive. Everyone thought differently. This was more than forty years ago, remember, and in the Cathedral Close of Rosington.

Nowadays I think David and Janet were both in prison. But neither of them could see the bars.

12

It became increasingly obvious that something would have to be done about Mr Treevor.

He and I, a pair of emotional vampires, arrived on the same February afternoon and more than three weeks later we were still at the Dark Hostelry. I flattered myself there was a difference, that at least I did some of the housework and cooking. I sold my engagement ring, too. I'd never liked the beastly thing. It turned out to be worth much less than Henry had led me to expect, which shouldn't have surprised me.

Mr Treevor did less and less. He took it for granted that we were there to supply his needs – regular meals, clean clothes, bed-making, warm rooms and a daily copy of *The Times*, which for some reason he liked to have ironed before he would open it.

'He never used to be like that,' Janet said to me on Thursday morning as we were snatching a cup of coffee. 'He hardly ever read a paper, and as for this ironing business, I've no idea where that came from.'

'Isn't it the sort of thing they used to do in the homes of the aristocracy?'

'He can't have picked it up there.'

'Perhaps he saw it in a film.'

'It's a bit of a nuisance, actually.'

'A bit of a nuisance? It's a bloody imposition. I think you should go on strike.'

'I think his memory's improving. That's something, isn't it?'

I wondered whether it would ever improve to the point

where he would be able to remember who I was from one day to the next.

'He told me all about how he won a prize at school the other day,' Janet went on, sounding as proud as she did when describing one of Rosie's triumphs at St Tumwulf's. 'For Greek verses. He could even remember the name of the boy he beat.'

'He's getting old,' I said, responding to her anxiety, not what she'd said. 'That's all. It'll happen to us one day.'

Janet bit her lip. 'Yesterday he asked me when Mummy was coming. He seems to think she'd gone away for the weekend or something.'

'When's he going home?'

'On Saturday,' Janet said brightly. 'David's offered to drive him back.'

Early on Friday morning all of us realized that this would have to be postponed. Even on the top floor I heard the shouting. By the time I got downstairs everyone else was in the kitchen. Even Rosie was huddled in the corner between the wall and the dresser, crouching to make herself as small as possible.

Mr Treevor was standing beside the table. He was in his pyjamas, but without his teeth, his slippers and his dressing gown. He was sobbing. Janet was patting his right arm with a tea towel. David, also in pyjamas, was frowning at them both. There was a puddle of water on the table, and the front of Janet's nightdress was soaked. The room smelled of singed hair and burning cloth.

Afterwards we reconstructed what had happened. Mr Treevor had woken early and with a rare burst of initiative decided to make himself some tea. He went downstairs, lit the gas and put the kettle on the ring. It was unfortunate that he forgot you had to put water in the kettle as well. After a while, the kettle started to make uncharacteristically agitated noises so he lifted it off the ring. At this point he forgot two other things – to turn off the gas, and to cover the metal handle of the kettle with a cloth. The first scream must have been caused when the metal of the handle burnt into his fingers and the palm of his hand.

David stared at me. 'We must have a first-aid box some-where, mustn't we?'

'Phone the doctor,' I said to him. 'Quickly.'

'But surely it's not a –'

'Quickly. Mr Treevor's had a bad shock.'

He blinked, nodded and left the room.

I pulled a chair towards the sink, and with Janet's help drew Mr Treevor down on to it. I turned on the tap and ran cold water over his hand and arm.

'Janet, why don't you take Rosie back to bed and fetch a blanket? Have you got any lint?'

'Yes, it's –'

'You'd better bring that as well. And then what about some tea?'

There's a side of me that derives huge pleasure from telling people what to do. No one seemed to mind. Gradually, Mr Treevor's sobs subsided to whimpers and then to silence. By the time the doctor arrived, all four adults were huddled round the kitchen boiler drinking very sweet tea.

The doctor was Flaxman. I recognized his name from Janet's letters – he had been helpful when she was pregnant. Later I came to know him quite well. He had a long, freckled face, flaking skin and red hair. He examined Mr Treevor, told us to put him to bed and said he would call later in the day.

In the afternoon, Flaxman returned. He spent twenty min-utes alone with Mr Treevor and then came down and talked to us in the sitting room. David was still at the Theological College.

'How is he?' Janet asked.

'Well, the burns aren't a problem. He'll get over those. It could have been worse if you hadn't acted promptly.'

'We've Mrs Appleyard to thank for that.' Janet smiled at me.

Flaxman sat down. He didn't look at me. He began to write a prescription.

'Would you like a cup of tea? Or some sherry? It's not too early for sherry, is it?'

'No, thanks.' He tore off the prescription and handed it to

Janet. 'These will help Mr Treevor sleep, Mrs Byfield. Give him one at bedtime. If he complains of pain, give him a couple of aspirin. Tell me, where does he live?'

'He has a flat in Cambridge.'

'Does he live alone?'

'There's a landlady downstairs. She cooks for him.'

'How long will he be staying with you?'

Janet wriggled slightly in her chair. 'I don't really know. My husband was going to take him back tomorrow but in the circumstances, I suppose –'

'I'd advise you to keep him here a little longer. I'd like to see him again over the next few days. I think his condition needs assessment. Perhaps you'd let me have the address of his GP.'

'He wasn't properly awake this morning,' Janet said, clutching at straws. 'He's not been sleeping well.'

'The sleeping tablets will help that. But the point is, he needs looking after. I don't mean he needs to be hospitalized, but he needs other people around to keep an eye on him.'

'Is – is this going to get worse?'

'It may well do. That's one reason why we need to keep an eye on him, Mrs Byfield – to see if he is getting worse.'

'And if he is?'

'There are several residential homes in the area. Some private, some National Health.'

'He'd hate that. He'd hate the loss of privacy.'

'Yes, but his physical safety has to be the main concern. Could he live with you or some other relative?'

'Permanently?'

'If you don't want him to go into a residential home, that would probably be the best solution, Mrs Byfield. At least until his condition deteriorates a good deal more.'

'But – but what exactly's wrong with him?'

'At this stage it's hard to be categorical.' He glanced quickly at us both. 'But I think he's in the early stages of a form of dementia.'

There was a long silence. I wanted to say to Janet, *You've got enough on your plate*, but for once I kept my mouth shut.

Then she sighed. 'I shall have to talk to my husband.'

13

Janet and I went to Mr Treevor's flat on Saturday. We drove over to Cambridge, another small victory for me hard on the heels of my display of Girl Guide first aid. In a sense I was beginning to shed my burdens just as Janet was shouldering more.

David had assumed that Janet would go by bus. It was after all cheaper than going by train.

'Why not the car?' I said on Friday evening, emboldened by my Girl Guide expertise and by a substantial slug from the gin bottle in my bedside cupboard.

'Janet doesn't drive.' David hardly bothered to glance at me. 'I'd take you myself, of course, but unfortunately I've got my classes in the morning and then there's a meeting first thing in the afternoon. The Finance Committee.'

'I'll take her,' I said.

This time David looked properly at me. 'I didn't realize you drove.'

'Well, I do. But what about insurance?'

'It's insured for any driver I give permission to.'

'There you are. Problem solved.'

'But have you driven recently, Wendy? It's not an easy car to drive, either. It's –'

'It's a second series Ford Anglia,' I interrupted. 'We had one for a time in Durban, except ours was more modern and had the 1200 cc engine.'

'I see.' Suddenly he smiled. 'You're a woman of hidden talents.'

I smiled back and asked Janet when she would like to go.

I felt warm and a little breathless, which wasn't just the gin. That's biology for you. David upset a lot of men in his time but I never knew a woman who didn't have a sneaking regard for him, who didn't enjoy his approval.

Janet and I had six hours of freedom. The charwoman agreed to come in for the day and keep an eye on Mr Treevor and Rosie. Rosie liked the charwoman, who gave her large quantities of cheap sweets which Janet disapproved of but dared not object to.

The road from Rosington to Cambridge is the sort of road made with a ruler. The Fens could never look pretty, but the day was unseasonably warm for early March and the sun was shining. It was possible to believe that spring was round the corner, that you'd no longer be cold all the time, and that problems might have solutions.

Mr Treevor's flat was the upper part of a little mid-Victorian terraced house in a cul-de-sac off Mill Road, near the station. I hadn't known what to expect but it wasn't this. The landlady, the widow of a college porter, kept the ground floor for herself. Mr Treevor and the widow and the widow's son shared the kitchen, which was at the back of the house, and the bathroom which was beyond the kitchen, tacked on as an afterthought.

The landlady was out. Janet let herself in with her father's key and we went upstairs. I must have shown what I was feeling on my face.

'It's a bit seedy, I'm afraid,' she said.

'It doesn't matter.'

'You didn't think he'd live somewhere like this, I suppose? He wanted to stay in Cambridge, you see, and it was all he could afford when Mummy died.'

Janet took me along the landing to the room at the front, which was furnished as a sitting room. It smelled of tobacco, stale food and unwashed bodies.

'She gives him his breakfast and an evening meal,' Janet said, meaning the landlady, 'and she's meant to clean for him as well and send his washing to the laundry.' She threw up one of the sash windows and cold, fresh air flooded into the room. 'I don't think she does very much. That's one reason why I didn't warn her we were coming.'

'I'm sorry. I – I suppose there was nowhere better available.'

'Beggars couldn't be choosers.' She turned round to face me. 'There was enough money when I was growing up. My mother was always working and she was good at her job. They were queuing up for her. And Daddy had a little money of his own. Not much, about a hundred a year, I think. They didn't have pensions or anything like that. I think they more or less lived up to their income.'

'It's all right,' I said awkwardly, because I was English and in those days the English hated talking about money, especially with friends. 'I quite understand.'

Janet was braver than me, always was. 'When Mummy was ill, the translation work dried up and they had to live on Daddy's capital. So what with one thing and another there wasn't much left when Mummy died.' She waved her arm. 'But he had this. He could be independent and he loves Cambridge.'

I said, suddenly understanding, 'You and David are helping to pay for this, aren't you?'

She nodded. 'Only a little.'

'That's something,' I said. 'You won't have to any more.'

But I knew as well as she did that they would have to pay for other things now, and in other ways.

John Treevor was still alive and less than twenty miles away in Rosington. Yet as we moved around his flat, sorting his possessions, it was as if he were already dead. His absence had an air of permanence about it.

His possessions dwindled in significance because of this. People lend importance to their possessions and when they're dead or even absent the importance evaporates. I remember there was a thin layer of grime on the windowsills, dust on the books, holes in most of the socks.

'It would be much simpler if we could just throw it all away,' Janet said as she closed the third of the three suitcases we'd brought with us. 'And what are we going to do about his post? He's not going to want to write letters.'

While I took the suitcases down to the car, Janet went through the drawers of the desk. When I came back there was a pile of papers on top and she was looking at a photograph, tilting it this way and that in front of the window.

'Look.'

I took it from her. The photograph was of her when she was not much older than Rosie, a little snapshot taken on the beach. She was in a bathing costume, hugging her knees and staring up at the camera. I handed it back to her.

'It was before the war. Somewhere like Bexhill or Hastings. We used to go down to Sussex to stay with my grandparents. I thought it was heaven. Daddy taught me to swim one summer, and he used to read me to sleep.' Her voice was trembling. 'There was a collection of fairy stories by Andrew Lang, *The Yellow Fairy Book*. I'd forgotten all about it.'

She foraged for her handkerchief in her handbag and blew her nose.

'Why did it have to happen to him?' she said angrily, as though it were my fault. 'Why couldn't he just have grown old normally, or even died? This is nothing. It's neither one thing nor the other.'

I said nothing because there was nothing to say.

Janet left a note for the landlady. I took her out to lunch and afterwards we walked in the pale sunshine through St John's College and on to the Backs. It wasn't much of an attempt at consolation but it was the only one I could think of.

Now the decision had been made, David felt there was no point in delay. Over the next few weeks we sold or gave away or threw away two-thirds of the contents of the flat.

Mr Gotobed, the assistant verger, helped David bring the rest of Mr Treevor's belongings back to the Dark Hostelry. Puffing and grunting, the two men carried some of the furniture – the desk, the chair, the glass-fronted bookcase – up to Mr Treevor's bedroom to make it seem homely. Janet arranged photographs on the desk, herself and her mother, both in newly cleaned silver frames. She brought her father's pipe rack and tobacco jar, not that he smoked any more, and put them where they used to stand on his desk.

I'm not sure this was a good idea. One morning, shortly after we'd finished the move, Mr Treevor emerged from the bathroom as I was coming down the stairs from my room. He laid his hand on my arm and looked around as if checking for eavesdroppers.

'There's funny things happening in this house,' he confided. 'They've got the builders in. They've been changing my room. It must be at night because I've never actually seen them at work. I've seen one of them in the hall, though. Furtive-looking chap.' He padded across the landing towards his room. At the door he glanced back at me.

'Better keep your eyes skinned, Rosie,' he hissed. 'Or there's no knowing what they'll get up to. Can't be too careful. Especially with a pretty girl like you.'

Rosie?

14

I have to admit the Cathedral came in handy when it was raining. You could walk almost the length of the High Street under cover. Or you could cut across from the north transept to the south door and avoid going right the way round the Cathedral outside. And sometimes if the choir was practising or the organ was playing I'd sit down for a while and listen.

That's where Peter Hudson found me.

It was raining heavily that morning, silver sheets of icy water sweeping across the Fens from the east. I had been to the Labour Exchange in Market Street. The woman I talked to disapproved of me. Was it my lipstick? The tightness of my skirt? The fact I'd forgotten to bring my gloves? I suspect she labelled me as louche, dangerously sophisticated and a potential husband-snatcher. Which tells you as much about the competition as it does about me.

At present the Labour Exchange had only two jobs for which I was suitably qualified. They needed someone behind the confectionery counter in Woolworth's. Or, if I preferred, I could earn rather more if I worked shifts at the canning factory on the outskirts of town. Neither of them had anything to be said for them except money, and there wasn't much of that on offer either.

I was beginning to think I'd have to go back to London. I didn't want to do that, partly because I thought Janet needed me but more because I knew I needed her. It wasn't just the breaking up with Henry. It was as if every mistake I had ever made in my life had come back to haunt me. It was rather like when you leave a hotel and they present you with a bill that's three times larger than you thought it was going to be.

I entered the Close by the Boneyard Gate from the High Street and ducked into the north door of the Cathedral to get out of the rain. Actually, it wouldn't have taken me much longer to stay in the open and reach the Dark Hostelry. But Janet was there and I wanted a moment or two by myself to catch my breath and decide what I was going to say to her.

Walking into the Cathedral was like walking into an aquarium, as if you were moving from one medium to another. Here the air was still, cool and grey. Gotobed, the assistant verger, gave me a quick, shy smile and scurried into the vestry. The building smelled faintly of smoke, a combination of incense and the fumes from the stoves that fired the central heating. I remember these stoves far better than anything else in the Cathedral. They were dotted about the aisles like cast-iron birdcages. The stoves were circular, domed, about the height of a man but much wider. Perched on top of each one was a cast-iron crown which would have fitted a very small child.

The choir was rehearsing behind the screen dividing the space beneath the Octagon from the east end. I couldn't see them but the sound of their voices welled into the crossing and poured into transepts and nave. Gotobed came out of the vestry, but this time he didn't look at me because he was on duty, carrying his silver-tipped wand of office and conducting Mr Forbury in a procession of one back to the Deanery.

I sat down on a chair, wiped the rain from my face and tried to think. Instead I listened to the sound of the voices spiralling up into the Octagon below the spire. The nearest I came to thinking was when I found myself wondering what Henry was doing at this moment, and where, and with whom. He must have found another woman by now, someone else willing to make a fool of herself because he flattered and amused her.

Then I noticed Canon Hudson coming out of the vestry. To my annoyance he came over towards me. That was one of the problems of Rosington. I had been used to the anonymity of cities.

'Hello, Mrs Appleyard. Enjoying the singing?'

'I don't know what it is but it's very restful.'

'We're rather proud of our music here. If you're here over Easter, you should –'

'I don't think I will be,' I said roughly, the decision suddenly made.

'You're leaving us?'

'I need to find a job. There's nothing down here. Or rather, nothing that appeals.'

He sat down beside me and folded his hands on his lap. 'And what exactly are you looking for, Mrs Appleyard?'

'I don't really know. But my husband's left me so I'm going to have to make my own living now.' I wished I could take the words back. My private life was none of his business. Janet had told other people that my husband was 'away'. I glanced at my watch and pantomimed surprise. 'Oh! Is that the time?'

'Difficult for you,' he said, ignoring my attempt to wind up the conversation. 'Am I right in thinking you'd prefer to stay in Rosington for the time being?'

'Well, it's a possibility.'

'You say you have no qualifications.'

'Apart from School Certificate.'

'And have you ever worked?'

'Only in my father's shop for a few years before I married. He was a jeweller.'

'What did that entail?'

I nearly told him to mind his own business, but he was such a gentle little man that being unkind to him seemed as wantonly cruel as treading on a worm. 'It varied. Sometimes I served in the shop, sometimes I helped with the accounts. I did most of the inventory when we sold the business.'

The music spiralled round and round above our heads. Just like me, it was trying to get out.

'How interesting,' Hudson said. 'Well, if you really are looking for something local, in fact I know of a temporary part-time job which might fit the bill. It's actually in the

Close and to some extent you could choose the hours you work. But I don't know whether it would suit you. Or indeed whether you would suit it.' He smiled at me, taking the sting from the words. 'I want someone to catalogue the Cathedral Library.'

I stared blankly at him. Still smiling, he stared back.

'But I wouldn't know where to start,' I said. 'Surely you'd need a librarian or a scholar or someone like that? It's not the sort of thing I could do.'

'How do you know?'

'It's obvious.'

'Mrs Appleyard, what's obvious to me is that it could suit us both if you were able to help. So it's worth investigating, don't you think?'

I shrugged, ungracious to the last.

'Why don't you have a look at the library now? It won't take a moment.'

He was a persistent little man and in the end it was easier to do what he wanted than to refuse. He fetched a key from the vestry and then took me over to a door at the west end of the south choir aisle. He unlocked it and we stepped into a long vaulted room.

Suddenly it was much lighter. On the east wall, high above my head, were two great Norman windows filled with plain glass. A faded Turkish runner ran from the door along the length of the room's long axis towards a pair of tables at the far end. On either side of the runner were wooden bookcases, seven feet high, dividing the room into bays. The temperature wasn't much warmer than in the Cathedral itself, which meant it felt chilly even to someone inured to the draughts of the Dark Hostelry.

'Originally the room would have been two chapels opening out of the south transept,' Peter Hudson said. 'It was converted into a library for the Cathedral in the eighteen-seventies. No one knows for sure, but we think there must be at least nine or ten thousand books here, possibly more.'

We walked the length of the room. I looked at the rank after rank of spines, most vertical, a few horizontal, bound in leather, bound in cloth. The air smelled of dust and dead

73

paper. I already knew I didn't have the training to do a job like this and probably not the aptitude either. But what I saw now was the sheer physical immensity of it.

One night at Hillgard House, Janet and I had sneaked out of our dormitory, slipped down the stairs and out of a side door. The sky was clear. We were in the middle of the country and in any case there was a blackout because it was wartime. We lay on our backs on the lawn, feeling the dew soaking through our nightdresses, and stared up at the summer sky.

'How many stars are there?' Janet murmured.

And I'd said, 'You could never count them.'

Terror had risen in me, a sort of awe. Facing all those books in the Cathedral Library I felt the same awe, only once removed from panic. Like the night sky, the library was too big. It contained too many things. I just wasn't on the right scale for it.

'I'm sorry, I don't think this will work.'

'Let's sit down and talk about it,' Hudson suggested.

At the end of the room were two large tables and an ill-assorted collection of what looked like retired dining chairs. Behind the tables was a cupboard built along the length of the wall. Hudson pulled out one of the chairs and dusted it with his handkerchief. I sat down.

'It's such a big job, and anyway I wouldn't know how to do it. I expect a lot of the books are valuable. I could damage them.'

He dusted another chair and sat down with a sigh of relief. Clasping his hands on the table, he smiled at me. 'Let me tell you what the job would entail before you make up your mind.'

'Aren't there medieval manuscripts? I wouldn't have the first idea how to read them.'

'The Cathedral does possess a few medieval manuscripts and early printed books. But they're not here. They're either under lock and key in the Treasury or they're on loan to Cambridge University Library or the British Museum. Nothing to worry about there.'

'If you say so.'

'You see, this library is a relatively recent affair. What happened was this – in the nineteenth century Dean Pellew left the Cathedral his books, about twelve hundred volumes. That's the nucleus of the collection. He also left us a sum of money as an endowment. So the chapter has a separate library fund which is there for buying new books and which can also be used for paying an assistant to manage the day-to-day work of the library. When the endowment was set up it was arranged that one of the canons should be the librarian and oversee the running of it. My immediate predecessor took over in 1931. He died in office last year so he had a long run for his money. But he didn't do much with the library.' Hudson smiled at me. 'And for the last ten years of his life, I doubt if he gave it a thought. Somehow it came to be understood that Cathedral librarian was one of those honorary posts. We've got enough of those on the Foundation, heaven knows. And then I took over.'

'Janet said there's a possibility the books might be given to the Theological College Library.'

He nodded. 'The dean and chapter have decided to close the Cathedral Library. It's not been formally announced yet but it's an open secret. The legal position's rather complicated – it's a question of diverting the endowment to something else relating to the Cathedral. And then there are the books, which is where you would come in. They're hardly ever used here, and frankly it's a waste of space having them here.'

'I wouldn't have thought space was a problem in this building.'

'You'd be surprised. It's our duty to make the best use of our resources we can. But to go back to the books. One possibility is that we give some or all of them to another library, and yes, perhaps the one at the Theological College might be appropriate.'

I noticed he did not mention the possibility that the Theological College might close.

'Or we may sell some or all of them. But we can't really decide what to do until we know what we've got. There's never been a complete catalogue, you see.' He stood up and lifted down a heavy foolscap volume from a shelf. He blew off the dust and placed it on the table. 'Dean Pellew's original collection is listed in here. Just authors and titles, nothing more, and I'd be surprised if we've still got them all. And then over the years there've been one or two half-hearted attempts to record acquisitions as they were made. Some of them are in here.' He tapped the book. 'Others are in the filing cabinet by the door.'

Hudson sat down again. He took out a pipe, peered into its bowl and then put it back in his pocket. I wondered what he would pay me and whether it would be enough to allow me to stay on in Rosington. He was going bald on top. Next I wondered whether he and his wife were fond of each other, and what they were like when they were alone together. Her name was June. She was one of the few ladies in the Close who not only recognized me but said hello when we met.

'Couldn't you get someone from a bookshop to look at the books?'

'We could. They would certainly do a valuation for us, I imagine. But we don't even know if we want to sell them yet. And if we wanted a catalogue, we'd have to pay them to do it.' He hesitated, and added, 'There's another reason why I'd like the books catalogued before we make up our minds what to do with them. There are a few oddities in the library. I'd like a chance to weed them out.'

'What do you mean exactly?'

'Apparently my predecessor found a copy of Mrs Beeton's *Household Management*. One or two novels have surfaced as well. Perhaps my predecessors muddled up some of their own books with the library's.'

'Look, it's very kind of you, but I still don't think I'd be suitable. I've never done anything like this before.'

He beamed across the table. 'Personally I've never found that a good reason not to do something.'

Hudson was persistent, even wily. He proposed I try my hand after lunch at half a dozen of the books under his supervision. If the results were satisfactory to me and to him then he suggested a trial period of a week, for which he would pay me three pounds, ten shillings. If we were both happy after this, the job would continue until the work was finished. All it needed, he said, was application and intelligence, and he was quite sure I had both of those.

The week passed, then another, then a third. It was easier to carry on with it than to try to explain to Hudson yet again why I wasn't suitable. The money was useful, too. I worked methodically round the room, from bookcase to bookcase. I did not move any of the books except when reuniting volumes belonging to a set. I used five-by-three index cards for the catalogue. On each card I recorded the author, the title, the publisher and the date. I added a number which corresponded to the shelf where the book was to be found and I added any other points which seemed to me to be of interest such as the name of the editor, if there was one, or the name of the series or whether the book contained one of Dean Pellew's bookplates, and had therefore been part of the original endowment.

It was surprisingly dirty work. On my first full day I got through several dusters and had to wash my hands at least half a dozen times. At Janet's suggestion, I bought some white cotton dusting gloves.

I reserved a separate table for the books which were in any way problematical. One of these was *Lady Chatterley's Lover*, which I found halfway through my second week sheltering in the shadow of Cruden's *Concordance*. I flicked through the pages, feeling guilty but failing to find anything obscene. So I borrowed it to read properly, telling my conscience that it wouldn't matter two hoots to Hudson if I found it today or next week.

I watched the cards expanding, inching across the old shoebox I kept them in until that shoebox was full and Canon Hudson found me another. My speed improved as I went on. The first time I managed to dust and catalogue fifty books in a single day, I went to the baker's and bought chocolate eclairs. Janet and Rosie and I ate them round the kitchen table to celebrate the achievement. As time went by, too, I needed to refer fewer and fewer queries to Canon Hudson.

At first he came in once a day to see how I was getting on.

Then it became once every two or three days or even longer. There was pleasure in that too.

'You've got a naturally orderly mind, Wendy,' he told me one day towards the end of April. 'That's a rarity.'

Henry would have laughed at the thought of me in a Cathedral Library. But the job was a lifeline at a time when I could easily have drowned. I thought it came to me because of the kindness of Canon Hudson, and because I happened to be in the right place at the right time. Years later I found out there was a little more to it.

It was in the early 1970s. I met June Hudson at a wedding. I said how much the job in the Cathedral Library had helped me, despite everything, and how grateful I was to her husband for offering it to me.

'It's Peter who was grateful to you, my dear. At one point he thought he'd have to catalogue all those wretched books himself. Anyway, if anyone deserves thanking it ought to be Janet Byfield.'

'What do you mean?'

'It was her idea. She had a word with me and asked if I would suggest you to Peter. She said she hadn't mentioned it to you in case it didn't come off. But I assumed she'd have said something afterwards.'

'No,' I said. 'She never did.'

That increased my debt to Janet. I wish I knew how you pay your debts to the dead.

15

Then there was the business about the bishop's invitation. It was delivered by hand through the letter-flap from the High Street while Janet and I were having tea in the kitchen. She ripped open the envelope, which had the arms of the see on the back, read the note from Mrs Bish and pushed it across the table to me. She had asked the Byfields to dinner.

'That means *he's* asked us,' Janet explained. 'David will be pleased.'

'What's he like?'

'He was the Suffragan Bishop of Knightsbridge before he came here.' Janet blushed as she usually did when she was going to say something unkind. 'And some people say he was better at the Knightsbridge part than the bishop part.'

'You mean he's a snob?'

On that occasion she wouldn't say more. But after meeting the bishop once or twice I knew exactly what she meant. Like so many people in those days, he secretly felt that the Church should be a profession confined to gentlemen. His chaplain was a young man named Gervase Haselbury-Finch, who looked like Rupert Brooke and had a titled father, qualifications which as far as the bishop was concerned made up for his lack of organizational abilities. I don't mean to imply there was anything improper about the bishop's behaviour, not in the sense that makes tabloid headlines. He was married and had three grown-up children.

'The bishop likes to have little chats with David,' Janet went on. 'He says things like, "I'm expecting great things of you, my boy." He's very much in favour of keeping the

Theo. Coll. going and he thinks that David would make a marvellous principal. So that's something in our favour. A very big something.'

'Is that how they choose someone?' I said. 'Because the bish likes their face?'

'Well, there's more to it than that. Obviously. But it helps.'

'It's not exactly fair.'

She made a sour face. 'The Church isn't. Not always.'

'It's like something out of the Middle Ages.'

'That's exactly what it is. You can't expect it to behave like a democracy.'

Later that evening we discussed the invitation over supper. David already knew about it because he had met the bishop at evensong. The only other people invited were the Master of Jerusalem and his wife. It turned out that the bishop had been at Jerusalem College too.

'I haven't anything to wear,' Janet said.

'Of course you have.' David smiled at her. 'Wear what you wore for the Hudsons. You'll look lovely.'

'I always wear that.'

'They'll notice your face not your dress.'

'Your mother had a very pretty dress at our engagement party,' Mr Treevor put in. 'I wonder if she's still got it. Why don't you ask her? Are there any more baked beans?'

Afterwards David took his coffee to the study and Mr Treevor went upstairs. Janet shook a small avalanche of powdered Dreft into the sink and turned on the tap so hard that water sprayed over the front of her pinafore and on to the tiled floor.

'What's up?' I said.

'It'll be ghastly. They'll make me feel like a poor little church mouse. I can never think of anything to say to the bishop. He pretends I must be frightfully intellectual because he's read some of Mummy's translations. So he tries to have conversations about the theme of redemption in Dostoevsky's novels and the irrationality of existentialism. It's dreadful. Meanwhile the women look at my shoes and wonder why they clash with my handbag.'

'Don't go,' I said.

'I've got to. David will be so upset if I don't. The bishop wants me to come, you see, and the bishop's word is law. And what about you?'

'Don't worry about me. I'd much rather stay at home.'

I hadn't been included in the invitation – I'm not sure the bish knew of my existence, not then. This suited me very well. Someone had to keep an eye on Rosie and Mr Treevor. Anyway, in my bedroom I had the bottle of gin and the unexpurgated *Lady Chatterley's Lover*. What more could a girl want?

'I suppose I could wear my blue dress. But there's that stain on the shoulder.'

'You can borrow my shawl if you like.'

In the end, though, Janet didn't go after all. On the day of the dinner party she developed a migraine. She had had them occasionally since we were children, usually when under strain. When I came back for lunch and found her flat out on the sofa, I made her go to bed and arranged to collect Rosie from school. David came in later, with just time to bathe and change before going out again. I told him what had happened, and said there was no chance that Janet would be well enough to go out to dinner.

'I'll go up and see her,' he said. 'Perhaps she's feeling better.'

'She's not. And if you try and persuade her she is feeling better, it'll only make her feel worse.'

'That's plain speaking.'

I sensed the anger in him. I even took a step backwards and felt the edge of the hall table pushing into the back of my thigh. 'That's what we do up in Yorkshire, David. Honestly, I don't mean to be rude, but I know what she's like when she has these migraines. And this one's a stinker.'

'I'll go and see her now.'

'But please let her stay in bed.'

He stared at me. There was so much anger in his face now that just for a moment I was frightened, physically frightened. He could strangle me now, I thought, and no one could stop him.

'I'll see how she is,' he said in a tight voice.

'While you're upstairs, perhaps you could say good night to Rosie. She was asking after you earlier.'

The jab went home. I saw it in his face. He went upstairs without another word. I felt guilty because I had been unkind to him and angry for being scared. I tend to attack when I feel defensive. I told myself that it wasn't as if he didn't deserve what I'd said about Rosie. David knew, and I knew, that Janet thought he should try to spend a little more time with her. He doted on her as he doted on Janet. But he was a busy man, convinced of the importance of what he was doing and in his heart of hearts he was a complete reactionary. Looking after children was something that you left to women. That was what they were for, along with the other marital duties which he probably assumed had been ordained by God and man since time immemorial. I wonder now if David was a little scared of young children. Some adults are.

The upshot of that was that Janet didn't go to dinner with David and David didn't say good night to Rosie. I went up later after he had left the house and found Rosie still awake.

'Your light shouldn't be on,' I said.

She stared at me without saying anything. She was a child who knew the power of silence.

'What are you reading?'

Rosie angled the book towards me. It was a big illustrated volume called *Tales from the New Testament*, an impeccable choice for a clergyman's daughter. It was open at one of the colour plates. The picture showed the Angel Gabriel talking to the Virgin Mary. The caption read, 'Hail, thou that art highly favoured, the Lord is with thee: blessed art thou among women.'

She looked up at me with bright, excited eyes. 'He looks like Daddy. The angel looks like Daddy.'

'I suppose he does a bit, yes. Except the angel's got fair hair and it's rather long.' I tried to make a joke of it. 'And, of course, Daddy doesn't wear a white dress or have wings.'

'He sometimes wears a sort of white dress in church.'

'Yes, I'm sure he does.'

'Grandpa said he saw an angel.'

'What?'

'He told me. He looked out of his window and there the angel was, walking in the garden.'

'How interesting. Now, why don't I read you a story, just a quick one, and then you can settle down?'

I read her the story of the feeding of the five thousand, which I chose on the grounds that it was short and contained no angels whatsoever. Some children like to sit with you, or on you, while you read to them. Rosie preferred me to sit in the chair by the window. She said it was so she could watch my face.

Later, when the story was over, I tucked her up and kissed the top of her head.

'Auntie Wendy?'

'What?'

'Was Lucifer an angel?'

'I don't know.'

'He'd be a sort of naughty angel. A wicked one who lives in hell.'

'You'll have to ask Daddy. He'll know.'

'Yes,' Rosie said. 'He knows all about God and things like that.'

Mr Treevor had settled into his new home surprisingly quickly. As long as there were no major deviations from the routine he had established he seemed quite content. Janet worried that he might try to repeat his mock-suicide attempt but there were no more incidents like that. (Janet asked him on several occasions why he'd done it. Twice he said it was a joke to amuse Rosie. Once he couldn't remember doing it at all. And the last time he said it was to see how much people loved him.)

If anything Rosie rather liked him. Perhaps it was because he was the nearest available man in the absence of a father. Sometimes he would go and say good night to her and an hour or so later Janet would find them both asleep, Rosie in bed and Mr Treevor in the armchair by the window. It was rather touching to see them together, asleep or awake. They didn't communicate much and they made few demands on each other, but they seemed to enjoy being in the same room.

The next day when the migraine had subsided, I told Janet what Rosie had said.

'An angel? Daddy must have been dreaming.'

'Most people settle for gnomes in the garden. I think an angel's rather classy.'

'Perhaps it was the milkman. He usually wears a white coat.'

'But he doesn't come to the garden door.'

'Daddy's getting a bit confused, that's all,' Janet said. 'Dr Flaxman said this might happen.'

Nowadays they would be able to narrow it down and perhaps delay the dementia's progress with drugs. Mr Treevor could have had a relatively early onset of senile dementia, either Alzheimer's or Multi-Infarct Dementia. Alzheimer's can be a pre-senile dementia as well. He wasn't a drinker so it can't have been alcoholic dementia. Other dementias can be caused by pressure in the brain, perhaps from a tumour, or by rare diseases like Huntington's or Pick's. But Pick's and Huntington's usually start when their victims are younger. If it was Huntington's it would have shown up when Rosie had the tests when she was an adult, even if she was not a carrier. The other main dementias, Creutzfeldt-Jakob disease and Aids dementia, developed later than 1958.

The worst thing, Janet said, was he knew what was happening. Not very often, but sometimes. He wasn't a fool by any means. And occasionally he was capable of acting completely rationally. That was why we took the story of the robbery seriously.

It happened while he was alone in the house. David and I were at work. Janet had gone to collect Rosie from school. When they got back they found Mr Treevor in a terrible state, trying to phone the police.

According to him, he had been dozing in his room when he heard somebody moving around downstairs. Thinking it was Janet, he had gone on to the landing and called downstairs, asking when tea would be ready. He heard footsteps, and the garden door slam. He looked out of the window and saw a man walking quickly down the garden and through the gate into the Close.

'He's been here before,' Mr Treevor said when he was retelling the tale for us at supper. 'I'm sure of it. He's stolen several of my things in the last few weeks. Those maroon socks, you remember, Janet, the ones Mummy knitted, and my propelling pencil.'

'The pencil had fallen down the side of your chair,' Janet reminded him.

He waved aside the objection. 'There's a ten-shilling note went from my wallet. That's what he took today.'

Janet glanced at me. I had been there yesterday morning when he'd produced a ten-shilling note and given it to Janet because he had a sudden urge for a box of chocolates.

'This man,' David said. 'What did he look like?'

'I only saw him from the back. Just a glimpse. A small dark man.' Mr Treevor stared thoughtfully at David and added, 'Like a shadow. That's it, David, tell the police that. He was like a shadow.'

16

Early in May the weather became much warmer. I no longer had to wear a coat and two cardigans when working in the library. The big room filled with light. The index cards marched steadily across the shoeboxes and everywhere I looked there was evidence of my industry. I felt better in other ways, too. On some days I hardly thought about Henry at all.

One Tuesday afternoon I was sitting at the table when I heard the door opening at the other end of the room. I assumed it was Canon Hudson or Janet or even Mr Gotobed, the assistant verger, who had a habit of popping up unexpectedly in the Cathedral or the Close. I turned in my chair and found myself looking up at David.

'I hope I'm not interrupting you. The dean's trying to track down a model of the Octagon, and there's a possibility it may be in here.'

I screwed the cap on my fountain pen. 'Not that I've seen, I'm afraid. But please have a look.'

He glanced round the library and smiled. 'It's looking much more organized than when I last saw it.'

'So it should be,' I said. 'Now what about this model?'

'The dean thought it might be in one of the cupboards.'

He nodded towards the long cupboard behind the table where I worked. It was about six feet high and built of dark-stained pine. Canon Hudson had told me that before the room was converted to the library, it had been used as the choir vestry and the cupboard had probably been built to house cassocks and surplices. It was full of rubbish now, he'd said, and when Gotobed had a spare afternoon he would investigate it properly. I'd tried the doors but they were locked.

David produced a key and unlocked the nearest door. Then he opened the other two, pulling open the three sets of double doors so the whole cupboard filled with light. What I noticed first was the skeleton of a mouse lying at the foot of one of the doors. Dust was everywhere, soft and gritty. I saw a bucket, a small mountain of prayer books, an umbrella stand, a stack of newspapers, an object like a wooden crinoline with a torn surplice draped over it, a clump of candlesticks, some of which were taller than me, a lectern, empty bottles and a cast-iron boot-scraper. I bent down to pick up one of the newspapers. It was a copy of the *Rosington Observer* from 1937.

'There we are.' David lifted the ragged surplice from the ecclesiastical coat hanger. 'Extraordinary, isn't it? I wonder who made it.'

'Is *that* it?'

He shot me an amused glance. 'Were you expecting something more lifelike? This shows what you don't see – the skeleton supporting the whole thing.' He flapped the surplice at the model, dislodging some of the dust. 'It's very elegant. A mathematical figure in wood. If I get the dust off, do you think you could help me lift it out?'

I ended up doing the dusting myself. Then we lifted the model out of the cupboard. It stood like the skeleton of a prehistoric animal on the library carpet.

'It's as if it's got eight legs,' I said.

'Each of them rests on top of one of the pillars below. They're beams supporting almost all the weight. Amazing, really – nearly sixty feet long, and they taper from just over three feet at the base to twelve inches at the top where they meet the angles of the lantern.'

His long fingers danced over the wooden framework. I didn't understand what he was saying. I really didn't try. I was too taken up watching how his hands moved and the expression on his face.

'And then look how they twisted the lantern itself round

so its sides are above the angles of the stone Octagon below. It splits the weight of each angle of the wooden Octagon between two pairs of these main beams that run down to the piers of the stone Octagon. Its legs, as you said.' Suddenly he broke off, frowning. 'But there should be a spire. Where do you think it's got to?'

I pointed into the cupboard at what I had assumed was an umbrella stand. Admittedly it was a peculiar shape for the purpose but it did have a broken umbrella jammed into it. With a cry of triumph David lifted it out. I applied the duster and then he raised it on top of the model of the Octagon. It slotted into place. We both stood back to admire it. The whole model now stood over six feet high. Nearly two feet of this was the slender framework of the spire, also octagonal.

'It's based on the Octagon at Ely,' David was saying. 'Ours is five or ten years later and rather smaller. In one sense it looks as if Ely was the apprentice work. Ours is much lighter – physically lighter, and also the windows in the lantern are larger. And we've got a spire which here is an integral part of the design.'

He was like a boy in his pleasure. It had never struck me before how attractive enthusiasm can be, the sort of enthusiasm that reaches out to other people.

'What are you going to do with this?' I asked him.

'We're planning an exhibition. The dean thinks we should do more to attract the tourists. Without the income we get from them it would be very difficult to run this place. Do you think I could leave it in that corner for now? He'll want to come and see it. But would it be in your way?'

We moved the Octagon where he suggested. David glanced at the table where I worked, which was underneath one of the windows.

'How are you getting on?'

'I'm nearly halfway, I think. I had to have a week off over Easter.'

'Any surprises?'

'*Lady Chatterley's Lover*.'

He stared at me, then threw back his head and laughed. 'What did you do with it?'

'I gave it to Canon Hudson.' I decided not to mention that I had read it first. 'Apparently it's the unexpurgated 1928 edition and it might be worth something.'

'But we'd have to sell it anonymously.' He gestured towards my card index. 'I'd like to have a look through there sometime, if I may.'

My excitement drained away. Indeed, up to that moment I hadn't been aware I was excited, only that I was enjoying myself. But now it was spoiled. Suddenly it seemed improbable he was interested in what was in the library for its own sake. Perhaps this was something to do with his campaign for the Theological College.

'I'm sure Canon Hudson wouldn't mind,' I said.

'I'd better leave you to your labours.'

At the door he paused. 'By the way, I should thank you.'

'It's nice to have an excuse for a break.'

'I don't just mean now. I mean at home. I don't know how Janet would have managed without you. Especially with her father around.'

I felt myself blush. I couldn't stand much more of this new David, considerate, enthusiastic and worst of all grateful.

'Of course, I'm not sure how long he'll be with us,' he said, and the old David emerged once again. 'In the nature of things it can't be for ever.' Then he smiled and the gears of his personality shifted again. 'Bless you,' he said, as priests do, and slipped out of the library.

I think coincidence is often a label we attach to events to confer a fake significance on them. But it makes me feel uncomfortable that on the same afternoon, a few minutes after David left, I had my first encounter with Francis Youlgreave.

I was cataloguing Keble's three-volume *Works of Richard Hooker*. On the flyleaf of the first volume, opposite the bookplate of the dean and chapter, was the name F. St J. Youlgreave. Presumably Youlgreave had owned the book and later presented it to the library.

There was a strip of paper protruding from the second volume. I took it out. The top was brown and flaky where it had been exposed to the air but most of the strip had been trapped between the pages. It looked like a makeshift bookmark torn from a larger sheet. Both of the longer edges were ragged. One side was blank. On the other were several lines of writing in ink that had faded to a dark brown.

> . . . a well-set-up boy perhaps twelve years old. He said he was going to visit his sister and their widowed mother who lodge in Swan Alley off Bridge Street. His name is Simon Martlesham and he works at the Palace where he cleans the boots and runs errands for the butler. It is curious how people of his class, even the younger ones, smell so unpleasantly of rancid fat. But when I gave him sixpence for helping me back to the house, he thanked me very prettily. He may be useful for . . .

Useful for what?

I made a note of where I had found the scrap of paper and put it to one side to show Canon Hudson. I didn't like the comment about the smell of rancid fat. I wondered what the boy had told his mother and sister when he finally reached home in Swan Alley. I made a note of Youlgreave's name on the index card for the *Works of Richard Hooker*.

I went back to the pile of books on my table and worked for another half an hour. I was on the verge of going out for a cigarette and a cup of tea when the door opened and Janet came in. She was rather pale and breathing hard.

'Help!' she said. 'You'll never guess what David's done. He's asked Canon Osbaston to dinner.'

17

Canon Osbaston, the principal of the Theological College, was the man whose job David wanted.

He had a taste for Burgundy and on Saturday morning David spent a good deal of money at Chase and Cromwell's, the wine merchants in the High Street. He also showed an uncharacteristic interest in the food Janet was intending to serve. David was trying to butter up the old man but I don't think he realized it. He could be astonishingly obtuse, especially where something he really cared about was concerned.

In honour of Canon Osbaston's visit we were going to use the dining room. I spent part of the morning polishing the table and cleaning the silver. What we needed, I thought, was a well-set-up boot boy to take care of these little jobs about the house.

Janet was unusually quiet at lunch. She wasn't irritable but her attention was elsewhere and there were vertical worry lines carved in her forehead. I assumed it was because of this evening. After lunch David went to play tennis at the Theological College. It was a fine day so I volunteered to take Rosie for a walk to give Janet a clear run in the kitchen. Rosie agreed to come on condition we went down to the river and fed the ducks. She was always a child who negotiated, who made conditions.

We walked down River Hill to Bishopsbridge. From there we went along the towpath until we found a cluster of mallards, two couples and their attendant families. We crumbled stale white bread and fed them.

'Would those ducklings taste nicer than ducks?' Rosie asked.

'I hadn't really thought about it.' The idea of eating one of those fluffy little objects, halfway to being cuddly toys, seemed absurd. 'Not as much meat on them as the older ones.'

'We like lamb instead of sheep, and veal instead of cow,' Rosie said. 'So I wondered.'

What she said made perfectly good sense. I was pretty sure that if a cannibal had a choice of me and Rosie on the menu he'd go for Rosie. I turned away from the ducks, looking for a change of subject. That's when I saw the Swan.

It was an L-shaped pub built of crumbling stone with an undulating tiled roof in urgent need of repair. A weather-beaten sign hung from one of the gable ends. I towed Rosie away from the river. There was a yard dotted with weeds in front of the pub, partly enclosed by the L. On one of the benches beside the front door an old man was sitting in the sunshine with his pipe and an enamel mug of tea.

'Hello,' I called out. 'It's a lovely afternoon.'

After a pause he nodded.

'I was wondering, is there somewhere called Swan Alley near here?'

'There is,' he said in a broad Fen accent, 'and then again there isn't.'

Oh God, I thought, not another old fool who thinks he has a sense of humour. 'Where is it?'

He took a sip of tea. 'Just behind you.'

I saw a piece of wasteland used as a car park, separated from the towpath by a mechanics workshop built largely of rusting corrugated iron.

I turned back. 'So it's not there now.'

'Just as well. Terrible place. Whole families in one room, and just a cold tap in the middle of a yard for all of them to share.' He shook his head, enjoying the horror of it. 'My old mother wouldn't let me go there because of the typhoid. They had rats as big as cats.' He studied me carefully to see how I took this last remark.

'How wonderful. That must have been a record, surely?'

'What was?'

'Having rats that size. I hope someone had the sense to catch a few and stuff them. Is there a museum where you can see them?'

'No.'

'What a pity.'

He started to light his pipe, a laborious procedure which told me the conversation was over. I felt a little guilty for spoiling his fun but not much. Rosie and I walked up the lane towards Bridge Street.

'Would baby rats be nicer to eat than full-grown ones?' Rosie asked, though unfortunately not loud enough for the old man to hear.

We crossed Bridge Street and went through the wrought-iron gates that led into the lower end of Canons' Meadow. The ground rose steadily upwards towards the Cathedral and, to the left of it, a mound of earth covered with trees, once the site of Rosington Castle. We walked up the gravel path to a gate into the south end of the Close. Canon Hudson was standing underneath the chestnuts on the other side talking to the bishop.

I tried to slip past them, but the bishop saw Rosie and beckoned us over. He was a tall, sleek man with a pink unlined face and fair hair turning grey. He was wearing a purple cassock that reminded me of a wonderful dress I'd once seen in a Bond Street window.

'Hello, Rosie-Posie. And how are you today?'

She beamed up at him. 'Very well, thank you, sir.'

Hudson introduced me to his lordship, who congratulated me briefly on my work in the library and then turned back to Rosie.

'And how old are you, my dear?'

'Four, sir. I'll soon be five. Not next week, the week after.'

'Five! Gosh! That's *very* grown up. What presents are you hoping to get?'

'Please, sir, I'd like an angel.'

'A what?'

'An angel.'

The bishop patted her shining head. 'My dear child.' His eyes swept from Hudson to me and he murmured, smiling, 'Trailing clouds of glory, eh?' Then he bent down to Rosie again. 'You must ask your daddy and mummy to bring you over to my house one day. You can play in the garden. It's lovely and big, and there's a swing and a pond with some very large goldfish. When you come I'll introduce you to them. And Auntie Wendy can come too. I'm sure she'd like to meet my fishies as well.'

And so on. The bishop seemed to have at his command an effortless flow of whimsicality. In an open contest he'd have knocked spots off J. M. Barrie. If anyone had told me at Rosie's age that I looked like the Queen of the Fairies I'd have curled up with embarrassment. But she accepted it as her due.

'I'm glad we bumped into each other,' Hudson said to me while the episcopal gush flowed on. 'I meant to drop in yesterday. Everything all right?'

'Fine, thanks.'

'I gather David found a model of the Octagon in the wall cupboard. Something for the dean's exhibition.'

'It was quite exciting, actually. It made a change from cataloguing books. Mind you, I'm not sure I'd have known what it was if he hadn't been there.' One memory jogged another. 'By the way, I came across a scrap of paper with some writing on. It was in a book that once belonged to someone called Youlgreave.'

'Ah yes. That would probably be Francis Youlgreave. He was the canon librarian about fifty years ago. What exactly did you find?'

'It looked like part of a letter or diary. Something about giving a boy sixpence for helping him.'

'He was a bit of an oddity, Canon Youlgreave. He had to retire after a nervous breakdown. If you come across anything else of his I'd like to see it. Would you make sure you do that?'

It wasn't what he said so much as the way that he said it. Hudson looked so mild and inoffensive that those rare times when I saw his other side always came as a shock. His voice was sharp, almost peremptory. He had just given me what amounted to an order.

'Of course,' I said. 'But now we mustn't keep you any longer. Come along, Rosie, we mustn't be late for tea.'

I dragged Rosie away from her mutual admiration society, said goodbye and walked towards the Cathedral and the Dark Hostelry. When we reached home, I opened the gate in the wall and Rosie ran ahead of me into the house. I found her and David waiting for me in the hall.

David was still in his tennis whites and his racket was on a polished chest near the door. I noticed that he'd knocked the vase of flowers on the chest, and a few drops of water glittered on the dark oak. Stupid man, I thought. If we didn't wipe off the water soon, it would leave a mark.

'Wendy, there you are.' His voice was casual to the point of absurdity, a tangle of elongated vowels and muted consonants. 'I thought I'd take Rosie downstairs and give her some tea.'

My face must have shown my surprise. But I managed a smile. 'OK. How nice.'

He moved towards the stairs to the kitchen, towing Rosie. 'Oh, by the way,' he said, interrupting Rosie who was telling him about the bishop and his fishies. 'Janet asked if you could pop up and see her if you had a moment. She's in our bedroom, I think.'

David give Rosie her tea? It was unheard of. Without taking off my hat, I went quickly upstairs and tapped on Janet's door. I heard her say something. I twisted the handle and went in. She was sitting on the window seat looking at the Cathedral.

'Are you all right?' I said, walking towards her.

She turned to look at me. The tears welled out of her eyes and ran down her cheeks.

'Wendy,' she said, 'I don't know what I'm going to do.'

I watched the tears running down her cheeks. 'What's wrong?'

She shook her head.

I went to her, put my hands on her arms and drew her towards me. She laid her head on my shoulder and began to sob. Between the sobs she muttered something.

'I can't hear you. What did you say?'

She lifted her tear-stained face. 'I can't bear it.' She hiccuped. 'Another one.'

'Another *what*?'

Janet pulled away from me and blew her nose. 'Another baby. I think I'm pregnant.'

18

Wine had a curious effect on Canon Osbaston, like water on a wilting plant. After two glasses of sherry and the first glass of Burgundy he moved on to a higher and more active plane of existence. As something of a connoisseur of the effects of alcohol, I watched with interest.

Osbaston had a big, unwieldy body, a long scraggy neck and a small bald head. My first impression was that he was like a tortoise, and this was not just because of his appearance. It was also because of the way he moved. You felt he should be encouraged to spend the winter in a cardboard box in the garage.

By the time we reached the veal cutlets, we were all rather merry. There were only the four of us round the table. John Treevor was capable of casting a blight on any social occasion, but fortunately he had been persuaded that he would be more comfortable having a tray upstairs. David was charming – he wasn't in competition with Osbaston, quite the reverse. I had fortified myself with a slug of gin beforehand so I was ready to relax and enjoy myself. So was Janet once the main course was on the table. With the second glass of Burgundy, Osbaston told an elderly joke involving chorus girls which was actually quite funny.

'Delightful to see such charming young ladies in the Close,' he boomed across the table to David. 'That's what the Theological College lacks, you know – a woman's touch. Mrs Elstree does her best, I'm sure, I don't want to imply she doesn't. But it's not the same. Mark you, there's bags of room for a family in the principal's quarters.' He nodded and if nods were words this one would have said, *A nod's as good as a wink*. The little head swivelled to face Janet. 'Which reminds me – how's young Rosie?'

'Asleep, I hope. She's very well.'

'A lovely name for a lovely child.' He swallowed more wine. 'It always reminds me of that story about dear old Winnington-Ingram when he was Bishop of London. Do you know it?'

'I'm not sure I do,' David said.

'I had it from his chaplain. The bishop was a great believer in cold baths, you see, and their moral value. One day he was talking in the East End and telling his audience how splendid it was to have a daily tub. Most of them didn't even have running water in their own homes, but I doubt if that occurred to the old boy. "And when I get out of my bath," he told them, "I feel rosy all over." At which a voice at the back of the hall pipes up, "'oo's Rosie, then?"'

We laughed enthusiastically. David turned the conversation to the previous occupant of the Principal's Lodging, a married man with a family.

'Yes, one of the daughters kept the library in order. What was her name? Sibyl, I think.' Osbaston inclined his head to me. 'Just as you are doing here in the Cathedral Library, Mrs Appleyard. Do you think librarianship is a job that women are particularly suited to? One could define it as a specialized form of housekeeping applied to books. It requires efficiency, a tidy mind. Splendid womanly virtues. Don't you agree?'

'Yes, indeed,' I said. 'In my experience, men tend to be both inefficient and untidy.'

His little brown eyes gleamed in the candlelight. 'Too true, Mrs Appleyard, too true.'

David got up to fetch the second bottle of Burgundy from the sideboard. Janet looked anxiously at me. I raised my glass to her and drained the rest of the wine.

Osbaston leant towards me. 'Once you've finished with the Cathedral Library, Mrs Appleyard, perhaps we should ask you to put our library in order for us.'

'So you've suffered from male librarians as well?'

'I think you'd find we're a little better organized than the

Cathedral Library.' He turned back to David. 'The last time I was in the Cathedral Library I happened to open Lowther Clarke's *Liturgy and Worship* to check a reference and I found half of it had been eaten.' There was a rumbling from deep in his interior. 'Mice, I suppose. I expect they found it pretty hard going. But undoubtedly edifying. No, Mrs Appleyard, you'd find our library much less daunting.'

'If the libraries are merged,' David said, 'Wendy's help could be particularly useful.'

'Doesn't that depend on Canon Hudson?' Janet said.

Osbaston nodded. 'And on others. We mustn't count our chickens, eh?'

'No news on that front, I suppose?' David asked, gesturing with the bottle towards Osbaston's glass.

'Not as far as I know. I gather Peter Hudson's rather taken up at present with the exhibition. Another of the dean's bright ideas.' While Osbaston's glass was being refilled he switched his attention to Janet and me. 'Trollope was perfectly right, I'm afraid. Cathedral closes are breeding grounds for eccentricity. Present company excepted. Let's hope the dean doesn't make an exhibition of *himself*. Ha, ha.'

Janet smiled politely.

I said, 'I gather some of the canon librarians have been a little eccentric. Francis Youlgreave, for example.'

'Oh, him.' Osbaston waved David and the bottle towards me. 'Mad as a March hare. Of course, he wrote poetry, which may explain it. Have you read any of his stuff?'

'I don't think I have.'

'There's quite a well-known one, "The Judgement of Strangers". Let's see, how does it go?' His voice dropped in pitch. *'Then darkness descended; and whispers defiled The judgement of stranger, and widow, and child.* Something along those lines.'

'What's it about?'

'No one's quite sure. My predecessor claimed it was based on a story Youlgreave found in the Cathedral archives. Something to do with a woman heretic being burnt at the stake. Can't say I've ever come across it.' Osbaston sipped his wine. 'Pity he didn't stick to poetry. He would have been all right then.'

'What do you mean?' Janet asked. 'What happened to him?'

'Went round the bend, my dear, had to resign. Unfortunately it wasn't something that could be hushed up. But they must have seen it coming. If only they'd managed to persuade him to take leave of absence. The trouble was, they say the dean was a bit of a weakling, afraid of his own shadow. And I think there might have been a family connection between them. Anyway, Youlgreave was allowed to stay in residence far longer than he should have been. There were complaints, of course, but it's actually quite hard to get rid of a canon. We're protected by statute, you see. Finally the poor fellow lost all touch with reality and he simply had to go. Caused quite a scandal at the time, I believe.'

'But what did he do?' I asked.

'He preached a sermon in favour of ordaining women priests.' Another rumble of laughter erupted from deep in the interior. 'Can you believe it?'

After dinner David took Osbaston into the drawing room and gave him a glass of brandy while Janet and I cleared the table and made the coffee.

'It seems to be going quite well,' Janet said as she piled plates into the sink.

'If Osbaston has any more to drink we'll probably have to carry him home,' I said. 'Who'd have thought it?' I noticed Janet was leaning against the draining board. 'Are you OK?'

She glanced back at me. 'Just tired.'

I made her sit down at the kitchen table. All the standing up couldn't be good for her and she had been up since half past six. I suggested she went to bed but she wouldn't hear of it.

'It would be rude.'

'It would be common sense.'

She shook her head. 'I'm all right. I'll be fine after a little rest.'

I gave up. It had always been impossible to deflect Janet from something she considered to be her duty. Probably the woman they burnt at the stake suffered from a similar mentality.

I picked up the tray and we went into the drawing room. Osbaston and David broke off their conversation as we came in. They looked like conspirators. I wondered if they'd been scheming about the Theological College. Ever the little gent, David sprang up to take the tray from me.

'I was just telling David,' Osbaston said, rolling the brandy round his glass, 'my housekeeper can remember Canon Youlgreave.'

'Really?'

He eyed me in a speculative way I suddenly recognized. It was as if someone had thrown a glass of icy water in my face. The sort of life Henry and I had led contained a great many men who looked at me as Osbaston did. 'It's not that surprising,' he said, settling his glasses on his nose. 'I've never dared ask Mrs Elstree how old she is but she can't be much less than seventy. Youlgreave must have died about fifty years ago.'

'It's hard to think of someone alive actually knowing him. He's like a character out of history, somehow.'

Osbaston allowed one of his rumbles to emerge. 'You must come and meet her. Why don't you all have tea with me tomorrow? Mrs Elstree makes very good –'

There was a loud crash above our heads. Janet was into the hall first, with the rest of us close behind.

Mr Treevor was standing at the head of the stairs. His feet were bare and his greasy hair stood up around his head. His pyjama jacket was undone, revealing a tangle of grey hair, and his trousers sagged low on his hips.

'Daddy, what's wrong?' Janet cried. 'Are you all right?'

'There was a noise, footsteps, just like before,' Mr Treevor said in a thin whine. 'I went to see if Rosie was all right but I couldn't find my glasses. I must have – must have knocked something over. Janie, where *are* my glasses?'

As if on cue, Rosie began to cry.

19

In the end I talked to David about Janet. He didn't like it and nor did I. I was beginning to feel like an interloper in their marriage, in more ways than one.

It was after breakfast the next day, Sunday, which happened to be the fifth anniversary of my marriage to Henry. No one else remembered this and I did my best to forget it. David came back from celebrating the early communion service full of the joys of this world and the next. While he worked his way through two cups of coffee, two boiled eggs and several rounds of toast, Janet pecked at a slice of bread and butter. After I'd washed up I cornered him in his study where he was reading a book and making notes.

'Janet's not well,' I told him. 'She needs to rest.'

'What's wrong with her?'

'She tired herself out yesterday killing the fatted calf. And she was tired beforehand. And then there's her condition.'

His eyes were drifting back to the book on his desk.

'She's pregnant, David. And in the first three months women are particularly delicate. If she works too hard there's a danger she might lose the baby.'

That got his attention. 'I hadn't realized. In fact . . .' His voice tailed away and I laid a private bet with myself that he had been about to say, *In fact I'd forgotten she was pregnant*. He looked at me. 'What do you advise?'

'I think she should go back to bed. She's getting ready for church at present. Tell her you think she ought to rest. It's what she needs. I can do lunch. There are plenty of leftovers.'

'Do you think she'll be well enough to have tea with Canon Osbaston?'

'She's not *ill*, David. She's just tired and I really think she needs a day off. Rosie and I can come if you want.'

In one way it worked out very well. Janet spent most of the day in bed and the rest of us muddled along reasonably happily. In retrospect, I think Rosie may have been withdrawn. Usually she enjoyed being with her father but when we walked to the Theological College for tea with Canon Osbaston, it was my hand she decided to hold. None of this seemed significant then and even now I wonder if I'm reading too much into it. That's the trouble with trying to remember things – you end up twisting the past into unrecognizable shapes. I just don't know what happened the previous evening. If anything.

I do know the weather was wonderful that afternoon. I haven't imagined the feeling of sun on my arms as we walked through the Close and down to the Porta. Ink-black shadows danced along the pavement. We passed Gotobed planting pansies in his window box. He pretended not to see us. He was a large man who hunched his shoulders as if trying to make himself small. His face was delicate, with big ears and a tiny nose and chin. I thought he looked like a mouse and perhaps felt like one too. He would talk to me when I was by myself but I think he was scared of David. He was certainly terrified of the head verger, a swarthy man named Mepal who rarely spoke, but I think everyone was a little afraid of Mepal, including the dean.

Immediately outside the Porta was Minster Street, which ran along one side of a small green before plunging down Back Hill to the station and the river. On the other side of the green stood the Theological College, a large redbrick building surrounded by lank shrubberies like coils of barbed wire.

David guided us up the drive and round to the lawn at the back. Four pink young men were playing lawn tennis. A little further on, four more were playing croquet. The Principal's Lodging, a self-contained wing of the main building, was beside the croquet lawn.

Canon Osbaston was dozing in a wing armchair in front of

open French windows. The room behind him was long, high-ceilinged and densely populated with large brown pieces of furniture. He must have heard our footsteps on the gravel because his eyes flickered open and he struggled out of the chair.

'Must have nodded off. Meant to have the kettle on before you arrived. Is Janet with you?'

'She's a little unwell,' David said.

'Nothing serious, I trust. Such a pleasant evening.' He leered at me. 'I wonder if you would give me a hand making the tea, Mrs Appleyard? I'm afraid it slipped my mind yesterday evening, in the – ah – heat of the moment, that Mrs Elstree has Sunday afternoons off. She visits her widowed sister, I believe.'

'Perhaps Rosie can help as well,' I said. 'Many hands make light work.'

In the end, all four of us went into the kitchen. I felt as though I'd awakened a Sleeping Beauty. I wished I could find a way to send him to sleep again. We found that Mrs Elstree had left everything ready for us in the kitchen. Ten minutes later, we were sitting in deckchairs on the lawn.

We drank lapsang souchong and ate most of a Victoria sponge. It was warm in the sun and I felt pleasantly tired. Osbaston found Rosie some paper and a pencil and once she had finished her cake she sat on the lawn in the shade of a beech tree and drew.

The young men played croquet and tennis, and watching them gave me something to do with the forefront of my mind. Occasionally some of them would wander over to have a few words with Osbaston or David. More than one of them looked at me in a way that gave me pleasure. I might have no taste for elderly clergymen but after the dreariness surrounding the end of my marriage it was nice to be admired again, even by theological students.

David and Osbaston were talking about the syllabus for next year – something about the pros and cons of increasing New Testament Greek at the expense of Pastoral Theology. It was one of those lazy conversations full of half-sentences which happen when people know each other very well, so much so that each is usually aware what the other is about to say. I looked at David through half-closed eyes.

Before I knew what was happening, I found I had drifted into a daydream in which I was married to him and Rosie was our daughter. That was enough to make me sit up with a jerk. I hate the way the mind plays tricks when you're relaxing. I went into the house to powder my nose. By the time I came out the tennis and the croquet were finished and it was time to go. The men were turning their thoughts towards evensong.

'You must come and meet Mrs Elstree some other time, Mrs Appleyard,' Osbaston said. 'In the meantime I found something else which might interest you.' He pottered through the French window into his drawing room and came out a moment later with a hardback book bound in blue cloth. 'I thought I'd seen something about that fellow Youlgreave recently, and I was right. I looked it out after breakfast this morning. Do borrow it, if you'd like. I've put a marker in.'

I took the book and opened it automatically to the title page. *The Journal of the Transactions of the Rosington Antiquarian Society 1904.*

'I think it may be what gave him the idea for that judgement poem,' Osbaston said. 'You remember, the story about a heretic being burned? Take it with you, my dear, and study it at your leisure.' He edged a little closer to me. 'Perhaps we could discuss it when you come and meet Mrs Elstree.'

I smiled at him. 'Thanks.' I looked around for a diversion and found Rosie. 'What a nice drawing. May I see it?'

With obvious reluctance she gave it to me. David and Osbaston came closer and together we looked down at the sheet of paper in my hands. It was a child's drawing with no sense of perspective or proportion. After all, Rosie wasn't yet five, though in some ways she was very mature for her age. The pencilled figures were like stick insects with a few props attached. But you could see what Rosie had been getting at. A man wearing a white dress and a pair of wings was about to plunge a sword shaped like a cake slice into a small person with long hair cowering at his feet.

'Let me guess,' said Canon Osbaston, his head swaying

towards Rosie. 'Could this be the sacrifice of Isaac?' He frowned and a heavy forefinger stabbed the man with the sword. 'But in that case this must be Abraham, despite the wings. After all, it can hardly be the Angel of the Lord.'

20

Osbaston had marked a letter, one of a number printed at the end of the *Journal*. I read it after supper when David was working in the study. Janet was trying to reconcile the butcher's bill with what we had actually received and said she would look at it later.

CORRESPONDENCE RECEIVED BY THE EDITOR

From the Revd Canon F. St J. Youlgreave:

Sir,
I write to apprise you and other members of the Society of an interesting discovery I have made in my capacity as Cathedral Librarian. I had occasion to examine the binding of a copy of the Sermons of Dr Giles Briscow, the Dean of Rosington in the reign of Queen Elizabeth, which was in a decayed condition, with a view to seeing whether it should be rebound. I discovered there were annotations on the end-paper at the back of the book. These are in a Secretary hand which I judge to be of the first half of the seventeenth century. The writing is in Latin and appears to have been copied from an older work, perhaps a Monkish Chronicle dealing with the history of the Abbey of Rosington.

Evidence on the flyleaf at the front of the book suggested to me that the volume had once been in the possession of Julius Farnworthy, who of course was Bishop from 1619 to 1628, and whose tomb is in the South Choir Aisle. It is possible, even probable, that Bishop Farnworthy, or one of his contemporaries at Rosington, was responsible for the memorandum inscribed on the end-paper.

For the time being I have entrusted the book to an acquaintance who has some skill at palaeography and who is also in a position where he may conveniently examine the Farnworthy Collection in the British Museum Library. First, however, I took the precaution of copying the memorandum in full. When the results of the palaeographical examination are known, and when I have had an opportunity to complete other researches, I hope to be in a position to present a paper on the subject to the Society. I intend to assess the authenticity and provenance of this curious discovery, and also to sketch in the background of the events which it describes insofar as this proves possible to do. In the meantime, I hope you will permit me to whet the appetite of my fellow members of the Society with my rendering of the memorandum into English.

'In the third year of King Henry's reign, plague swept this part of the country. Merchants and pilgrims alike dared not cross the Great Causeway for fear of infection. Houses were left empty, fields untended and animals starved for want of feeding.

'Men said openly that the devil was abroad in the land.

'In the village of Mudgley, the parish priest died in much agony. His housekeeper stood at the cross and told those that remained alive that the Devil had carried away his soul, but at the same time an Angel had protected hers. And she uttered this blasphemy: that the Angel had told her she was chosen among all women to be His first priest of her sex. And the Angel ordained her, saying unto her, "Am I not greater than any Bishop?"

'Whereupon the woman led the people into church and celebrated Mass. Hearing this, the Abbot, Robert of Walberswick, sent men to bring her to Rosington where she was tried before God and man for blasphemy. But the Devil would not leave her. She would not confess her sins nor repent of her evil so they burned her in the marketplace. Her name was Isabella of Roth.'

Robert of Walberswick was Abbot from 1392 to 1407. The third year of King Henry's reign must refer to Henry IV and therefore date this episode to 1402. It is not clear whether the village mentioned is Mudgley Burnham or Abbots Mudgley. The Latin shows no signs of the influence of the Renaissance and it contains many characteristically Mediaeval contractions and turns of phrase. At present, at least, we can only speculate why the unknown writer of this memorandum should have wished to copy the passage. The whereabouts of the original is equally mysterious.

If I may be permitted to end on a personal note, you will notice that Roth is mentioned. I can only assume that this is the village of Roth in the County of Middlesex. Strange to say, this is a locality I know well, since my family has resided there for more than forty years.

I am, Sir, etc.

F. Youlgreave

I also found Youlgreave's poem, 'The Judgement of Strangers', in an anthology of Victorian verse in the dining room bookcase. If I hadn't read the letter, I don't think the poem would have made any sense to me at all. But if you assumed it was Isabella's story, then everything fell into place. Well, perhaps not everything because some of it was almost wilfully hard to understand. But you could see that the poem might be an impressionistic account of a woman being martyred for her beliefs in a vaguely medieval setting.

I read both the poem and the letter again when I was in bed with rather a large nightcap. The gin gave a slight hangover later and probably caused the nightmare which woke me covered in sweat in the early hours. I dreamed I was in Rosington marketplace. Someone was burning rubbish near the cross and people were shouting at me. Just before I woke up, I glanced into a litterbin fixed to a lamppost and found a doll with no arms staring up at me.

'Theologically the idea's completely untenable, as Youlgreave would have known,' David said. 'The notion of women priests simply doesn't make sense.'

'Why?' I asked, not because I cared one way or the other. It was just that I wanted to keep David talking, and he was particularly appealing when he became passionate about something.

He glanced up at the Cathedral clock. 'I don't want to go into it now. There isn't time and it's a very complicated subject.'

'Come on. That's no answer.'

He stopped at the door to the cloisters. We had been walking round the east end of the Cathedral on our separate ways to work. It was another beautiful day. A wispy cloud hung behind the golden weathercock at the tip of the Octagon's spire. Every detail of the stonework was crisp and clean. A swallow appeared round one of the pinnacles at the base of the spire, banked sharply and swooped down the length of the nave towards the west end. Suddenly David smiled, and not for the first time I thought that there is something cruel about beautiful people. Their beauty sets them apart from the rest of us. From the beginning they are treated differently.

He said, 'I don't believe a woman can be a priest any more than she can be a father.'

'But being a priest's a job. If you can have a woman on the throne, why can't you have one in the pulpit?'

'Because God chose to become incarnate in a patriarchal society. He chose only male apostles. Just as he wanted a woman, the Virgin Mary, to have the highest possible human vocation.'

'We're not living in first-century Palestine any more.'

'I don't think God's choice of time and place was an accident. It would be absurd for a Christian to think that. There's nothing in Scripture to support the idea of women priests. So we can only conclude that a male priesthood

110

is what God wanted. If it were just a matter of human tradition, of course it could be changed. But it's not. It's a divine institution.'

'I'll have to take your word for it. But can't the Church sometimes admit it's got it wrong? After all, it's changed its mind before. For instance, you don't go around burning people at the stake any more just because they don't agree with you.'

'The two things aren't analogous.'

You can't argue with fanatics, I thought. If David wanted to inhabit a fairy-tale universe conducted by fairy-tale laws, that was his business.

'I've got to do some work,' I said. 'I'd better go. Thanks for the theology lesson.'

For an instant I thought he looked disappointed, like a dog deprived of a bone. Perhaps he had seen me as a potential convert, the prodigal daughter on the verge of a change of heart. We said goodbye and he walked on towards the Porta and the Theological College.

I ducked into the cloisters and walked slowly towards the south door of the Cathedral. On my way I passed the entrance to the Chapter House, a large austere room with a Norman arcade running round the walls below the windows. Nowadays the chapter met in more comfortable surroundings and the room was used mainly for small concerts and large meetings. They were going to use the room for the exhibition. Hudson was in there talking to the dean, and he gave me a wave as I passed the doorway.

Before I started work I got out a couple of histories of Rosington and one of the county. There were references to Mudgley, both Abbots and Burnham, and to outbreaks of plague in the fourteenth and fifteenth centuries. But I found nothing about Isabella of Roth, women priests or angelic visitations.

After that I catalogued half a dozen books. But my attention kept wandering back to Francis Youlgreave and Isabella and to the boy called Simon, the one Youlgreave thought might be 'useful'. Finally I decided that I would take my coffee break early and skip the coffee part of it.

111

Instead I went to the public library which was housed in a converted Nissen hut in a street off the marketplace. Janet had taken me to join the library a few weeks before but I had never used it. The librarian in charge was a thickset man with a face like a bloodhound's and thick, ragged hair the colour of wire wool. I asked him if they had anything on Francis Youlgreave.

'About him or by him?'

'Either.'

'We've got a book of his poetry.'

'Good. Where can I find it?'

Wheezing softly, he stared at me. 'I'm afraid it's on loan.'

I felt like a child deprived of a treat. 'Can I reserve it?'

The book was called *The Tongues of Angels*. 'Is there a biography?' I asked as I handed the librarian the reservation card and my sixpence.

He glanced at my name on the card. 'Not that I know of, Mrs Appleyard. But he's in the *Dictionary of National Biography*, and there's also something about him in a book we have called *Rosington Worthies*. Chapter nine, I think. You'll find it in the reference section under Local History.'

I was impressed and said so.

'To be honest, I hadn't heard of him until last week. But someone happened to be asking about him.'

'Would that have been Canon Hudson, by any chance?'

'It wasn't him. No one I know.'

It was another little mystery, and one which irritated rather than intrigued me. I was surprised to find I didn't like the idea of someone else being interested in Francis Youlgreave. I felt he ought to be mine. A substitute for Henry, perhaps, safely dead and therefore able to resist the lures of widows with more money than morals.

I thanked the librarian, went into the little reference department and dug out the bones of Youlgreave's life. But, like the model of the Octagon we'd found in the library, the bones didn't give much idea of the finished article.

Francis Youlgreave was born in 1863, the younger son of a baronet. He published *Last Poems* in 1884 while he was an undergraduate at St John's College, Oxford. After coming down from the university he decided to go into the Church. These are facts, you can look them up for yourself in the *Dictionary of National Biography*. He was in fact one of the first ordinands at Rosington Theological College. Several curacies followed in parishes on the western fringe of London.

In 1891, still in London, Francis became the first vicar of a new church, St Michael's, Beauclerk Place, which is west of Tottenham Court Road. (That's how I came to think of him, by the way. As Francis, as if he was someone I knew.) In 1896 he published his second volume of poetry and then *The Four Last Things*. Four years later he became a canon of Rosington. Osbaston had been right about a family connection. The dean at the turn of the century was a cousin of Francis's mother.

His last book, *The Tongues of Angels*, was published in 1903. The following year ill health forced him to retire. He went to live in his brother's house, Roth Park in Middlesex, where he died on 30th July 1905. Nowadays he was best known for the one poem 'The Judgement of Strangers', said to have been admired by W. B. Yeats.

At lunchtime there were usually only the three of us at the Dark Hostelry. Rosie was at school and David had lunch at the Theological College. Janet had found time to read Youlgreave's letter in *The Journal of the Transactions of the Rosington Antiquarian Society*. While we ate cold lamb and salad I told her about the failure of my attempt to find out more about Isabella. Meanwhile Mr Treevor chewed methodically through an immense quantity of meat.

'Why are you doing this?' Janet asked.

'It's such a strange story. And I can't help feeling sorry for the woman.'

'If she ever existed.'

'I think she did. Why would Francis have invented something like that?'

Janet looked across the table at me. 'I don't know. So you think the poem *was* inspired by Isabella?'

'Of course. Have you read it?'

'Not yet. I'll look at it after lunch.'

'The poem's in three parts.' I held up my hand and ticked off the fingers. 'First the soldiers come for her when she's in

113

church. Then there's the trial scene. And finally there's the bit at the end where she's burnt at the stake.'

'When was it written?' Janet said.

'It was one of the poems in *The Four Last Things*, which was published in 1896. So –' I broke off as the implication hit me.

'And when did he write this letter to the Antiquarian Society?'

'In 1904. He'd become a canon of Rosington in 1901.'

Janet smiled at me. 'Then isn't it a little hard to see how a discovery he claimed to have made in the Cathedral Library could have inspired a poem published at least five years earlier?'

'Is there any more lamb?' asked Mr Treevor, looking at the remains of the joint.

For a moment I felt ridiculously depressed. Then I cheered up. 'I know – Francis was at the Theological College here. That must have been in the eighteen-eighties. So he could have come across the book then. Perhaps the students were allowed to use the Cathedral Library. And then he found it again when he came back to Rosington. That makes sense, doesn't it? He'd be bound to look for it.'

For a moment Janet concentrated on carving the meat. 'Why does it matter?'

'It's quite interesting. Especially in view of that sermon of his, the one about women priests that made them give him the sack. There must be a connection.'

'More?' Mr Treevor suggested.

Janet went back to the carving and Francis Youlgreave slid away from us, back into the void he had come from. Instead we talked about the Principal's Lodging at the Theological College, and whether it would make a better family home than the Dark Hostelry.

I was glad of the change of subject. I didn't want to think too much about why Francis was interesting me, or to allow Janet to delve too deeply into my motives. All right, I was bored. I needed stimulation. But another reason for my interest is painfully obvious now. But believe me, it wasn't then – in those days I fooled myself as well as everyone else.

I wanted to find a way of impressing David Byfield. I wanted to make him take notice of me. How better to do this than by making a scholarly discovery? It makes me squirm to think about it. I wouldn't say I was in love with David. Not exactly. What I felt about David had a lot to do with wanting to get back at Henry. But it wasn't entirely that. The thing you have to understand about David, the real mystery perhaps, is that despite his arrogance and his habit of patronizing the little women around him, he was actually very sexy.

Living in the same house I couldn't avoid him. Once I saw him naked. Despite its size there was only one bathroom at the Dark Hostelry. I came down one morning in my dressing gown, opened the door and there he was – standing in the bath, the water running off his white body, reaching for a towel draped over the washbasin. As the door opened, he stopped moving, apart from his head turning towards the door, and in that instant he was like a statue of an athlete, a young god frozen in time.

'So sorry,' I blurted out. I closed the door and bolted back to my room on the next floor. If it was anyone's fault it was his, because we always locked the door of the bathroom. But somehow I felt the blame was mine, that I had been prying like a Peeping Tom. Twenty minutes later we met at breakfast and both of us pretended it hadn't happened. I wonder if it stuck in David's memory over the years as it has in mine.

21

The dean's exhibition was taking shape in the Chapter House. Janet told me that the idea had aroused considerable opposition because it smacked of commercialism. I was never quite sure whether the opposition was on religious or social grounds. In the Close, it was often hard to tell where the one stopped and the other began.

The dean had financial logic on his side. There was death-watch beetle in the roof of the north transept. The windows of the Lady Chapel needed re-leading and the pinnacles at the west end were in danger of falling into Minster Street. The available income barely covered the running costs, according to David, and was incapable of coping with major repairs or emergencies. Opening the Chapter House for an exhibition might be the first step towards setting up a permanent museum. The real question was whether the tourists would be prepared to pay the entry fee for what was on offer.

'If this works, the dean's talking of having a Cathedral café,' David told us one evening. 'It makes a sort of sense, I suppose. Why should the tea shops in the town reap all the benefit from the Cathedral's visitors?'

'But where would they put it?' Janet asked.

'If they close the library there would be plenty of room there.'

'But that's inside the Cathedral.'

He shrugged. 'They could move the exhibition into the library and use the Chapter House or somewhere else in the Close for the café.'

The collection included a good deal of medieval stonework

– fragments of columns, tombstones and effigies, some of the grander vestments from the great cope chest, fragments of stained glass, and of course the model of the timber skeleton of the Octagon which David had found in the library cupboard. Canon Hudson asked me to keep an eye out for attractively bound or illustrated volumes in the Cathedral Library, particularly ones with a Rosington connection. I tried to make David laugh by suggesting they used the *Lady Chatterley* I had found, but he preserved a stone face and said he did not think it would be suitable.

The whole thing was done on the cheap. The dean had no intention of wasting money on new display cases or on extending the collection until there was evidence that the exhibition would make a profit. They had decided against hiring staff, too. One by one, the ladies of the Close were recruited for the exhibition rota. There was to be a grand opening in June with the bishop. The *Rosington Observer* had promised to send a photographer.

'I'm sorry you got landed with this as well,' Janet said to me on the evening of the day I was asked to join the rota. 'I don't think David should have asked you.'

'I don't mind. Anyway, it may never happen.'

'What do you mean?'

'I may not be here by then. This job isn't going to last for ever.'

Janet looked at me and I saw fear in her eyes. 'I hope you don't go. Not yet.'

'It won't be for a while,' I said, knowing that I would never be able to resist Janet if she asked for my help, if she asked me to stay. 'Anyway, the cataloguing may take longer than I think. You never know what's going to turn up.'

Or who. When I left the library the following afternoon I found Canon Osbaston loitering in the cloisters.

'Ah!' he said. 'Good Lord! I'd forgotten I might find you here, Mrs Appleyard. I was just examining the exhibition.'

Wheezing softly, he held open the door to the Close.

'You're going to the Dark Hostelry?'

'Yes.'

He fell into step beside me. 'Perhaps we might walk

together. I'm on my way to the High Street to buy some tobacco.'

We walked for a little while without talking.

Suddenly he burst out, 'Youlgreave was mad, Mrs Appleyard. Absolutely no doubt about it. Don't you find it rather warm for the time of year?'

'It's lovely, isn't it?' I said.

'Let's hope the sunshine lasts. We have a jumble sale for the South American Missionary Society on Saturday.'

Our progress through the sun-drenched Close was slow, a matter of fits and starts. We stopped while Osbaston mopped his face with a large handkerchief. In honour of the weather he was wearing a baggy linen jacket and a Panama hat with a broken brim.

'When you say "mad",' I said after a moment, 'what do you mean exactly?'

'I understand Canon Youlgreave was considered eccentric when he first came to Rosington,' Osbaston said, edging closer to me. 'And then he grew steadily worse. But it was in ways that made it difficult for one to insist on his having the appropriate medical treatment. When I arrived here in 1933 there were many people living who had known him and all this was common knowledge.'

'So what did he *do*?'

'It was a particularly distressing form of mental instability, I'm afraid.' Osbaston glanced at my face as if it was a pornographic photograph. 'It seems that his private life may not have been above reproach. And then there was that final sermon. Caused rather a stir – there were reports in the newspapers. They had to bring in the bishop and I believe Lambeth Palace was consulted too. Fortunately the poor fellow's family were very helpful. No one wanted any scandal.' The little head nodded on the great body. 'So we have that much to be thankful for, Mrs Appleyard. And we mustn't judge him too harshly, must we? I believe he was always very sickly even as a boy.'

By now we were standing outside the door in the wall leading to the garden of the Dark Hostelry.

'I must say goodbye, Mr Osbaston.'

He moistened his lips just as he had on Saturday night when he was about to take a sip of Burgundy. 'I thought I might have a cup of tea at the Crossed Keys Hotel. I don't suppose you'd care to join me?'

'That's very kind, but I should go. Janet's expecting me.'

He raised his Panama. 'Some other time, Mrs Appleyard. Delightful to see you again.' He ambled away.

Janet was on her knees weeding a flower bed near the door into the house. 'What have you got to smile about?' she said.

22

'How nice to see you again, Mrs Byfield,' Mrs Elstree said. 'Such a shame about the weather.'

'It's not a bad turnout all things considered,' Janet replied. 'By the way, this is my friend Mrs Appleyard. We were at school together. Wendy, this is Mrs Elstree.'

I shook hands with Canon Osbaston's housekeeper, a tall, drab woman who looked as though she had stepped out of a sepia-tinted photograph. She stared at the base of my neck. I wondered if my neck was dirty or if a button had come adrift and my bra was showing. But she smiled quite affably and then turned her attention back to Janet.

'Let's have some tea, shall we?' she suggested. 'I need to check they've remembered everything. I'm afraid some of our staff need watching like a hawk.'

The three of us made our way through the crowd to the urn controlled by the Theological College's cook. It was raining hard so the jumble sale was being held in the dining hall. Since the doors had only just opened, there wasn't a queue for tea. Most of the people here were middle-aged women in hats and raincoats, armed with umbrellas. They intended to let nothing get between them and a good bargain.

Janet insisted on buying the tea. Mrs Elstree examined the sugar bowl, felt the side of the urn and checked the level in the milk jug.

'Nothing to worry about, I'm glad to say,' she murmured in my ear. She had a Fen accent, its harsh edges softened by years of contact with clerical vowels. 'They know better than to try monkeying about with me.' She smiled at Janet's back

120

and lowered her voice still further. 'Lovely lady, Mrs Byfield. Such a nice family to have in Rosington.' Then, at a more normal volume, 'I understand you work in the Cathedral Library, Mrs Appleyard.'

'For the time being,' I said. 'Which reminds me, Canon Osbaston told me you might be able to tell me something about Canon Youlgreave. I came across something he'd written in the library a week or so ago.'

'He was a strange man and no mistake.' She lifted her eyes to my face. The pupils were large and black. 'Not that I knew him well, of course.'

'Where did he live?'

'Bleeders Hall. Where the Hudsons are now. I was working next door in the Deanery. Of course they did things in a lot more style in those days. The dean had a butler and kept his own carriage.'

'Really? And what was it like at Canon Youlgreave's?'

'I couldn't say. I never had any call to go there. Of course, Mr Youlgreave was a bachelor and didn't need the sort of establishment the dean did. But he had the house redecorated – I remember that. He lived in the Dark Hostelry while it was being done.'

Janet brought the tea. 'Who lived in our house?'

'Francis Youlgreave,' I said. 'But Mrs Elstree says it was only for a short time. Apparently he had the house the Hudsons have got.'

'He wasn't liked, I'm afraid,' Mrs Elstree said. 'And of course he went mad in the end. Not that we were surprised. We could see it coming.'

'Did you hear the famous sermon about women priests?'

She shook her head and then, as if to make up for this failure, added, 'They say he was over-familiar with the servants. And some of his ideas were very strange. You know he did away with himself?'

'No, I didn't.' I watched her spooning sugar into her tea. 'I thought he'd not been well for some time and he just died.'

'That's not what we heard. And him a clergyman. But it didn't happen here. It was after they got rid of him.' She took a sip of tea and then turned to Janet. 'What I say, Mrs

Byfield, is that you're bound to get a few rotten apples in every barrel.'

'I don't suppose you knew a boy called Simon Martlesham in those days. He worked at the Bishop's Palace.'

'Simon Martlesham? Oh yes.' She hesitated and stirred her tea again, quite unnecessarily. 'I think he used to run errands for Canon Youlgreave sometimes. But he left Rosington years ago. He lives in Watford now. My brother bumped into him in the Swan.'

'I know. The pub by the river.'

She nodded. 'His family used to live down there. There was his mother and sister. By that time he was at the Palace, of course, the servants lived in . . . I don't remember a father. I expect he was in the area and thought he'd go and see his old home. Not that there's much to see.'

People swirled between us. Someone jogged my elbow and tea slopped in the saucer and on the sleeve of my mackintosh. Other conversations began. Later Janet bought a knitted golliwog in a blue boilersuit for Rosie's birthday and I found a Busy Lizzie for the kitchen windowsill.

Afterwards as we were walking home arm in arm under one umbrella, Janet said, 'So you're still interested in Francis Youlgreave?'

'Just something to pass the time.' I was afraid that Janet would sense my ingratitude, my boredom with Rosington, my shabby little thoughts about David. I rushed into speech. 'I imagine Mrs Elstree can be rather terrifying. But she was very pleasant to us.'

'Mrs Elstree tries as hard as she can to be nice to me,' Janet said. 'That's because if David gets Osbaston's job, she hopes we'll keep her on.'

'And will you?'

'Not if I can help it. I think she's too used to running the place, too set in her ways. Mr Osbaston leaves everything to her. But she's right about the work involved.' She looked sideways at me. 'Actually, I don't think it would be much fun being the principal's wife.'

We hurried through the rain in silence after that. David was at home working on his book in the study and in theory keeping an eye on Mr Treevor and Rosie. In the Close a car passed us, splashing water over my shoes and stockings.

'Can you smell anything?' Janet asked when we were taking off our raincoats in the hall.

'Only damp.' I sniffed the air. 'And perhaps bacon from this morning.'

'No, it's something underneath that. Something not very nice. At least I think it is.'

It was the first time any of us mentioned the smell. Of course Janet must have imagined it or smelled something different from the later smell. There's no other explanation.

David came out of the study. 'Hello. How was it?'

'Much as you'd imagine,' Janet said. 'But wetter. Where's Rosie?'

'Somewhere upstairs with your father. I think they were going to play Snap.' Then his voice dropped a little in pitch. 'Ah – Wendy?'

Surprised, I looked away from my reflection in the mirror. I was wondering if my nose was unusually red. Was it becoming what my mother would have called a 'toper's nose'? I thought David was looking accusingly at me.

'I had a letter this morning,' he said. 'From Henry.'

I stared at him. I felt sick. What he'd said was as unexpected as a punch in the stomach. But David and Henry were friends, in the inexplicable way that men are friends. Which meant that it didn't necessarily matter that they hadn't seen each other for years, they rarely wrote to each other, and they had completely different outlooks on life. I wondered if they'd been plotting about me.

'He asked if you were here,' David went on.

I said nothing.

'I'll have to write back and say you are. Naturally.'

'All right.'

'He wants to see you. He says –'

'I don't want to see him,' I said loudly. 'Just tell him that. Now I'm going to get changed. I'm soaking wet.'

I ran upstairs, past the sound of giggling coming from Rosie's room and up the next flight of stairs to my own bedroom. When I got there I blew my nose and looked away from my reflection in the mirror on the dressing table. What I needed, I decided, was a very early nightcap.

Two days later, on Monday, I came across a copy of an Edwardian children's book in the library. It was by G. A. Henty and was called *His Country's Flag*. Though the spine had faded the colours of the picture on the jacket were still as vivid as the day it was new. The picture showed a young English boy in a red coat. He was harvesting a crop of frightened-looking Zulus with a sabre. I opened the book and there was that familiar handwriting on the flyleaf.

For Simon Martlesham on his thirteenth birthday with good wishes from F. Youlgreave. July 17th, 1904.

23

Rosie's fifth birthday was on Wednesday, 14th May. All of us except Mr Treevor got up a little earlier than usual so she could have her presents before going to school.

As I came downstairs I thought for an instant that I smelled something unpleasant, like meat that's beginning to go off. I remembered Janet mentioning a smell the previous Saturday when we returned from the jumble sale at the Theological College. But when I stopped in the hall and sniffed, there was nothing out of the ordinary. Only damp, old stone and yesterday's vegetables.

Rosie was very excited, darting round the kitchen like a swallow round the Octagon. On the table was a little heap of cards and presents.

'May I open them?' she demanded. 'May I, please?'

'Have some breakfast first,' Janet told her.

'I want them now. It's my birthday.'

'Yes, poppet, but you have to eat breakfast, even on your birthday.'

'Afterwards.'

'Now. Please, Mummy.'

They stared at each other. Janet looked away first, about to concede.

I picked up the card and parcel I had put on the table. 'Well, you won't be needing this then.'

Rosie looked up at me, her gaze both curious and calculating.

'This is for a little girl who does what her mummy tells her to do.'

I smiled at her, wishing I hadn't interfered. Rosie was Janet's business, not mine. A moment later Rosie sat down at her place and watched her mother pouring cornflakes into her bowl. If she had been a general, she would have called it a tactical withdrawal.

It took Rosie five minutes to eat her cereal and a slice of toast, and drink a glass of milk. Then she worked through the pile before her. First she opened the envelopes, glanced at the birthday cards and put them on one pile. The discarded envelopes went on another. But two postal orders and a Premium Bond went in a special pile of their own, weighted by a fork.

Next came the parcels. She allowed David to cut them open with scissors. The parcel which had come in the post contained a maroon cardigan.

'How nice of Granny Byfield,' Janet said without enthusiasm.

Rosie did not comment.

Now there were four parcels left, the ones from the adults in the house. First she opened Mr Treevor's. The old man had wanted to give Rosie an apple taken from the bowl on the dresser. Last night, he'd told Janet that an apple would be good for Rosie and would also be something she would enjoy eating. When he was a boy, he said, he had often wished for an apple but no one had ever given him one for his birthday. Janet said it was a lovely present and very thoughtful of him. But when she wrapped up the apple she added the blue golliwog she had bought at the jumble sale.

David's present was Lamb's *Tales from Shakespeare*, an illustrated edition with simplified language. Janet had bought her a new dress, very smart, in navy-blue needlecord covered with pale-pink horses and trimmed with pink lace. It had puffed sleeves and a Peter Pan collar. Rosie was enchanted. Before she went to school she took the dress up to her parents' room so she could put it on and look at herself in the big mirror.

But first she opened my present. I had asked Janet to find out what Rosie wanted. It turned out she wanted an angel. Janet and I decided that a doll might be an acceptable

126

compromise. In the toy shop in the High Street I'd found a rather expensive one with long blonde hair and blue eyes which opened and closed according to whether the doll was vertical or horizontal. The legs and the arms were jointed where they met the torso and the head swivelled on the neck. If you pressed the chest it croaked 'Mama'.

The doll came complete with a pink dress, underwear, socks and shoes. This didn't seem quite the right outfit for a celestial being, so I'd made a long white gown out of a couple of old handkerchiefs and embroidered an A for Angel in blue cotton over the heart, or rather over the place where the heart would have been if the angel had possessed one. We dressed the doll in the gown and packed away the pink clothes in an empty cigar box.

'They can be her trousseau,' Janet had said.

'Or her disguise when she goes out among humans,' I replied.

When Rosie opened the box and saw her angel lying there, she didn't say anything for a moment. Then, very slowly and very gently, she picked up the angel and cradled it in her arms.

'Do you like it?' Janet asked. 'Go and say thank you to Auntie Wendy.'

Still carrying the doll, Rosie came to stand by my chair and waited for me to kiss her cheek.

'Happy birthday,' I said. 'I'm glad you like it.'

Janet explained about the trousseau and how I'd made the gown and about the doll's saying 'Mama'.

Rosie nodded. 'But where are the wings?'

'Not all angels have wings,' I said.

'They do,' Rosie said.

'Ask your father, dear,' Janet suggested. 'He knows about this sort of thing. And I'm sure he'd like to have a good look at your angel.'

In fact, David's attention was now divided between *The Times* and a slice of toast and marmalade. But he allowed himself to be diverted for long enough to agree that angels didn't always have wings, which allayed Rosie's doubts for the time being.

'Auntie Wendy,' she said to me when she and Janet were leaving for school. 'My angel is my favourite present.'

On Rosie's birthday I did not come home at my usual time. I wanted her to have her birthday tea, with the cake, with Janet and David. It was her birthday and she deserved to have her parents all to herself. So at lunchtime I told Janet that I wanted to do some shopping and I would be a little later than usual.

Late in the afternoon I found another book that had once belonged to Francis Youlgreave, the *Religio Medici* by Sir Thomas Browne, in an edition published in 1889. I was keeping a separate list of everything that had been his, and I felt everything I found told me a little more about him. The book was bound in flaking leather that left crumbs of dead skin on my fingers, and the spine was cracked. I riffled through the pages, which rustled like leaves in autumn. I found a passage marked in the margin with a wavering line of brown ink.

> Nay, further, we are what we all abhor, Anthropophagi and Cannibals, devourers not onely of men, but of our selves; and that not in an allegory, but a positive truth: for all this mass of flesh which we behold, came in at our mouths; this frame we look upon, hath been upon our trenchers; in brief, we have devour'd our selves.

It took me a moment to work out what the writer was saying, and when I did I shivered. I thought of those pictures of snakes with their tails in their mouths.

'Not nice, Francis,' I said aloud. 'And why did you mark it?'

In the still air of the Cathedral Library, the words waited for an answer. Jesus, I thought with another shiver, I'm talking to myself, this is ridiculous.

I stood up and walked over to the old catalogue in the big foolscap volume. Here were listed the books in Dean Pellew's original bequest and a number of later additions. The last entry was dated 1899. No sign of the *Religio Medici*. I checked the cabinet by the door which contained the later records, equally patchy. The earliest of these was a commentary in German on the Pentateuch. The entry was dated November 1904 and was in a neat copybook hand, very unlike Francis's scrawl.

I now knew from the *Dictionary of National Biography* that Francis had come to Rosington in 1900 and had departed at some point in 1904. He might have left some books in the library, but I hadn't come across any trace of him in the various catalogues. It suddenly struck me that the catalogue entry for November 1904 might well mark the point when someone more conscientious had started to look after the collection. Which suggested Francis had probably been forced to resign in the late summer or early autumn of the year. Which in turn would make my job easier if I ever wanted to try to trace a public record of his last sermon.

Until then the idea of doing so hadn't occurred to me. But why not? Osbaston had said the sermon had been mentioned in the papers. It must surely have been reported in the *Rosington Observer*.

I glanced at my watch. I had planned to spend forty-five minutes dawdling round the shops before going back to the Dark Hostelry. But there was nothing I wanted to buy that couldn't wait.

The *Rosington Observer* had an office in Market Street. It was a weekly newspaper which told you all about markets and meetings, and announced auctions, births, deaths and marriages. Funerals were covered in obsessive detail. The main editorial policy was to mention the names of as many local people as possible and to include the word 'Rosington' at least once in the first sentence of every piece.

Two women sat behind a long, polished counter in the room overlooking the street. They were talking about some-one called Edna while one of them typed with two fingers and the other knitted. I asked if they kept old copies of the newspaper, and the knitter took me into a room at the back whose walls were lined with deep steel shelving. There was a table under the window with a single chair beside it. The newspapers were stacked in chronological order.

'They're filthy,' the woman warned me. 'I'll leave you to it. We close at five.'

I had my cotton dusting gloves, so the dust and the ink didn't bother me. I worked my way round the shelves to the pile that included issues from 1904. That was when I began to get suspicious.

First, there was no dust on the top of the pile. But there was on the piles to the right and the left, and indeed on every other pile in this part of the shelves. The pile covered 1903 to the first half of 1906, so you would have expected the issues for 1904 to be somewhere in the middle. But they weren't. They were on top.

I carried them over to the table and began to work back from November. I found a mention of Francis almost at once in a small item on the fifth page.

> The Revd J. Heckstall will give a series of four evening lectures on the Meaning of Advent, beginning Tuesday next at 7.30 p.m., at the Almonry. All are welcome to attend. These were previously advertised as being given by Canon Youlgreave. There will be a collection in aid of the Church Empire Society.

I worked backwards. In October the newspaper told its readers that Canon Youlgreave had resigned and left Rosington because of poor health, and that the dean and chapter thought it unlikely that his successor to the canonry would be appointed until the new year.

In September I expected to find details of the sermon that had led to the resignation and its consequences. Instead I found something that in a way was worse than nothing. Two issues had been mutilated. Someone had used a pen-knife to cut out a total of five items, two of them probably letters to the editor. They'd pressed so hard that the blade had sliced through two or three of the pages beneath.

I took the two newspapers into the front office. The knitter and the typist stopped talking and looked at me.

'They mustn't be taken out of the room,' the knitter said. 'It's the rules.'

I spread the papers out on the counter. 'Look. Someone's been cutting bits out.'

'People just don't care, do they?' the typist said. 'I mean, look at those Teddy boys.'

The knitter popped a peppermint in her mouth. 'Just couldn't be bothered to copy it out, I expect. Whatever it was.'

'Has anyone been in there lately?'

'Could have been done years ago.'

I doubted it because the cuts in the yellowing paper looked too clean. 'Perhaps. But has anyone been recently – in the last few weeks, say?'

'There was Mrs Vosper,' the typist said. 'Wanted to find out the date of her parents-in-law's wedding.'

The knitter gave a bark of laughter. 'A bit late for that.'

'And the solicitor's clerk came in on Friday, didn't he?' the typist went on.

'Which solicitor?' I asked.

'I don't know.'

'He *looked* like a solicitor's clerk,' the knitter explained. 'Quite a small man. Black jacket and pinstriped trousers.'

'And what did he want?'

'Didn't ask. We were too busy. A couple of people had come in to place advertisements, and someone else was moaning about something the editor had written, though why talk to us, I just don't know.'

'Anyway,' the typist said, regaining control of the conversation by raising her voice, 'why do you want to know?'

'It just seems an odd thing to do.'

'People do odd things every day,' the knitter said. 'You just wouldn't believe some of the stories we hear. You couldn't surprise us if you tried.'

'I don't suppose I could.'

The typist said, 'It's almost five o'clock. We have to close in a moment.'

So I went shopping after all. I bought cotton for Janet, a bar of chocolate for Rosie and a bottle of gin for me. At the wine merchant's, Mr Cromwell looked curiously at me, and for a moment I thought he was going to say something. Next time I needed gin I'd buy it in Cambridge.

And all the time I found it hard to concentrate because I was wondering who had been taking cuttings from the *Rosington Observer*, and why, and whether it was something to do with Francis Youlgreave.

It must have been almost six o'clock by the time I reached the Dark Hostelry. Janet rushed into the hall as I let myself into the house. When she saw it was me, disappointment flooded over her face.

'What's wrong?' A split second later, I asked, 'Where's Rosie? What's happened?'

'She's fine. She's in the kitchen. It's Daddy. You haven't seen him, have you?'

'No.'

'He was in the garden with Rosie while I was making the tea. When I called them in, only Rosie was there. She said he'd gone out. And that was nearly two hours ago. David's looking for him.'

Mr Treevor rarely left the house and garden, and when he did one of us always went with him. He hadn't been out by himself since he'd moved into the Dark Hostelry.

'He can't have got far. Have you told the police?'

'Not yet. David thought we should wait a little.'

We went down to the kitchen. Rosie was chatting to her new doll and did not look up as we came in. The remains of the birthday tea were still on the table. My bag clanked as I put it down on the dresser. I wondered if David had delayed calling the police because he was afraid of scandal.

'Rosie,' Janet said. 'Are you sure Grandpa didn't say where he was going?'

She glanced up, shaking her head. 'No, he didn't say where.'

There was a slight stress on the last word. That's what made me say, 'But did he say *why* he was going out?'

'He said he wanted to look for some wings.' Rosie stroked the doll's hair. 'For Angel. He said angels must have wings.'

At that moment we heard a key in the back door, the door that opened into the High Street and the marketplace. And then Mr Treevor was saying, 'I'm very hungry. Isn't it teatime yet?'

24

There was a devious side to David. The business about the phone call showed that.

Janet was on a committee, chaired by Mrs Forbury, the dean's wife, which met at teatime on Thursday afternoons at the Deanery. The Cathedral, Janet said, needed what Mrs Forbury called a Woman's Touch. So we used to refer to the committee members as the Touchies. They dealt with the flower rota, oversaw the cleaning and the maintenance of various fabrics, from altar cloths to choir boys' ruffs. There was even a sub-committee to deal with the complicated question of the manufacture, maintenance and disposition of kneelers. According to Janet, this was where an inner circle of Touchies decided all matters of importance.

That was why I left work early on Thursday afternoons. While Janet went to the Touchies, I gave Rosie and Mr Treevor their tea. Between four and five-thirty, I was usually the only responsible adult at the Dark Hostelry.

David knew this.

The phone rang while I was washing up. Rosie was playing with Angel at the kitchen table and Mr Treevor was dozing in his room. His adventure yesterday had left him tired out. David had eventually found him in the High Street. Mr Treevor said he wanted to find some ducks so he could feed them. There weren't any ducks in the High Street, and in any case he had nothing to feed them with.

I went up to the study, where the phone was. It was David's room, dark, austere and full of books, and it always made me feel like a trespasser. I picked up the handset and recited the number.

'Wendy,' Henry said. 'It's me.'

I felt sweat breaking out on my forehead and on the palm of my hand holding the telephone.

'Wendy, don't hang up, please. Are you there?'

I stared at a crucifix on the wall over the fireplace. Christ's brass face was contorted. The poor man really looked in pain.

'Wendy?'

'I've got nothing to say.'

'I'm sorry,' Henry said. 'I was a fool. I miss you. I love you.'

'Oh, bugger off.'

I put the phone down. I stood beside the desk and glared at the telephone. I was trembling and the tears blurred my vision. After a while the phone rang again. I let it ring. It went on for thirty-six rings. I felt like a piece of elastic, and each ring stretched me a little further. David must have arranged this. David and Henry were friends, and no doubt David felt it no more than his pastoral duty to do his best to help repair a failing marriage. When at last the ringing stopped, it was as if someone had turned off a pneumatic drill. I turned to go. Rosie was in the doorway, with Angel in her arms. I scowled at her.

'What are you doing?'

'The phone kept ringing.'

'Yes,' I said.

'So why didn't you answer it?'

'I – I was busy.'

Rosie pressed the doll's chest. 'Mama,' it said.

The little black monster started to ring again.

'Are you going to answer it now?'

I turned round and picked up the handset.

'Wendy?' Henry said. 'Can't we talk? Please.'

What was there to talk about, I wanted to say – divorce? Henry's wobbling buttocks bouncing on top of the Hairy Widow? The way my money had disappeared? But I couldn't say any of this because Rosie was still in the doorway.

'I need to see you,' he went on. 'Whenever you want. Couldn't we meet for lunch? I've got some of your things. A bit of jewellery.'

'I'm surprised you haven't sold it,' I said. 'Or perhaps you haven't needed to.'

'If you're thinking about that woman,' he said, 'I haven't seen her since the day on the beach. I promise you.'

I turned away from the door because I didn't want Rosie to see me crying.

'We could meet in Cambridge,' he suggested. 'Would that be easier for you? Please, Wendy.'

'London,' I said.

'All right. Can you manage Monday? We could meet at the Café Royal. What time would suit you?'

'Twelve-thirty,' I said. 'And if you aren't there when I arrive I won't wait. I've done enough waiting.'

I put the phone down. Rosie and I went back to the kitchen and I finished the washing up. Afterwards I went up to my bedroom and had an early nightcap. It seemed to me that I no longer had anything left to lose. It didn't matter if I made a fool of myself. I'd already done that in such a comprehensive way that any other follies barely registered.

So after I'd rinsed out the glass and done my teeth, I went back to the study and rang directory enquiries. It was very easy – they found the number almost immediately. I perched on the edge of the desk and listened to a phone ringing in a strange house in a strange town.

'Hello,' said a woman's voice, high and breathless. 'Who's speaking?'

'Hello,' I said. 'Could I talk to Mr Simon Martlesham?'

'Not here, you can't. We rent the house off him, you see.'

'Do you have a phone number or a forwarding address?'

'So you don't know him?'

'Not exactly. But we've a sort of mutual friend, and I've got something to return to him.'

'Hang on.' A moment's silence, then the rustle of paper. 'Are you ready?'

'As much as I'll ever be.'

She didn't laugh, but she gave me a phone number.

25

On Saturday morning there was a postcard from the library. The book I had reserved the previous Monday was now waiting for me. Immediately after lunch I went to fetch it.

It was another warm day and the same librarian was on duty. He was wheezing more than before and his wiry hair needed brushing. He was sitting at the table near the door, his hands fluttering over tray after tray of tickets. The library was almost empty because people were still at lunch. He looked up and the folds and wrinkles of his bloodhound face rearranged themselves into a smile.

'I've come to collect the book,' I said, and put down the postcard on his desk. 'That was quick.'

'We aim to please, Mrs Appleyard,' he said sadly. 'There's not much else one can do in this vale of tears, is there?'

'I can think of one or two other things,' I said.

He took a small green hardback from the shelf behind him and stamped it. I read the last due date, upside down, and worked out that the last borrower had taken out the book in the middle of last week.

'So who had it?' I asked. 'The man you mentioned before? The one who was asking about Francis Youlgreave?'

'What is it about Francis Youlgreave? Why's everyone so interested?'

'I can tell you why I am. I'm working in the Cathedral Library, and there are books that used to be his. So I'm just curious.'

'Just curious?' He had a way of speaking that made it sound as though he were testing everything, like a scientist with

137

a laboratory full of instruments. 'I told you before, I didn't know who the borrower was.'

'But wasn't the name on the ticket?'

'Of course. But I didn't see the ticket. Someone else stamped the book. It was a busy time, and she couldn't remember the name. It was returned at a busy time, too. She thought it might have been Brown. Or Smith. Not a name that stood out.'

So he'd bothered to ask. He was getting curious too.

'So you don't know if it was the same person?'

'It seems likely. The man I talked to was middle-aged. Small, dark. I think he wore glasses and had a bald patch. Dressed quite formally. Looked very respectable.'

'A black jacket and pinstriped trousers? A bit like a solicitor's clerk?'

'Something like that, I suppose. Not that I know any solicitor's clerks.'

I thanked him and put the book in my bag.

'By the way,' he said, 'are you by any chance related to *Henry* Appleyard?'

It was as if the bloodhound had slapped me.

'Yes. How do you know him?'

The librarian waved orange-stained fingers. 'We used to bump into each other occasionally.'

In the betting shop? In the pub?

He was waiting for me to explain. He was curious about that as well.

'I haven't seen him for a while,' I said. 'Anyway, thanks for the book. 'Bye.'

I walked back through the sunshine, stopping to buy a pair of stockings, very sheer and very expensive, and also some new lipstick. On my way to the Close I went through the market. There were stalls around the cross and the cobbles were strewn with rotting vegetables and cardboard. A rubbish bin attached to a lamppost reminded me of my dream, but this one didn't contain a doll, only a woman's shoe without a heel and crumpled newspaper greasy from wrapping fish and chips. I wondered whether Isabella of Roth had really died here over five hundred years ago and, if she had, whether any trace of her agony remained apart from Francis's letter in the *Transactions of the Rosington Antiquarian Society*. Pain mattered, I thought, it should be noticed and remembered. Did Henry and his Hairy Widow add up to a pain that mattered?

From the market, it was only a few yards to the back door of the Dark Hostelry in the High Street. I let myself in. The house was cool and quiet. Nobody was around. I went upstairs to take off my hat and gloves. I saw David, Janet and Rosie from my window sitting in the dappled shade of the apple tree. They looked like an ideal family, self-contained in their beauty. You didn't often see them sitting together.

I lay on my bed and resisted the temptation to have a nip of gin as a reward for not minding the fact that I wasn't part of an ideal family. Instead I looked at *The Tongues of Angels*. The pages smelled of tobacco, strong and foreign, like French or Turkish cigarettes. When I tried to read a poem called 'The Children of Heracles' I couldn't concentrate. So I put the book in the cupboard by the bed and went down to join the others.

David was in a deckchair with a book on his lap, his shirt open at the neck and the sleeves rolled up. He looked like Laurence Olivier in a very good mood. Janet was sitting on a rug brushing Rosie's hair. Rosie was in her new dress because she was going to a party later in the afternoon and was brushing Angel's hair, the strokes of her brush exactly in time with Janet's. I felt like a trespasser, just as I had in David's study the other day.

'Oh good,' Janet said. 'Do you think these ribbons match?'

David sat up. 'Come and sit here. I'll go on the grass.'

'Don't move, please. And the ribbons look fine to me.' I knelt on the rug beside Janet and lit a cigarette.

'David's just had a phone call from Gervase Haselbury-Finch,' Janet said. 'Do sit still, poppet. You know, the bishop's chaplain.'

'In a sense it concerns you,' David said, 'and anyway there's no reason why you shouldn't know about it. It seems that the bishop's definitely in favour of diverting the Cathedral Library's endowment to the Theological College. He's written to the dean and chapter about it.'

'How nice.' I couldn't think of anything else to say.

'Do sit still, poppet,' Rosie said to Angel.

'Gervase went to the same school as David,' Janet said, and went back to the brushing.

I flicked ash on a fallen leaf. 'It's a small world.'

'He's got no direct influence over what the dean and chapter decide,' David went on, leaning towards me, 'but they are bound to take notice of what he thinks. The point is, the bishop wouldn't suggest diverting the endowment unless he intended the Theological College to stay open.'

'But I thought you already knew he was in favour of that.'

'Yes – he's said as much to me. But this shows he's actually prepared to do something about it. It's a step forward, believe me.'

The Cathedral's clock boomed the half-hour. Janet stood up suddenly and brushed her skirt with her hand.

'We must go. Time to do your teeth, poppet.'

'Time to do your teeth, poppet,' Rosie echoed to Angel.

'Mama!' Angel replied.

They went into the house. David told me how it would be perfectly possible not just to keep the Theological College open but to expand the number of students. It was a question of attracting the right type of ordinand and he had a number of ideas how they could do that. Accommodation wouldn't be a problem – they could convert the attics into study bedrooms.

'We'll be back at about five,' Janet called from the house. She grimaced at me. 'I've been roped in to help with the games.'

David told me about a programme of visiting lecturers he planned, about changes in the course structure to reflect new trends in theology, and about improvements to the social and sporting activities of the college. He gesticulated with long, graceful hands.

'After all, it's not a nunnery,' he said. 'There's no reason why they shouldn't have a bit of fun.'

'Oh, yes,' I said. 'We all need that.'

While David talked I nodded and occasionally commented

or asked appropriate questions in the pauses. I was really engaged in admiring the line of his jaw, the colour of his eyes and his well-kept and beautifully shaped fingernails. I also wondered if he talked to Janet like this while they were alone. They didn't talk very much when I was there.

'By the way,' he said, leaning closer to offer me a cigarette, 'I know Henry was planning to ring.'

'Yes.' I sat up and shook my head to the cigarette. 'He phoned on Thursday.'

'Janet told me. Look, I hope you didn't mind my telling him when you might be in?'

'It's too late if I did,' I said. 'I'm going to see him on Monday.'

He nodded. 'I'm glad.'

'I don't know what I feel,' I said, suddenly reckless. 'It's all such a bloody mess.'

'Wendy,' he said, 'you know that –'

At this interesting moment the door to the house opened. We both turned, as if caught red-handed.

'He's out there,' Mr Treevor said in a thin, wavering voice.

'Who is?' David asked, standing up.

'The burglar. He was standing outside Chase and Cromwell's and looking up at my bedroom window.'

'The man you saw?' I said. 'The man like a shadow?'

'Yes. I told you. He's there. He's watching us. He's biding his time before he strikes again.'

'I don't think that's very likely, actually,' David said.

Mr Treevor pouted. 'He is. I saw him.'

'Why don't we go and see?' I suggested.

The old man's face crumpled. 'Don't leave me.'

'You can come as well.'

David sighed. 'This is absurd,' he murmured to me.

'Perhaps. But it won't do any harm, will it?'

'What are you whispering about?' Mr Treevor's voice rose to a squeal. 'Everyone's always whispering.'

'We're just talking about going out,' I said. 'Let's go this way.'

We went into the Close and walked down to the Sacristan's

Gate and into the High Street. It was Saturday afternoon so the pavements were crowded with shoppers. But I couldn't see a little man in black outside Chase and Cromwell's, or indeed anywhere else. Mr Treevor's head made jerky little stabbing movements as if he was pecking the air with his nose.

'He's not there now, is he?' David said.

'He was,' Mr Treevor cried. 'I saw him. I did, I did.'

'All right.' I patted his arm which was hooked round mine. 'Let's go home.'

It was quieter in the Close and he calmed down almost immediately. We walked arm in arm, three abreast, with Mr Treevor in the middle, our prisoner. Canon Hudson was coming in the other direction. He waved to us and we stopped to talk near the gate to the Dark Hostelry.

'I was going to phone you this evening,' I said to him after we had agreed how unseasonably warm the weather was and how well Mr Treevor was looking. 'Do you mind if I take Monday off? I have to go to London.'

'Of course. Business or pleasure?'

'Business,' I said, avoiding David's eyes.

There was a clatter behind us. I turned to see Gotobed coming from the north door, carrying a bucket and a small shovel. Usually he walked in a stately fashion in the Close, as though leading an invisible procession. But now he was hurrying.

'Are you all right?' Hudson called to him.

Gotobed veered towards him. 'I'm all right, sir. But there's them that aren't.'

'What do you mean?'

'You'd better look at this.'

He motioned Hudson to one side, turned his back on the rest of us and held up the bucket.

Hudson wrinkled his nose. 'Not a nice sight, I agree. But we get plenty of pigeons in the Close, and sometimes they die.'

'He was under the bench in the north porch, sir.'

'Looks as if he'd been there for some time.'

'He was tucked under one of the legs. I wouldn't have seen

him if I hadn't dropped my keys. He couldn't have got there by accident.'

'Perhaps a visitor pushed him under there to –'

'They did more than push him under the bench, sir,' Gotobed interrupted. His hands were trembling but there was no trace of his usual shyness. 'Have a proper look. Go on.'

Hudson peered into the bucket. 'Yes,' he said slowly. 'I see your point.'

'Let me see,' Mr Treevor said, pulling his arms free of David's and mine.

He skipped across the path to Hudson's side. David and I, taken by surprise, followed. I glanced into the bucket.

'Don't, Mrs Appleyard,' Gotobed said to me, his nose twitching. 'It's not nice.'

It was a very skinny, decaying pigeon with mangy feathers. One of its legs had been reduced to a stump. For an instant I thought it had died of natural causes.

Mr Treevor's head bobbed, and he turned away. 'Ugh!' he said. 'Isn't it time to go home? We mustn't be late for tea.'

The bucket swung in Gotobed's hand and the pigeon rolled slowly over. It was beginning to smell. Then I realized why it looked so skinny. There were wounds along its sides, ragged slits exposing flesh and bone and gristle. Someone had hacked the wings off the pigeon's body.

26

I felt like a fool on Monday morning. Part of me was also excited, as if I was going to a party.

When the train left Cambridge I went along the corridor to the lavatory. As I sat there I took off my wedding ring, which wasn't easy, and slipped it in my handbag. The skin where it had been was slightly paler than the rest of the finger. As far as the world was concerned, Mrs had turned into Miss, a magical transformation like frog into prince, or the other way round. Perhaps snakes felt this way when they sloughed off a dead skin, colder and suddenly more vulnerable, but also lighter than air.

I checked my make-up in the lavatory mirror for the third time since leaving the Dark Hostelry and then returned to the compartment. There were two men, one my age, one a little older, and they both glanced at me as I came in. The younger of the two was quite good-looking. He stared discreetly as I crossed my legs, and I was glad I was wearing the new stockings.

The Tongues of Angels was one of the two books in my shopping bag. I took it out and skimmed through the poems again. I thought I knew where Francis had found the title – I'd checked the phrase in David's dictionary of quotations. Almost certainly he'd taken it from the New Testament, from the opening sentence of the thirteenth chapter of I Corinthians. 'Though I speak with the tongues of men and of angels, and have not charity, I am become as sounding brass, or a tinkling cymbal.'

But the contents didn't have much to do with charity,

144

not on the surface at least. The poems were divided into seven sections. Each of the sections had the name of an archangel. Uriel, Raphael, Raguel, Michael, Sariel, Gabriel and Remiel. Oddly enough the poems themselves weren't about angels, arch or otherwise. They were mainly about children or animals, sometimes both. I'd read all of them at least three times but I still wasn't sure what most of them were really about.

But there was one thing I approved of. There was none of that J. M. Barrie nonsense for Francis. Quite the reverse. The children in 'The Children of Heracles' were cut up into little bits by their father, because a goddess had put him under a spell and made him think they were his enemies. Another poem was about the Spartan boy who ran with a fox gnawing his vitals and saved his country at the cost of his own life. At the end of it the fox ran off laughing. A third concerned a cat at the court of Egypt, a cat who was older and more mysterious than the Sphinx, a cat who watched with unblinking eyes as the children of the pharaoh died of the plague.

The longest poem was called 'Breakheart Hill'. It was about a hunt in a pseudo-medieval forest where people said 'prithee' and 'by our lady' at the drop of a hat, and varlets lurked on the greensward 'neath the spreading oaks. The quarry was a hart, the noblest in the country, and the king, his huntsmen and his hounds pursued it all day for miles and miles. At last the light began to fade and the king commanded the huntsmen to drive the stag up a steep hill near the royal hunting lodge, for it was time for it to die.

The king's son, who was on his first hunt, begged his father to spare the hart which had given them so much sport. But the king would not. The pack drove the stag up the hill, and there, on the summit, its great heart broke open and it died of exhaustion just before the hounds leapt at its throat. The young prince wept.

The king ordered his huntsmen to drive the dogs back. Then he took his son by the hand and led him to the stag. He drew his dagger, sliced open its breast and cut deep down to its broken heart. The king put his hand inside the broken heart and drew it out, dripping with blood. The prince watched. The king daubed blood on the boy's face and kissed his forehead.

> 'For hart's blood makes the young heart strong,' quoth he.
> 'God hath ordained it so. He dies that ye
> 'May hunt, my son, and through his strength be free.'

So what had angels to do with all this? Maybe Francis believed he'd cracked their code, and worked out what they talked about among themselves when not on official business. And their favourite topic of conversation turned out to be nasty anecdotes involving children and animals.

Or perhaps it was the other way round and the message was straightforwardly Christian. Heracles, the fox, the pharaoh's cat and the hunting king were all dominant types who either remained aloof from the crowd or got their own way. But was this of any use to them or anyone else, Francis was asking, without charity?

None of this made much sense. But with Francis I was used to that. I felt a kinship with him for that very reason. My life didn't make much sense either. At least I was going to London for the day. I crossed my legs again, glanced up at the younger man and caught him watching.

The train was slowing for Liverpool Street Station. I put the book in my bag and stared out of the window at bomb sites, the backs of grimy houses and new tower blocks. The last time I had seen this view I had been suffering from a king-sized hangover and more unhappy than I could ever remember being before. Life had improved. London was huge and full of possibilities. Excitement wriggled inside me as if the snake was escaping from another skin.

I took the tube to Chancery Lane. The noise, the crowds and the constant movement were partly scary and partly invigorating. So was the fact that no one knew who I was. I felt like someone who had emerged from months of seclusion – from a monastery, say, or hospital or prison. Rosington had been all three of those things to me.

When I left the station I had to ask directions to Fetter Passage. Not once but three times. It was that sort of place

– people thought they knew where it was but turned out to be wrong. I found it at last, a lane curved like a boomerang, north of Holborn in the maze of streets between Hatton Garden and Gray's Inn Road. On one side were warehouses and offices, and on the other a small Victorian terrace, now incomplete because a bomb had ripped out one end of it. Most of the houses had shopfronts. The one nearest the bomb site was the Blue Dahlia Café, the side wall shored up with balks of timber growing out of a sea of weeds. I lingered outside, looking through the window.

The café was about half full. The customers, men and women, seemed respectable. Office workers, I thought, perhaps having elevenses. Was one of the men Simon Martlesham? I went inside.

Layers of smoke moved sluggishly through the air. At the back was an archway masked by long multi-coloured strips of nylon which trembled in the draught. A radio played quietly. Few people were talking. A sad-faced woman was washing up at the sink behind the counter and a man was making sandwiches. They ignored me.

I waited at the counter. Eventually the woman dried her hands and shuffled over to me. She had sallow skin and black lank hair.

'My name's Appleyard. I've arranged to meet a Mr Martlesham here, but I'm a little early. Do you know him?'

She nodded.

'He's not here already?'

'You sit down and wait. You want something?'

I ordered coffee. She waved me to an empty table and said something in what sounded like Italian to the man making sandwiches. Then she slipped through the ribbons into the room beyond, her slippers slapping on the linoleum. A little man in a raincoat was reading a newspaper at the next table. He glanced up at me, squinting through his cigarette smoke, but turned away when I met his eyes.

While I waited, I dipped into *His Country's Flag,* the other book in my shopping bag. Soon I learned that young Harry Verderer had recently been orphaned, but his wealthy uncle intended to send him to Cape Town where there were openings at a bank with whom the uncle had connections. This was appropriate, because the man at the next table was going bald, and the patch of shiny skin on the top of his head was shaped rather like a map of Africa. Harry was frightfully cross because he wanted to join the army and become a hero like his father and grandfather before him. Instead he had to buckle down and do his duty at the bank for the sake of his kid sister Maud.

At that moment the woman brought my coffee. The man at the next table squirmed in his chair, brushing ash from his lap.

The ribbons fluttered again, and then I was no longer alone. A man limped towards my table, dragging his left leg across the floor. His left arm hung down at his side with a *Daily Telegraph* wedged near the armpit. He wore a worsted suit and carried a stick. His dark eyes were on the book, not me.

'Miss Appleyard?' He must have looked for a wedding ring.

'Mr Martlesham. And in fact it's "Mrs".'

We shook hands. I wondered why I'd been so keen to claim the 'Mrs' I could so easily have discarded with the ring.

Martlesham propped his stick against the table and sat down, lowering himself awkwardly into the chair. If his thirteenth birthday had been in July 1904, he must now be almost sixty-seven. He had neat, well-proportioned features and once must have been handsome. Still would have been if his face hadn't been lower on the left side than on the right. But the suit was brushed and pressed, his hair had been recently cut and his collar was spotless. He wore a gold tiepin, a horse's head inlaid with enamel. He smelled of shaving cream now, not rancid fat.

When he was settled, he glanced at the waitress and she went through the ribbons again.

'You've got them well trained,' I said.

'What?'

'The waitress. Is she fetching you something?'

'Coffee. Sorry. Is there anything else you would like?'

'No, thanks. Do you live near here now?'

'In a way.' He smoothed back his silver hair and nodded towards the book. 'Is that the one you mentioned?'

'Yes.'

Martlesham had sounded suspicious when I'd phoned him on Thursday, but had been too surprised to ask many questions. I hadn't been sure how he would take it – not everyone wants to be reminded of their childhood, me included. But he'd said he'd like the book, if it was all the same to me. I'd suggested the time for our meeting, and said I was coming up to Liverpool Street, and he'd suggested the Blue Dahlia Café. I assumed it was near where he lived or worked, but perhaps he had just thought it would be convenient for me.

'I don't mind telling you, that phone call of yours took me by surprise.' He had a strange accent, clipped as a suburban privet hedge, but the stroke had slurred his voice just as it had changed the shape of his face and crippled his left arm and leg. 'Still, it's very kind of you, I'm sure.'

'That's all right. I was coming up to town anyway.'

'Even so.'

'Actually, I was curious.'

'Why?'

'As I told you on the phone, I'm cataloguing the Cathedral Library.'

He nodded, impatiently. 'That's where you found the book.'

'Yes. By and large it's not exactly an exciting job. So anything out of the ordinary makes it more interesting. You see?'

'Can I have a look?'

'Of course.' I pushed the book across the table. 'After all, it's got your name in it.'

He opened the book and read what Francis had written on the flyleaf. I drew on my cigarette. I wasn't sure whom the book belonged to. I hadn't asked Canon Hudson if I could give it to Simon Martlesham. That would have involved showing him the inscription, and I was sure he would disapprove of my trying to find out anything to do with Francis.

The waitress brought Martlesham's coffee and a plate with two Rich Tea and two ginger biscuits on it. She stationed the

149

plate between us and went away. Neither took any notice of the other. They might have been mutually invisible.

He looked up and stared across the table at me. I was shocked to see tears in his eyes. No reason for him to be sad. Perhaps the stroke had affected his tear ducts.

'What I don't understand is how you found me,' he said. 'I forgot to ask. I mean, you just rang up out of the blue.'

'Mrs Elstree told me you lived in Watford. So I asked directory enquiries, and a lady who was your tenant gave me your London number.'

'Who's Mrs Elstree?'

'I don't know what her maiden name was but she knew you when you were a boy, when she worked at the Deanery. And she said her brother met you a year or two back, when you visited Rosington.'

'Oh yes. That'd be Alf Butler. The first and last time I've been back to Rosington. Just happened to be passing through and I thought I'd take a look at the old place. He was down by the Swan, and he recognized me right away.' He caressed the handle of the stick with his right hand. 'I looked different then.'

'You knew him when you were children?'

'Alf's parents used to have a little shop in Bridge Street. So Mrs What'sername must be Enid.' Martlesham gave me a crooked smile. 'I remember her. Always full of doom and gloom, that one.'

I smiled back. 'She's Canon Osbaston's housekeeper now. He's the principal of the Theological College.'

'Hang on a minute.' His forehead wrinkled. 'How come you were talking to her about me in the first place?'

'I wasn't,' I said. 'Not exactly. I was asking about Canon Youlgreave. Because he was the one who gave you the book.'

He moved sharply. The stick propped against the table began to slide. The coffee swayed in the cups. 'What's your interest in Canon Youlgreave, Mrs Appleyard?'

I caught the stick before it fell. A drop of coffee had fallen on the toecap of one of Martlesham's shoes. It looked like a grey star on a curved black mirror.

150

'He was the Cathedral librarian at one time,' I said. 'Some of the books I found used to belong to him. He seemed quite an interesting person.'

Martlesham stared out of the window. 'Compared to the rest of them, he certainly was that.' He turned back to me. 'Do you live in the Close, Mrs Appleyard?'

'I'm staying at the Dark Hostelry.'

'I remember. When I was a lad I think the precentor had it. Though Canon Youlgreave lived there for a few months, I remember. So is your husband a clergyman?'

'No.'

'Oh, really?'

I hurried on. 'I expect the Close has changed a good deal since you were there.'

'I doubt it. But I wouldn't know what it's like now. I haven't been there for years.' He glanced at me and went on, speaking more quickly than before, 'Never liked the atmosphere, to be honest. When I was growing up there wasn't much love lost between town and Close. Either you were one or t'other. Which made it awkward for the people like me. For the servants.'

'That's one thing that's changed.' I thought of Janet imprisoned in her own kitchen. 'I don't think there are many servants in the Close nowadays.'

'I was lucky,' he said.

'Because you worked at the Palace?'

He shook his head. 'Worst place of all. The bishop's butler could have given Stalin a few lessons. No, I meant I was lucky because I didn't have to work there very long. Not much more than a year. I've got Canon Youlgreave to thank for that. But I doubt if anyone remembers him now.' His voice roughened. 'Not as he really was. After all, it must be more than fifty years.'

'Some people do.'

'Not *him*. Not the man. If they remember anything, they'll remember what happened. But there was more to him than that. Those folk are meant to be Christians and yet they're as fond of scandal as anyone else.'

'More to him than what? You mean the poetry?'

151

'Yes, there's that. But I don't go in for that sort of thing myself. No, what I meant is that he did a lot of good in a quiet way. I know people thought he was strange. All right, he was a bit odd. But the long and the short of it is, if it hadn't been for him I wouldn't be here.'

'What happened?'

'I suppose you could say he took a fancy to me. First time we met was when he had a fall in the Close – he'd slipped on some ice and I helped him home. Later on he lent me some books. You know, encouraged me to think there was more to life than cleaning other people's boots.' He brought out a silver case and fumbled one-handedly for a cigarette. 'A lot of people were poor in those days. Really poor. Hard to imagine it now, isn't it? No one goes hungry any more. No one dies because they can't afford the doctor.'

'It's progress,' I said.

He nodded but his attention was elsewhere, on whatever he saw in his memory. 'Most people in the Close didn't give a damn about what was happening on their own doorstep. They'd only put their hands in their pockets if it was somewhere else. India, say, or even the East End. But they didn't want to see it themselves a few hundred yards from the Close.'

'In Swan Alley?'

'Maybe they thought poverty might be infectious, like the plague. Or maybe they'd have to realize it was their fault.' For a few words his accent changed – the vowels broadened and the Fen twang of his childhood emerged. 'But Mr Youlgreave wasn't like that.'

He put the cigarette in his mouth at last. I flicked the lighter under his nose.

After a moment I said, 'Did you hear that last sermon of his? The one that caused such a lot of fuss?'

'What sermon?'

'Apparently he said there was no reason why women couldn't be priests as well as men.'

Martlesham shook his head. 'I was in Canada by then. I'd lost touch with him. I heard him preach a sermon about

152

Swan Alley, though. Said it was a blot on God's earth. They didn't like that, either. He was a good man.'

A good man? So unlike the other epitaphs for Francis Youlgreave.

'What did you mean about scandal? You said that's what people would remember.'

'Scandal? That's the whole point. What scandal? If you ask me, it was all smoke, no fire. He didn't fit in, you see. And they made him suffer for it.'

Why didn't he fit in? Wasn't his father a baronet and his mother the cousin of the dean? Fifty years later I didn't fit in either. But at least I knew why. My lipstick was too bright and I'd mislaid my husband. And something else was niggling at me, something to do with now, with the Blue Dahlia Café.

'Mr Youlgreave paid for me to emigrate,' Martlesham went on. 'He had a friend on the committee of this organization, the Church Empire Society. If they liked you, if you had good references, they'd put up half the money if someone else would put up the rest.' He laid his right hand on the book, the cigarette still smouldering between his fingers. 'That's why I'm glad to get this. A bit late, but in a way that makes it all the better.'

'So you never had it at the time?'

He shook his head. 'Do you know where I was on my thirteenth birthday? In the middle of the Atlantic on the *Hesperides*. He probably bought it and forgot to give it to me before we sailed. But how did it get in the library?'

'There were several of his books there. He was ill when he left Rosington, so perhaps they just got left behind. It's nothing out of the ordinary. No one's sorted out that library for years and I've found all sorts of odd things.'

Like *Lady Chatterley's Lover*, for example, unexpurgated but disappointingly dull. Meanwhile my sense of unease was growing. I glanced round the room. What was so familiar about the Blue Dahlia Café? There were fewer customers now. Perhaps this was the lull before lunch. The waitress met my eyes for an instant and then looked away. The man with the bald patch like Africa turned another page of his *Daily Express*. I glanced at my watch. I was going to be late for Henry if I wasn't careful. Not that it mattered. He could wait or stay as he pleased.

'He wanted me to have a chance to make something of myself,' Martlesham was saying. 'In the colonies everyone was as good as everyone else. No one cared who your parents were. The Church Empire Society made sure you learned a trade.' He looked at his hands. 'I was a carpenter. Did quite well, too. I had my own little business in Toronto. Then came the war, the Great War, I mean, and that was the end of that.'

'You joined up?'

'Hard not to. So there I was, back in England. But at least I had a trade. Probably saved my life, that did. Most of the chaps I joined up with died in the trenches. Me, I spent most of the time on Salisbury Plain teaching heroes like them how to saw props for dug-outs.'

'It must have been nice to see your family again.'

'What family?'

'I thought – Mrs Elstree mentioned your mother, and a sister.'

He stubbed out his cigarette. 'Mother died before I went to Canada. As for Nancy, she was in Toronto. Mr Youlgreave saw to that as well.'

'She went with you?'

'Yes. The society had an orphanage. She was adopted almost as soon as we got there. Best thing that could have happened to her.'

'It must have been a wrench for you, though. Your last link with home.'

He shrugged. 'It's a long time ago. I can't remember. I didn't go back to Rosington. No point. Nothing to go back to. But I stayed here.'

'Why?'

'Met a girl at a dance in Winchester.' He was looking not at me but through me. 'It was Armistice Day. Vera.' He swallowed, and his eyes focused on me again. 'Died last year.'

'I'm sorry.'

'Anyway. So I let the house in Watford and moved back to

town. I've got the flat over the café. That's the story of my life, for what it's worth.' He smiled, revealing a sudden glimpse of the charm he must have had as a younger man. 'I don't know why a pretty young woman like you should bother to listen, but thanks. And I'm glad to have the book.'

'It was no trouble.' I looked at my watch again, this time more obviously. 'I really should be going. I've an appointment.'

'Hope I haven't made you late.' He pushed back his chair. 'Don't worry about paying for your coffee, Mrs Appleyard. Least I can do.'

'Thank you. That's very kind. Don't get up, there's no need.'

We shook hands, and I almost ran out of the café. It was half past twelve and I was going to be very late. Not that it mattered. Anyway, it wasn't that. It was because I'd suddenly realized why the Blue Dahlia Café was making me uneasy.

Turkish tobacco, or something very similar to it. Someone in the café had been smoking it. Perhaps even Martlesham himself. After all, there had been a touch of the dandy about him, from the tiepin to the glistening shoes, from the spotless collar to the silver cigarette case. It was perfectly possible that Francis Youlgreave himself had smoked cigarettes like that at the turn of the century, oval Sullivan Powells, perhaps, or Kyprinos from Cyprus.

The sort of cigarette that made the café smell like *The Tongues of Angels* in my handbag.

27

A gypsy was selling lavender at Piccadilly Circus.

'Have a sprig, sir,' she said to the man in front of me. 'Bring you luck.'

He side-stepped, trying to get round her, but she wouldn't let him. 'Just a little bit,' she whined, 'and bless you, so much luck.'

He brushed her arm from his sleeve and hurried towards the steps to the tube.

'God rot you in hell,' she shouted after him. Then she saw me and the anger left her face and the whine returned to her voice. 'A little bit of lavender, missy? Bring you luck. Young ladies need luck as well as a pretty face.'

I didn't want her to curse me. I felt I had enough bad luck to cope with already. Meeting Martlesham had settled nothing. It had just made matters worse. And now I had to deal with Henry.

I found my purse and gave the gypsy sixpence. A hand like a monkey's paw snatched the money and dropped the lavender in the palm of my hand. The hand was damp and left a smear of dirt on my pale leather glove.

I hurried up Regent Street. It was nearly ten to one. Still clutching the lavender, I hurried through the revolving door of the Café Royal.

If Henry had waited for me, I expected to find him in the bar. But he was standing just in front of me in the lobby and looking almost as dapper as Simon Martlesham in a dark-blue suit with a faint pinstripe. He had a white carnation in the buttonhole and a silk handkerchief poking out of the breast pocket. For an instant I saw him with Rosington eyes. Mrs Forbury and her Touchies would have thought him a bit of a cad.

'Wendy.' He lunged towards me. 'You're looking beautiful.'

I couldn't stop him embracing me but I turned my head and all he succeeded in kissing was my ear. He smelt familiar, but as smells from the past do. The sort of smells that belonged to you at another time, when you were another person.

'We must celebrate,' he was saying. 'Let's have a drink. Why are you carrying that bit of lavender?'

I looked at the sprig. I had been holding it so tightly that the stain had spread further. The glove was probably ruined.

'I bought it from a gypsy just now.'

'Not like you to be superstitious.' Henry was always quick. 'Is that the effect of Rosington?'

I shook my head and said what about that drink.

We went into the bar. I wrapped the lavender in a handkerchief and dropped it in my handbag. When the waiter came Henry ordered dry martinis.

'Just like when we first met,' he murmured.

'Don't be sentimental. It doesn't suit you.'

But I was glad he'd chosen dry martinis. I needed a slug of alcohol.

'We can have lunch here if you like,' he was saying. 'Or if you'd rather we could go somewhere else. I wondered about the Savoy, perhaps.'

'Where does all this money come from?' I asked. 'Your Hairy Widow?'

'I told you on the phone. I haven't seen her since – since the day I last saw you.'

Luckily the drinks arrived at this moment.

'Cheers,' Henry said, and we drank.

For the next few minutes, neither of us found much to say. We smoked cigarettes, finished our drinks and ordered another round. Henry asked how the Byfields were, and I said they were very well, and that Janet and David sent their love.

'How's Rosie?'

'Very well.'

'Isn't her birthday around now?'

'Last Wednesday.'

'She must be – ah –?'

'Five.'

'Perhaps I should send her a present.'

Once again the conversation languished.

'We should talk about the divorce,' I said at last.

'I meant what I said on the phone. I love you.' He sat up, squaring his shoulders. 'I was a bloody fool. Can't we start again?'

'There's no point. There'd be someone else. Some other poor fat widow with a big bank balance.'

'There won't. Because –'

'And where did you go to, anyway? Your solicitor told mine that you'd just vanished.'

'It was a business trip, and I was a little short of cash.' Henry stared at his hands. 'I left a letter with him for you. Did you get it?'

'I told my solicitor to put it in the wastepaper basket.'

It had been about the only useful thing poor Fielder had ever done for me. His unpaid bill was still in my bedroom at the Dark Hostelry. The amount seemed rather large for what he'd achieved.

I said, 'I'm saving up to divorce you.'

'Is there someone else?'

I stared at Henry. He had a little dimple in his chin which made him look like an overgrown baby. I had always found it rather attractive. I wondered what he'd say if I said, *Yes, there is someone else. David.*

'It's none of your business any more.'

'I owe you some money.'

'You owe a lot of people some money.'

'Do you remember Grady-Goldman Associates?'

'I'll hardly forget.'

He nodded. 'When Grady went bust I ended up with about thirty per cent of the stock in Grady-Goldman.'

Aloysius Grady lived like a rich man and talked like one too. He had wanted Henry to set up a European property portfolio for him and then to manage it on his behalf. Henry had put in a lot of work. He had even lent Grady a lot of money for him to give to his daughter, who was studying in the UK, and taken company stock as collateral on the loan. When the crash came, our money vanished and the stock plummeted.

'Just after you – you left,' Henry went on, 'I had a cable from Louis Goldman. A subsidiary of Unilever wanted to buy the company and the shares had gone through the roof. He was the other major shareholder, and he thought we could get them higher if we worked together.'

'Come on, Henry.'

'What?'

'This sounds like another one of your fairy tales.'

'It's not, I promise. That's why I had to leave the country. Louis bought me a ticket. It was all in that letter.'

I tried to remember the Grady-Goldman place. A big compound with a wire fence and lots of huts roofed in corrugated iron. A black watchman making tea. Grady's Rover driving into the compound in a cloud of dust. Cigar smoke catching the back of my throat in a small, hot office. And Grady himself, a big, balding man with wispy red hair who tried to pinch my bottom.

'What did they do? Why did Unilever want to buy them?'

'Machine tools,' Henry said. 'That's why Grady-Goldman seemed a good bet to me in the first place. There're not many people who make them south of the Sahara. Louis had got the company up and running again. They weren't into profit because of the debts Grady had left. But they had the trained workers, they had the plant, and they had the customers.'

'If you're trying to tell me your financial acumen has made you rich, I just won't believe you.'

'It wasn't my financial acumen. It was Louis's. But it was my luck.' He hesitated. 'To be precise, just over forty-seven thousand pounds' worth of luck.'

'Good God.' I thought about the sprig of lavender in my bag. It seemed to have worked retrospectively, and for the wrong person. 'What are you going to do with it?'

'I'm going to give you some.'

I said nothing.

159

'I've been thinking about all sorts of things lately,' Henry went on, sounding pleased with himself.

'Good for you. It's a big responsibility, isn't it, having all this money to waste?'

'That's just it. Change of plan. I've come to the conclusion that gambling as a career doesn't suit me. I'm thinking of becoming a schoolmaster again.'

I laughed.

'It's not such a silly idea. I was a schoolmaster when you first met me. I rather enjoyed it.'

'Henry,' I said. 'Have you forgotten what happened at the Choir School? They more or less chucked you out. No one's going to give you a job without a reference.'

He looked smug. 'I've thought of that. Though to be honest, I didn't have to do much thinking. Someone else did my thinking for me.'

'Like Louis Goldman? I wish you'd stop being mysterious.'

'You remember I taught at another school before Rosington? Veedon Hall. The Cuthbertsons want to sell up. A friend of mine who's still on the staff wrote to me out of the blue and asked if I knew anyone who might be interested in going into partnership with him. It's a going concern, waiting list as long as your arm, and old Cuthbertson always had a soft spot for me. The price is a snip, too. All it would take is thirty thousand.'

'Then there's nothing to stop you going ahead.'

'I don't want to do it by myself. I want us to do it.'

I shook my head.

'It wouldn't be like burying yourself in the sticks.' He stretched out a hand towards me which I pretended not to see. 'It's not far from Basingstoke. You could be up in town in no time.'

'It's too late.'

'I shouldn't have blurted it out like this. I'm sorry. Look, why don't you think about it for a few days? A few weeks, if you like. Talk to Janet. Let's go and have some lunch.'

After that, my mood changed. I don't know whether it was the alcohol or what Henry had said, but I felt much happier.

Perhaps the lavender was doing its job. We took a taxi to the Savoy and had lunch in the Grill Room. Henry wanted champagne.

'Not Veuve Clicquot,' I said. 'I've had enough of widows.'

So he ordered a bottle of Roederer instead. 'Talking of widows,' he said. 'That reminds me.'

He launched into a long, involved story about Grady's widow and her attempts to entrap a Unilever executive for herself or, failing that, for her daughter. He ended up making me laugh. Later I told him about the Dark Hostelry and my job. We compared notes about the inhabitants of the Close.

'There's no need for you to stay in that job if you don't want to,' Henry said over coffee.

'I need to earn my living now,' I said as lightly as I could.

He took an envelope from his jacket pocket and laid it on the table between us. 'That's up to you.'

'What is it?'

'A cheque for ten thousand.'

'You're paying me off? Is that what it is?'

'Don't be silly, Wendy. It's yours. I want you to have it.'

'A divorce settlement?' My voice was rising. 'Is that it?'

His lips tightened. 'At least you won't have to work in a dead-end job if you don't want to, and you won't have to live in Rosington.'

'I'm going to finish the job.'

'You don't *have* to. You can just walk away from it.'

'It wouldn't be fair to Hudson.'

'Wendy, you don't owe him anything. You've done some work for him, he's paid you for it, but there's no reason why you should work any longer than you want to.'

'I know, but I'd like to finish it.'

I watched Henry putting two cigarettes in his mouth, lighting them both and giving one to me. It seemed such a natural thing to do. He hadn't asked, either, just taken it for granted that as he was having a cigarette I would have one as well.

I said, 'Actually, there's another reason.'

'I thought there might be. There *is* someone else, isn't there?'

'It's none of your business. Not now.' Then I laughed at his face, which was pink with champagne and anger. 'OK, there is someone. His name's Francis Youlgreave.'

He ran a hand through his hair, leaving a tuft of it standing up, the way he always did when he was puzzled. 'Youlgreave? Who?'

'You might have come across him at Rosington.'

'The bastard,' Henry muttered.

'He's been dead for fifty-two years. He was one of the canons in the early nineteen-hundreds, and a minor poet as well. He caused a bit of a scandal and they made him leave.'

Henry's face brightened. 'Then Francis and I have got something in common. Besides you, I mean.'

'There's a lot of unexplained things about him. For example, no one seems to know whether he died naturally or committed suicide.'

'At Rosington?'

'No – he died a little later, after they'd made him resign. The story was that he was forced out because he preached a sermon in favour of having women priests.'

Henry raised his eyebrows. 'If you did that in Rosington even today you'd probably get tarred and feathered.'

'There was more to it than that. I keep finding traces of him *now*. But the strangest thing, the thing that worries me, is that something's going on, something I don't understand.'

'What do you mean?'

'Someone else is interested in Francis Youlgreave, someone else is trying to find out about him.'

'Well, why not?'

'No reason. But I think they're doing it secretly.'

'You don't sound very sure.'

I sighed. I wasn't sure. No one seemed to know the little man who looked like a solicitor's clerk, but that didn't mean he was trying to hide his identity. There could be a perfectly innocent explanation for his interest in Francis. And apart from him, what else had I got to worry me? The fact that Mr Treevor kept seeing little men hanging around the Dark Hostelry? Senile dementia does not make for reliable

162

witnesses. Or the pigeon with its wings cut off? Someone's idea of a joke, perhaps, or just a schoolboy with an absorbing interest in biology. Nothing necessarily suspicious, nothing to do with Francis. The smell of what might have been Turkish tobacco clinging to *The Tongues of Angels*? Coincidence.

'It's nothing,' I said. 'Anyway, thank you for lunch. I really ought to be going now.'

'Don't go yet. There's no hurry.'

'I want to go shopping before I catch the train back.'

'Where?'

'I thought I'd start in Piccadilly and walk up Bond Street and then down Oxford Street. And then I can catch a tube or a bus back to Liverpool Street.'

'Sounds arduous. Can't I come too? Carry the parcels? Fight off the footpads?'

'No, Henry. In any case, you'd be bored.'

'I'd like to buy you a present.'

'I don't want a present, thanks. I doubt if I'll buy anything. You wouldn't understand – I just want to look. Shopping in Rosington is like shopping in nineteen fifty-three.'

'I tell you what. I'll buy you some gloves.' He picked up the pair on the table. 'Look at those. Filthy. You *need* some more.'

'All right.' I smiled at him. If money was no object I might as well make the most of it. 'In that case you can buy me a pair from the Regent Glove Company. But they won't be cheap.'

'I should hope not.'

Henry paid the bill and we walked up to the Strand. He wanted to hail a taxi but I had a fit of remorse and wouldn't let him.

'Listen, Henry, you're taking taxis everywhere, you've just given me lunch at the Savoy, you're about to buy me the most expensive pair of gloves I've ever had – the way you're going, that money will be gone in a few months. And why do we need a taxi? There's nothing wrong with a bus.'

'I think Rosington must have given you ideas below your station.' But he took my arm and we walked towards the bus stop. 'After you've done your shopping, let's have a

163

drink before your train. Perhaps even dinner. Or what about a show?'

'Stop it, Henry. Anyway, I won't have time.'

'We could just have a quick drink at Liverpool Street if you want.'

'I don't think that would be a good idea.'

'Why not?'

I stopped so sharply that a man behind us bumped into Henry and swore.

'Henry, nothing's changed. It's over between us. I promised I'd see you for lunch but that's all.' I thought of the Hairy Widow and hardened my heart. 'I'm not going to meet you for a drink.'

He stared at me, looking hurt and angry at the same time. 'But Wendy –'

'I'm sorry, there's nothing you can say that will change my mind.'

I pulled my arm away from his and we walked the rest of the way to the bus stop in silence.

It was about a minute later I changed my mind. The bus came almost at once. It was a double-decker, and I led the way upstairs. I wanted to look out of the window at the streets of London, pretend to be a tourist and not have to talk to my husband.

Henry followed me up the stairs. He was closer than I liked. His nearness oppressed me. It made me nervous and also gave me a pleasure I didn't want. I turned round, meaning to glare at him. As I turned, something caught my eye.

Passengers were still filing on to the platform of the bus. I was just in time to see a small, dark man in a raincoat moving towards a seat on the lower deck. He wasn't wearing a hat. He was bald.

From my vantage point on the stairs, I saw quite clearly that the bald patch was roughly the shape of a map of Africa.

28

The western side of the Cathedral's spire was coated with evening sunlight as heavy as honey. I walked up from the station, occasionally glancing down at my new gloves, which were fine black suede, lined with silk. It was almost a crime to wear them.

In one way it had been a mistake to see Henry, I knew, like scratching a scab until the blood welled up again. On the train I'd kept thinking of him bouncing on top of his Hairy Widow. Henry with his bare, wobbling bottom like a plump baby's, and the widow waving her legs in the air and wearing those oh-so-desirable, dark-blue, high-heeled shoes. It was there in the photograph, captured for all eternity in black and white, in my bedside table at the Dark Hostelry.

I trudged slowly up the hill towards the Porta. I wasn't drunk and I didn't have a hangover, though this was a matter of luck rather than good judgement. But I wasn't exactly sober either. It was more than alcohol. Emotions can intoxicate you as well, even sadness.

Part of the sadness, tied up with Henry in some inexplicable way, was the knowledge I was here in Rosington again. That was one reason why I was walking slowly. I felt as though I were thirteen years old and trying to postpone the moment when I had to go back to Hillgard House at the beginning of term.

The first person I saw when I went into the Close was Mr Gotobed. He was sitting on a bench beside the door of his house, reading the sports page of the *Rosington Observer* and stroking a large ginger cat. He was still in his cassock, which he wore when he was being a verger and conducting the clergy about the Cathedral. When he heard my footsteps, he glanced over the top of the paper.

'Mrs Appleyard.' He stood up quickly, dislodging the cat. 'Lovely evening.'

'Isn't it?' The cat rubbed itself against my leg so I bent down and stroked it. 'This is a fine animal. Is he yours?'

'My mother's. He's not bothering you, is he?'

'Not at all.' The cat purred like a distant aeroplane. 'What's his name?'

'Percy.' Gotobed was blushing. 'My mother says it ought to be spelt with a U and an S.'

I stared blankly at him for a moment. His blush deepened. Then I realized that Gotobed had made a joke. 'Oh, I see! Pursy. Because of his purring. Very good.'

'She's ninety-three, my mother,' confided Gotobed. 'But she's still got her sense of humour and she's as bright as a button. Which reminds me. I told her about that pigeon. You remember?'

'It's not something you're likely to forget in a hurry.'

'Sorry – maybe I shouldn't have mentioned it.'

'No, I'm interested. What did your mother say?'

'She said perhaps there's a loony on the loose in the Close. Like there was last time.'

'Last time?'

'Fifty or sixty years ago. Someone started doing things to animals and things. Not at all nice.'

'What exactly happened?'

He clasped his hands in front of him and his nose twitched. He looked so unhappy I would have liked to stroke him rather than Pursy.

'It's all right,' I said. 'You don't have to worry about shocking me. It just can't be done.'

He gave me a tentative smile. 'If you're sure you want . . . Well, they found a rat without any legs outside Bleeders Hall one morning. And there was a headless cat in the north porch. Mother wasn't sure, but she thought there might have been a bird without any wings as well.'

'And did they ever find out who was doing it?'

'Turned out to be one of the canons. He'd gone queer in the head, poor chap.' Gotobed was staring at me now, his eyes clear and intelligent. 'You wouldn't have thought many people would remember it now. It's a long time ago. But if someone did, they might be trying to play games with us, don't you think? Like pretending to be a ghost.'

'Do you believe in ghosts, Mr Gotobed?'

'Not me, Mrs Appleyard.' He slapped his hand against his thigh, and there was a *crack* that bounced off the wall of the Porta. 'I only believe in what I can see and touch.'

I made a rapid calculation. If Mrs Gotobed was now ninety-three, she must have been about forty when Francis had left Rosington. 'Was your mother living in the Close then?'

'I don't rightly know. It must have been around then she married Dad. But the way she talked about it, everyone knew what was going on.'

'She must remember a lot about the old days.'

'She remembers more about what happened when she was a girl than what happened yesterday. You know what these old folks are like.' Gotobed beamed like a proud parent. 'Of course, she gets a bit muddled. Thinks I'm Dad sometimes.'

'Do you think she might let me talk to her?' I added hastily, 'I'm interested in the old days because of the Cathedral Library and the dean's exhibition.'

'I could ask her. Mind you, she doesn't see many people now.'

I told him it didn't matter and said good night.

The Cathedral clock struck half past eight. The swallows and martins were doing their evening acrobatics around the Octagon. I walked slowly, aware of my tiredness. In London, I'd found it hard to concentrate on the shops. I suppose the alcohol hadn't helped. And meeting Henry had made me weary too, and so in another way had that business with Simon Martlesham and the little man on the bus.

No doubt tiredness was the reason why I felt someone was watching me. The feeling increased as I neared the door to the cloisters. It was almost as if Francis were pursuing me rather than the other way round. Which was absurd. Ghosts were no more plausible than gods and the idea that either of them, should they exist, should be interested in the living was equally silly. I remembered the lavender in my bag and wondered why I'd been fool enough to buy it.

Better to concentrate on the questions belonging to the here and now. What was Simon Martlesham up to? Was the little bald man the one who had borrowed the library book and stolen cuttings from the 1904 backfile of the *Rosington Observer*? And was he also the man Mr Treevor had seen in and outside the Dark Hostelry, the little dark man who looked like a ghost?

Now the Cathedral was between me and the sun. The path round the east end was in shadow. I walked more quickly. I was within fifty yards of the door to the garden of the Dark Hostelry when I heard the wings.

At first I thought one of the swallows had swooped down to hawk for insects near the ground, and that it had passed close to my ear. But the wing beats were slower and deeper than a swallow's could ever be and I swear I felt the air move. On the other hand, I was in a suggestible mood and everyone knew that the acoustics of the Close were almost as strange as the acoustics of the Cathedral itself. The Close was a network of stone canyons with a battery of idiosyncratic sound effects. David said there was a spot outside the north door where a whisper could be heard clear as a bell at the Sacristan's Gate.

All this galloped through my mind in not much more than a second. I looked up, half expecting to see a bird darting away. There was nothing. A trick of the mind, I told myself; I was tired.

I pushed open the gate of the Dark Hostelry. The sun was on the upper windows of the house and they gleamed like slabs of polished brass. The garden was in shadow. I noticed, as I had on that first day three months ago, how impossibly neat and tidy it was. The Byfields couldn't afford a gardener, and it was all Janet's work. How did she manage, especially now she was pregnant? And why did she bother? She had always been neat, in her possessions as well as in her person. At Hillgard House, her locker in the fourth-form common room had been displayed to all of us as a model of what a locker should be.

I made a resolution that in future I should at least mow the lawn. I walked up the path. I had missed supper but I didn't mind that. It was a long time since lunch at the Savoy but I wasn't hungry.

As usual the door was unlocked. I stepped into the hall. The house was silent. There was definitely an unpleasant smell now. Perhaps it was the drains or a rat had died under a floorboard. But there were no floorboards in the hall, only stone flags. David would have to talk to the chapter clerk.

For a moment I was seized with a dread that history was about to repeat itself, that soon there would be a child's scream from upstairs. The doors to the sitting room, the dining room and the study were all open. I left my hat on the hall table and went down to the kitchen to show Janet my new suede gloves.

She was sitting at the table with the tradesmen's account books in front of her. The books were closed and she was smoking a cigarette. She looked very pale.

'Hello. How did it go?'

'Glad it's over.'

She started to get up. 'I'll put the kettle on.'

'Don't bother.' I sat down beside her. 'Are you all right?'

'Tired. I thought I'd take the weight off my feet.'

'You ought to be in bed.'

'I'll perk up in a moment.'

'Where's David?'

'There's a meeting at the Theo. Coll.' She pushed the cigarettes and matches towards me. 'But tell me, how was Henry?'

'He bought me some very nice gloves.'

Janet stroked them. 'They're beautiful. I won't ask how much they cost.'

'And he also gave me this.'

I took the envelope from my handbag and passed it to Janet. I watched her opening it, watched her eyes widening.

'Wendy, is this a joke?'

'I don't think so.' I explained about Louis Goldman and about Henry going to South Africa. 'Anyway, if I pay it in I'll soon find out.'

169

'If?'

I concentrated on lighting a cigarette. Then I said, 'He wants to buy a share in a prep school, Veedon Hall, the one he used to teach in before he came here. He asked if I'd come back, if we could start again.'

'And will you?'

'I don't know.' I blew out smoke. 'Half of me thinks, what's the point? You can't take away the past. I'm not even sure I want to.'

Janet said nothing.

'You think I should go back to him, don't you?'

'I don't know.' Suddenly her face began to crumple like a sheet of paper. 'I don't know what I think about anything.'

'It'll be all right. Don't worry.'

She sniffed and a tear fell on the table, just missing Henry's cheque. 'It's probably because I'm pregnant. It's as if all your emotions suddenly belong to someone else.'

I leant across the table and put my arm round her. Her shoulders were shaking.

'Sorry,' she said, 'sorry. I'm not really like this, but I think I must have been bottling it up until you came back. I don't want to bother David with it at present, he's so busy.'

'It's not your fault. Blame the baby. My mother had a craving to eat grass when she was pregnant with me.'

She clung to me for a moment and then relaxed. How could David leave her in this state?

'You've been doing too much,' I said harshly.

'Don't be cross.'

'I'm not cross with you. I'm cross with me.'

'Don't be silly.' She pulled away and looked at me. 'What is it? Something's wrong, isn't it? Was it seeing Henry?'

'I thought it was over. I thought I was past the worst.' I stubbed out my cigarette, wishing the ashtray was the Hairy Widow's face. 'But on the train coming back I kept thinking about – about that woman. At least David doesn't . . .'

'David's got God instead.' She smiled at me to show the words were meant as a joke.

'I'd like to kill the wretched woman,' I said. 'And torture Henry for a very long time.'

'Of course you would.'

'I must be going round the bend. When I was walking through the Close this evening I had the strangest feeling. I heard wings. It was as if a bird swooped down behind me. Not a swallow or anything like that. Something much larger.'

'It's the acoustics. And you're tired.'

'That's what I told myself.' I looked at her. 'And to be honest I had too much to drink in London. I don't suppose that helped.'

'Don't worry. It's a difficult time.'

'But it's always difficult.'

'You need an early bed. We all do.'

Neither of us spoke for a moment. It was the first time I'd mentioned the drinking, though she must have known about it. But Janet never tried to change me. She always took me as I was. She let me believe I was the strong one.

After a moment she looked at her watch. 'I must go and check on Rosie. I promised I'd go up in ten minutes after I settled her down, and that was ages ago.'

'I'll go.' I stood up, eager to show that I wasn't a complete failure. 'I bought a couple of postcards for her, and if she's awake she can have them now. I need to take my things up anyway.'

I went slowly upstairs, back to that faint but definitely increasing smell in the hall. The sun was completely behind the Cathedral now and the whole house was in shadow. On the next flight, I heard Rosie giggling, an unusual sound – she was not a child that laughed much, partly because she had too much sense of her own dignity. I walked along the landing to the open door of her room. The curtains were still open and through the window I saw the Octagon and the spire, dark against a darkening sky. Rosie giggled again.

'Hello, Rosie, I've –' I broke off.

The room was full of soft, grey light. It was perfectly obvious that there were two heads on the pillow.

'Mr Treevor,' I said.

He sat up in the bed. Rosie was still laughing, snuffling with excitement. Mr Treevor wore his maroon striped pyjamas. His hair looked like a wire brush and he was not wearing his teeth. His eyes were huge in his shrunken face.

'What are you doing here?'

'I was cold,' he said, pushing out his lower lip. 'Rosie's keeping me warm.'

'I'm tickling Grandpa,' Rosie announced, 'and Grandpa's tickling me.'

'Nice and warm now,' Mr Treevor said.

'Then perhaps you'd better go to bed,' I suggested. 'I think it's time for Rosie to go to sleep.'

He extricated himself with some difficulty from the bedclothes. In the end I had to help him. He tottered out of the room and across the landing. He and Rosie did not say good night to one another. His door closed with a gentle click. I decided the postcards could wait until the morning.

'Are you all right?' I asked Rosie as I tucked her in again.

She nodded, settling her head into the pillow. Her face rolled towards me. The excitement had faded away.

'Where's Mummy?'

'Downstairs. She'll be up to see you soon.'

'But why isn't she here *now*?'

'She will be. She –'

'But I want her.'

'Why? For a particular reason?'

'She always came to see me before.'

'Before what, dear?'

'Before you came.'

'And she does now. But I happened to be passing, and I heard you and Grandpa, and –'

'You take Mummy away from me,' she interrupted. 'You stop her seeing me. You *make* her stay downstairs.'

'Don't be silly, Rosie. You know that's not true.'

She put a thumb in her mouth as though corking it would stop further words falling out. In the fading light her face had become the colour of lard, like one of the marble monuments in the Cathedral and just as hard. I stroked her hair. She turned her head away, dislodging my hand.

'Mummy,' she muttered, so quietly I could pretend not to hear her. 'I want Mummy.'

Didn't Rosie understand I was trying to *help* Janet? Did she really believe I had taken her mother away from her? The trouble with children, I thought, is that they see things differently from grown-ups, and it's so easy for them to get hold of the wrong end of the stick.

She muttered something else, in an even lower voice, and this time I really couldn't hear what she said. Not for sure. But it might have been, 'I hate you.'

'Mummy will be up very soon. Don't worry about anything, and sleep tight.'

I squeezed Rosie's shoulder and left the room. Least said, soonest mended. I'd let Janet know that Rosie had wanted her, I thought, as I climbed the stairs up to the second floor and my own bedroom. But perhaps it would be better not to mention Mr Treevor and the tickling. Janet would worry that Rosie might have been scared. She would be concerned about her father, at this further sign that he was growing worse.

This was 1958. We were more innocent then. And adults can get hold of the wrong end of the stick, too.

29

In the morning I went back to work. My visit to London seemed to have given me extra energy. I catalogued more books than ever before. This was despite the fact that I had three visitors.

The first was Canon Hudson, who wanted me to check a draft of the pamphlet for the exhibition in case there were any errors.

My next visitor was Mr Gotobed who stood in the doorway fiddling with the badge of the Cathedral which he wore on a chain round his neck as part of his verger uniform.

'I mentioned to Mother what you said, Mrs Appleyard.' He gabbled the words out as though they were hot. 'She says she'd be pleased to see you if you'd like to drop in for a cup of tea tomorrow afternoon. But she says she hopes you won't mind her not being up and dressed. Of course, if you can't spare the time –'

'It's very kind of her. Please tell her I'd love to come.'

Mr Gotobed coloured. 'Mother's a bit deaf, I'm afraid, so you may have to speak quite loudly.'

'That's all right. Tell her I'm looking forward to it.'

Finally, just as I was thinking of packing up at the end of the day, Canon Osbaston arrived. Under his arm was a large flat package wrapped in brown paper and tied up with string.

'Good afternoon, Mrs Appleyard. I hope I haven't interrupted your labours at a crucial point.'

'Not at all.' I watched him moving down the library, deliberate as a tank.

'Mrs Elstree knew I would be passing nearby and she entrusted me with an errand.'

He ran out of breath and began to puff. I drew out a chair for him and he sat down heavily and laid his package on the table. It was a big chair but his body overflowed around it. He took out a handkerchief and dabbed the bald patch on his little head.

'Dear me, Mrs Appleyard, it is still unseasonably hot.'

'One of the advantages of working here is that the temperature never gets that far above freezing.'

He chortled like a schoolboy in a Billy Bunter story. 'Very droll, Mrs Appleyard. And how are your researches into Canon Youlgreave progressing?'

'Slowly,' I said, playing safe.

He edged his chair a little closer to mine and leant towards me. 'It's really very odd, but someone else has been asking questions about him.'

'Asking you?'

He shook his head. 'Mrs Elstree. Apparently a man came up to her as she was leaving the Theological College one day. It was in the morning, she was going shopping. He said he was writing a book about him. According to Mrs Elstree, he looked quite respectable but he certainly wasn't her idea of a writer.'

'How strange. Did she say anything else about him?'

'Not really. She sent him off with a flea in his ear.' Canon Osbaston settled his glasses more firmly on his nose so he could see me better. 'I wondered if he might be some sort of journalist. But why would a journalist be interested in Canon Youlgreave?'

'I've no idea,' I said with perfect truth.

'Of course, in your case it's very different. In a sense you're treading in his footsteps. Which brings me to my reason for being here.' He smiled, and if tortoises have teeth they must be just like Canon Osbaston's. 'Mrs Elstree was up in the attics the other day. There's a possibility that we may convert some of them into study bedrooms. Be that as it may, she chanced upon something she thought might interest you. As she knew I was practically passing the library door, she asked me to deliver it.'

He moved the parcel a little closer to me. Clearly I was expected to examine it there and then. This took some time because Canon Osbaston felt that dealing with knots was a man's responsibility. This meant he had to find his penknife, cut the string, close the knife, roll the string into an untidy ball and unwrap the brown paper, a process that is far less tedious to describe than it was to watch. The result of his labours was a framed photograph measuring perhaps fifteen inches by twelve. The frame was heavy and dark, its varnish dulled, and the photograph itself was spotted with damp. It showed about twenty people on the lawn in front of a building, which I recognized almost immediately as the Theological College. They were on the croquet lawn in front of the French windows of the Principal's Lodging. On the far left of the photograph were branches from what must have been the beech tree under which Rosie had sat drawing a picture of an angel with a sword.

Several of the people in the photograph were wearing costumes of some sort. Of those who weren't, three of the men were dressed as clergymen.

Canon Osbaston leant closer still. His breath was sour, smelling of ginger. He tapped a long knobbly forefinger against one of the clergymen.

'According to Mrs Elstree, that's Canon Youlgreave.'

So at last I saw Francis, though not as clearly as I would have liked. He was the smallest of the men and he stooped towards the camera as if he'd seen something rather interesting at the base of the tripod. He was wearing a hat, but what I could see of his hair was dark. His nose was long and his eyes were dark, blank hollows.

Canon Osbaston leant a little closer and peered at the photograph. As he did so he rested his right hand as if for support on my left knee.

'Have you noticed the curious clothing, Mrs Appleyard? I wonder if they were engaged in a dramatic production of some sort.'

'Excuse me,' I said, 'your hand.'

He glanced down at his hand and my knee as though seeing them for the first time. 'Good heavens! I'm so sorry.'

He removed the hand, although without obvious haste, and gave me another of his tortoise smiles. 'I think the clergyman in the centre must be Canon Murtagh-Smith, one of my predecessors.'

I stood up, moved round the corner of the table and stretched. 'Pins and needles,' I explained.

'How tiresome. I believe regular exercise is the only answer. As for the third clergyman, both Mrs Elstree and I are baffled. In those days we had our own chaplain, so it may be him, or perhaps one of our lecturers.' Seizing the back of his chair with one hand and resting the other on the table, he pushed himself to his feet. 'But I mustn't keep you any longer from your work, Mrs Appleyard.'

'Do thank Mrs Elstree for me. And tell her I know Mrs Byfield will be interested to see the photograph as well.'

'Yes, indeed,' said Canon Osbaston, his eyes bright with understanding. He knew as well as I did that Mrs Elstree had produced the photograph for Janet, not for me. It was Janet who might be the wife of the next principal.

He shuffled down the library, gave me a wave and left. I turned back to the photograph. There were several children in it, including two little girls in white dresses. One of them was standing next to Francis, part of her shielded from the camera lens by his right arm. I stared at her, wishing there were more detail in the print. Then I remembered the magnifying glass in the tray where I kept my pens and pencils. I could see everyone a little more clearly under the glass. If only I could climb into the photograph, I thought, I would understand everything. As it was, all I really discovered was that the two little girls seemed to have white protuberances attached to their shoulders. A moment later, I realized what they were. Wings.

The little girls were dressed up as angels.

30

'You're a big girl,' Mrs Gotobed observed. 'That's nice.'

'Mother!' Mr Gotobed set down the tea tray on a brass table between my chair and his. 'She doesn't always realize what she's saying,' he murmured to me.

'Like me,' Mrs Gotobed continued. 'Wilfred's father used to say I was built like a queen.'

'How lovely.' Nobody had ever told me I was built like a queen but I wished they had.

Mrs Gotobed nodded. She was sitting in a wing armchair with her feet up almost on top of the little coal fire that smouldered in the grate. Her legs were covered with a crocheted blanket. She was wearing what looked like a tweed coat. Her face was long and bony, with pale, dusty skin like tissue paper.

'Milk, Mrs Appleyard? Sugar?'

Watched by Pursy, who was lying in a patch of sunlight on the window ledge, Mr Gotobed blundered around the over-furnished little room. He was wearing an apron over a dark suit made of stiff, shiny material that looked as if it would stand up by itself if its owner suddenly evaporated. The tea service was bone china speckled with little pink roses. We had lovingly laundered napkins, so old that their ironed creases were now permanent, apostle teaspoons, two sorts of sandwiches and two sorts of cake.

'You've gone to an awful lot of trouble,' I said as I accepted a fishpaste sandwich.

'It's no trouble,' Mrs Gotobed replied. 'Wilfred enjoys it. I always say he'll make someone a lovely wife.'

'Mother!'

For the moment we devoted ourselves to eating and drinking. The Gotobeds' house was next to the Porta. Through Pursy's window I saw the Theological College across the green. Rain fell steadily from a sky the colour of the slates of the college's roof. As I watched, two familiar figures emerged from the driveway, the one sheltering under an umbrella held over him by the other.

'There's the bishop,' I said.

Mrs Gotobed looked up. 'And Mr Haselbury-Finch. The dean and Canon Hudson went in a little earlier.'

'Mother knows everything that's going on,' said Mr Gotobed proudly. 'Inside or outside the Close.'

Directly opposite Pursy's window was another which overlooked the chestnuts, the entrance to Canons' Meadow and the road up to the cloisters and the south door.

'So you live in the Dark Hostelry with Mr and Mrs Byfield?'

'That's right.'

'They're a handsome couple. And that little girl of theirs is a beauty. I saw you and her the other day talking to His Lordship and Canon Hudson.'

'Mrs Appleyard is working in the Cathedral Library for Canon Hudson,' Mr Gotobed said in a loud voice, speaking in the vocal equivalent of capital letters.

'I know that, dear. I'm not stupid.'

'No, Mother. Try a slice of this fruit cake, Mrs Appleyard. It was made by one of the Mothers' Union ladies.'

'Just a small slice,' I said. 'I mustn't spoil my supper.'

Mr Gotobed cut three substantial slices and handed them round. Once again silence descended. It was clear that in this household eating and talking were not combined.

'Not bad,' Mrs Gotobed said, wiping her fingers on her napkin, 'though not as good as the ones I used to make. They don't put in enough fruit nowadays.'

'Mrs Appleyard,' announced Mr Gotobed, 'is very interested in the *old* days.'

'There's no need to shout, Wilfred.'

'Because of working in the library and helping with the

exhibition. You remember the exhibition, Mother? The one the dean's having in the Chapter House.'

She sniffed. 'Next thing we know they'll be selling cups of tea in the Lady Chapel. I don't know what your father would have said.'

'The dean and chapter have to make ends meet, same as everyone else.'

'It's not right,' Mrs Gotobed said. 'It's the thin end of the wedge, you mark my words.' She cast her eyes up to the ceiling as if searching for consolation there. 'You'd think they'd remember Jesus throwing the moneylenders out of the Temple, being educated men and all.'

'That's not the same thing at all, Mother.'

'Why not?'

I said, 'You must have seen a lot of changes over the years, Mrs Gotobed.'

'Changes?' She snorted, then began to choke. But a second later I realized she wasn't choking, she was laughing. After a moment, she brushed the tears from her eyes with a grubby forefinger. 'This is the sort of place where everything changes and everything stays the same.'

'Now, Mother, that doesn't quite make sense. Do you mean –'

'Mrs Appleyard knows what I mean.'

'Were you thinking about the pigeon your son found?' I asked.

'Oh, that. I suppose so. That and other things.'

'Mr Gotobed said you'd told him it'd happened before, about fifty years ago.'

'Not pigeons, I think.' She took a sip of tea and stared into the glowing coals of the fire. 'I remember a cat. That had lost its head. They found it in the north porch. And there was a rat, too – they found that in Canons' Meadow. And I think there was a magpie that had lost its feet. No pigeons, though.'

'And they found who was responsible?' I prompted. 'One of the canons who wasn't quite right in the head?'

'Oh, no.' Mrs Gotobed held out her cup to her son. 'More.'

He took the cup. 'But, Mother, I'm sure you said –'

'You're getting muddled again, Wilfred.'

She turned to me. 'He sometimes says it's me that's muddled, Mrs Appleyard, but half the time it's him.'

'I'm sure you said it was one of the canons.'

'I said they *thought* it might be one of the canons, Wilfred. That's a very different thing. There was a lot of gossip, I remember, a lot of wagging of nasty tongues.'

'Was the canon Mr Youlgreave?'

'Yes, that's the name. How do you know?'

'Just a guess. He used to be the Cathedral librarian so I've come across a few references to him.'

'They didn't like him, that was the long and the short of it. He tried to rock the boat, Mrs Appleyard, and nobody likes people like that.'

'How did he rock the boat?'

'There used to be some dreadful places in Rosington then. Down by the river. He made a fuss about them, tried to get something done.'

'Like Swan Alley.'

'How do you know about Swan Alley?' she snapped.

'Someone mentioned there was slum housing down there.'

'All the land down there was owned by the dean and chapter. They'd let it out, of course, but it was still their land. So they didn't like him pointing the finger. Well, they wouldn't, would they? It's human nature, isn't it? Mind you, Canon Youlgreave did have some funny ideas. They got rid of him in the end. Ganged up on him, I shouldn't wonder. He wasn't a well man.' She shook her head sadly. 'But such a lovely gentleman.'

Mr Gotobed was looking bewildered. 'So it wasn't him after all.'

'What?'

'Cutting up birds and things.'

'How can it be? He's been dead for fifty years.'

'Not now, Mother. Then.'

'There's a copycat about if you ask me.' She stared dreamily into her teacup and then looked at me. 'Like I said, Mrs Appleyard, things don't change, not around here. I said as much to Dr Flaxman only the other day.'

'But who would want to copy something like this?' I asked. 'And who would know about it in the first place?'

'Plenty of people,' she shot back. 'You'd be surprised. Fifty years isn't really a long time.'

'Not when you're your age, Mother,' said Mr Gotobed, beaming nervously and brushing the crumbs from his apron. 'Next thing we know we'll be seeing your telegram from the Queen and your photo in the *Observer*. That *will* be a treat.'

She shook off his interruption like a fly. 'Fifty years isn't long in Rosington.' She waved a hand at the window overlooking the Close. 'Especially out *there*.'

'Just some lad, I expect,' Mr Gotobed said. 'Fiddling around with his penknife. I dare say he didn't mean any harm.'

Mrs Gotobed wrinkled her nose, sipped her tea and wrinkled her nose again. 'This is stewed, Wilfred. That's not very nice for our visitor, is it? Couldn't you make some fresh?'

In an instant Mr Gotobed was on his feet, apologizing, gathering teacups, dropping teaspoons on the carpet, and denying that making a fresh pot would be in the slightest bit troublesome. He picked up the tray and then realized he would have difficulty opening the door. I stood up to do it for him. He edged out of the room, keeping as far away from me as possible.

'Close the door,' Mrs Gotobed told me. 'There's a draught.'

On my way back to the chair, I paused by the mantelpiece. There was a photograph of a boy in a chorister's cassock and ruff.

'Is this Wilfred, Mrs Gotobed?'

She nodded. 'He cried when his voice broke. Always was a silly boy. But kind-hearted, I'll say that.'

I sat down. Now we were alone, she looked younger, as if age was part of a disguise she wore when her son was in the room.

'Have you lived in this house a long time?' I asked.

'That's one good thing about a place like this, about it not changing. They'd had a Gotobed in the Close for the past hundred years, so they didn't want a change when his dad died. Just as well. I don't know what he'd have done otherwise. I don't know where we'd have lived.'

A short, uncomfortable silence followed. Pursy woke and looked first at Mrs Gotobed and then at me. Coals settled in the grate, and the window looking out on the Close rattled in its frame as a squall of rain spattered against the glass.

'If it wasn't Canon Youlgreave cutting up animals,' I said, 'then who was it? Did you ever find out?'

She glanced at me, her face at once sly and unsurprised. 'Not for certain.'

'But you had an idea?'

'There was a boy.'

'Can you remember his name?'

'Simon. Was it Simon?' Her head nodded on to her chest and her eyelids closed. 'Don't mind me if I nod off,' she mumbled. 'And don't go. Wilfred will bring the tea, that will wake me up.'

'Simon who?'

'Simon,' she repeated. 'Good-looking boy. He went away.'

Then the door opened and Mr Gotobed walked backwards into the room carrying the tray. For the rest of my visit the three of us took part in short, intense bursts of conversation, punctuated with pauses when Mrs Gotobed nodded off for a moment.

She was curious about Mr Treevor. She had heard that he was living in the Dark Hostelry.

'I thought I saw someone who might be him the other day,' she said. 'Old gentleman, with a big head, not too steady on his pins. Went into Canons' Meadow. He was by himself.'

'Mr Treevor doesn't go out much,' I said. 'Not by himself.'

But he had gone out on his own on Rosie's birthday. He said he'd gone to feed some ducks.

'That's Mother all over,' Mr Gotobed whispered as he showed me out of the house. 'Likes to know everything about everyone.'

It was only as I was walking back through the Close that I realized Mrs Gotobed had asked me very few questions about myself, and none about how I came to be living in the Dark Hostelry, or the whereabouts of my husband. She must have known that Henry had been sacked from the Choir School. She must have noted my surname. If she asked no questions, then presumably she knew the answers already.

At the Dark Hostelry I found Janet, Rosie and Mr Treevor in the kitchen. Rosie and Mr Treevor were eating cheese on toast. Rosie's doll was on the chair beside her.

'How did it go?' Janet asked.

Rosie pressed the doll's chest. 'Mama!' it said.

'Angel wants more,' Rosie interpreted.

'Coming, darling,' Janet said mechanically.

'It was interesting.' I sat down at the table. 'And she was very protective of Wilfred.'

'Wilfred?'

'Mr Gotobed to you. Mrs G. was a hen with one chick. I think I was being sized up.'

Janet giggled. 'As a future Mrs Gotobed?'

It was the first time I had heard her laugh for days. 'I don't think the current Mrs Gotobed would approve of a woman in my situation.'

I tried to speak lightly but Janet wasn't fooled. All the laughter drained from her face.

'Did you learn anything about Francis Youlgreave?' she asked.

'Not really. Except Mrs Gotobed's a supporter. A real gentleman, she said. She thinks he wasn't liked in the Close because he ruffled too many feathers about the slums by the river. Apparently the dean and chapter owned the freehold.'

I didn't mention Simon. David had told Janet about the pigeon Mr Gotobed had found, but I hadn't yet passed on Mr Gotobed's information that someone else, fifty years earlier, had a penchant for cutting up small animals in the Close. The Byfields had other things on their minds at present, and also I didn't think Janet would thank me, or that David would approve. When I was in Rosington that year, I often had the feeling he was looking for reasons to disapprove of me.

'So Canon Youlgreave remains a man of mystery,' Janet said, cutting the slice of bread into two, half for Rosie, half for Angel.

'What about mine?' Mr Treevor demanded.

'Just coming, Daddy.'

There was something in her voice that alerted me. 'How have you been?'

Janet pushed her hair from her forehead. 'Fine, really. A bit tired.'

Our eyes met. She was tired, so she should rest. But how could she rest with these people in this house?

I said, 'When the weather's cleared up, I'll mow the lawn.'

Janet began to speak, but was interrupted by the slamming of the door in the hall above. She straightened up. Suddenly the tiredness was smoothed away.

'David's home early,' she said. 'That's nice, isn't it, poppet?'

Rosie nodded.

'You've got crumbs on your chin,' Janet went on. 'Wipe them off with your napkin and sit up.'

Rosie obeyed.

Usually David would come down to the kitchen to say hello when he got back from the Theological College, if only for a moment.

Janet took some toast from the grill, added a layer of grated cheese and slid it back. 'I'll just pop up and see if he needs a cup of tea.'

'I'll keep an eye on the toast,' I said.

I listened to Janet's slow footsteps on the stairs to the hall. A moment later I gave Mr Treevor his second slice of cheese on toast.

'Thank you, Mummy,' he said, and seized it with both hands.

He had almost finished by the time Janet came back downstairs. I knew by her face something was wrong.

'Janet –'

'There was a meeting of the trustees this afternoon,' she said dully. She leant on the table, taking the weight from her feet. 'They've decided to close the Theological College after all.'

31

I was still angry on Thursday morning when the parcel came.
I was in the drawing room doing the dusting. The postman
knocked at the back door and David answered. He brought
the parcel up to me, which I suppose was meant as an olive
branch. I recognized the handwriting at once and so I expect
did he.

He gave me the parcel and said, 'Wendy, I must apolo-
gize.'

'What for?'

'Last night. I know I was upset but I shouldn't have taken
it out on you.'

'And on Janet and Rosie,' I reminded him, rubbing salt into
the wound. I was in no mood for an apology, and I thought if
David was going to put himself on a pedestal as a clergyman,
he should have had all the more reason to act like a civilized
and Christian human being.

'Yes,' he said mildly. 'You're right.' But the Olivier nostrils
flared momentarily and I realized that I was trespassing
yet again on the wrong side of an invisible line. Not that
I cared. 'In any case,' he went on, 'it was unforgivable
of me.'

Suddenly there was no longer any satisfaction in attacking
him. 'It's all right. Anyway, it's not me you have to worry
about, is it? It's Janet.'

He nodded curtly and left the room. I knew it was pointless
to goad him, but if he was angry with me then I was angry
with him. There hadn't been much point in his shouting at
Janet over supper last night, or in his storming out of the

kitchen in the middle of the meal and slamming the door behind him.

If David hadn't been a priest, if he hadn't been a man who habitually kept his emotions so tightly under control, it would have been less shocking. After he'd left, Janet had wept into a tea towel, Rosie had played with Angel in the corner by the dresser, and Mr Treevor had quietly finished off all the untouched food on everyone else's plates.

I sat down on the sofa, turning Henry's parcel over and over in my hands. On Monday Henry had said he wanted to buy a birthday present for Rosie and in the end there hadn't been time that afternoon. He had the cheek to ask me to do it for him, but I'd refused.

It was odd seeing my name in Henry's handwriting, as subtly unsettling as receiving a self-addressed envelope. I undid the string and unwrapped the brown paper. Inside were three books and a letter. *Noddy Goes to Toyland* and *Hurrah for Little Noddy* were by Enid Blyton. He had written Rosie's name inside but in a way they were meant for me. The third book was a slim green volume almost identical to the library book in my bedside cupboard upstairs. It was a copy of Francis Youlgreave's *The Tongues of Angels*.

I opened the letter, which was written on notepaper from Brown's Hotel. He was obviously still doing his best to run through the £47,000 as soon as possible.

My dear Wendy

I hope Rosie likes the Noddy books. Noddy looks like an odious little twerp to me, but perhaps I'm not the best judge.

Anyway, over to Youlgreave. I've done a little checking. There is a Farnworthy collection listed in the catalogue of the British Museum Library – mainly theology. It doesn't include the sermons of Dr Giles Briscow, though the library does have a late-seventeenth-century copy of that. So presumably it's not the one that Youlgreave had, if Youlgreave's ever existed.

Now for the big news. On Tuesday I went to the Blue

Dahliah only to find your little bald man just leaving. I followed him back to Holborn. He's got an office over a tobacconist's. Harold Munro, Ex-Detective Sergeant Metropolitan Police, Private Investigations & Confidential Enquiries Undertaken. That's what it said on his card in the tobacconist's window. And I know it's him, because he came into the shop for some cigarettes while I was there and the tobacconist called him Mr Munro.

Munro asked the tobacconist to take any messages the next day, that was Tuesday, because he had to be out of the office. The tobacconist said where was he going, and hoped it was somewhere nice. And Munro said it was a place called Roth, up the Thames near Shepperton.

There were footsteps in the hall and I looked up. Mr Treevor had come up from the kitchen and was moving towards the downstairs lavatory.

'Mr Treevor?' I called.

He paused, his hand on the lavatory door. 'Yes?'

'You know the man you saw watching the house from the High Street?'

'I've seen him before,' Mr Treevor said. 'I'm pretty sure he's a ghost.'

'Was he bald?'

'Might have been.' Mr Treevor twisted the handle of the lavatory door. 'Yes, I think he was.'

'And can you remember the shape of his bald patch? You must have seen it from above when he was in the High Street.'

'It wasn't a nice shape. He wasn't a nice man.'

'Was it triangular? A bit like a map of Africa?'

'I expect so,' said Mr Treevor obligingly, vanishing into the lavatory and locking the door behind him.

I went back to Henry's letter.

So next morning I went down to Waterloo and caught a train for Shepperton – Roth is too small to have a station. In fact, Roth hasn't got much of anything besides a church, a bus shelter and a pub. It's one of those villages that got swallowed by the suburbs and apart from a whacking great reservoir and one or two fields that the builders forgot, all you can see are houses.

But there's a sort of green where the bus shelter is and the pub. This seems to be the centre of the place and I reckoned if Munro came to Roth he'd probably come there sooner or later. I spent about an hour having a cup of coffee in a ghastly little café, all chintz and horse brasses. No luck there. When it was opening time, I pottered along to the pub. Luckily our Harold had had the same idea. He was talking to an old codger in the snug, so I nipped into the lounge bar, got myself a drink and settled down for a spot of eavesdropping.

I wonder if he's ex-Metropolitan Police because they kicked him out for inefficiency. I sat at the bar pretending to read the paper. I could hear some of what they were saying. Munro seemed to be asking about the Youlgreaves. They mentioned someone called Lady Youlgreave who lives in the Old Manor House (just down the road). Unfortunately some people came in and I couldn't hear very well, because people were talking loudly on the other side of me.

But I heard the name Francis Youlgreave several times. The old codger was rabbiting on about a place called Carter's Meadow. I think Youlgreave may have upset a neighbour by doing something beastly to a cat there.

Munro left soon afterwards. The last I saw of him, he was walking fast down the road to the station.

I didn't want to follow, because I thought it might make my interest in him a little too obvious. So I had a look at the church, which is small and old. Francis Youlgreave is buried here – there is a memorial tablet in the chancel to him. All very discreet – just the family crest, his name and the dates of his birth and death.

The only other thing was the poems. There was a box of second-hand books near the door, threepence each, all profits to the Church Restoration Fund. One of them was some poems by Francis Youlgreave, which I thought you might like. I had a look at it on the train back to town, and I couldn't make head or tail of it. Nutty as a fruit cake, as your mother used to say.

On Thursday, I'll try and find out something about Martlesham and I'll give you a ring in the evening. With luck you'll get this before I phone.

I meant everything I said on Monday. I know I've been a bloody fool but don't let's throw it all away. If you haven't cashed that cheque, please do.

All my love,

Henry

I don't know why, but that letter made me want to cry. I suppose it underlined how far Henry and I had travelled since we married, and especially since I found him with his Hairy Widow on the beach.

I went up to my room with the parcel. I'd have to find some paper to wrap up the present for Rosie. The house was very quiet. Janet had taken Rosie to school, David was in his study and Mr Treevor was in his room. I mounted the second flight of stairs up to my landing. When I put the books in my bedside table, I noticed the sprig of lavender resting on Henry's cheque beside the gin bottle. I didn't feel lucky. Just miserable.

I lit a cigarette. I was in no hurry to go to work. I stared at the photograph Canon Osbaston had lent me. It was propped up on an old washstand in the corner of the room behind the door. The trouble was, nothing made sense, then or now. What the hell were Martlesham and Munro up to? If they wanted to find out about Francis, why couldn't they do it openly? Perhaps there was some obvious explanation staring me in the face which I couldn't grasp because I was too busy making a mess of my life and watching Janet and David making a mess of theirs. Where did the mutilated pigeon come in? And what about the little man Mr Treevor saw, the little man like a shadow who might or might not be the same as, or at least overlap with, Harold

Munro, the private investigator with a bald patch the shape of Africa?

I picked up the photograph and took it to the window so I could see it better. There, according to Mrs Elstree, was Francis Youlgreave. Hero or villain? Madman or saint? If I could climb into the blurred monochrome world of the photograph and talk to him for five minutes, I would at least find the answers to those questions. And perhaps I would also find the answers to others in the present.

I stubbed out my cigarette and got ready to go to the library. When I went downstairs I found David in the hall. He was wearing his hat and raincoat and bending over the oak chest. He poked his umbrella between it and the wall.

'What's up?' I asked. 'Lost something?'

'It's this smell.' He jabbed the umbrella viciously downwards. 'I wondered if there's something got trapped down here. I can *feel* something.'

'Why don't we move the chest out?'

'It may not be terribly pleasant. If it's a dead rat, for example. And wouldn't the chest be rather heavy for you?'

'No, it wouldn't,' I said. 'But are you sure you can manage?'

Those nostrils flared, but he bit back the temper and nodded. There were handles at either end of the chest. We lifted it a few inches away from the wall, easy enough with two of us, though hard for one person to do without scraping the chest on the flagstones.

Wedged in the angle between the wall and the floor was a mass of feathers and bone. The smell was suddenly much stronger.

David said, 'What the hell –?'

I touched his arm. 'We must get it out of the way before Janet sees it.'

Not it – them.

As if on cue, the kitchen door slammed, and we heard Janet's footsteps coming up the stairs to the hall.

32

'He'll have to go,' David said. 'You must see that, Janet.'

She chewed her lower lip. 'We don't know it was him.'

'Who else could it have been?' He sighed, rather theatrically. 'Rosie?'

'Of course not.'

'It's a symptom of severe mental illness. He needs to be under proper medical supervision.'

'But he'd *hate* it if we put him in a home.'

There was a sudden rushing of water and the bolt on the door shot back. Mr Treevor slipped out, walking backwards as if from a royal presence, peered into the empty lavatory and carefully closed the door. Only then did he turn round and see the three of us.

The chest was still pulled away from the wall. David and Janet were facing each other across it. I was on my hands and knees, eavesdropping while sweeping up the mess with the coal shovel and brush from the drawing room fireplace. The smell was worse, so I was breathing through my mouth. I tried not to look too closely at the wings because I thought there might be maggots.

Mr Treevor was carrying *The Times*. He tapped it importantly and said, 'Good morning. I can't stop and chat, I'm afraid. I must check my investments.'

'Daddy –' Janet began.

He paused, his foot already on the first stair. 'Yes, dear?'

'Nothing.'

He smiled at all three of us. 'Oh well, I must be on my way.'

We listened to his footsteps mounting the stairs and waited for the slam of his bedroom door. I shovelled the wings on to a sheet of newspaper, part of yesterday's *Times*, and wrapped it into a parcel. I could cover it with brown paper and string, put a stamp on it, and send it through the post. To Henry? To his Hairy Widow? I shook my head to shake the madness out of it. Perhaps madness was infectious, and this house was riddled with its germs.

David glanced at his watch. 'We'll talk about it this evening,' he said to Janet. 'But I'm afraid he can't stay here.'

'It could have been anyone,' Janet burst out. 'We don't lock the door in the day. They could have just walked in.'

'Why should they bother?' David picked up his briefcase. 'I have to go. Canon Osbaston's expecting me.'

He and David were meeting to discuss ways of reversing the decision to close the Theological College. The trustees' change of heart was due to the diocesan architect's unexpectedly gloomy report on the fabric of the Theological College. Apparently it needed thousands spent on it, quite apart from the cost of the proposed modernization programme. But there were a number of other considerations which had not been taken into account. David had lectured Janet and me about them last night. There was the question of whether the trustees were legally entitled to close down the college and divert its endowment to the wider needs of the diocese. In any case, shouldn't they seek a second opinion from another, and more objective, surveyor? There was also the point that one of the trustees had been absent. It might be possible to raise extra funds from sources outside the diocese. And then there was the bishop. David was seriously disappointed in him. Instead of throwing his weight behind the Theological College, as he'd led everyone to expect he would do, he had abstained when it came to the vote. But if there were a new vote, he might be persuaded to change his mind.

'It's the dean and Hudson who are the real problem,' David had told us, not once but several times. 'Not that report – they're just using it as an excuse. But they don't realize what they're destroying. Once the college is closed, they'll never be able to get it started again.'

I watched him through the glazed door as he strode down the garden path to the gate into the Close, the rain pattering on his umbrella. What he hadn't mentioned last night, but what Janet and I knew, was that if his career was a boat, it had just hit a rock. The principal's job would have been perfect for him, and according to Janet it would have almost certainly led to higher things.

But with that no longer a possibility, what was David going to do? He couldn't stay here as a minor canon for ever. Unless a friendly bishop could be persuaded to pull a tasty rabbit out of a hat, at best he'd have to become a chaplain to a school or college and at worst he'd end up as a parish priest in the back of beyond.

I put the parcel in the dustbin. Before going to the Cathedral Library I had a cup of coffee with Janet because that was the only way I could persuade her to sit down for ten minutes.

'I'm sorry about David being so rude,' she said. 'He's so upset he doesn't know what he's doing.'

'It's not surprising.'

'But it's not fair of him to take it out on everyone.'

'I'm not sure I'd behave much better if I was in his shoes. Losing a job you've –'

'It's not just the job. It's Peter Hudson.'

'I don't understand.'

Janet wrinkled her forehead. 'He's the only person in the Close David really admires. He says he's got a first-class brain.'

'Lucky him.'

'David respects him. He'd like Peter to *like* him.'

'So it must have made it worse that he was the one who wanted to close the Theo. Coll.?'

She nodded. 'I think he hoped that Peter would change his mind at the last moment. Not that there was ever much chance of that.'

'Men can be such babies.' I took our cups and saucers to the sink.

'The funny thing is, I think Peter *does* like David. June said something once . . . Wendy, leave the washing-up. You must go to work.'

Janet became almost cross when I tried to help, so I left her in the kitchen, with the suds up to her elbows. At the library, I began with the proofs for the Chapter House exhibition, which didn't take long. Despite his poetry, Francis hadn't earned a place in the dean's roll of honour. When I'd finished, I took the marked-up proofs to the Chapter House. Canon Hudson was there with Mr Gotobed, directing two of the Cathedral workmen as they moved display cases around the big room. Mr Gotobed beamed shyly at me as I came in.

'Thank you for tea yesterday,' I said. 'It was nice meeting your mother too.'

Hudson looked sharply at me. I was about to give him the proofs when I saw that there was another person in the Chapter House. Mr Treevor perched like a little black bird in one of the niches which ran round the walls below the great windows. He was very close to the model of the Octagon and was staring at it with huge, fascinated eyes.

'Thanks for doing that.' Hudson skimmed through the proofs. 'Not too many problems, then?'

'No. Is Mr Treevor all right?'

'He's no bother.' Hudson looked up. 'He wandered in a few minutes ago.'

'It's just that he doesn't normally go out by himself now.'

'Then if Mrs Byfield is at the Dark Hostelry, perhaps you could take him home? I wouldn't like her to be worried.'

I went over to Mr Treevor, laid a hand on his arm, smiled at him and told him it was time to go. He nodded and put his arm through mine. In the archway leading to the cloisters he stopped to wave at the men in the Chapter House. They waved back.

Outside it was still raining. I put up my umbrella. The pair of us walked slowly through the Close.

'I saw him going into the Chapter House,' Mr Treevor confided.

'Who?'

'The dark little man. I saw him in the garden, you see, so I followed him. He went into the Chapter House but he must

195

have gone when I wasn't looking. He wasn't there when we left.'

'Do you see him a good deal?'

Mr Treevor considered the question. There was a drop of moisture on the end of his nose and I didn't think it was rain. I watched it trembling and wished it would fall.

'Yes, he's often around. You don't think he could be my brother?'

'I didn't know you had one.'

'Nor did I, but I think I might. It's possible they didn't tell me. And it would make sense, wouldn't it?'

In the Dark Hostelry, we found Janet in the kitchen scrubbing the floor. She hadn't noticed her father's departure.

'You shouldn't be doing that,' I said. 'Leave it for the charwoman.'

'I was going to,' Janet said, 'but Daddy spilled porridge on the floor this morning and then Rosie stepped in it.'

'Then you should have asked me.'

'I can't ask you to do everything. It's not fair.'

'Why not? After all, you won't be pregnant for ever. Anyway, I must run. I'll see you at lunchtime.'

'You know I've got the Touchies this afternoon?'

Mr Treevor wandered into the kitchen. He drew back the sleeve of his jacket and ostentatiously consulted his wristwatch. 'I see it's lunchtime. I've washed my hands.'

Janet glanced at her own watch. 'Did you forget to wind your watch last night? It's only quarter past ten.'

'But I'm hungry.'

'That's all right, Daddy. Don't worry. You can have some bread and dripping to be going on with.'

Mr Treevor looked at his watch again. 'But I was sure it was one o'clock.'

'What's on your wrist?' Janet said, taking a step nearer to him. 'Have you cut yourself?'

He held out his arm, and stood, head bowed, waiting for her to examine it. Janet pushed back the watch. The strap had partly concealed a gently curving scratch about two inches long. Part of it had been deep enough to draw blood, now dried. The blood was on the inside of Mr Treevor's shirt cuff. The second hand was still sweeping round the dial of the watch. The hour and minute hands stood at seventeen minutes past ten.

'How did you do that?' asked Janet.

'I must have caught it on a nail when I went out for my walk.'

Janet and I exchanged glances. Mr Treevor sat down at the kitchen table and asked how many slices of bread and dripping he could have. I went back to work. For the next two hours I catalogued library books. There were no surprises either, not unless you count a bound volume of *Punch* for 1923. I was bored, but the boredom was a kind of relief. It was better to be bored than to worry about Janet and about Mr Treevor and his ghostly brother and about what Simon Martlesham might be up to.

At a quarter to one I locked the library and went back to the Dark Hostelry for lunch. We had bread and soup, followed by cheese and fruit. Mr Treevor ate in silence as though his life depended on it. Janet and I made sporadic attempts to start a conversation, but our minds were on different things and in the end we gave up.

After lunch I washed up while Janet went to lie down for half an hour. I took her a cup of tea, but she was so deeply asleep I tiptoed away without waking her.

I had my own tea in solitary state in the drawing room. I fetched *The Tongues of Angels* to read, the copy Henry had sent me. It was just possible, I thought, I might be able to trace the former owner of the book, who might have known him. Or there might be marginal notes. Or the book might turn out to be Francis's own copy.

But Francis hadn't read this book. No one had – the pages were still uncut. I fetched the paperknife from Janet's bureau and worked my way through, reading scraps of verse as I turned each page. There were my old friends Uriel, Raphael, Raguel and Co. There were the children of Heracles, sliced into bits by their dreaming spellbound father. There was the cat watching the pharaoh's children die, and the slaughter of the stag on Breakheart Hill.

I turned back to the beginning of the book and noticed

something I'd missed when I'd looked at it before. There was an epigraph, and I knew at once where it had come from, knew the very book Francis had taken it from.

> Nay, further, we are what we all abhor, Anthropophagi and Cannibals, devourers not onely of men, but of our selves; and that not in an allegory, but a positive truth: for all this mass of flesh which we behold, came in at our mouths; this frame we look upon, hath been upon our trenchers; in brief, we have devour'd our selves.

I'd found this very passage marked in the *Religio Medici* which had once belonged to Francis. It was an oddly intimate discovery, as though I had sliced open his mind with Janet's paperknife, and now I was seeing something that perhaps only he himself had seen before.

I turned the page and glanced at the table of contents. For one vertiginous moment I thought I was falling. Or rather that everything else was falling away from me. It was exactly the sensation I had felt on the afternoon near the beginning of my stay in Rosington when David had taken Janet and me up the west tower of the Cathedral. This time there was no Janet to put her hand on my sleeve and murmur that if tortoises waddled, they would waddle like Canon Osbaston. I shut my eyes and opened them again.

Nothing was altered. I hadn't imagined it. The table of contents wasn't as it should have been. As before, it listed all the poems in the collection under their appropriate angelic sub-heading. But there weren't seven archangelic sub-headings now, as there were in the copy of the book I had borrowed from Rosington Library. There were now eight. The new sub-heading came at the end – 'The Son of the Morning', which sounded like a suitable pseudonym for an angel – and it contained only one poem, 'The Office of the Dead'.

I think now that the oddest thing of all was the violence of my reaction. The poem shocked me before I'd read it, before I knew why it was shocking. It didn't make sense, any more than the fact I had smelled something unpleasant in the hall before Mr Treevor could have put the pigeon's wings there. There are some things I still don't understand.

I turned back to the title page. At last I saw what should have stared me in the face as soon as I opened Henry's parcel. I had expected this book to be called *The Tongues of Angels*. After all, it looked like *The Tongues of Angels* and Henry had said it was *The Tongues of Angels*. And most of its contents were identical in every way to those of *The Tongues of Angels*.

This book was called *The Voice of Angels*.

I turned back to the title page. Instead of being published by Gasset & Lode, *Voice* had been 'privately printed for the author'. Everything else was the same as far as I could tell – the date, the typeface, even the paper.

I turned the pages to the end of the book. The new section had its own epigraph, taken apparently from the fourth section of the *Celestial Hierarchies* of Dionysius the Areopagite, whoever he was.

> They, above all, are pre-eminently worthy of the name Angel because they first receive the Divine Light, and through them are transmitted to us the revelations which are above us.

The poem was long and very obscure, even by Francis's standards, and written in the painfully archaic language he had liked so much. I skimmed through it. As far as I could tell, it was in the form of a conversation between the poet and a passing angel. The angel told Francis why he'd left his principality and come down among the sons and daughters of men. The angels had the gift of eternal life, it seemed, and they wanted to share it with a handful of suitably qualified humans. In fact, according to the angel, he and his friends had just about everything in their gift.

I didn't like the poem – it made me feel uncomfortable, and I certainly didn't begin to understand it. On the whole, I thought it was just another version of the old Christian claptrap about death being just a gateway to eternal life. What was so wonderful about life that you should want it to go on for ever?

I closed the book with a snap and tossed it on to the table by the sofa. It slid across the polished wood and almost fell off. Why had Francis bothered to print a separate edition of

The Tongues of Angels? Was there something about 'The Office of the Dead' that he didn't want the rest of the world to see? If so, what? Or was it simply that Gasset & Lode had refused to print it in the commercially published edition because it was such a bad poem?

The rain had stopped at last and a pale sun was trying to force its way through the clouds. I decided to have a walk before I went back to work. I needed to clear my head. I put on my hat and raincoat and went into the Close. There was a farm on the other side of the Theological College. If the ground wasn't too muddy I'd get out of the city for half an hour and walk among fields, dykes and hedgerows that sloped down to the Fens.

But I never even left the Close. Just as I reached the Porta, I heard the tinkle of a handbell, uncannily similar to the one we used in the Dark Hostelry to let people know a meal was ready. Then came a jangling crash. I looked towards the Gotobeds' cottage. One of the first-floor windows was open. A hand fluttered in the room behind the window.

I walked over to the cottage and looked up. 'Hello, Mrs Gotobed. How are you?'

The hand appeared again, beckoning me. I couldn't see her face, but the sound of her voice floated down to me.

'The door's unlocked. Come upstairs.'

I picked up the bell from the flagstone path, went inside and up the stairs to the little sitting room. There were several changes since I had seen it last. For a start, Mrs Gotobed was sitting at the window overlooking the Close with Pursy on the ledge between her chair and the glass. Secondly, the room had not been smartened up for a visitor. The remains of her lunch were on a tray beside her, the commode was uncovered, and she looked as if she hadn't bothered to brush her hair since yesterday.

'Is there something I can do?' I asked.

'Have you seen him?' she hissed at me.

'Mr Gotobed? Not recently, not since this –'

'Not him. That man who was trying to get in.'

'What man?'

'There was a fellow in a black overcoat trying to get in.'

Her voice was shaking, and she looked older than she had yesterday. 'I've never seen him before. Though I didn't get a good look at him, me being above and him wearing a hat.'

'What happened?'

'He knocked on the door. I was asleep, nodded off after my dinner, didn't hear him at first. Then I looked out to see who it was and there he was. He tried the door handle. He was about to come in, murder me in my sleep, I shouldn't wonder. I called down, "What do you think you're doing?" and he glanced up at me and scarpered. Out through the Porta, and the Lord knows where he went then. If I'd been a couple of years younger, I could have got to the other window to see where he went.'

'It's all right,' I said, drawing up a chair and sitting beside her. I took one of her hands in mine. Her skin was as cold as a dead person's. 'Would you like me to fetch Mr Gotobed, or the police?'

She shook her head violently. 'Don't go.'

'I won't. Can you remember anything else about this man?'

Her fingers gripped mine. 'Black hat, black coat. I think he was a little fellow, though I can't be sure as I was above him, you see.' She breathed deeply. 'Bold as brass,' she muttered. 'In broad daylight, too, and in the middle of the Close. Wouldn't have happened when I was a girl, I'll tell you that. It's been one of those days, Mrs Appleyard, I don't mind telling you. I was all shook up to start with, but I didn't expect something like this.'

'Shall I make you a cup of tea?'

'Later.'

'I'm sure he won't come back. Not now you've frightened him off.'

'How can I be sure of that?'

There wasn't any way you could be sure. Once you're frightened, you're frightened and common sense doesn't come into it.

'Could the man have been a tramp?'

'He could have been a parson for all I know. All I saw was the black hat and black coat, I told you.' Suddenly she paused and stared at me. 'Tell you one thing, though, his shoes were clean. If he was a tramp, he was a very particular one.'

Another possibility was that Mrs Gotobed had misinterpreted the situation altogether. Perhaps it had been a door-to-door salesman paying a perfectly innocent call. He might have been as frightened of her as she was of him.

'What a day, eh?' said Mrs Gotobed. 'First poor Pursy, and now this.'

We both looked at the cat who was still sprawled at his ease on the window ledge. He had taken no notice of either of us since I had come in.

'He came in this morning like a bat out of hell,' Mrs Gotobed said. 'Through the kitchen window, we keep it open a crack for him, and Wilfred said he broke a vase he was in such a hurry. Came streaking up here and jumped on my lap. He doesn't do that very often unless he wants something. Cats aren't stupid.'

She rested her hand on Pursy's fur. He turned his head and stared out of the window, ignoring her. It was only then that I saw that his left ear was caked with blood.

'What happened to him?'

'Must have got into a fight. The other fellow nearly had his ear off.'

I scratched the cat gently under its chin with one hand and with the other smoothed aside the matted fur round the base of the ear. It looked as if a single claw had sliced through the skin near where the ear joined the scalp. A claw or a knife? At least the blood had dried and if the wound wasn't infected it should heal easily. Pursy pulled his head away from me and examined me with amber eyes.

'Poor little fellow,' Mrs Gotobed mumbled. 'When he was a kitten, he was such a scrap of a thing. Just like a little baby.' Her hands turned and twisted in her lap. 'You've not had children then, you and Mr Appleyard?'

'No.'

'Not yet,' she amended. 'Don't leave it too long. I didn't have Wilfred till I was forty, and then it was too late to have more.' Her jaw moved up and down, up and down as if she were chewing her tongue. 'I never had much time for children. But it's not the same when it's your own. You feel differently somehow. And it never goes away, neither. Sometimes I look at Wilfred and I feel like he's a baby all over again.'

'I'm sure he's a good son.'

'Yes. But that's not to say he isn't a silly boy sometimes. I don't know what he'll do without me to look after him, and that's the truth. Lets his heart rule his head, that's his problem. If he could find himself a nice wife, I'd die happy.'

I wondered if she suspected I was dallying with her son's affections and was therefore warning me off. For a moment we sat in silence. I stroked Pursy, who rewarded me with a purr.

'This cut,' I said. 'I think this might have been done with a knife.'

Mrs Gotobed wrinkled her nose. 'Shouldn't be surprised. They're everywhere, you know.'

'Who are?'

'Mad people. Ought to be locked up.'

'Does this remind you of what happened before?'

'That pigeon Wilfred found?'

I nodded.

'What I'd like to know is where the wings went.'

'And it's not just the pigeon, is it? What about fifty years ago and all the things that happened then?'

Her shoulders twitched. 'Same thing, another person.'

'You said in those days a boy was doing it. A boy called Simon.'

'Did I?'

'It couldn't be him, could it?'

She shook her head. 'He went away. Years ago.'

'But he might have come back.'

'Why would he do that? Nothing to come back *for*.'

'I don't know. Was his surname Martlesham, by the way?'

'Might have been. I can't remember. Why?'

'I found something in the Cathedral Library which mentioned him meeting Canon Youlgreave. Was there a boy called Martlesham?'

'Oh, yes.'

'Who was he?'

'He used to clean the boots and things at the Palace.'

'Where were you living then?'

'Down by the river.'

'In Swan Alley?'

She sighed, a long broken sound like rustling newspaper. 'No – Bridge Street. Over a shop.'

'Not far away. Did you know the Martlesham family?'

'Everyone knew the Martleshams.' She licked her lips. 'The mother was no better than she should be. Called herself missus but she was no more married than I was in those days.'

'Let's see if I've got this right. Simon was the eldest, and he worked at the Palace. And then there was a sister?'

'Simon was always going to make something of himself. Ideas above his station. Nancy must have been five or six years younger. Funny little thing, black, straight hair, always watching people, never said very much. Never heard her laughing, either, not that there was anything to laugh about in Swan Alley.'

'What happened to them?'

'The mother died in childbirth. Don't know who the father was. It was around that time Simon went a bit queer in the head. But Canon Youlgreave helped him.'

I waited. Pursy's paw dabbed at a fly on the windowpane. The sun had broken through the clouds. There was a big puddle near the chestnuts and two schoolboys in short trousers were trying to splash each other.

'He heard their mother had died, and he helped Simon emigrate. Paid for him to learn a trade, as well. And he found someone to adopt Nancy.'

'So Nancy emigrated as well?'

'Might have.' Blue-veined lids drooped over the eyes. 'I can't remember.'

The front door opened. I turned in my chair, half fearing and half hoping that the little man in black had come back. But Mrs Gotobed didn't stir. There were footsteps on the stairs, heavy and confident. Then Mr Gotobed came into the room. He saw me, and the air rushed out of his mouth in a squeak of surprise.

'It's all right,' I said. 'Your mother's had a bit of a shock, but she's all right now.'

'It's all wrong,' Mrs Gotobed said, 'frightening people like that.'

33

As the evening went on, I felt increasingly annoyed with
Henry. It was true that we hadn't arranged a time for him
to ring, but I naturally assumed he'd phone while Janet was
out with the Touchies, as he had last week. He didn't.

I made beans on toast for Rosie and Mr Treevor. I banged
the plates down on the table, not that they noticed, and had
a minor tantrum when I couldn't find the vegetable knife.
They didn't notice that either. It was stupid, but I wanted to
talk to him. He might be able to make more sense out of *The
Voice of Angels* and what Mrs Gotobed had said than I could.

After I'd washed up and done the vegetables for the
grown-ups' supper, I fetched the book and went through
'The Office of the Dead' again. There were some grisly
bits which reminded me of 'The Children of Heracles' and
'Breakheart Hill'. Blades sliced through flesh, bones cracked
asunder. There was a particularly disgusting passage about
a bleeding heart. I was trying to work out what the angel
wanted the poet to do with this when Mr Treevor tottered
into the kitchen.

'Am I Francis Youlgreave?' he asked.

'No,' I said. 'You're John Treevor.'

'Are you sure?'

'Absolutely sure.'

'It's only that I thought someone said I was Francis
Youlgreave. But if you're sure I'm not I must be John
after all.'

'Who said you were Francis Youlgreave?' I asked.

'Someone I saw this morning. When I was out.'

'In the Chapter House, do you mean?'

'Yes. He was the little man near the winkle thing.'

'The what?'

'You know, that thing that's a bit like a willie when it's big.' He stared at me, his face suddenly aghast. 'Oh dear. Shouldn't I have said that?'

'It's all right. Don't worry. The thing to remember is, you're John Treevor.'

'Yes,' said Mr Treevor. 'I know.'

He went upstairs again, leaving me to remember the scene in the Chapter House with the model of the Octagon, which was like no willie I'd ever seen. Besides Mr Treevor, the other men in there had been Mr Gotobed, Canon Hudson and two of the Cathedral workmen. Mr Gotobed and the workmen were all big and burly. Canon Hudson was small but not particularly dark. I gave up the puzzle just as the garden door opened and Janet called downstairs that she was back.

'That was extraordinary,' she said when she came down to the kitchen. 'You'll never guess who the Touchies talked about.'

'Henry?'

'Francis Youlgreave.' She filled the kettle at the sink, raising her voice to be heard over the rushing water. 'According to Mrs Forbury, they used to call him the Red Canon.'

'How does she know?'

'Because she grew up in Rosington. Her father was the vicar of St Mary's.'

'She can't have known him personally, can she? She doesn't look much more than fifty.'

Janet shook her head. 'She remembers people talking about him when she was growing up. Did you know he used to smoke opium?'

'She's pulling your leg.'

'She wasn't. *She* believes it, and so do all the other Touchies.'

'The Red Canon – so he was a Socialist?'

Janet shrugged. 'Or he had one or two vaguely Socialist ideas. I doubt if they'd seem very radical now. There was that business about the slums near the river. Youlgreave

207

made himself unpopular by going on about it ad nauseam at chapter meetings. And what was worse, much worse, he was far too free and easy with the servants. Mrs Forbury said he invited working-class children into his house and gave them unsuitable ideas.'

'What does that mean exactly?'

'She was far too coy to say. But she mentioned his experiments with animals. Someone claimed he'd cut up a cat, so people started talking about witchcraft. There were complaints to the dean, who was in a very awkward position because Youlgreave was some sort of cousin. But he had to do something about it because the police were involved. Not officially, I think, but someone had a word in the ear of the chief constable.'

'They certainly laid it on with a trowel,' I said. 'So he's a drug addict and a revolutionary, and practises black magic on the side.'

'He was also a heretic as well, or the next best thing. When he preached that sermon about women priests, he played into everyone's hands. Mrs Forbury said it was so obviously loopy, it made his position untenable.'

'That's Rosington logic,' I said. 'They could cope with drug-taking and witchcraft, but they couldn't let him get away with heresy.'

'One of those people who live in the wrong time.'

'And the wrong place. Don't forget the place.'

All at once I felt depressed. It seemed to me that whatever Francis had been guilty of, he wasn't alone with his guilt. I thought of the Touchies smacking their lips around a tea table in the Deanery. How did you calibrate guilt? How did you measure one guilt against another?

'I don't suppose they mentioned the names of any children, did they? A boy called Simon Martlesham?'

'I don't think so. And *was* there a boy? I thought Mrs Forbury said something about a little girl.'

Then Rosie came downstairs and we started talking about other things. One of them was Mr Treevor. I didn't tell Janet about his willie-winkle remark because that would have only added to her worries. But she was concerned that he'd gone out by himself again this morning. I suggested we start locking the doors, even when one of us was at home, so he couldn't slip out without our knowing.

Underneath this was the other conversation that we weren't having. Finding the wings this morning had brought matters to a head. Though I wasn't going to say so to anyone, least of all Janet, for once I agreed with David. Mr Treevor ought to go into a home, for his sake and everyone else's.

I knew he would be miserable, but if he stayed here he wouldn't be particularly happy either, and he'd make at least two other people miserable as well. And, as the dementia took hold, there was always the risk that he'd do something far worse than he'd already done. At the back of my mind was the possibility that he might already have done worse things than kill a pigeon and cut off its wings.

'And it's going to be difficult when the baby comes,' Janet was saying. 'I'll have to go into hospital for a few days, I can't see any way round that.'

'I'll come and hold the fort if you want.'

I saw alarm flicker in Janet's face. She was looking over my shoulder. I turned. Rosie was in the room, sitting on the floor with Angel on her lap in her corner by the dresser. She met my eyes and I knew she had heard us talking about the baby, and understood what it meant as well. Whatever else Rosie was, she was never stupid. Janet and David had decided not to tell her about it until the pregnancy was past the first twelve weeks.

'Oh,' Janet said. 'I didn't see you down there, darling. I wish you wouldn't sit on the floor. You'll get your school dress dirty.'

'All right.'

She got up and wandered round the table, a thumb in her mouth.

'Where are you going?' Janet said.

'Up to my room.'

Rosie broke into a run as she reached the doorway. Her feet pattered up the stairs.

'Oh, Lord,' Janet said. 'This would happen now.'

The evening continued to roll downhill. David came home

but communicated mainly in grunts before going to ground in the study. Rosie had a tantrum, which ended in her lying rigid and bright red on the floor, screaming as loudly as possible. Mr Treevor climbed into his bed and pulled the covers over his head. David came out of the study and shouted upstairs, 'Can't you control her, Janet? I'm trying to work.' Meanwhile, I made an egg-and-bacon flan with too few eggs and not enough bacon.

I went upstairs for a bracing nip of gin. I hadn't touched my bottle since the trip to London on Monday but these were special circumstances. On the first-floor landing I heard voices in Rosie's room and paused to eavesdrop.

'Are we really having a baby?' Rosie was saying in a singsong, babyish voice.

'Yes, darling,' Janet said. 'Isn't that nice?'

'Will it be a boy or a girl?'

'We don't know yet. We have to wait till it comes. We can't be absolutely sure it's coming yet – that's why Daddy and I haven't told you before. Would you like a little brother or a little sister?'

'Rosie doesn't want a baby,' she said in the same silly voice. 'Angel doesn't want one, either. Never, never, never.'

Things improved slightly at suppertime, partly because of the gin. Mr Treevor was lured out of bed at the thought of food. Rosie was so exhausted that she fell asleep. Even David cheered up a little, after drinking two glasses of sherry before we ate. Meanwhile, Janet carried on as usual. She was, of course, the one person in the house who wasn't allowed to be depressed or have tantrums, or act strangely or brace themselves with fortifying nips of gin. Someone at the Dark Hostelry had to be reliable, and we had chosen her.

After supper, she went up to check on Rosie and settle Mr Treevor. I washed up, made coffee and took it up to the drawing room. David was reading *The Voice of Angels*. I poured the coffee. He looked up as I handed him the cup.

'Thanks. Is this yours?'

'Yes. Henry sent it. He found it in a box of second-hand books.'

'It's absolute tosh, isn't it?' He smiled up at me as he spoke, making it obvious that the sting in the words was not directed at me. 'I knew Youlgreave was eccentric, but I hadn't realized he was quite such a bad poet.'

'I think he was very unhappy,' I said.

'Quite possibly. But is that an excuse?'

Part of me was annoyed with David for criticizing Francis, and another part of me had treacherously abdicated its responsibilities and turned into a mass of goo because he'd smiled at me. I sat down and lit a cigarette. David shut the book and put it gently on the side table by his chair. He always treated books as though they were infinitely fragile.

'Why are you spending so much time on Youlgreave?'

'I'm interested in him,' I said, blowing smoke out of my nostrils like an outraged dragon. 'He was an interesting person.'

David smiled at me again. He opened his mouth to speak but then Janet came back into the room. I finished my coffee and said there was something I needed to do upstairs. I wasn't sure whether the result of leaving David and Janet alone would be a quarrel or a reconciliation, but I knew I had to let them try and find out.

On the first floor, Rosie's room was dark and silent. Mr Treevor's door was closed. I went upstairs to my room. The first thing I did was open the bedside cupboard and take out the gin bottle. The cupboard smelled of lavender. The light gleamed on the green glass like the smile on the face of a welcome friend. I poured myself a comfortable inch and sat on the bed, sipping slowly and feeling liquid fire run down my throat and into my belly. Who needed babies when you had London Dry Gin?

Bloody Henry.

So I took out the photograph of Henry and his Hairy Widow and looked at it again, something I'd sworn not to do. I looked at her legs waving in the air and his quaking bottom between them and thought I would probably need another glass of gin in a moment. To delay this, I put the photograph away and looked around for a distraction.

My eyes fell on the other photograph, the one of the clergymen and the children in front of the Theological College. I lifted it down from the washstand and held it under the bedside light. Francis, the little man with the long nose and the black shadows where his eyes should be, was face to face with me.

I rubbed the glass with my finger, trying to see him better. Once again, I wished I could pass through it into that world and find out what they were doing in the photograph and who they all were. I took another sip of gin and at that very moment, as though the liquid brought inspiration with it, I realized that there was a way.

I turned the photograph over. The frame was wooden, and the photograph was backed by a thin sheet of plywood held in place by tacks. I levered some of them up with a nail-file and then pulled out the plywood. I pushed the glass up from underneath and pulled out the cardboard, the mount and the photograph in one go. I peeled the photograph and mount away from the cardboard. There was writing on the back of the photograph. I had gone through the glass.

In that other time it was high summer. 'Tableaux Vivants at the Principal's Garden Party: first prize Oberon, Titania, and attendant fairies. August 6th, 1904.'

Not angels after all.

Underneath, written in the same faded brown ink, were the names. 'The Revd Canon Murtagh-Smith, Principal – the Revd J. R. Heckstall, Vice-Principal, Canon Youlgreave . . .' But it was the name next to his that leapt up at me.

'N. Martlesham'.

In my haste I knocked the glass as I turned the photograph over. Drops of gin slopped on to the frame. So that was Nancy, the little girl standing literally in Francis's shadow. She was the real mystery, not Simon, not Francis. What was a little girl from Swan Alley doing with wings sprouting from her shoulders at a Theological College garden party?

There was something else, too, something whose unsettling significance gradually crept over me. I reached for my glass. At that moment the phone began to ring downstairs.

I went on to the landing and hung over the banisters. David went to answer it in the study. The ringing stopped, and a moment later David came out and called softly up to me.

By the time I reached the hall, the drawing room door was tactfully closed and he and Janet were on the other side.

'Wendy, darling!' said Henry's disembodied voice.

'A character in *Peter Pan*.'

It was an old joke, dating back to the days of our engagement. It wasn't funny any more. Instead it had become a sort of emotional nursery food, something one of us would produce when the other was feeling low, a way of saying everything was all right and some things never change. I don't know what made me produce it then, and if I could have withdrawn the words I would have done. They were implying quite the wrong thing to Henry.

'How are you, dearest?' he burbled. 'Have you had the parcel?'

'It came this morning,' I said. 'Listen, I need to see you. Can I come up to town tomorrow?'

'Wonderful! Come tonight. I'll hire a car and come and fetch you.'

'I don't mean like that. Listen, there're several things I want to do.'

'Concerning your friend Francis?'

'Yes. That book you sent me was very interesting. It's not like the one I got from the library after all. The title's different, and there's a poem in it which isn't anywhere else. I'll come up on the same train – can you meet me at Liverpool Street?'

'Of course I can. But what's –?'

'The most important thing to do is talk to Simon Martlesham. So we need to go to the Blue Dahlia. But first I'd like to –'

'Hang on. Why do you want to see Martlesham again?'

'Because he told me he had his thirteenth birthday on the *Hesperides* in the middle of the Atlantic.'

'What's wrong with that?'

'He said his sister Nancy was with him on that voyage, and we know that his birthday was in July 1904 from that children's novel Francis was going to give him.'

'So?'

'I've just found a photograph that shows Nancy on the lawn of the Theological College. It's dated the sixth of August. So why was Simon lying? And what happened to Nancy?'

34

I wish I hadn't gone to London, not on Friday.

The shouting started a little after six o'clock. I was in that uncomfortable state between sleep and waking and at first I thought it came from my dream. I was with Simon Martlesham on the *Hesperides* and there were icebergs ahead and he and everyone else said we were going to sink. And I kept saying but it's July so there can't be any icebergs.

I snapped into consciousness. I'd slept badly all night. Too excited, I supposed, and too curious. There was also the question of Henry. I was half looking forward to seeing him and half reluctant.

After a second or two, I realized the shouting wasn't in the dream. I scrambled out of bed and struggled into my dressing gown. At this stage I couldn't make out the words, or even who was shouting. I opened my door and went on to the landing.

'You disgusting old man.' David's voice. 'Get into your room and stay there.'

A keening sound like the wind in the chimney. Mr Treevor?

Running feet, bare soles thudding on the linoleum, then Janet saying, 'What is it, what is it?'

I paused at the head of the stairs. She wouldn't want me down there, not now.

'What's he *done*?' she said.

'God knows,' David snarled. 'He was in bed with Rosie. Cuddling her.'

'He was probably just lonely or cold. You know how fond of –'

'There's nothing to discuss. He has to go.'

The keening rose in volume.

'David, I –'

'It's a question of what's best for him as well as for everyone else in this house. In the long run it's kinder to everybody if he goes into a home.'

'What's *happening*?' moaned Mr Treevor.

'Shut up and get in your room,' roared David.

The door slammed.

'You can't do this,' Janet said.

'Can't I?' David said. 'Why not?'

I slipped back into my room and shut the door very quietly. I climbed into bed, lit a cigarette and told myself that Janet loved David. If I was really Janet's friend, I couldn't come between her and him, however well-meaning I felt my intervention was. Two's company in a marriage. The Hairy Widow had taught me that.

I don't know what David actually saw. I never dared ask him then or later. The possibility that there might have been some sort of sexual contact between Mr Treevor and Rosie didn't even occur to me, not until years later. I thought he'd just been monkeying about in some way and that his actions showed that he'd sunk still further into his second childhood. But if this had happened now, over forty years later, I would automatically have placed a sexual interpretation on it. Whether I would have been right to do so is another matter. I just don't know what was going on in Rosie's bedroom.

All I know is that I heard David shouting and that hindsight can play tricks on you just as any other kind of vision can.

So I pretended I'd heard nothing. It was the action of a coward, a well-mannered guest and even a loyal friend. I was all three of those, though not usually at the same time. I stayed in bed until my alarm went off. When I went downstairs, only Janet and Rosie were in the kitchen.

'Sleep well?' Janet asked.

'Like a log, thanks. And you?'

'Not bad.' Janet patted her tummy. 'Felt a bit queasy but it didn't come to anything. Unlike yesterday. I don't know if that's progress or not.'

'David not down?'

'He was up early. He went to do some work at the college. He's going to see the diocesan architect today.'

'It's a very worrying time,' I said.

'I expect something will come up. David's already put out a few feelers.'

Breakfast went on as usual. Janet took a tray up to Mr Treevor. She asked if I needed sandwiches for London and sent her love to Henry. She carefully avoided saying anything I could have interpreted as a hope that he and I would get back together again. And I carefully avoided mentioning the shouting. Our friendship was about what we didn't say as well as what we did.

'There's no real urgency about going to London,' I said as I was washing up. 'Perhaps I should go next week. It's not a bad day and I could give you a hand in the garden.'

'The garden can wait. You go to London and enjoy yourself. Have you told Canon Hudson, by the way?'

'No, not yet. I'll phone after breakfast. But I do wonder if I should mow the lawn instead.'

Janet looked up through the basement window of the kitchen. If you leaned forward far enough you could see a rectangle of sky above the roofs of the houses on the other side of the High Street. 'Anyway, I think it might rain. There's really no point in your staying.'

'Let me take Rosie to school before I go. There's plenty of time.'

She agreed to that, saying that she was a little tired. Now I wonder if she knew me better than I knew myself, and she allowed me to walk Rosie to school to soothe my conscience.

When I got back I phoned Simon Martlesham and arranged to meet him in the Blue Dahlia at two-thirty. His clipped voice showed no sign of surprise. He bit back emotions as well as words. When he asked why I wanted to see him, I said I'd found something to do with his sister, something which would interest him. And then I put the phone down. I know it was melodramatic of me, but I felt that Simon Martlesham had been making a fool out of me, and now it was my turn.

I borrowed a music case from Janet to carry the photograph and the two books, *The Tongues of Angels* and *The Voice of Angels*. On the train to London I read the poems again, but the more I read them the less I understood them. At one point I persuaded myself that 'The Office of the Dead' was a punning title, meaning both a funeral service for the dead and the job the dead did for the living. But if Francis was not only mentally unbalanced but also taking opium, it was quite possible that the poem was never anything more than nonsense.

The train journey passed quickly. Travelling to London already seemed like a habit, and an enjoyable one at that. Whatever I decided to do about Henry, I had established that a life outside Rosington was a possibility.

Henry was waiting at the barrier, which surprised me a little because punctuality was not one of his virtues. He took my arm and insisted on carrying the music case.

'What do you want to do?' he asked. 'A cup of coffee?'

'I'd like to go to the Church Empire Society, please.'

'I beg your pardon?' We stopped to allow a porter wheeling a barrow to go by. 'What on earth's that?'

'The organization that sent Simon Martlesham to Toronto, with a little help from Francis Youlgreave. And according to him, his sister went into one of the society's orphanages.'

'Can't we phone them up?'

I had looked up the Church Empire Society in David's copy of *Crockford's Clerical Directory*. There was an address in Westminster, but no telephone number.

'I think a personal visit would be better.' I smiled at him. 'I thought you'd enjoy being a relative trying to trace your long-lost uncle and aunt.'

He smiled back. 'And who will you be?'

'I'll be your little wifey, of course. Reluctantly indulging my husband's whims.'

'I'd like that.'

Once again our eyes met. This time neither of us smiled.

We took a taxi from the station. On the way I told Henry what I knew about Simon and Nancy Martlesham's emigration.

As we were coming down to Blackfriars, Henry said, 'I went to Senate House yesterday afternoon.'

'What senate?'

'It's the University of London Library in Bloomsbury. I thought I'd see if I could track down anything about Isabella of Roth. No luck.'

'I'm not surprised. She was probably one of Francis's inventions.'

'But I did find something that might be relevant in *English Precursors of Protestantism in the Later Middle Ages*.' He looked smugly down his nose at me. 'Murtagh-Smith and Babcock, London 1898. Perhaps I should give up teaching and become a scholar instead.'

'What was the name of the first author?'

His smile faded. 'Murtagh-Smith. Ring a bell?'

'He was the principal of the Theological College in Youlgreave's time. Anyway, what did he have to say?'

'Not a lot that helped, I'm afraid. But apparently at the end of the fourteenth century, the Lollard Movement was trying to reform the Church. They had lots of revolutionary ideas – they thought people should read the Bible in their own language and that warfare was unchristian. Oh, and they didn't like the Pope, either. They thought every Christian had the right to work out what they really believed by reading the Bible and meditating on it. According to Murtagh-Smith and his friend, the Peasants' Revolt was partly to do with the Lollards. The government didn't like them, naturally, and in 1401 they passed the first English law to allow the burning of heretics.'

'Well, it fits so far. But were the Lollards in favour of women priests?'

'I doubt it. But they didn't approve of clerical celibacy.' He grinned at me. 'They claimed it led to unnatural lusts. But this is the point. Murtagh-Smith says that several people

218

were burned at the stake for preaching Lollard heresies in Rosington.'

'When?'

'In 1402.'

'Same date. But nothing about women priests?'

He shook his head. 'Perhaps that was another of Francis's little ideas. Just a little modification of history. After all, that's what poetic licence is all about, isn't it?' Suddenly he changed the subject. 'Do you think it's a good idea to go to this society? What are you trying to prove?'

'That Simon Martlesham was lying.'

'He might have made a mistake. Anyway, what's the point in turning over stones? It's not going to help anyone now, is it?'

I didn't answer. I stared out of the window. We were on the Victoria Embankment now, with Big Ben rearing up ahead. How could I explain to Henry that when everything was wrong in my life Francis had thrown me a line, a thread of curiosity. More than that – I felt about Francis as I'd felt about Janet, all those years ago at Hillgard House. He was weak, and I wanted to protect him.

'Sorry,' said the new, reformed Henry. 'I don't want to be nosy. It's none of my business.'

The Church Empire Society occupied a shabby little house in a street off Horseferry Road. There were two dustbins and a bicycle in what had once been a front garden. I rang the bell and a moment later it was answered by a tall tweedy lady, very thin, with a sharp nose and chin set between cheeks that bulged, as though crammed with illicit sweets.

Henry raised his hat. 'Good morning. So sorry to bother you. But I wonder if you could help us.'

Suddenly, and quite unexpectedly, Henry and I were a team again, just as we had been with his clients. I didn't have to do much because Henry did most of the talking – I was cast in the role of the grumpy wife, who thought it stupid that her husband should waste so much time chasing after a family black sheep. So he had a double claim on the tweedy lady's sympathy.

She was the sole permanent employee of the society and

her name was Miss Hermione Findhorn. Her office occupied the front room on the ground floor. It must have been about twelve feet square and there was barely room for two people, let alone three. This was because the office, and as far as I could see the whole house, was filled with outsized paintings and pieces of furniture.

'I'm frightfully sorry, Mr Appleyard,' Miss Findhorn said in a voice which seemed to emerge from her nose. 'The problem is, we were bombed. We used to have a rather larger house in Horseferry Road. We managed to save quite a lot, as you can see.' She waved a chapped hand with bitten fingernails around the room, around the house. 'But alas, our records were stored in the attics and we recovered none of them.'

Henry persevered. Miss Findhorn said it was perfectly possible that the society had arranged for the passage of two orphan children to Toronto in 1904. In those days, they trained young people for useful trades. They had in fact maintained an orphanage in Toronto. Unfortunately that had been closed in the 1920s. But they'd managed to save the scrapbooks which in those days the society maintained to record its achievements. Miss Findhorn produced a tall, leather-bound volume covering 1904. She and Henry turned the pages. I knew from the way Henry was standing that he had found nothing, that this was a waste of time. Then he stiffened, and pointed to a clipping. I craned my head to see what he was looking at. A name leapt up at me.

Sir Charles Youlgreave Bt.

'There was someone of that name in Rosington,' Henry said casually. 'Canon Youlgreave, I think it was. I wonder if there's a connection.'

'Quite possibly,' said Miss Findhorn, angling her glasses so she could read the newsprint. 'Sir Charles was on our Committee of Management. Usually members sit for three years, and I think in those days they often took a personal interest in the young people they helped. Perhaps Canon Youlgreave suggested your uncle and aunt as suitable candidates.'

'Very likely,' Henry said.

We said goodbye and found another taxi in Horseferry Road. Henry suggested lunch at the Ritz, but I wouldn't let him. In the end we went to a chop house off the Strand, a dark, low-ceilinged place divided up into wooden booths so you could be private if you wanted to be. We got there before one, so we found a quiet table without difficulty.

'Are you still wasting money at Brown's Hotel?' I asked.

'I'm leaving today.' Henry offered me a cigarette. 'I'm going to find a nice little private hotel with a landlady who'll mother me.' He leaned forward with his lighter. 'You're wearing your wedding ring today.'

It was part of my social camouflage in Rosington. I said, 'I needed it for Miss Findhorn. After all, we were supposed to be man and wife.'

'We still are. Have you paid in that cheque yet?'

'No.'

'Why not?'

'I don't know if I want to.'

'But it's ten thousand pounds. Where is it?'

'In my bedside cupboard.' *With a sprig of lavender on top to make it smell better.*

'Listen, Wendy, it'll be safer if you have it. Then I can't spend it. And it's only fair.'

'I thought you were going to buy a share of that school.'

'I am. It's all going ahead. I promise. But if I've got this extra money, I'll just waste it.'

I smiled at him. 'I'll see.'

'You've changed.'

'And why do you think that is?'

Suddenly we were on the verge of a quarrel neither of us wanted. He must have sensed it as well because he threw a question about Janet and David at me. Soon I was telling him about the Dark Hostelry, about the collapse of David's hopes for the Theological College and about the odd behaviour of Mr Treevor.

Later I showed him the two books, *Tongues* and *Voice*, and also the photograph. Henry read 'The Office of the Dead' while demolishing a helping of steak-and-kidney pudding.

'In a way, it's like Christianity gone mad.' He sat back and wiped his mouth with his napkin. 'You eat the body and blood, and in return you get eternal life.' He glanced down

221

at the open book. 'Or the secret of youth or something. Hard to know exactly what he *does* mean.' He turned over a page. 'And what's all this stuff about the angel sitting at his shoulder telling him what to write? It makes it sound as if he's got his own personal Angel of the Lord. He must have been completely round the bend.'

'I don't know. He was obviously a bit eccentric –'

'That's one way of putting it.'

'But you can't deny he did a lot of good. Some of his ideas were just a little ahead of his time.'

'And ours,' Henry said. 'I can imagine how David feels about women priests.'

'What worries me is the girl.' I pointed to the little figure beside Francis. 'What happened to her? Why should Martlesham lie about it?'

'There's probably a perfectly innocent explanation. Anyway, he might have made a mistake.'

'About something like that, his own sister coming with him to Canada?'

'It happened over fifty years ago, Wendy. And he's had a stroke since then, remember.'

Henry ordered more beer and by common consent we talked about other things, mainly about his plans for Veedon Hall. We both skated round my role in these, if any. At ten past two we went back to the Strand and took a taxi to the Blue Dahlia Café.

As we drew up outside, Henry touched my arm. 'Look!'

I followed the direction of his pointing finger. There were several people walking down Fetter Passage but I recognized none of them.

'Right at the end,' Henry said. 'Just turning the corner.'

'Who?'

'I'm sure it was Munro.'

'What do you think?' Henry said as we stood on the pavement after paying off the taxi. 'Martlesham's got Munro to follow us after we leave him?'

I shook my head. 'More likely he's been following us already.'

'But how?'

'If Martlesham told him I was coming to see him this afternoon, all Munro needed to do was go to Liverpool Street and keep an eye on trains from Rosington.'

Fetter Passage was very quiet after the bustle of Holborn. But was someone watching us, Munro or a colleague? I glanced up at the windows above the café, wondering which belonged to Martlesham's flat.

Henry said, 'In that case he'll know about the Church Empire Society.'

'And what about if he was in the chop house? If he was in the booth next to ours, he might have heard something.'

'Nothing we can do about it now.' He looked up and down the terrace. 'Bit of a dump.'

'But not as bad as Swan Alley.'

I opened the door of the café. The ribbons swayed like seaweed across the archway at the rear of the room. We had arrived in the dead time between lunch and tea and there were few customers. The sad-faced woman was cutting bread at the counter. She didn't look up as we came in.

'I've come to see Mr Martlesham,' I said to her.

'I tell the boss you're here.'

Without meeting my eyes, she put down the knife and shuffled through the archway. A moment later, she parted the ribbons again and beckoned us.

Beyond the archway was a small room used for serving food. Immediately opposite us was an open door leading to a kitchen. She gestured to another door on our left.

'Knock,' she commanded.

I tapped on the door and I heard Martlesham telling us to come in.

The room was equipped as an office with what looked like cast-off War Department furniture. Martlesham was sitting behind the desk and facing us. Behind him was an open window looking into a sunny yard full of bicycles and dustbins. He didn't get up, but stared past me at Henry.

'Who's this?'

'My husband, Henry Appleyard. Henry, this is Mr Martlesham.'

Henry smiled and extended his hand across the desk. Martlesham shook it for the shortest possible time.

223

'You'll excuse me if I don't get up. Please sit down.'

I chose a hard chair in front of the desk. I felt as though he was interviewing me. I said, 'Do you own the café?'

'I own the whole terrace.' He sounded bored with his possession.

I heard Henry suck in his breath beside me.

'It must mean a lot of work for you,' I said, not because it was an intelligent thing to say but because it was the first thing that came into my mind.

'Not really. I have someone to take care of the details. It's a long-term investment, really.'

'You're planning to develop the site?' Henry said.

'Yes. Everyone's on short tenancies except for a couple of leaseholders at the far end of the terrace. I'm waiting for them to die or move.' He gave us a twisted smile. 'And they're probably waiting for me to do the same.'

A fleck of ash marred the brilliantly white surface of his left-hand shirt cuff. He put down his cigarette and carefully brushed it off. There was a freshly ironed handkerchief in the breast pocket of his jacket and his hands had been manicured. I wondered who looked after his appearance now Vera was dead. Perhaps he had planned Fetter Passage to be a nest egg for their shared old age. For the first time it struck me that Vera's death might have had something to do with his hiring Munro. Perhaps he'd wanted to find out if he still had a family. It isn't easy to be lonely. I knew all about that.

'What did you want to see me about?'

'About Nancy,' I said. 'I wondered if she might have any memories of Canon Youlgreave.'

He shrugged. 'Quite possibly. But you'd have to find her.'

'So you don't have an address?'

He shook his head. 'I told you, she was adopted almost as soon as we got to Toronto. The couple who took her were moving down to the States, and the lady at the orphanage said it would be better for her if she didn't have any contact with her old life.'

'That must have been terrible for both of you.'

His heavy lids drooped over dark eyes. 'Better than Swan Alley, Mrs Appleyard, I tell you that. She was going to a good home, with good people. I had a job, somewhere to live, prospects. They didn't give us much time to think about it, anyway. After the *Hesperides* docked, I saw her maybe twice in the next six weeks. Then that was that.'

'That's a pity,' I said.

'Why?'

'Because if you had an address for her, she might have been able to explain this.' I lifted Janet's music case on to the desk and took out the photograph. I put it in front of him, on his unblemished green blotter. 'But perhaps you can explain it instead.'

Slowly he put on a pair of glasses. For what seemed like several minutes he stared down at the photograph. His expression didn't change. Henry fumbled in his pocket and a moment later lit a cigarette. As if the flare of the match was a signal, Martlesham raised his head and transferred his stare to me.

'Well?'

'I wondered if you recognized it.'

'The place? No, I don't.'

'It's Rosington Theological College. The lawn at the back.'

'Very possibly. I never went there. Wasn't it that redbrick place near the Porta?'

'Do you recognize anybody?'

'There's Canon Youlgreave, of course. And that man there, the old clergyman, wasn't he another canon? Some of the ladies look familiar but I wouldn't be able to put a name to them, not now.'

'What about the children?'

For the first time there was a hint of anger in those dark eyes. 'Why are you asking me all this?'

'Look at the girl next to Canon Youlgreave,' I said.

He glanced down, then back to me. He said nothing.

'Is that your sister?'

'Could be.' He spoke as though I were grinding the words out of him one by one. 'Hard to tell.'

'She's dressed up, Mr Martlesham. Looks like a pair of wings. Does that ring any bells?'

'Maybe they were doing some kind of play. Canon Youlgreave

was always involved in anything artistic, you see, being a poet. Maybe not a play. Might have been dancing, or something, and they needed a little girl.'

'According to the writing on the back, it *is* your sister.'

He looked at me as if I'd stung him. Then, clumsily with his one good hand, he turned the photograph over. He read the row of names on the back.

'So you knew it was Nancy all along, Mrs Appleyard.' He glared at me and I was suddenly glad that Henry was in the room. 'Why come and pester me about it?'

'Because of the date at the top.' I watched him looking at it. Then I went on, 'Your birthday was on the seventeenth of July. According to you, you and your sister were in the middle of the Atlantic on the *Hesperides* on that day. So what's she doing with a pair of wings on the lawn of the Theological College over two weeks later?'

Martlesham took off his glasses, folded them and put them away in their case. Only then did he look at me. 'I must have made a mistake about the date.'

'We can easily check that,' said Henry suddenly. 'The date of the sailing would have been in the newspapers.'

Martlesham ignored him. 'Or whoever wrote the names on the back made a mistake. Simple as that. Or they put the wrong date.'

'I don't think that's very likely, Mr Martlesham. You thought that was Nancy and there are plenty of people in Rosington we can ask, people who will remember her as she was then. There's Mrs Elstree, for one. And I expect we can check when the principal's garden party was. If we need to.'

Martlesham sighed and reached for his cigarette case. He said in a low voice, almost as if talking to himself, 'I could ask you to leave.'

'And then your private investigator could follow us and see what we did next.'

'What are you talking about?'

'Harold Munro, ex-detective sergeant, Metropolitan Police.'

'Never heard of him.'

'Who else would bother to hire him?'

'How should I know?' He tapped a cigarette on the case and put it in his mouth. 'Anyway, what's he been doing?'

'He's paid several visits to Rosington in the last few weeks. He's stolen cuttings about Francis Youlgreave from the backfile of the *Rosington Observer*. He borrowed a copy of one of Youlgreave's books from the public library. He tried to question a number of people, including Mrs Elstree, and nearly frightened one old lady to death. He's been seen watching the Dark Hostelry, it's even possible he's been inside the house. He followed me after I met you here on Monday and he's got an office in Holborn. My husband saw him ten minutes ago at the other end of Fetter Passage.'

'Very mysterious, Mrs Appleyard. Sounds like a job for the police, especially if you think this man's broken into the Dark Hostelry.'

I picked up the photograph and returned it to the music case. His hand twitched as I picked it up, and for a moment I wondered if he would try to stop me taking it.

'What would you think, Mr Martlesham?' Henry said. 'If you were in our position.'

'I'd think it was time to stop poking my nose in other people's business.'

'You haven't any children, have you?'

Martlesham shook his head.

'And your wife has just died, Wendy tells me,' Henry went on. 'It would be very natural if you wanted to trace members of your family.'

'Well, I don't,' Martlesham said. 'What would be the point?'

'I would have thought the answer to that was obvious,' Henry said gently. 'It's not much fun being by yourself.'

Martlesham fiddled with his lighter. Then he looked at me and sighed. 'You've got it all wrong. I suppose there's no reason why you shouldn't know. I don't want to trace Nancy now for the same reason that I didn't want to trace her when I came to England in 1917. I don't want to *embarrass* her. That's the long and the short of it.'

'Embarrass?' I said. 'I don't understand.'

His mouth twisted. 'The last thing she said to me was, "You sold me. I hate you."'

'At the orphanage?' I said.

'There never was any orphanage, Mrs Appleyard. And she didn't come to Canada, either. She stayed here. That's why she's in that photo.'

He lit the cigarette at last and puffed furiously. Smoke billowed across the desk, pushed by the draught from the window. I sniffed.

Virginia tobacco, not Turkish.

35

'Did you believe him?' asked Henry.

'I don't know.' I stroked the cool, silky glass in front of me. 'I'm sure some of it was true. The question is how much.'

Henry was good at finding nice little pubs. He'd found one near Liverpool Street Station, a place of engraved mirrors, burnished brass, dark, gleaming woodwork and stained-glass lights in all the windows. The downstairs bar was full of office workers snatching a quick drink before going home. Henry and I were in the little upstairs bar, which was much quieter. We had a table in the window and could talk without the risk of being overheard. Not that there was any sign of Harold Munro.

'I think he's a gambler by nature,' Henry said. 'You don't start life in Swan Alley and end up fifty years later with a slice of Holborn unless you're prepared to take chances.'

'So what are you saying?'

Henry shrugged. 'Just that he may have been taking another gamble with us. Admitting part of the story as a way of keeping the rest of it concealed. I mean, he couldn't really get away from the date on that photograph. You set a trap for him and he walked right into it. When you come down to it, there's very little he told us that can be proved. Anyone who could have supported the story is dead.'

'Except perhaps the sister.'

Henry cocked an eyebrow, a trick I'd seen him practise in the mirror. 'You think she's still alive? After what Martlesham told us?'

The story had emerged by fits and starts. It was as if

Martlesham was in the witness box, reluctantly disgorging information, volunteering nothing, and leaving the cross-examining counsel to do as much of the work as possible. The Martlesham children's mother had died in childbirth. At the time there wasn't a man living with them. 'Pregnancy scared them off, I reckon,' Simon told us. 'And she was getting very sickly.' He never actually said, but it was clear that Mr Martlesham had not been seen for many years. Simon hinted that his parents might not have been married and there was even some question as to whether his father was also Nancy's.

Simon had met Francis during the winter before his mother's death. The relationship sounded innocent, even praiseworthy. Francis lent Simon books and encouraged him to go to evening classes in English literature and arithmetic. He invited both Simon and Nancy to tea at the Dark Hostelry, where he was living at the time. Francis was looked after by two elderly servants, a cook-housekeeper and a maid who disapproved of the Martlesham children.

'For me and Nancy,' Martlesham said, 'it was like a glimpse of paradise. Sitting on a comfortable chair in a clean house. Afternoon tea with sandwiches and as much cake as you wanted to eat. Youlgreave gave me a penknife and let me carve my initials on a walnut tree in the garden, to show how well I could make the letters. He used to put Nancy on his knee and read us stories. Is the walnut tree still there?'

'No,' I said. 'There's only an apple tree now.'

When the mother died – 'I heard her screaming,' Martlesham remarked in a matter-of-fact voice – the only other relative in Rosington had been an aunt, the mother's elder sister who worked in a haberdasher's in the High Street. 'She'd come a long way from Swan Alley, Aunt Em had,' Martlesham said. 'Us kids were just a burden to her. And she was walking out with someone she wanted to marry, a very respectable man with a house and everything. She didn't want us queering her pitch. Hard woman. But I can't say I blame her.'

That was when Francis had stepped in. He helped to pay for the mother's funeral. One evening he called on Aunt Em with a proposal. He was willing to arrange for Simon to go to

Canada, where he could learn a trade and make a fresh start in life. And he had an even more alluring offer for Nancy. A lady and gentleman who lived near his brother's house in Middlesex were unable to have children. They wanted to adopt a little girl and bring her up as a lady. Nancy would be perfect for them. She was quick, intelligent and pretty. Her eyes were the same colour as the lady's. She would live in a house with a big garden and have a pony and a room of her own.

'Aunt Em was pleased, of course, then she said I was old enough to make up my own mind. Nancy said she wanted to stay with me, but there was nothing I could do for her. Or not for years, until I got myself established. No, it was the right choice, no doubt about that.'

'You said she accused you of selling her,' I said. 'What did you mean by that?'

His face darkened. I guessed he hadn't meant to tell us that, that the words had slipped out. He wasn't angry, I realized a moment later, he was embarrassed.

'Just before I left Rosington, Mr Youlgreave gave me fifteen pounds.' He hesitated, selecting the right words. 'To help me settle in Canada. But Nancy was only a kid, she misunderstood what was going on.'

Now, in the upstairs room of the pub, Henry said, 'We've only Martlesham's word that Nancy was adopted. As we've only got his word about so much else. There's another reason why he might not have tried to get in touch with his sister when he got back to England. Perhaps he knew there was no point.'

'How do you mean?'

'What if he *knew* she was dead?'

'That's horrible.'

'It's where all this is going, if you ask me.' Henry lit two cigarettes and passed one to me. 'There was a very strange side to Francis Youlgreave – that's obvious from the poems. And Martlesham got very worked up when you asked him about the animals.'

He had come the nearest I'd seen him to losing his temper. He said that was typical of all he hated about Rosington.

People had said that Canon Youlgreave was mad, going around cutting up animals for sadistic reasons of his own. But he, Simon Martlesham, knew better, and so did many other people, including Canon Youlgreave's servants. Mr Youlgreave had an interest in animal physiology. Once or twice Simon Martlesham had helped him to dissect small animals. There was one occasion when Simon had found a drowned kitten floating in the river and had fished it out for Youlgreave, who had rewarded the boy with half a sovereign for his pains. But the twisted minds of others had soon interpreted this absolutely innocent scientific enquiry into something sinister.

'Call themselves Christians?' Martlesham had said, just as he had done on the first occasion I met him and echoing Janet a few hours earlier. 'They were no more Christian than this desk is. And from what you say, it sounds like things haven't changed.'

'Suppose he's feeling guilty?' I said to Henry, wondering if there was time for another drink. 'He's had a stroke, he's lost his wife, he's got no children. Suppose this is the first time in his life he's had time to think about what he did to his sister. I think he needs to find out if she's still alive.'

'Because he wants to see her again?'

'Not necessarily. He might just want to reassure himself that Francis was telling the truth, that she was adopted, that she did grow up to be a lady. He feels guilty. He simply doesn't *know* what happened to her.'

Henry picked a shred of tobacco from his lip. 'I suppose it would explain a lot. The private investigator going to Roth, going to Rosington, taking an interest in us. This isn't just about Youlgreave.'

'If she – she died in 1904, do you think *The Voice of Angels* tells us anything about how?'

'For God's sake, Wendy.' Henry stared at me. 'You're not suggesting that Youlgreave took that tripe *literally*?'

I shrugged and pushed aside my empty glass. 'It's time I went.'

There was a scrap of pleasure to be derived from the knowledge that I'd shocked Henry. It was usually the other way round. He walked with me to the station. I wouldn't let him see me on to the train. At the barrier, I paused to say goodbye. Suddenly he leaned forward and put his arms around me. He was clumsy about it, which was unlike him. He tried to kiss my lips. I turned aside so he kissed the lobe of my right ear instead. I pulled his arms away from me and stepped back.

'Wendy, listen, when can I see you again?'

'I don't know. I expect I'll be coming up to London sooner or later.'

'Can't we fix a time? If it would help, I could come to Rosington.'

If Henry was seen in Rosington, the Touchies would really have something to gossip about and he'd run the risk of being snubbed as he came round every corner.

'I don't think that would be a good idea.'

'I thought perhaps the wedding ring meant –'

'You thought wrong.'

'Wendy, please –'

Suddenly furious, I turned on my heel and left him. I had my ticket punched at the barrier and walked up the length of the train. I knew Henry was still watching me but I didn't turn round and wave.

How dared he think he could snap his fingers and I'd come running back? Damn Henry, I thought, as I squeezed myself into a compartment already crowded with commuters, damn Francis and damn everything.

Between Cambridge and Rosington I indulged in an unpleasant fantasy conversation with Henry. I told him that I fancied his friend David much more than him, that David was much better looking and had a much nicer body. David's bottom didn't wobble, I told Henry, and his skin wasn't so flabby it looked as if it needed ironing. I knew I'd never say any of these things, and I felt rather sick for even thinking them.

At Rosington, I walked quickly up the hill and went into the Close by the Porta. There was no sign of Mr Gotobed, or indeed of anyone I knew, and for that I was glad. I didn't want to make conversation.

I opened the gate to the Dark Hostelry garden. Rosie's

tricycle was standing on the lawn. Janet made a fuss about things being left out in the garden overnight, so I picked it up and put it in the little shed in the corner by the honeysuckle.

The garden door was unlocked. I went into the hall.

'Nurse!' called a man's voice from the landing on the floor above. 'Is that you?'

Dr Flaxman's head appeared over the banisters. He frowned when he saw me.

'Come up here,' he barked. 'Come and make yourself useful.'

36

It wasn't just the baby that died.

Janet's miscarriage was the turning point of the whole business. Until then, I'd never thought much about miscarriages. They were something that happened to queens in the history books whose husbands were desperate for an heir. Or to characters in novels. Or to quiet little women I didn't know very well because they didn't go out much. A miscarriage was hard luck for all concerned, I assumed in so far as I thought about it at all, but not the end of the world.

It was a day or two before I learned the full story. On Friday morning, after I had left for London, Janet had finished the housework before going into the garden to mow the lawn. The pains started coming at teatime. They grew steadily worse in the early evening. David was late home, and both Rosie and Mr Treevor were demanding food and attention and I wasn't there to share the load. Janet meant to sit down and rest for a moment, but every time she was about to do so there would be another demand.

'Anyway, I thought I was just having a few twinges,' she wailed to me when I went to see her on Saturday morning in hospital. 'It's like the curse – you carry on and sooner or later they go away. But this time they didn't. They got worse.'

Janet had gone to the lavatory and that was when she realized that things were very wrong. Even then, she wouldn't phone David. She phoned the doctors' surgery instead, and was lucky enough to catch Flaxman as he was about to go home. That was the only piece of luck she had that day.

'It's all my fault,' she said in the hospital. 'I killed him.'

235

'Look,' I said awkwardly, 'that's nonsense. It wasn't your fault. And in a way it wasn't a proper baby yet. You don't even know it was a boy.'

'Of course it was a proper baby,' she snarled at me. 'And I know it was a boy, I always did. His name was going to be Michael. *Michael.*'

For a moment she held my eyes with hers. She looked as if she wanted to strangle me. Then she started crying again and held out her arms, asking for comfort.

Later she told me what Dr Flaxman had said when he had visited her earlier in the morning. 'He told me I had to put it behind me and get pregnant again. What does he know? He made it sound as if I'd had a tooth out and another would grow in its place.'

No matter how often I told her not to be silly, no matter how often I told her the miscarriage was nobody's fault, no matter how often she said that she quite agreed, she still felt she was to blame on some level I couldn't reach. In the end, no one reached her there.

In the meantime I rather enjoyed myself. I had the agreeable sense that other people thought I was rising to the crisis. I tried to comfort Janet. I looked after Rosie and Mr Treevor, whose needs were almost identical. I ran the Dark Hostelry after a fashion. And I listened to David when he needed to talk.

'I had a note from the bishop this afternoon,' he told me on Saturday evening. 'Asking after Janet, and so on. But he said that there's a combined living becoming vacant at the end of the summer. Asked if I might be interested.'

'Where is it?'

'Tattisham with Ditchford. It's about thirty miles away. Near Wisbech.'

'So it's in the depths of the Fens?'

He nodded. 'You can't get much more remote. It would be a struggle financially too – the stipend's nothing special and one would have to run a car. I don't know how Janet would manage. There would be no one for her to talk to.'

Nor for David, I thought, who was one of those people who wherever they live never quite leave university.

'Still, perhaps she would like the change,' he went on. 'A chance for a new start. How's Rosie, do you think? This must be very unsettling for her.'

'She's OK, I think,' I said with the assurance of the childless. 'Of course, she's very young, and children that age are self-absorbed.'

'Does she know about the baby?'

'I told her Mummy had to go into hospital, and that she wouldn't be having a baby after all.'

'How did she take it?'

'In her stride.'

This was entirely true. When I told Rosie the news, she smiled up at me and said, 'Good.' I thought David might find this upsetting. Now I'm old and times have changed, I see things rather differently. It strikes me as faintly ridiculous that Janet and I, two grown women. should have spent so much time and effort worrying about David's feelings. We treated him as if his heart was made of eggshells.

Janet came home on Sunday morning with orders to rest as much as possible for a few days. She was very weak and still depressed. Flaxman told us that the best thing to do was to try to jolly her out of it, and David and even I colluded with this. I think this was probably the worst thing we could have done. Every time David or Flaxman said, 'Never mind, Janet, you'll soon get over it, and then you can get pregnant again and have another baby', he was telling her that she wasn't allowed to mourn for the one she'd just lost. No one else was mourning, not really. We were being relentlessly bloody jolly. So Janet had to grieve inside herself, and confined griefs grow bitter.

On Sunday afternoon Janet said to me, 'I'm worried about David.'

'Because of Tattisham with Ditchford?'

She shook her head. 'Because I'm ill, I won't be able to – well, he'll have to do without it for a while.'

'I'm sure he'll manage.' It would have grated if either of us had used the word sex.

'It's different for men, I suppose.'

'Each to his own,' I said, wondering whether Henry was

doing without it at present and why he hadn't phoned me. I'd tried to phone him at Brown's on Saturday but he had already paid his bill and left the hotel. He had not left a forwarding address. Perhaps he'd had enough of me.

Sunday went from bad to worse. Mr Treevor went to bed early, Janet had her supper in bed, and David and I ate in the kitchen. Afterwards David went upstairs to collect Janet's tray. A moment later I followed him up because he had forgotten to take Janet's coffee. I found David ushering a whimpering Mr Treevor across the landing. The old man wasn't wearing his teeth and his face had collapsed in on itself.

'What's up?'

'He was in Rosie's room again.' David glared at me as if it was my fault. 'I'm not having this.'

Suddenly Mr Treevor flung himself on his knees and embraced David's legs. 'Don't send me away,' he wailed. 'Please don't put me in a home.'

I tried to help him to his feet but he clung to David.

'Come on, Mr Treevor,' I urged him. 'Why don't you get into bed and I'll bring you a nice warm hot-water bottle and a cup of cocoa?'

'Don't send me away!'

I noticed that Rosie was watching from the doorway of her room. It could only be a matter of seconds before Janet appeared.

White-faced, David bent down, gripped Mr Treevor's wrists and broke his hold. He pulled the old man to his feet. David's eyes were so bright that it seemed to me that it wasn't him looking through them but someone else.

'Get back in your room,' he said softly, and his fingers squeezed the frail old wrists until Mr Treevor squealed. 'You've caused enough trouble.'

He pushed Mr Treevor away from him. The old man would have fallen if I had not put out an arm to steady him. He stared at David as if he was seeing his son-in-law for the first time, which in a sense of course he was.

'I wish I was dead,' Mr Treevor said. 'Please kill me. I don't want to live.'

'Of course you do,' I said briskly, taking him by his arm and drawing him towards his room. 'We all love you very much, Mr Treevor, but we're all a bit upset now because Janet's not well. But things will seem much better in the morning.'

Suddenly the fight went out of him. I led him into his room. He allowed me to put him into bed. I tucked him in.

'Night, night,' I said. 'Don't get out of bed again, and I'll come and see you soon.'

He held up his face to me. 'Kiss,' he ordered.

I bent down and kissed his forehead. It was like kissing an old newspaper. Then I went back to the landing, which by now was empty. I peeped into Rosie's room. She was in bed, pretending to be asleep with Angel on the pillow beside her. Rosie had never held up her face and asked me to kiss her. Janet and David's door was closed and I heard voices on the other side.

I felt very sorry for myself. So I went down to the drawing room, mixed myself a large gin and Angostura, stretched out on the sofa and lit a cigarette. Things would get better, I told myself without conviction. I thought that David had behaved appallingly. And I also thought that, given the right circumstances, or rather the wrong ones, I might have behaved in exactly the same way.

After a while, he came downstairs. I didn't bother to take my feet off the sofa or try to hide the glass. He sat down beside the empty fireplace.

'I'm sorry about that,' he said. 'I lost my temper. I shouldn't have done that with anyone, but with poor John it's even more inexcusable.'

I lit another cigarette and let him stew.

'You won't know, but I've caught him in with Rosie before. It's – ah – not normal behaviour – a symptom of course of the dementia.'

'But it was all harmless, really, wasn't it? He wasn't hurting her.'

'I don't think we need discuss this further. It's a medical matter. In point of fact, Janet and I had already decided he would have to go into a nursing home. There's no question about it now. I'll ring Flaxman in the morning.'

There was a silence. I searched desperately for something worth saying.

'Are you sure it's the best thing to do?'

'Are you implying it isn't?' His voice hardened, and the stranger looked out of his eyes. 'John can only get worse. He needs trained help. And Janet and I have to think of Rosie as well.'

I nodded. 'I know. And you're right. But he's going to be so upset.'

'It's a question of what's best for all concerned.' David's voice was gentler now. 'Naturally we'll visit him regularly. But the probability is that he soon won't recognize any of us, so it really doesn't matter where he is.'

This time the silence was longer.

'I never asked,' David said abruptly. 'How was Henry when you saw him the other day?'

'Much the same. He sent his regards.'

'And is he helping with your researches?'

It was odd that David couldn't mention my search for Francis without sounding patronizing about it, even when he was trying to be nice to me.

'Very well, thank you,' I said primly. 'But now there's another puzzle. Someone else is interested.'

'In Youlgreave?'

'Yes. They've hired a private investigator called Harold Munro to dig around.'

David frowned. 'But that's absurd. You don't hire a detective to find out about a dead poet.'

'No. Henry said much the same thing on Friday evening.'

'So he knows about this?'

What David meant was that if Henry knew about Harold Munro, then the private investigator couldn't be dismissed as a fantasy created by a credulous woman.

'It was Henry who followed Munro and found out who he was,' I said.

'In London?'

'Yes. But Munro's also been to Rosington. It may have been him watching the Dark Hostelry the other day – you remember when Mr Treevor saw a man staring up at the house?'

'Do you think he might be interested in you rather than Youlgreave?'

'He borrowed one of Youlgreave's books from the public library. He took cuttings about him from the *Rosington Observer*. He's even been pestering Mrs Gotobed and Mrs Elstree.'

'How very odd. Perhaps we should have a word with the police.'

'And tell them what?' I asked. 'Has anyone committed a crime?'

Once again David shrugged. I knew his mind had wandered off to something else, probably the Theological College or his brilliant career rather than Mr Treevor, Janet or the dead baby. So I sat there nursing my glass and wondered if there had in fact been a crime, not in 1958 but over fifty years earlier.

David would have said I was imagining things. But I hadn't imagined Nancy Martlesham, who to all intents and purposes had vanished in a puff of smoke from the lawn of the Theological College on August 6th, 1904.

37

I had talked to Canon Hudson over the weekend and he told me to take as much time off work as I needed. On Monday morning I walked Rosie to school. David had already gone to the Theological College, so it meant leaving Janet alone at the Dark Hostelry with Mr Treevor.

'Are you sure you can manage?' I asked her.

'I'll be fine. Anyway, I'd like to stay with Daddy.'

Mr Treevor had refused to get out of bed. David had already phoned Dr Flaxman about a nursing home.

It was a fine morning. Rosie answered my attempts at conversation with monosyllables. When we reached the gates of St Tumwulf's, she didn't want me to come in. But she gave me Angel, and watched carefully as I stowed the doll in the shopping bag I had brought for the purpose. She allowed me to drop a kiss on the top of her shining head. I watched her walking through the playground, which was full of children standing or playing in groups. She didn't talk to any of them, just threaded her way among them to the door of the school.

It was nearly a mile back to the Close. I spent most of the time thinking about the shopping and the menus for the next few days, and also thinking about how strange it would be to sit down to meals in the kitchen without John Treevor in the Windsor chair at the end of the table.

After crossing the main road, I passed St Mary's and went into Palace Square. Directly in front of me was Minster Street with the west front of the Cathedral rearing up on the far side of it. I was just in time to intercept Mrs Elstree.

'Hello,' I said. 'How are you?'

'Very well, thank you.' She made to move on, without even asking how Janet was. I hadn't seen her for a few days. and in the interval she seemed to have become more sepia-tinted than ever, as if she was gradually losing all her colours except brown.

'There was something I wanted to ask you,' I said.

'I'm afraid I'm in a bit of a hurry.'

'It was about the Martlesham children, Simon and Nancy. Apparently they had an aunt who worked at a haberdasher's.'

'Really?'

By now she was past me and moving away towards the High Street. I turned and walked beside her.

'I wondered if you could remember anything about her.'

'It's a very long time ago, Mrs Appleyard. I'm afraid I can't help you. Now you must excuse me.'

She hurried on. Short of seizing her arm, there wasn't much I could do to stop her. I thought I knew what had happened. Now the decision had been taken to close the Theological College, there was no longer any need for Mrs Elstree to waste unnecessary time and effort on the Byfields, let alone on me as Janet's friend. Unless there was more to it than that – had Mrs Elstree decided that she had had enough of talking about Francis Youlgreave?

But there was someone else who might remember the Martleshams' aunt. I walked along Minster Street and into the Close by the Porta. But Dr Flaxman's Riley was parked outside the Gotobeds' house. I moved towards the chestnuts, meaning to cut through the cloisters. I heard a door slamming behind me.

I looked back. Dr Flaxman walked round his car and came towards me, moving as usual at one-and-a-half times the speed of a normal person.

'I think I've found a room for Mr Treevor,' he said, touching his hat with a forefinger. 'Would you tell Mrs Byfield? It's in the Cedars, so it should be quite convenient.'

'Where's that?'

'On the outskirts of town. A couple of hundred yards beyond the infants' school. But the room won't be ready until the beginning of next week. The Byfields will need to phone the matron. I wonder whether in the meantime we should take him into hospital. I'd like to have a proper look at him, and it would be one less thing for Mrs Byfield to worry about.'

'Do you want me to mention that to her now as well?'

'Please. She may want a word with her husband. Tell her to ring the surgery as soon as possible and let me know if it suits.'

He nodded and turned back to his car.

'Is Mrs Gotobed all right?' I said quickly. 'I was wondering about calling on her this morning.'

'I wouldn't do that if I were you.' He jingled his car keys in his hand. 'I've just been to see her – she had one of her turns in the night.'

I went back to the Dark Hostelry. Mr Treevor was still in his room but Janet had dragged herself down to the kitchen, where she was sitting at the table and staring at the washing up from breakfast which I hadn't yet had time to do.

'You should be back in bed,' I said, 'or at least resting.'

'There's so much to do.'

'Yes, and I'm doing it. It's all arranged.' I put the kettle on. 'Go on – put your feet up in the drawing room and I'll make us some coffee.'

She did as I asked. I washed up while the water was coming to the boil. I took the coffee upstairs and gave her Dr Flaxman's message.

'I still think we should keep him for a little bit longer,' she said. 'I'd feel so guilty if he went now. Perhaps if I had a week or two to talk to him about it.'

'It wouldn't do any good.' I lit a cigarette and perched on the window seat with my coffee. 'He's already too much for us to cope with.'

Janet lay back on the sofa twisting a damp handkerchief between her fingers. I felt I was failing her, and she felt she was either failing her father or failing David and Rosie. That was silly. The only person who was failing was Mr Treevor himself, and that through no fault of his own.

'Janet, trust me. This is the right decision. And in a week or two you'll agree. It's just that you feel ghastly at present, because of the baby.'

The tears overflowed. I knelt by the sofa and put my arms around her. This is what Flaxman and David never understood. Janet needed to cry. Someone she loved had died. The fact that the person was less than three months old and she had never seen him was beside the point.

After a while Janet drew away from me and blew her nose. 'I *despise* people who dissolve into tears at every possible opportunity.'

'You cry all you want,' I said.

I turned away so she wouldn't see the tears in my own eyes and took a sip of cold coffee. My cigarette had burned itself out in the ashtray on the window seat. I picked up the packet and shook out another. As I did so I heard the clack of the latch on the gate. I looked out of the window. The dean's wife came in from the Close and strode down the path towards the house.

'Oh, damn and blast,' I said viciously, channelling all my anger towards the woman in the garden. 'It's Mrs bloody Forbury. Shall I head her off? I'll tell her you're resting.'

Janet shook her head. 'I'd better see her. It's very kind of her to come.'

'More like nosy.'

'I'll have to see her sooner or later so I might as well get it over with.'

I wiped the scowl off my face and went to answer the door. Mrs Forbury swept past me into the hall.

'Good morning. It's Mrs Appleyard, isn't it?'

'Yes, indeed.' I added, not to be outdone, 'And you must be Mrs Forbury. I believe Janet's mentioned you.'

She was already stripping off her gloves. I took her into the drawing room. Janet asked if I would make some fresh coffee. When I came back, Mrs Forbury was describing how her mother treated miscarriages with wonderful sang-froid, insisting that they were tiresome but hardly serious, like the common cold. Janet took it well, though there was a brief chill between the two women when she said she didn't think she would be up to coming to the Touchies at the Deanery on Thursday afternoon, and that she might not be able to do the flowers in the Lady Chapel next week.

In a perverse way, dealing with Mrs Forbury seemed to do Janet good. She treated her in much the same way as she had treated Miss Esk, our headmistress at Hillgard House, with an appearance of deference masking a calm determination to get her own way as far as was possible. Nor did the dean's wife bear her any ill will for this. Quite the reverse. It made me realize that Janet fitted in here. Mrs Forbury liked her. Janet could be trusted to play by the rules of the Close. Janet suited Rosington in a way that I never could.

Mrs Forbury mellowed. She even accepted one of my cigarettes.

'I don't usually smoke before lunch but I'm feeling a little naughty today.' She sat back, smoke dribbling from both nostrils, and bestowed a smile on me. 'Janet tells me you've found traces of the Red Canon in the Cathedral Library.'

'A few books. I gather he was still talked about when you were a child.'

She chuckled. 'Hardly surprising, Mrs Appleyard. He caused a few ripples in his time, I'm afraid. It wasn't just his Socialist ideas, though those were bad enough. In religious terms he became very eccentric indeed. My poor dear father used to say that he should never have been allowed to stay for as long as he did. Especially after the business with the animals.'

'The ones that were cut up?'

Mrs Forbury raised her eyebrows. 'You *have* been doing your homework. If I remember rightly, there was some question as to whether he did it himself or whether he encouraged a boy from the town to do it for him. Anyway, it was all rather unpleasant. He was far too friendly with those children.'

'Children?'

'There was a little girl as well.' Her eyes met mine for an instant and slid away. 'The boy's sister. Canon Youlgreave made rather a pet of her, rather like Lewis Carroll and that Oxford girl. You know, the one they say was Alice. But that was rather different, of course – after all, Alice was the daughter of a don.'

'What happened to the children?'

'Heaven knows.' Mrs Forbury stubbed out her cigarette. 'Went back to where they came from, I suppose.' She snorted with laughter but her face wasn't amused. 'My old nanny used to say that if I was naughty the Red Canon would come and take me away. There was a lot of talk, I'm afraid.' She helped herself to one of the Rich Tea biscuits which I had brought out in her honour. 'But eventually they persuaded Mr Youlgreave to resign his canonry and leave Rosington, and then everything calmed down.'

So perhaps the sermon in favour of women priests had only been their excuse for easing him out of Rosington, a convenient ecclesiastical scandal used as a smokescreen for something worse. But had he left Rosington with or without Nancy?

Mrs Forbury glanced up at the mantelpiece at a little silver clock Janet had salvaged from her father's possessions. 'I must fly. I haven't even begun to think about lunch.'

I saw her out of the house. On the doorstep she beckoned me to follow her outside.

'I'm glad you're here, Mrs Appleyard,' she murmured, though there was no risk of Janet overhearing us. 'If ever Janet needed a friend, it's now.'

I blinked. 'I'll do my best.'

'I'm sure you will. This can't be an easy time for her, what with her father and the Theological College closing.' Her face suddenly puckered, and wrinkles appeared so she looked like a pink walnut. 'I've had three miscarriages myself so I know what it's like. One tries to be cheerful about these things but it's not easy. Keep an eye on her, won't you?'

She patted me on the arm and marched down the path to the gate. Momentarily flabbergasted, I stared after her. I'd long since written off Mrs Forbury as a snobbish, domineering, insensitive cow. She might be all of these things but now I'd learned she was something else as well. It was unsettling. I wished people didn't have to be so messy and confusing.

I went back into the house to find that Mr Treevor had crept downstairs to the drawing room. He had made an attempt to dress himself. His flies were undone and the bottom button of his cardigan had been pushed through the buttonhole at the top. He was sitting in the chair where the dean's wife had sat, and his trousers had ridden up to reveal the fact that he was wearing only one sock. As I came in, he turned eagerly towards me.

'Is it lunchtime, Mummy?'

'No, dear,' I said. 'Not yet.'

Janet exchanged glances with me. Then she said, 'Daddy, there's something –'

'Daddy?' he said wonderingly, looking around the room. 'Where?'

Janet looked at me again and gave a tiny shake of her head.

'I thought you meant *me* for a moment.' Mr Treevor frowned and nibbled his lower lip, just as Janet sometimes did. 'But I'm not Daddy, am I? I'm Francis.'

38

Several hours later, just before David came home, Janet finally managed to tell Mr Treevor that he was going into hospital. He took it badly, both at the time and afterwards. I'm not even sure he understood what she was saying to him but he must have sensed her distress.

'I feel like a murderer,' Janet said to me afterwards. 'How can we do this to him?'

When David came home he did his best to reassure both Janet and Mr Treevor, but his best wasn't good enough in either case. Rosie sensed the strain and started to play up, spilling her milk on the kitchen table and talking in a babyish lisp very unlike her normal precise voice. I took her upstairs, bathed her and read her one of the Noddy books which Henry had sent.

Hurrah for Little Noddy was about a little puppet who lived in Toyland. The plot involved the theft of a garageful of cars by a gang of sinister goblins. Noddy was wrongfully accused of the crime and flung into jail. Fortunately his best friend, a gnome named Big Ears, was able to clear his name. After the arrest of the goblins, Noddy was rewarded with a car of his own. If only life were that simple, I thought.

While I read, Rosie cuddled Angel and stared at me with large eyes. As I was nearing the end, I heard Janet coming upstairs with Mr Treevor. He was sobbing quietly. 'I wish I was dead,' he said. 'I wish I was dead.'

I raised my voice and hurried on with the story.

'It doesn't make sense,' Rosie said when I had finished. 'What doesn't?'

'This book. How could they think he'd stolen all the cars? There're at least six in the picture. He couldn't drive them all at once.'

'Perhaps they thought he drove them away one by one. Or he had some friends who came and helped.'

'It's silly.' Rosie shut the book with a snap. 'Doesn't make sense. I don't like that.'

'Nor does anyone.' I got up and closed the curtains. 'Time to settle down now. I'll ask Mummy and Daddy to come and say good night, shall I?'

'Why does Grandpa want to die?'

I hesitated in the doorway. 'I don't think he does really.'

'But he keeps saying he wants to. Is it nice being dead?'

Rosie wasn't my child so I didn't say what I thought. 'When you're dead you go to heaven. That's what Mummy and Daddy believe.'

'I know that. But is it *nice*?'

'Very nice, I expect.'

If it existed, it couldn't be much worse than the life that some people left behind them. Like poor Isabella of Roth, if *she* had existed, burning to a cinder in Rosington marketplace for believing the wrong thing at the wrong time about something that didn't exist in the first place.

'Do they have nice food in heaven?' Rosie asked, settling herself down in bed.

'I'm sure they do. Nothing but the best.'

'Angels eat food too, don't they? It's not just for the dead people?'

'You'll have to ask Daddy. He's the expert. Now, sleep well and see you in the morning.'

I bent to kiss her. Rosie's nightdress and the doll's angelic uniform blended with the pillowcase and sheet. For an instant in the half-light it looked as if there were two fair disembodied heads resting like head-hunters' trophies on the pillow. A memory stirred. Someone's father at a party in Durban, talking about head-hunters and why they did it.

The phone began to ring. I heard Janet talking in Mr

250

Treevor's room and David's footsteps crossing the hall. I went down to the drawing room. A moment later, David poked his head around the door.

'It's Henry.'

I went into the study, wishing I'd had time to have a drink or a cigarette, or even to touch the sprig of lavender for luck. It wasn't easy seeing him again. I had grown used to his absence.

'Wendy!' Henry's enthusiasm bubbled down the line. 'How are you, darling?'

'All right, thanks.' I was so glad to hear him that I decided to postpone reminding him that I wasn't his darling any more. 'What have you been up to?'

'I'll tell you in a minute. What's up with David?'

'I'm sorry,' I said. 'I tried to let you know.'

'Let me know what? What's happened? Are you OK?'

'It's not me. When I got back on Friday, I found that Janet had lost the baby.'

Henry whistled. 'It never rains but it pours, eh?'

'There's more. Mr Treevor's going into hospital tomorrow morning, and then to a nursing home next week. Permanently.'

'Sounds quite sensible – I'd have thought that would be a relief.'

'It is sensible and it will be a relief, but it doesn't stop Janet feeling awful about it. And Mr Treevor hasn't taken it well, either.'

'Why didn't David say something to me? I'm meant to be his friend.'

'You know him. His idea of a heart-to-heart chat is to ask you if it's stopped raining yet.'

Neither of us spoke for a moment. It was a trunk-call. I wondered how much the silence was costing.

'Wendy?'

'What?'

'I'm sorry about the other day. At Liverpool Street. I shouldn't have said all that.'

'It's all right.' I felt a surge of pleasure I didn't want to think about too much. 'I got a bit carried away too.'

251

There was another pause. I heard the scrape of a match as Henry lit a cigarette.

'I bet the atmosphere's pretty grim. You must need a holiday.'

'Sounds wonderful. When Janet's better I think I'll probably have one.'

'Have you paid in that cheque yet?'

'No.'

'Damn it. Why not?'

'I haven't had time.'

'Would you like me to do it for you?'

I laughed. 'It's not like you to be careful with money.'

'I'm a reformed character nowadays. Economizing like mad. I've left Brown's.'

'I know. I tried to phone you on Saturday.'

Another expensive silence went by.

'I thought about phoning,' Henry said at last. 'But I wasn't sure you'd want to hear from me.'

'Where are you staying?'

'That's why I was phoning you, actually. To let you know. I've got a room at the Queen's Head.'

'Where's that?'

'It's the pub at Roth.'

'What on earth are you doing there?'

'Sleuthing. That's the technical term, isn't it? I had to go somewhere, so I thought why not here? The Queen's Head is very cheap, compared to Brown's at any rate. The food's not bad, and it turns out they've got quite a good cellar. I went to church yesterday – the vicar's about ninety-nine and quite inaudible – and I've had tea at the café on the green, which is run by some terrifyingly refined ladies.'

'How long are you staying?'

'I haven't made my mind up. Why?'

'I just wondered –'

'You see, dearest,' Henry said quickly, 'without your organizational powers I go to pieces. I need you to make the decisions. I wish you were here.'

'So do I.' I'd spoken without thinking but immediately realized I might have given him the wrong impression. I

252

rushed on before he had time to comment. 'Have you got anywhere? With the sleuthing, I mean.'

'I tried to call at the Old Manor House this morning. I had it all worked out. I was going to be an architectural historian writing an article about interesting houses in the area. But I didn't have a chance to say anything. A woman in a pinny answered the door and said Lady Youlgreave wasn't at home. And there were a couple of dogs, too.' His voice became plaintive. 'Savage brutes. One was an Alsatian. It kept trying to bite me.'

I don't think anyone except myself knew that Henry was afraid of dogs. When he was a kid he had been bitten in a sensitive place by a long-haired collie.

'I tried the library, though, and that wasn't a complete wash-out. There was a pile of old newspapers on a table at the back. The local rag, the *Courier*.'

'Don't tell me. For 1904 or 1905?'

'Both. The librarian just said that another reader had left them out.'

'So Munro's been back to Roth?'

'Presumably. Though nothing had been cut out. No chance, I suppose. I had a look through. There was a certain amount about the Youlgreaves and Roth Park, charitable stuff mainly, but nothing about Francis leaving Rosington.'

'The Youlgreaves probably owned a chunk of the newspaper.'

'And hushed up the Rosington business as far as they could?' Henry said. 'Maybe. He was mentioned in December 1904, though, as one of a list of local worthies who gave money to the village school. Then there's nothing till the report of his death the following summer.'

'That's something. What exactly happened?'

'There was an inquest but the official line was that it was a pure accident. Youlgreave's room was quite high up in the house and apparently he fell out of his window one night. A maid found the body the following morning. Accidental death. That was the story. The coroner said he must have leant out a bit too far trying to get a breath of air. It was a very warm night.'

253

'When are you going back to London?'

'Tomorrow morning, probably. Any chance of your coming up to town in the next few days?'

'Not really. There's too much I need to do here.'

'How would it be if I came to see you?'

'In Rosington?' I couldn't keep the disbelief out of my voice. 'They've got long memories here, you know. If Oliver Cromwell turned up, they'd probably present him with a bill for damaging the carvings in sixteen forty-something.'

'I don't mind that. Why don't I come up tomorrow? I've got a date with the Cuthbertsons but I can easily put them off. We could have lunch at the Crossed Keys.'

'The Cuthbertsons?'

'I told you – they own Veedon Hall. I'd arranged to run down and spend the day with them looking over the school and so on. But they won't mind if –'

'You mustn't cancel that.'

'All right, then I'll come and take you to lunch on Wednesday. So that's settled. I've looked up the trains. There's one that gets to Rosington at about twelve-thirty-five.'

'But Janet –'

'She can come too, if you like. And David, I suppose. Though I'd much rather it was just you.'

I gave in, mainly, I told myself, because it would mean I wouldn't have to cook lunch.

'That's wonderful,' he said. 'And afterwards we can go to the bank and pay in your cheque.'

I couldn't help myself. I laughed. Henry was like a terrier with a sense of humour. He made me laugh and he never let go.

He cleared his throat. 'Anyway, I'd better leave you to make cocoa or whatever you do for fun at this time. I love you. I'm going to put the phone down now so you don't have to reply to that.'

There was a click and the line went dead. I stared at the handset for a moment and then replaced it on its base. I felt happier than I had done for months, which was stupid of me. I heard Janet's footsteps on the stairs and went to tell her that Henry had invited us to lunch the day after tomorrow. She must have had a bath while I was on the phone because she was already in her nightclothes – a dressing gown over a cotton winceyette nightdress, cream-coloured and with a pattern of small pink bows. It was a thick winter dressing gown, which made me think that even a bath had failed to warm her up. But her face lit up when I told her Henry was coming.

'How lovely,' she said. 'I'm so glad.'

'It doesn't mean anything's changed,' I warned her. 'But there's no reason why we shouldn't behave like civilized human beings, is there?'

'No, of course not.'

'It's Tuesday tomorrow,' I said hastily, knowing I was beginning to blush, and seizing on an exit line. 'I'd better put the rubbish out.'

I was still feeling happy when I went to bed that night. Before going to sleep, I reread 'The Office of the Dead' whilst smoking a final cigarette.

> *Enough! I cried. Consume the better part,*
> *No more. For therein lies the deepest art . . .*

The words triggered the memory that had begun to surface when I was talking with Rosie. Or rather parts of a memory, about the conversation with someone's father in Durban. The man who knew about head-hunting.

It had been at one of Grady's parties. This one had been just before the company crashed, and with it Henry's investment. My memory of it was partial because even by Grady's standards, the party had been particularly drunken.

The ex-colonial administrator had stuck out because he didn't resemble any of the other guests. He was somebody's father on a visit from England. He was a little, hunched man with a creased yellow face. I remember him early on in the evening standing in a corner with a glass of orange juice in his hand watching us making fools of ourselves. I felt sorry for him because I thought he was obviously lonely, and anyway I was trying to escape from Grady, so I went to talk to him. I asked him if he was bored.

'No,' he said. 'It's fascinating.'

'What is?'

He smiled up at me and gestured with his glass towards the crowd of people swirling through the room and spilling on to the terrace and down into the garden and around the pool. 'All this. Ritual behaviour is one of my interests.'

I laughed. 'You're teasing me.'

He shook his head and explained that his work had encouraged him to develop an interest in anthropology.

'Yes, but that's about savages – primitive people, I mean.'

'All human societies have their rituals, Mrs Appleyard, however sophisticated they may appear to be on the surface. Think of the ritual mourning we indulged in when the King died. And look at this – intoxication, formalized sexual display and childish games, many of them of an aggressive nature. I could give you plenty of parallels from tribal cultures in West Africa.'

'But that can't be the same,' I said. 'Their reasons for doing it must be completely different from ours.'

'Why?'

'Because we're Europeans and they're Africans.'

'It makes no difference. That is one of the interesting things that anthropology shows. On a ritual level, human societies are strikingly similar in many respects. Take cannibalism, for instance.'

I made a face at him. 'Rather you than me.'

'I don't mean cannibalism from necessity or inclination, of course, where eating other human beings is a matter of survival, or an addition to the diet. No, I mean ritual cannibalism, which has nothing to do with nourishment. It's often allied to head-hunting. I came across a certain amount of it in West Africa and also in the East Indies. There were various reasons for it, but the most common, found in most cultures at some point or another, is that by eating something of a person you acquire his soul, or perhaps a part of him you particularly value. His courage, for example, or his prowess in battle.'

'Not in Europe, surely? Or at least not since we all lived in caves and went around knocking each other over the head with rocks.'

'There's evidence to show that the practice persisted in England and Scotland until the Middle Ages. And there were cases in other parts of Europe much later than that. There was one in the Balkans, in Montenegro, in 1912. And a diluted version of this lasted much longer. Think of hair, for example. Other people's hair.' He smiled grimly at me. 'You wouldn't necessarily eat it, of course, not nowadays. But I can remember my aunts wearing mourning brooches and rings containing locks snipped from the loved one's head. What they were really doing, of course, was carrying around a little bit of the soul of a person they'd lost. Rather like the head-hunters do in parts of Borneo. More genteel than eating his brain as they might have done at another time or in another place, but the principle's exactly the same.'

The rest of what he'd said had been drowned in dry martinis or lost in the blue haze of cigarette smoke. It didn't matter. The question was what had Francis wanted that a child might possess? Youth, health and life? Had Francis believed that the purpose of dead children was to feed the living with life? How did that compare with buying a sprig of lavender from a nasty old woman in the hope it would bring you luck?

I turned over the pages of *The Voice of Angels* until I came to 'Breakheart Hill'.

> *'For hart's blood makes the young heart strong,' quoth he.*
> *'God hath ordained it so. He dies that ye*
> *'May hunt, my son, and through his strength be free.'*

Time sanitizes all but the most dreadful horrors. There I was, entertaining the bizarre idea that a clergyman of the Church of England might have considered eating bits of children in the crazy belief that this would somehow extend his life. But it was only a speculation, and the fact that Francis had died more than fifty years ago removed it one stage further from here and now. So I felt pleased with myself. I was even looking forward to telling Henry about the idea tomorrow.

I put out the cigarette and settled down. I thought of Henry briefly, that he had his good points as well as his bad, then I slid into a deep sleep. There must have been dreams, though I don't remember any of them, and they must have been happy ones because I was still feeling happy when I woke up.

It was one of those times when there's very little transition between sleep and being awake. It's like swimming up from the bottom of a pool, the sense of urgency and speed, the sense of breaking out of one element into another.

The room was full of light. I knew it was still early because the light had that soft, almost colourless quality you get in the hour or two after dawn. I opened my eyes and saw Janet in the doorway. She was wearing a long pale-blue nylon nightdress and her hair was loose and unbrushed.

'Wendy,' she said. 'Wendy.'

I sat up. 'What is it?'

She seemed not to have heard me. She looked so cold, an ice woman. You could see the shape of her body through the nylon of the nightdress. With a twist of envy I wondered if she'd bought it to make herself look pretty for David.

'Janet, what's happened?'

'Wendy.' She took a step into the room, then stopped and blinked. 'Daddy's *dead*.'

39

Blood is the colour of a scream.

Neither of us said anything as we stood in the doorway looking down at the body of John Treevor. But that's what I thought. *Blood is the colour of a scream.* There was nothing logical, nothing rational, about it. I couldn't scream for fear of waking Rosie.

Who would have thought he had so much blood in him?

Really we should get the sheets and the pillowcase in a bath full of cold water as soon as possible. Soak blood in cold water, said my mother, who was a sort of walking housewife's manual. But the bedding was so saturated I doubted if they would ever be clean again. And there was nothing we could do about the mattress. It wasn't just the cover. The blood would have soaked right into the horsehair.

I knew Janet was right, that he was dead. He was so very still, you see, and the blood had stopped flowing.

There were red splashes on the bedside rug. The rug would have to go, too. Mr Treevor's false teeth, clamped for ever shut, were in the glass on the bedside table. His knees had drawn up under the eiderdown. He was lying on his back and it looked as if he had two open mouths, one redder than the other. All the redness cast a sombre glow through the room, neutralizing the pale dawn light.

On the rug was a knife, the vegetable knife we'd lost. Oh well, I thought, that's something. None of the other knives in the kitchen drawer were nearly as good for peeling potatoes. Mr Treevor's eyes were open and he stared up at the ceiling towards David's heaven. Except that David was far too sophisticated to believe in a common-or-garden traditional heaven located above the sky.

Janet stirred. 'At least he's at peace now.'

Peace? Is that what you call it? 'I'm going to be sick.'

I pushed past her, went into the bathroom and locked the door. When I came out, Janet was waiting for me on the landing. She had a key in her hand and the door to Mr Treevor's room was closed. Without exchanging a word we went down to the kitchen.

I filled the kettle and put it on the stove. While Janet laid the tea tray, I leant against the sink and watched her. I remember how she fetched the cups and saucers and aligned them on the tray, how the teaspoons were polished on the tea towel, how the milk jug was filled and then covered with a little lacy cloth designed to keep out the flies. I remember how deft her movements were, how she made a little island of order amid all the chaos, and how beautiful she was, though she was still pale and her face was rigid with shock.

She must have sensed me watching her, because she glanced up and smiled. For an instant it was as if she'd struck a match behind her face, and the flame flared, warmed the chilly air for a moment, and died.

I made the tea. Janet poured it and added three teaspoonfuls of sugar to each cup.

'It's my fault,' she said after the first sip.

'Of course it isn't.'

She shook her head. 'He couldn't face going away. We were putting him out like a piece of rubbish for the dustmen. My *father.*'

'He was going into hospital for his sake as much as for yours.' I reached across the table and touched her hand. 'You know how he's been lately. He could have done this at any time, for any reason. Or for no reason at all. He wasn't himself.'

Janet gasped, a single, ragged sob. 'Then who was he?'

'At one point he thought he was Francis Youlgreave,' I said. 'Listen, all I'm saying is that part of him had already died. The important part, the part that was your father.'

Janet took a deep breath. 'I must phone someone. Dr Flaxman, I suppose.'

I touched the key lying between us on the table. 'You've locked the bedroom door?'

She nodded. 'In case Rosie –'

'What about David?'

Janet blinked, wrinkled her forehead and looked up at the clock on the dresser. 'He'll be getting up in a moment to say the morning office.'

'Janet, why did you go into your father's room?'

'I woke up and I couldn't get back to sleep. I – I thought I'd just peep in and see if he was all right. He was so upset. When do you think –?'

'I don't know.' I remembered how still everything had been in Mr Treevor's bedroom, how the blood had soaked into the bedding, how dark the blood had been. 'Probably hours ago.'

'What a way to end.'

'If he'd had the choice, he'd probably have preferred it. I'd much rather go like that than get more and more senile.'

Water rustled in one of the pipes running down the wall. Janet pushed back her chair.

'That's David,' she said.

I wondered why she'd come to me not him after she found her father.

Death wasn't something I'd had to deal with very often. I hadn't had the practice. I didn't know the procedures. I thought that Mr Treevor had somehow cheated death by killing himself. Part of me, the little selfish child that lives within us all, was glad he was dead. In the long run, it would save everyone a lot of trouble.

I just wished he hadn't made such a mess of his exit. Literally. Why hadn't he done it sensibly and discreetly somewhere in the wings of our lives? A nice quiet overdose, perhaps, almost indistinguishable from a natural death, or at least something Janet could have told herself was an accident, like stepping in front of a bus. At times like this I was glad of the privacy of the mind. If my thoughts had been public property, the world would have labelled me a psychopath.

Janet slipped away to talk to David. I went upstairs to dress. Afterwards I took another cup of tea into the drawing room and smoked a cigarette. David was now in the study talking on the phone. The doors were open and I could hear what he was saying.

'No, there's no doubt at all, I'm afraid . . . can't you come sooner than that?'

I stared through a window at a garden varnished with dew. The spire gleamed in the early morning sun. Francis must have stood in this room, looked out of this window, seen this view.

'I appreciate that,' David was saying. 'Very well . . . Yes, all right, I'll ring them straightaway . . . Goodbye.'

He put down the phone and came to join me in the drawing room.

'Flaxman can't manage it before half past eight.'

'I'll take Rosie to school.'

'Thanks.' I doubt if he heard what I'd said. 'Poor Janet,' he went on. 'All this on top of the miscarriage.'

'I think she needs to be in bed.'

'Would you tell her about Flaxman? I'd better phone the police, and the dean.'

I persuaded Janet to go back to bed. Then I got Rosie up, made breakfast and walked her to school. It felt unnatural to be doing normal things. Everything should have become abnormal in deference to Mr Treevor's death. But Rosington ignored his absence. The city was the same today as it had been yesterday, which was *wrong*.

I looked at Rosie as we drifted down the hill towards St Tumwulf's. She had Angel clamped under her arm and she was sucking her thumb. The doll was wearing its pink outfit because it was moving in disguise among mortals, and so she matched Rosie in her pink gingham school dress. I thought Rosie was paler than usual. She'd been as fond of Mr Treevor as anybody.

During breakfast, David had told her that Grandpa had gone to heaven in the night.

'Will he be coming back?' she had said.

'No,' David replied. Rosie nodded and went back to her cornflakes.

At the school gates, I asked Rosie if she was feeling all right.

'*I'm* all right. But Angel's got a tummy ache.'

'A bad one?'

'A little bit bad.' Rosie's face brightened. 'I'm going to finish sewing Angel's shawl today and it'll go nicely with her dress. That'll cheer her up.'

'She'll look very pretty.'

'We're sisters now,' Rosie told me. 'Both in pink.'

'Makes the boys wink, doesn't it?'

She gave me the doll and went into the playground. It seemed to me the other children parted before her like the Red Sea. I found the headmistress in her office, told her what had happened and asked her to keep an eye on Rosie.

'A death in the family, in the home,' the headmistress said. 'It's a terrible thing for a child.'

When I got back to the Dark Hostelry, I found Dr Flaxman in the drawing room talking to David and Janet.

'I'd better have the key,' he was saying. 'If you wouldn't mind.'

David frowned at him. Janet moved along the sofa and patted the seat beside her. I sat down.

'I don't understand,' David said.

'It's common practice in cases like this, Mr Byfield.'

'What do you mean?'

'Cases where the coroner will have to be notified.'

'I can understand that of course, but –'

'And particularly where there's an element of doubt about the death.'

'I should have thought that was plain enough.'

Flaxman's eyes flickered towards me and then returned to David. 'Perhaps I could have a word in private.'

Janet said, 'That's not necessary. Whatever you can say to my husband you can say to Mrs Appleyard and me.'

David nodded. 'Of course.'

'Very well.' Flaxman continued to speak to David, ignoring

Janet and me. 'It's possible that Mr Treevor killed himself. But any death like this needs careful investigation.'

'Surely you're not suggesting –?'

'I'm not suggesting anything,' Flaxman said. 'I'm just doing my job. May I use your phone?'

People came and went, doing their jobs, while we sat by and watched. Dr Flaxman waited until two uniformed police officers appeared on the doorstep. David took the police to see Mr Treevor. They didn't stay long in the room and they said very little. But when they came out, one of them went away and the other lingered like a ghost on the landing in front of Mr Treevor's door.

I took him up a cup of coffee and a biscuit. He looked at me as if I were a Martian and blushed. But he said thank you and then broke wind, which embarrassed him more than it did me.

Our next visitors were also police officers. But these were detectives in plain clothes. Inspector Humphries was a tall, hunched man with short, fair hair which looked as if it would be as soft as a baby's. He had a broken-nosed sergeant called Pate, all bone and muscle. I later discovered Pate played fly-half for the town's rugby football fifteen. David introduced me and explained that his wife was in bed.

Humphries grunted. 'Perhaps you'd like to take us upstairs, sir,' he said. 'Who was it who actually found the body?'

'My wife. Then she woke Mrs Appleyard and me.'

'I see.' The inspector had a Midlands accent and a way of mumbling his words that made it sound as if he was speaking through a mouthful of thick soup. 'And when was Mr Treevor last seen alive?'

'About half past ten the previous evening. My wife looked in to say good night.'

Humphries grunted again. We had reached the landing. At a nod from the inspector, the constable on guard unlocked Mr Treevor's door. I heard Pate sucking in his breath. Then the two detectives went into the room and closed the door behind them. Then the doorbell rang and David and I went downstairs and answered it together.

The doorbell kept ringing all morning. First there was

another doctor, the police surgeon. Then came Peter Hudson, who asked if there was anything he could do and said that he would take over David's responsibilities at the Cathedral for the time being. Later on in the day we found in our letterbox a stiff little note from the dean, addressed to Janet, expressing polite regret at the death of her father.

Canon Osbaston turned up in person, suddenly frail, his little head wagging like a wilting flower on the long stalk of his neck. David put him in the drawing room and I brought him a glass of brandy.

'Poor Janet,' he said, 'it's so very hard. Sometimes it seems so meaningless.'

'Yes,' said David.

'So pointless,' Osbaston murmured. 'It really makes one wonder.' Then he glanced at his watch, finished his brandy and struggled to his feet. 'Give my love to Janet and let me know if there's anything I can do. But I'll call again tomorrow, if I may. Perhaps I'll see you at evensong, David.'

In that moment I liked him better than I had ever done.

June Hudson appeared just as Osbaston was leaving. She was holding a large earthenware dish.

'Just a little casserole,' she said, handing it to me. 'I thought you might not have time to cook a proper meal tonight.' She shifted from one foot to the other. 'And how's Janet?'

'Very shaken, naturally,' David said. 'She's resting now.'

'Let me know when you think she might like a visitor.'

'You're very kind.' David made it sound like an accusation.

June Hudson smiled at us both and almost fled down the garden towards the gate to the Close.

Shortly after this, they took the body away. They brought an ambulance into the Close and backed it up to the gate into our garden. People lingered to watch, swelling to a small crowd when the police raised screens. Sergeant Pate suggested that it might be better if we kept out of the way. So the three of us sat in Janet and David's room and tried to resist the temptation to peer out of the window.

We heard the tramp of feet on the stairs. They took away the mattress and the bedding as well as the body. They also removed some of Mr Treevor's possessions. They gave David a receipt. Janet wanted to say goodbye to her father, but David wouldn't let her. He said there would be other opportunities. He meant when the mortuary had cleaned him up.

'I'm trying to remember him now as he used to be,' Janet said carefully, like a child repeating a lesson. 'Before Mummy died.'

Then it was time for me to collect Rosie. David offered me the use of the car but I refused, because it was garaged at the Theological College and fetching it would have meant one of us having to walk through the Close. Besides, I thought it would be better for Rosie if everything that could be normal was normal.

I met no one I knew on my way to school with Angel. None of the mothers and grandmothers at the school gate talked to me, though one or two of them gave me curious looks. They did that anyway. When Rosie came out I gave her the doll.

'I've done the shawl,' Rosie said. 'It's pink. I've got it in my satchel. Where's Mummy?'

'She's having a rest at home.'

'But it's daytime.'

'You know she hasn't been very well recently. And of course she's very sad at present because of Grandpa.'

'Grandpa's in heaven,' Rosie announced, with a hint of a question mark trailing at the end of the sentence.

'Yes, that's what Daddy said.'

She took my hand because it was less effort for her if I towed her up the hill to the town. 'Angel says, perhaps he went to hell.'

'Why would he go there?'

'If you do bad things, you go to hell.'

'Did Grandpa do bad things?'

Rosie conferred silently with her doll. 'Angel doesn't know. What's for tea?'

'That's something *I* don't know. I expect we'll find something.'

We didn't talk for the rest of the way. There was a men's outfitters with a large plate-glass window in the High Street, and as usual Rosie lingered as we passed to admire her reflection. The proprietor was fetching a rack of ties from the window display for a customer standing a yard or two behind him. It was the dean. For an instant his eyes met mine and then he turned away to examine a glass-fronted cabinet containing cufflinks and tiepins.

We went into the Close by the Sacristan's Gate. Mr Gotobed was shooing a group of schoolboys off the sacred grass around the east end of the cathedral, the skirts of his cassock fluttering in the breeze. He turned as he heard our footsteps on the gravel, abandoned the children and walked quickly and clumsily towards us.

'Mrs Appleyard.'

I smiled at him.

'Mother and me were sorry to hear about Mr Treevor. She asked me to send her condolences.'

'Thank you. I'll tell the Byfields.'

His eyes were full of yearning. I told him Rosie needed her tea and that I had to rush.

When we got home, Rosie went up to see her mother. There was a knock on the garden door. A small man with no chin and a very large Adam's apple was standing on the doorstep. He waved at me. When I opened the door he edged forward, smiling, and I automatically stepped back into the hall.

'*Rosington Observer*, miss. I'm Jim Filey. I called about the sad fatality.'

'I see.'

'I gather there'll have to be an inquest. Very distressing for the family, I'm sure.' He pulled out a notebook. 'And you are?'

It was the way he stared at me that made up my mind. He was younger than me and acting like a hard-bitten newshound. I didn't like anything about him, from his over-greased hair to the fussy little patterns on his gleaming black brogues.

'My name's none of your business.' I began to close the door. 'I'll say goodbye.'

'Here, miss, wait. Is it true Mr Treevor cut his throat?'

'I'd like you to go, Mr Filey.'

But he was no longer looking at me. He was looking over my shoulder, into the hall.

'Get out,' David said very quietly.

I stepped aside from the doorway. David moved towards Filey. For an instant I thought that he was going to hit the reporter. Filey took a couple of steps backwards. David shut the door and locked it. Filey scowled at us through the glass and then walked rapidly down the garden to the gate.

'Thanks,' I said. 'He was beginning to be a pest.'

'You shouldn't have to put up with that sort of thing.'

He had calmed down now. The whole episode had lasted less than a minute. What really shook me was not that nasty little reporter but what I'd glimpsed in David. There was so much rage in him. Perhaps that was why he needed to believe in God, to find something greater than himself that would contain and repress whatever was swirling around inside him and trying to find a way out.

I said, 'This may be a sign of things to come.'

His eyebrows shot up. 'Surely not?'

I'd lowered my voice to a whisper, as had he. 'This is going to get in the newspapers.'

'You may be right. I'd better phone my mother.'

He returned to the study to phone Granny Byfield. I went downstairs to the kitchen. I wanted to talk to someone who didn't belong in Rosington, who wasn't part of the little world of the Close. That wasn't the whole truth – I wanted to talk to *Henry*.

In the kitchen I opened the larder door and wondered what to do for Rosie's tea. At least we had the Hudsons' casserole for supper. All at once the idea of living in Henry's prep school seemed wonderfully attractive. At least there would be staff to take care of the cooking and cleaning, the washing and ironing.

I turned round to put a loaf of bread on the table. For a moment I thought Mr Treevor was sitting in the Windsor chair at the end of the table. Suddenly the knowledge that he would never be there again, demanding a second helping before some of us had even started our first, made my eyes fill with tears.

40

On Wednesday morning our first visitor was Mrs Forbury. She came through the gate to the Close, glancing over her shoulder like a thief as she slipped into the garden.

'It's the Queen Touchy,' I told Janet, who was lying on the sofa in the drawing room. 'I'll send her away.'

'No, don't,' Janet said. 'It's kind of her to come.'

You can never predict how people are going to react. When Mrs Forbury saw Janet lying there in her dressing gown, she bustled over to her, put her arms around her and gave her a hug. Janet hugged her back and started to cry.

'There, there,' said the Queen Touchy. 'There, there.'

'Would you like some coffee?' I said.

Mrs Forbury looked over Janet's head at me. 'I'd better not, thank you. I mustn't stay long. I just popped in on impulse, you see, and Dennis wouldn't know where to find me if – if he happened to want me.'

In other words, she hadn't told her husband she was coming here. She didn't stay long. She slipped out of the house as furtively as she'd come in. When she said goodbye, Janet clung to her hand. At the time I couldn't understand it, but now I think that Janet and Mrs Forbury were joined together by dead babies.

'It *was* kind of her,' Janet said when I came back.

I nodded offhandedly, miffed that I had been temporarily dislodged from my position as Comforter-in-Chief.

'I must do a bit of shopping this morning,' I said. 'You remember that Henry's coming?'

'David will stay with me. You go out to lunch with him by yourself. It'll do you good.'

'But what about you?'

'I'll find something. I'm not very hungry.'

'But Janet –'

'I'm not ill. I wish you wouldn't mother me.'

The doorbell rang again.

I went into the hall. Inspector Humphries and Sergeant Pate were standing with their backs to the house, apparently admiring the sun-filled garden. When I opened the door they turned together to face me in a movement so synchronized it might have been choreographed.

'Good morning, Mrs Appleyard,' Humphries mumbled, his lips scarcely moving. 'Is Mr Byfield in?'

'I'm afraid you've missed him. He's at the Theological College.'

'May we come in?'

I stood back to let the two men into the house.

'Who is it?' Janet called from the drawing room.

'The police.'

Humphries moved so that he could see Janet on the sofa through the doorway of the drawing room. 'Mind if I have a word, Mrs Byfield?'

The policemen sat down one on either side of the fireplace. I perched on the arm of the sofa. Pate took out a notebook and fiddled with the piece of elastic which held it together.

Humphries cleared his throat. 'I'm afraid I shall have to have a look in Mr Treevor's room again, Mrs Byfield. And perhaps elsewhere in the house.'

'All right.'

I said, 'Is there something in particular you're looking for?'

'One or two things we'd like to clear up,' he said, still looking at Janet.

'Such as?' Janet asked.

'If you don't mind, I'd rather talk to your husband about this,' Humphries said.

'Why?'

'Well, there are some things that aren't suitable for ladies, really.' He stirred in his chair. 'No need to make things worse than they are, is there?'

'Mr Treevor was my father,' Janet said. 'I want you to talk to *me*.'

I saw Pate wince, as though expecting an explosion. Humphries ran his fingers through his baby-soft hair. But he didn't clam up. Quite the contrary.

'Very well, Mrs Byfield, I'll tell you what I would have told your husband. There's some doubts about the circumstances of your father's death. You know what a pathologist is?'

'Of course I do.'

'He had a look at the body last night. Now, when someone cuts their throat, you normally get a clean cut and they arch their heads back, which means the carotid arteries slip back. And that means that the knife misses them, so there's less blood than you'd expect. Follow me so far?'

For a moment the scene in Mr Treevor's room flashed in vivid technicolour behind my eyes.

'There was quite a lot of cuts on your father's throat, and a lot of blood. The bedclothes were in a mess, too, which suggests he struggled. Tell me, Mrs Byfield, was your father right-handed or left-handed?'

'Right-handed,' she muttered, and Sergeant Pate had to ask her to repeat her answer.

'If a right-handed person is cutting his throat, Mrs Byfield, he usually does it from left to right. Understand? But the cuts on your father's throat were from right to left. So. Perhaps you can see now why I wanted to talk to your husband, and why we'd like to have a look around a little more, and ask a few questions.'

I stood up. 'This is absurd,' I said. 'You know Mr Treevor wasn't a well man. As Dr Flaxman will tell you, he was going senile. He wasn't acting normally. Nothing he's done in the last few months could be called *normal*. So it hardly seems strange that the way he killed himself was rather unusual.'

Inspector Humphries had stood up as well. With his head hunched forward on his shoulders, he looked like a bird of prey in an ill-fitting suit. 'Unusual, Mrs Appleyard? Oh yes,

271

very unusual. For example, this is the first suicide I've seen where the perpetrator killed himself, then got up and washed the knife, left it on the floor at least a yard away from the bed, climbed back into bed and carried on with being dead.' He sucked air between his teeth. 'Very unusual indeed, I'd say. Wouldn't you agree, Sergeant?'

Janet shifted her body on the sofa. 'What would you say if I asked you to leave?'

'I'd say that was your right, Mrs Byfield, but if you do it won't take me long to come back with a search warrant. And if this goes any further, your refusal will look very bad. Whatever happens there will have to be an inquest, you know. It will probably be adjourned so we can make further enquiries.'

Janet sighed. 'You can look round, if you want.'

'Good.'

'Do you want me to go with them?' I said to her.

Janet shook her head. 'It doesn't matter.'

Neither of us spoke for a moment when Humphries and Pate left the room. We heard their heavy footsteps on the stairs and the key turning in the lock of Mr Treevor's room.

'Why was he so unpleasant to you?' I asked.

She looked at me for a long moment. 'Why should he be nice?' she said at last. 'They'll look everywhere.'

'Everywhere?'

'Of course they will. It's their job.'

I wanted to laugh. What would they make of the bottle of gin in my bedside cupboard, not to mention the sprig of lavender resting on a cheque for ten thousand pounds?

'Janet, you don't think –'

'I don't know what to think.' She swung her legs off the sofa. 'I'd better ring David.'

There was another ring at the doorbell.

It was a boy with a telegram addressed to David and Janet. Janet tore open the envelope, read the message and passed it to me.

ARRIVING 12.38 TRAIN. MOTHER.

'Damn it,' Janet said, running her fingers through her hair. 'I thought this might happen.'

'It must be the train Henry's on. Ask David to bring round the car, and I'll meet them both if you want.'

'We'll have to make up a bed for her, and then there's supper.'

At least David's mother had given us something to do, something to distract us from the heavy feet moving about upstairs, and what the presence of the police officers might mean to all of us. While Janet phoned David, I explained what had happened to Inspector Humphries and made up the bed for old Mrs Byfield in the little room next to Rosie's. Mrs Byfield was a demanding visitor, and Janet asked me to make sure there was a hot-water bottle to air the bed, and on the bedside table a carafe of water, a glass and a tin of biscuits in case she should feel peckish in the night. She might be chilly at night, so extra blankets had to be found and a fire had to be laid.

While I was doing this, David came home, and I heard his raised voice first in the hall and later in Mr Treevor's room. I was glad to see him, because we soon had other distractions in the shape of two more journalists, whom David turned away, and the bishop's chaplain. I stood on the landing and eavesdropped on his conversation with David in the hall below.

'I say,' said Gervase Haselbury-Finch, 'this is awful. The bishop sent me round to say how sorry he is. He says you and Mrs Byfield are much in his mind at present. And in his prayers, naturally.'

'How very kind of him,' said David in a voice that suggested the opposite. 'Do thank him.'

'Um – I should say – the chief constable telephoned him this morning.'

'Really?'

'I gather there are one or two things that the police will have to clear up about Mr Treevor's death. He – the bishop, that is – would very much appreciate it if you could keep him informed.'

'I'm sure he would,' said David.

'There are wider issues to be considered.' Haselbury-Finch was almost gabbling by now. 'The bishop feels that the matter could be a sensitive one for the diocese, even for the church as a whole.'

'Thank him for his advice, Gervase. In the meantime, I have got rather a lot to do.'

'Eh? Oh yes, I see. You must be awfully busy. I'll say goodbye then.'

The garden door opened and closed. I went downstairs and found David lighting a cigarette.

'I heard that,' I said.

'I could have strangled him,' David said, and to my surprise smiled at me. 'Not poor Gervase. The bishop.'

'I'd better go down to the station.' I studied my reflection in the hall mirror. I would have to go as I was. There was no time to repair make-up or brush hair.

'I'll see if I can get rid of the policemen before my mother comes. I'm sorry you're being dragged into this. Just drop my mother off here and then go and have lunch with Henry. Try and forget all about it.'

'Not so easy.'

'No.'

We seemed to have blundered into a world where the ordinary rules were temporarily suspended. So I said, 'What do you think really happened to Mr Treevor?'

David rubbed his forehead. 'God knows. It simply doesn't make sense.'

Our eyes met. I felt sick. It was as if we were all in a lift going down a shaft, and the cables had snapped and we were falling, and all we could do was pretend we were calm and wait for the crash at the bottom.

David let me out of the back door into the High Street. The car was parked in the marketplace. I drove down River Hill and cut through Bridge Street to the station. I was a few minutes late and when I got there I found Mrs Byfield asking a porter to be more careful with her suitcases while Henry was pretending to be absorbed in a poster advertising the Norfolk Broads.

Henry pecked my cheek. 'I'm so sorry. How are David and Janet?'

'I'll tell you later.'

'There were journalists on the train.'

I smiled at Granny Byfield. To look at her was to get an impression of what David would look like when he was old. I introduced myself, and then Henry. She had met us at David and Janet's wedding but we had not lingered in her memory. I drove them back to the Dark Hostelry. Henry tried to make conversation – he'd have tried to talk to a Trappist monk – but Mrs Byfield kept him in his place with monosyllabic replies and the occasional glare.

We parked in the marketplace. Mrs Byfield gazed out of the window while she waited for Henry to fetch the suitcases from the boot and me to open the door for her. Her hip was painful and I had to help her out.

'I'm sure I've seen that woman before,' she said, leaning heavily on my arm. 'Do you know her?'

I was just in time to see a small woman wearing a dark-blue headscarf going into the Sacristan's Gate.

'No, I don't think so.'

'I never forget a face,' announced Mrs Byfield. 'I probably met her when I've stayed here before.'

'Damn,' I murmured.

'I *beg* your pardon.'

Jim Filey was leaning on the back doorbell of the Dark Hostelry. There was another man with him, a camera and flash slung round his neck.

Henry followed my gaze. 'Trouble?'

'What is it?' demanded Mrs Byfield.

'There's a journalist and a photographer outside the house.'

At that moment the door opened and I glimpsed David's face. The flash went off.

'Intolerable,' Mrs Byfield said. 'It shouldn't be allowed.' She limped down the pavement towards the Dark Hostelry, with Henry and me trailing behind her. She tapped Filey on the arm with her stick. 'Excuse me, young man. You're blocking our way.'

Filey swung round. So did the photographer, raising his camera. There was another flash.

'Come in, Mother,' David said. 'These gentlemen are just leaving.'

'Mrs Byfield?' Filey said, his Adam's apple bobbing in excitement. 'I wonder if you'd care to comment on the tragic death of your daughter-in-law's father. Was he someone you knew well?'

'I don't want to talk to you, young man. I shall complain to your editor.'

Filey jotted something down in his notebook. 'Have you come down to stay with your son and his family, Mrs Byfield?'

She compressed her lips as if to stop the words falling out. David took her arm and drew her gently into the house. I followed, with Henry dragging the cases behind me. David shut the door and put the bolts across.

'Well!' Mrs Byfield said. 'This is a fine welcome, I must say.'

'It's getting worse.' David kissed his mother's cheek.

'Worse?'

'They were peering through the kitchen window just before you came.'

'But when all's said and done, it's none of their business.'

'That's not how they see it, Mother.' He hesitated and then went on, 'It seems that there's a possibility that Janet's father didn't commit suicide after all.'

She frowned. 'Some kind of accident?'

'The police think not.'

'But that's ridiculous.' She was nobody's fool and saw where this was leading. 'Then someone broke in. A thief.'

'Perhaps. Janet's father did say he'd seen a strange man in the house, but we rather dismissed that. As you know, he hadn't been himself in the last few months.'

'I'd like to sit down now.' She looked tired and old.

'Come up to the drawing room. Let me take your coat.'

'Where's Janet?'

'Resting in bed.'

Granny Byfield grunted as she moved towards the door to the stairs, either because of the pain from her hip or because she disapproved of Janet's resting in bed.

David looked at Henry and me. 'I'm sorry about this. Why don't you two go to lunch?'

276

'Isn't there something I should do here?' I said. 'Your mother will need some lunch as well.'

'Just go,' David said wearily. 'Please. I'll need to talk to her, and it'll be easier if there's no one else around.' He glanced at his mother, who had begun the long haul up the stairs, and turned back to us. 'I'm sorry to sound so unwelcoming.'

I don't know why, but I put my hand on his shoulder and kissed his cheek.

41

A few minutes later Henry and I slipped into the High Street and walked down to the Crossed Keys. I thought the lobby of the hotel smelled faintly of Turkish tobacco, but no one I recognized was there or in the bar.

The big, panelled dining room was almost empty. We ate tinned tomato soup, a steak-and-kidney pie with far too much kidney, and a partially cooked bread-and-butter pudding. Not that it mattered. Neither of us had much appetite. We had a couple of gins beforehand and shared a bottle of claret with the meal.

While we ate, or rather for most of the time failed to eat, I told Henry what had happened. It wasn't until the pie arrived that I realized something that should have struck me at the station. I laid down my fork.

'You *knew*,' I said. 'You knew about Mr Treevor.'

'There was something in the *Telegraph* this morning. Not much – police are investigating the death of a sixty-nine-year-old man in the Cathedral Close at Rosington. That sort of thing. They didn't mention him by name but they made it clear he was a resident. So I was half expecting it. And then I asked the ticket collector at the station, and he confirmed it.'

'Filey.'

'Who?'

'He's a reporter on the local paper. He was the one asking the questions when we arrived at the Dark Hostelry. I bet he sold the story to the *Telegraph*.'

'How's Janet taking it?'

'Not very well. It's come on top of David losing his job, and the miscarriage. It would be bad enough if he had just died. But to have it happen like this . . . David's been good. I think they've learned who their friends are.' I thought of the dean's wife. 'And sometimes they're not who you'd expect.'

We sat in silence for a moment. There had been a party of rowdy men, perhaps journalists, in the bar, but the only other person in the dining room was a well-dressed woman sitting twenty feet away with her back to us and staring out of the window into the street. I thought she might be the woman that Mrs Byfield had recognized in the High Street, but I wasn't sure.

Henry broke the silence. 'No sign of Munro?'

'It seems rather unimportant now, whatever he and Martlesham are up to.'

Henry glanced across the table at me. 'After what happened to Janet's father?'

I nodded.

'I suppose they are unconnected.'

'They must be.' I pushed aside the small mountain of bread-and-butter pudding. 'Martlesham hadn't got anything to do with Mr Treevor. They probably didn't even know of each other's existence.'

Henry shook his head. 'Not necessarily. When Munro came to Rosington, he might have been finding out about the Dark Hostelry as well as about Youlgreave. So Martlesham could have known about Mr Treevor. I bet it was an open secret in the Close that he was going senile. And Munro would have told Martlesham.'

I thought about the stroke-blighted man we had met. 'Martlesham was hardly in a position to nip down to Rosington and cut somebody's throat, even if he had a motive for doing it.'

'No. I agree.' Henry threw down his napkin and reached for his cigarettes. 'Nothing quite fits. I wish you'd come away with me. *Now.* Not go back to that bloody house. I don't like thinking of you there.'

'I've got to stay. They need me.' I gave him a weak smile. 'Besides, Granny Byfield will fight off any intruders.'

'But this could go on for ever.'

'Nonsense.' I glanced at my watch. 'Listen, we can't stay too long. I've got to collect Rosie from school.'

'I'll come with you.'

'There's really no need. I'll take the car.'

'I'd like to come. And I'm going to book myself into a room here.' He flapped a hand at the smoke between us. 'Have you paid that cheque in yet?'

I shook my head.

'Then that's something else I can do, isn't it? You see – I can make myself useful.'

'Henry –'

'Wendy.'

We looked at each other across the table.

'Yes?'

'I wish,' he said, and stopped.

'I do too.' For an instant I laid my hand on top of his and watched the expression of shock leap into his eyes. I moved the hand away. 'I don't think I want any coffee.'

'What about a small brandy?'

'Not for me.'

When we got back to the Dark Hostelry, we found Janet crying on the sofa, David looking harassed in the hall, and Granny Byfield standing in the doorway between them, explaining what she was going to do. She glanced at us as we came up the stairs from the kitchen.

'I'm sure Mr and Mrs Appleyard will agree with me.'

'Agree with what?'

'That the Dark Hostelry is no place for a child at present.'

'I take your point, Mother,' David said. 'But the question is whether Rosie would find it more upsetting to go back with you than to stay here.'

'I'm surprised at you,' she fired back.

'Take her,' Janet said.

David slipped past his mother into the drawing room. 'Darling, are you sure?'

Janet blew her nose. 'Your mother's right. Especially *now.*'

Now that the police were treating Mr Treevor's death as suspicious.

280

Granny Byfield wheeled on Henry and me. 'The sooner the better, don't you agree? I wonder if one of you would be kind enough to drive us to the station. I'll get ready to leave while you pick Rosie up from school. There's a train back to town at ten to four.'

'I'm coming as well,' Janet said.

'Where?' Granny Byfield asked.

'To the station, of course.'

The old woman nodded. 'But you won't come up to town with us?'

'No,' Janet said.

Janet and I went upstairs to pack a suitcase for Rosie.

'Are you sure this is sensible?' I murmured.

'She's right. I don't like to have to admit it but she is.'

'They needn't go by train. If you want I could drive them, and you could come too.'

Janet thought about it for a moment and then shook her head. 'It would only prolong the agony.'

'Where exactly does she live?'

'She's got a flat in Chertsey. It's quite large, and very nice.'

I knew her well enough to understand what she wasn't saying. 'But no place for a child?'

'As Granny Byfield has said herself. More than once. But at least she'll be away from all this. No, don't pack Angel. Rosie will need her on the train.'

I carried the suitcase down to the kitchen. Janet launched into a desperate conversation with Granny Byfield about Rosie's likes and dislikes. Semolina would make her sick, and she wasn't very fond of porridge. Could she have the landing light on when she went to sleep? She usually had a glass of orange squash in the middle of the morning and the middle of the afternoon.

'We'll see,' Granny Byfield said. 'I don't approve of cosseting children.'

Henry and I slipped out to fetch the car.

'Poor Rosie,' Henry said as we walked up the High Street. 'I'd pay quite a lot of money to avoid a few days alone with Granny B.'

281

'She's a tough little kid.'

'She'll need to be.' He touched my arm. 'Funny how they vary – kids, I mean. I wonder what a child of ours would be like.'

'I wonder.' I stopped by the car and unlocked the driver's door. 'By the way, aren't you going to have to buy a toothbrush and so on if you're staying the night?'

Henry accepted the diversion and we moved on to safer subjects. We drove down to St Tumwulf's and collected Rosie. She was shy at first with Henry but willing to flirt with him – she always preferred men to women. Then I told her that Granny Byfield had come to take her on a little holiday. Her face froze for a moment as though briefly paralysed.

'Can Angel come?' she said at last.

'Oh, yes.'

I drove round to the High Street door of the Dark Hostelry. There were no journalists, which was just as well. Granny Byfield was not in a mood for compromise, she would probably have attacked them with her umbrella. Janet and I loaded her into the car while David put the suitcases in the boot.

David said, 'Wendy, if you don't mind, I'll take them down to the station.'

'Is this wise?' his mother said through the open window of the car. 'Having both Mummy and Daddy there might give Rosie a bit of a swollen head.'

'I don't think so,' David said.

He started the engine. His mother was beside him in the front. Rosie sat in the back holding Angel, both in pink to make the boys wink.

We're sisters now.

As the car drew away from the pavement, Janet glanced up at me, her face unsmiling. No wave, no words, just an expression that said, *Now I have lost two children.*

Henry and I went back to the Dark Hostelry. As I was unlocking the back door, Henry brushed my arm.

'Look. There he is. I'm sure it's him.'

I swung round. A large black car had just passed us, moving slowly up the High Street towards the marketplace. I glimpsed the profile of a man sitting in the front passenger seat. The driver was very small and his head was turned away from us, towards the passenger. It was impossible to see clearly because of the reflections in the glass.

'Munro?' I said.

'I think so.'

'Who's driving?'

'It looked like that woman. The one who was having lunch in the Crossed Keys.'

'Perhaps she works for Martlesham too.'

The car turned left and vanished round the corner.

'Hell of a car,' Henry went on. 'A Bentley. He must be simply rolling. Do you think Martlesham could have been in the back?'

'I don't think anyone was.'

He looked at his watch. 'I need to draw some cash. We've just got time before the bank closes.'

'Do you still have an arrangement here?'

He shook his head. 'But I can give you a cheque made out to you and you can draw the money out of your account.'

'All right.' I patted my handbag. 'I've got a cheque book.'

We walked down the High Street to Barclays Bank. It was a dark, gloomy building both inside and out. Henry and I sat facing each other at one of the tables in the banking hall and wrote our cheques. I reached for a paying-in slip.

'Wouldn't this be a wonderful opportunity to pay in that cheque for ten thousand?' he suggested.

'I've not made up my mind about that yet.'

'Then pay it into your account and make up your mind afterwards.'

'Don't try and bully me.'

'After all, your handbag might be stolen.' He slid the new cheque across the blotter to me. 'And there's the other one.'

I don't know what I would have done if we hadn't had the interruption. I'd been dimly aware of a tall man in a dark suit standing at the counter with his back to us. At that moment, he turned around, sliding a wallet into the inside pocket of his jacket. It was the dean. Mr Forbury saw me at the same time that I saw him.

'Good afternoon, Mrs Appleyard.' He nodded in a stately way.

Henry pushed back his chair and stood up, his hand outstretched. 'Good afternoon, Mr Forbury.'

As chairman of the Choir School governors, the dean had had a good deal to do with Henry's resignation. But Henry wasn't the sort of person to bear a grudge. He wouldn't have wanted this meeting, but now it had happened he was going to make the best of it.

'Good afternoon.' If the dean's face had been a pool of water, you'd have said it had frozen over. 'Goodbye, Mrs Appleyard.'

He ignored Henry's hand and stalked out of the bank. I noticed that the tips of Mr Forbury's ears were pink.

'Horrible man,' I said.

Henry shrugged. 'It had to happen sooner or later.'

He spoke lightly but I wasn't fooled. Henry liked people to like him. It was his little weakness. The episode with the Hairy Widow hadn't just been about money.

'The bank's going to close in a moment,' I said. 'We'd better get a move on.'

He was always quick to seize an advantage. 'You'll pay in both cheques, won't you?'

I scribbled the long row of noughts on the paying-in slip. Just because of the dean.

'Good girl,' Henry said.

I stood up. 'Don't push your luck.'

We were the last customers to leave the bank. I stood in the doorway searching for my keys in my handbag and listening to the heavy doors closing behind us and the soft metallic sounds of turning locks.

'Excluded from paradise,' Henry said. 'Again.'

'We'll have to go back through the Close. I haven't got my back-door key.'

The Boneyard Gate was only a few yards from the bank. As we went through the archway, the full length of the Cathedral was in front of us, stretching east and west like a great grey curtain.

Henry said, 'It will get worse, you know. Much worse.'

'That business with Mr Treevor?'

He nodded. 'You don't have to stay here.'

'I do.'

We walked a few yards in silence. Our squat shadows slithered along the path in front of us. The sun was in the south-west and another shadow lay beside the nave of the Cathedral like a canal of black water.

Henry glanced at me and smiled. 'By the way, now David's mother's gone, there must be a spare room at the Dark Hostelry. Do you think Janet might let me ask myself to stay?'

I smiled back. 'Nothing to do with me.'

At that moment Mr Gotobed shepherded a group of tourists out of the north door. They broke away from him and scuttled down the path round the east end, towards the cloisters and the Porta. I raised a hand in greeting.

'Do you mind if I have a word with him?'

'With Gotobed? Why?'

'His mother's ill. I'd like to know how she is.'

'It's hard to believe you've actually met the mother.'

'Why?'

'It's rather like someone claiming they've met a leprechaun. No one ever sees her, you see, not close up. The boys used to claim she died years ago, and that Gotobed –'

'She certainly wasn't dead when I had tea with her.' I opened my bag. 'Look – here are the keys. Why not make yourself useful and put the kettle on?'

I veered across the close-cropped grass towards Mr Gotobed, who was still standing at the north door. Henry had irritated me. I liked the Gotobeds. They weren't there to be laughed at.

As I drew near, Mr Gotobed bobbed his head as though I were the dean and he had come to conduct me from the vestry to my stall.

'How's your mother?'

'As well as can be expected, thank you. She's had these turns before but this one's worse.'

'She's still at home?'

'Won't go to hospital. Put her foot down. Doctor says it's best to let her be. But people come in to help.'

285

Mr Gotobed was very pale, his skin dry and flaking. There were more lines than ever before. He blinked often, the sandy eyelashes fluttering like agitated fingers.

'Is there anything I can do?'

'You've got enough on your plate.'

'I'd like to help.'

He looked at me. 'Thank you. It might cheer her up to see you. But perhaps you wouldn't want to –'

'I'll come. When's the best time?'

'Could you manage this evening? About six o'clock?'

I nodded.

'The nurse comes to settle her down about six-thirty. But by six I will have given her tea, and as a rule she's quite perky after that. It's a good time.'

'I'll be there.'

'Don't be surprised at the change. Her mind wanders more. You know?'

'I know,' I said.

We said goodbye. Mr Gotobed went back into the Cathedral and I walked on to the Dark Hostelry. On the way it occurred to me that Mr Gotobed hadn't called me 'Mrs Appleyard' once. He hadn't been nervous, either, or embarrassed. Between them, Mr Treevor and Mrs Gotobed had succeeded in dissolving the formality between us.

I don't know what made me stop at the gate of the Dark Hostelry. Some people claim we have a sixth sense that tells us when we're being stared at, which strikes me as an old wives' tale. Nevertheless, something made me look over my shoulder.

At first sight I thought the green between the Cathedral and the Boneyard Gate was empty. Then a movement near one of the buttresses caught my eye. Someone was standing in the great pool of shadow that ran the length of the Cathedral.

Not standing – walking. The sun was in my eyes. It was as if a drop from the pool of shadow had broken away and taken independent life. The smaller shadow became a man in dark clothes. Around him glowed the brilliant green of the lawn. He was coming towards me, but he must have seen me

286

watching because he swung away towards the Boneyard Gate as if trying to avoid me.

Francis?

Then I blinked. It was Harold Munro, dressed as usual in his drab, old-fashioned clothes. He might be flesh and blood but he had no right to haunt us.

'Hey! You!'

At my shout he stopped. He stared across the lawn. I began to walk, almost run.

'Mr Munro! I'd like a word with you.'

He said nothing, just waited, cigarette in hand. A moment later I was within a yard of him. Because of my heels I was an inch or two taller than him. In my stockinged feet we would have been about the same size. There were flecks of dandruff on his black jacket and his pinstripe trousers needed pressing. He wore a grubby hard collar and a greasy, tightly knotted tie. A silver chain stretched across the front of his black waistcoat. The bald patch the shape of Africa glistened with sweat. The only cool thing about him were his eyes, which were grey and slanting.

'Why are you spying on us?'

'Me, miss?'

Anger bubbled out of me, surprising me as much as it surprised Munro. 'You can go back to Simon Martlesham and tell him we're sick and tired of having you turn up like a bad penny round every corner. And what's more, you can tell him I'll be notifying the police about a suspicious character hanging round the Close and harassing old ladies.'

I paused, partly because I had run out of things to say and partly because I wanted to hear his reaction. But he said nothing. He sucked on his cigarette and stared up at me with his little grey eyes while the sweat ran like tears down his cheeks.

'So you'll tell Martlesham?' I put my hands behind my back because they had clenched into fists. 'I've had enough. We've had enough. Can't you see?'

Munro nodded.

'He's looking for his sister, isn't he? That's what this is all about.'

He bobbed his head again and smiled – not at me but at something he saw in his mind. He flicked the cigarette end into the air. We watched it falling to the ground. Then he slipped away, a black shadow gliding silently across the grass towards the Boneyard Gate.

I sniffed the air like a rabbit scenting danger. I smelled Turkish tobacco.

42

The little sitting room was even more crowded than before because they'd moved a bed into it. A bank of coal glowed in the grate. The windows were closed. The smells of old age were stronger. The body was decaying in advance of death.

Mrs Gotobed's tissue-paper skin covered the bones of her face like a sagging tent. 'Wilfred, go and have your tea,' she said.

'I'm all right.' Mr Gotobed smiled uneasily at me. 'Mother likes to make sure I'm eating properly.'

'That's why you must have your tea. Mrs Appleyard will sit with me.'

'Of course I will.'

Mr Gotobed left the room.

'I don't know what he'll do when I'm gone,' Mrs Gotobed said as soon as the door had closed. 'No more sense than a new-born baby.'

'How are you?'

'Tired. Very tired. Sit by the window where I can see you.'

I sat on a hard chair near the window overlooking the Close. Pursy stared incuriously at me from the window seat. A golden slab of sunshine poured through the opposite window. Dust swam in the air and lay thickly on the horizontal surfaces. I wished I could turn back time for Mrs Gotobed, and for myself, until we reached a golden age when pain had not existed. The lids fluttered over Mrs Gotobed's eyes.

'Still looking for Canon Youlgreave?' she said.

I nodded. 'In a way.'

'He was a good man, a good man.' The eyes were open now to their fullest extent. 'Do you hear what I say? A *good* man.'

What I say three times is true. But why was it so important to her even now, when the life was almost visibly seeping out of her.

'What about the Martlesham children's aunt? What happened to her?'

The old woman's shoulders twitched.

'*You* must have known her.' Urgency made me raise my voice. 'What was she like? What did *she* feel about the children?'

Mrs Gotobed shook her head slowly from side to side. She blew out through loosely closed lips, making a noise like a dying balloon.

'I'm a fool, aren't I?' I said. 'It was you all along. You were the aunt.'

She continued to blow out air. Then she stopped and smiled at me. 'I wondered if you'd ever guess.'

'You didn't want the children. You had a good job, and then you were getting married. Would they have been in the way?'

'I was his queen,' Mrs Gotobed mumbled. 'Last chance for me. But I knew Sammy didn't want the children. Can't say I blamed him. *Her* children, especially.'

'Your sister's?'

'Everyone knew what she'd been like. Better off dead, that one. Bad blood.'

'Canon Youlgreave helped.'

'He was very kind. And there's no denying the money came in handy.'

'Simon went first?'

'Couldn't wait. He left just after his ma died, before me and Sammy got engaged. Nancy lived with me for a bit after that.' She screwed up her face. 'I told you, I had lodgings in Bridge Street. Landlady kept complaining about the children. Couldn't abide the trouble and the mess they made, and the noise, and she wouldn't look after them when I was at work. *I'll thank you to remember I'm not a nursemaid*, that's what she

290

said. Silly woman, with a front tooth missing . . . I can see her now. Wilfred never made much noise. He always was a quiet boy, right from the start.'

'Nancy,' I reminded her, trying to keep her to the point. 'What was *Nancy* like?'

There was a pause. Then Mrs Gotobed said slowly, as though the words were being pulled out like teeth, 'Out for what she could get. Nice as pie with Mr Youlgreave, oh yes, but when she was at home with me it was another matter. Nasty piece of work when all's said and done.'

'When did she leave?'

'Sammy and me were wed in the autumn. October the fourteenth. It was before that.'

'And before Canon Youlgreave left Rosington?'

'I think so. But it can't have been long before. He said he'd give Sammy and me a wedding present, and he did – he sent us some money. But he'd gone by then.'

'Where did he take Nancy?'

'To a lady and a gentleman who were friends of his. No children of their own, he said. They were going to bring her up a lady. Always had the luck of the devil, that one. Trust her to fall on her feet.' The eyelids drooped again. 'Little bitch.' The lids flickered. 'Sorry. It slipped out. Really, I'm sorry.'

'It doesn't matter.'

'No one else knew, apart from Sammy. Not about the money. Not about the children. Sammy thought it was for the best. We said I'd had them adopted by relations in Birmingham. It was for their own good.'

'You never heard from them again?'

'I did from Simon. He sent me a letter from Canada. And I'm sure Mr Youlgreave wouldn't have hurt the kiddies, he was a clergyman. Anyhow, why would he do them any harm?'

There were footsteps on the stairs. Suddenly her face became cunning.

'You won't tell Wilfred? You promise? A Bible promise?'

'Of course I won't tell him,' I said. And the fact that she needed me to say that made it obvious that she must have at least suspected that Nancy was not going to live in a gentleman's house and grow into a fine lady.

The door opened and Wilfred Gotobed edged into the room. 'Are you all right, Mother?'

She was still looking at me. 'When will this end? I've had enough.'

I stood up. 'I hope I haven't tired you.'

The old woman shook her head.

'Does Mother the power of good to see a new face,' Mr Gotobed said. 'Doesn't it, Mother? When you're feeling better, we could get a wheelchair and –'

'Goodbye, dear,' Mrs Gotobed said to me, and turned her head away.

'Goodbye.'

'It was a long way from Swan Alley,' she said as I reached the door. 'You'll remember that, won't you?'

I nodded. Mr Gotobed stumbled towards me but I said I would see myself out.

A moment later I was breathing the sweet, fresh air of the Close. They said there was one law for the rich and one for the poor. Perhaps rich and poor had different moralities as well.

Now I knew or could guess what had happened in 1904. Perhaps Francis had buried what was left of the body in one of the gardens of the Close. Or put it in a weighted sack and dropped it in the river like a litter of unwanted kittens. No one had wanted to know what he had done, not to Nancy Martlesham, because she wasn't the sort of little girl who belonged in the Close or anywhere else.

I felt no sense of achievement. It wasn't just that I liked old Mrs Gotobed and I did not like what I'd heard of Nancy Martlesham. There was another problem. Something niggled. Something didn't make sense. And I didn't think I would ever see Mrs Gotobed again, and so I would never find out what it was.

43

It was as if they sensed blood. During that long evening, the reporters seemed to be everywhere. Two of them tried to talk to me on my way back to the Dark Hostelry. As I unlocked the garden gate, the photographer raised his camera. While Henry and I were making supper, they rang the back-door bell seven times. Until I drew the kitchen curtains, they crouched down on the pavement of the High Street and peered through the window.

We ate on trays upstairs in the drawing room. None of us said very much, Janet least of all. Her pale, perfect face gave nothing away. At one point David and Henry tried to have a conversation about cricket. I wanted to kick both of them.

Halfway through the meal the phone rang. Henry went to answer it. He'd started answering the phone after David swore at one of the reporters. Janet wouldn't let us take the phone off the hook because Granny Byfield or Rosie might try to get in touch.

This time it wasn't one of the journalists, it was the dean. David went to talk to him and came back looking even angrier than before.

'He suggests we ask the police if we can move out for a while. He feels we'd be happier. And that this sort of attention is bad for the atmosphere of the Close.'

'It mightn't be a bad idea.' I looked from Janet to David. 'You won't get any peace here, not for a day or two. You could take the car.'

'Wouldn't it cost a lot of money?' Janet said vaguely, as if she was thinking of something completely different.

'Blow the money,' Henry said.

David put down his tray on the carpet and picked up his cigarettes. 'Perhaps we *should* go away. It's like living in a goldfish bowl.'

'You must let me know if I can help,' Henry said to David, in the awkward voice he used when he wanted to do someone a good turn.

'We'll manage, thanks.'

Janet stood up suddenly, knocking over an empty glass. 'You all seem to have made up your minds about what we're doing. I'd better go and think about what needs to be packed.'

She closed the door behind her and we listened to her feet on the stairs.

David cleared his throat. 'Yes, no time like the present.'

He and Henry continued to talk about cricket. When it comes to burying heads in the sand, a man can out-perform an ostrich any day. I found Janet in Rosie's room. She was sitting on the bed, her hands clasped together on her lap, staring out of the window. I sat beside her and the bed creaked. When I put my arm around her she felt as cold and stiff as a waxwork.

'Listen,' I said. 'You know what they say – the darkest hour's before dawn.'

'I thought I'd better see if there was anything of Rosie's we should send on.'

'I thought you were packing for you and David.'

'Rosie's more important.'

'I'm sure she's all right.' I gave Janet's shoulder a little shake. 'Ten to one, you'll find that Granny Byfield's met her match.'

'You're too kind to me. You've always been too kind for me. I'm not worth it.'

'Don't be silly.'

A door closed downstairs. The men's footsteps crossed the hall. They were talking about the last test match in the West Indies.

'Silly to worry, isn't it?' Janet said. 'It doesn't change anything.'

'Would you like a hand with the packing?'

'I don't even know if we're going anywhere yet.'

'I really think you should.'

She turned her head and smiled at me. 'You're right. No point in staying here. But if you don't mind, I think I'll do it tomorrow. I'm feeling rather tired.'

I remembered belatedly that she was still coping with the miscarriage. I persuaded her to have a bath and go to bed. I went downstairs and bullied the men into making themselves useful. Half an hour later I took Janet some cocoa. She was already asleep. On impulse, I bent down and kissed her head. Her hair wasn't as soft as usual. It needed washing.

I went to bed early myself. After a long bath, I got into bed to read. I flicked over the pages of *The Voice of Angels*. The poems were nasty pretentious rubbish, I thought, sadistic and unnecessarily difficult. But as well as all those things, they were also sad. As I picked my way through the verses, I hardly noticed the rest, only the sadness.

I heard footsteps on the stairs, my stairs, the ones to the second floor. There was a tap on the door and I said, 'Come in.'

Henry smiled uncertainly at me from the threshold. He had a bottle of brandy under one arm and was carrying a couple of glasses.

'David's gone to bed. I saw your light was on. I wondered if you'd fancy a nightcap.'

I nodded and moved my legs so he could sit on the end of the bed. He poured the drinks and passed me a glass.

'Cheers.'

I said, 'Not that there's much to be cheery about,' and drank.

'David's in an awful state.'

'Is he? I thought he was concentrating on cricket this evening.'

Henry shrugged. 'It's what he doesn't say. I suggested they go to London. They could see Rosie.'

'That's assuming Inspector Humphries lets them.'

'Do you think . . . ?'

I took another sip. 'I don't know what to think. But if Humphries is right, Janet's father didn't kill himself.'

'It doesn't bear thinking about.'

'Do you know, before he died, Mr Treevor was beginning to think he might be Francis Youlgreave?'

'He was going senile. Wendy?'

I looked at Henry. 'What?'

'I'm sorry. Sorry for everything.'

He patted my leg under the bedclothes. We sat there for a moment, as awkward as teenagers. I thought about my schoolgirl passion for David and decided that even though it hadn't actually come to anything, I didn't have much to be proud about either. And I also thought about the Byfields and Mr Treevor and Francis Youlgreave. There was too much suffering in the world already. I held out my hand.

Henry took it and kissed it. Then our lips were kissing and we both spilt our glasses of brandy.

'Phew,' Henry said, as the bottle rolled off the bed and fell to the rug without breaking. 'And thank God I put the cork in it.'

In the morning, we were still together, naked in that narrow bed, and the brandy bottle was still where it had fallen. It was like that other morning when Janet came into my room to tell me that Mr Treevor was dead. The light had the same pale, colourless quality.

But it was David, not Janet, in the doorway. He was in his pyjamas, unshaven, his hair tousled.

Henry grunted and turned towards the wall. I looked at David and he looked at me.

'It's Janet,' he said. 'This time it's Janet.'

PART III

The Blue Dahlia

44

Time doesn't heal, it just gives you other things to think about.

'How are you feeling?' Henry said, speaking gently so as not to startle me.

'I'm fine, thank you.'

'Are you sure?'

'Darling, I wish you'd stop treating me like a restive horse.'

He had been like this since we had discovered I was pregnant. I'd never seen him so excited, so happy. I was less certain about my own feelings. Over the years I had grown used to not being pregnant. So the possibility that I might be had been unsettling, like a threatened invasion. And the knowledge that I actually was left me breathless with excitement and fear.

'Would it be better if I drove?' Henry asked.

'If you drive I'll be holding on to the seat for the whole journey.' I changed down for a corner and threw a smile at him. 'I feel much more secure if I've got the steering wheel.'

We drove for a moment in silence through the gentle Hampshire countryside. It was September, and the afternoon still had the warmth of summer. I kept the speed down, dawdling along the A31 in our new Ford Consul, because we'd been invited to tea and I didn't want to be early. Granny Byfield liked punctuality in others.

'I wish the old hag wasn't going to be there,' Henry said. 'It'll be bad enough as it is.'

'Not for you, surely. At least you've talked to David on the phone.'

'It's not the same. The sooner he gets another job, the better.'

'And for Rosie.'

I didn't want to see David, and I wanted to see Rosie even less. They would remind me of Janet.

'If it's a girl,' I said, 'I'd like to call her Janet.'

Henry touched my hand on the steering wheel. 'Of course.' He squeezed my fingers for an instant. 'Darling, at least we're making a fresh start now. Everything else is in the past.'

'Yes, Henry,' I said, and added silently to myself, *They're all in the past, Francis, Mr Treevor and Janet, and even your Hairy Widow with those wonderfully frivolous navy-blue shoes.* You can never really go back to what you once were, not unless you grow senile like Mr Treevor. You can never forget what you and others have done.

Granny Byfield's flat in Chertsey was in a small block near the centre of the town. David answered the door. I was shocked at the change in him. He had never been fat, but he had lost a lot of weight in the last few months. Suffering had made him less handsome than he had been, but in a strange way more attractive. He brushed my cheek with cold lips.

'You look fit,' Henry said.

They shook hands awkwardly.

'I managed to do quite a lot of walking up in Yorkshire.' David had spent nearly two months immured in an Anglo-Catholic monastery, a sort of gymnasium for the soul which Canon Hudson had found for him. 'Mother and Rosie are in the sitting room. By the way, she doesn't like one to smoke.'

Granny Byfield and Rosie were sitting at a tea table in the bay window. The room was large for a modern flat, but seemed smaller because it was filled with furniture and ornaments, and because the walls were covered with dark, striped paper like the bars of a cage.

Rosie had Angel in her arms. The doll was in her pink outfit, now rather grubby. Rosie seemed unchanged from that time six or seven months ago when I had first seen her in the garden of the Dark Hostelry. She was wearing a different dress, of course. This one was green with white flecks – I remembered Janet making it for her. But she must have grown a little since then, because the dress was getting small for her.

We shook hands with Granny Byfield, who looked us up and down but did not smile. I bent and kissed the top of Rosie's head.

'Hello, how are you?'

Rosie looked up at me. She said nothing. I hugged her, and it was like hugging a doll, not a person.

'You must answer when you're spoken to, Rosemary,' Granny Byfield said. 'Has the cat got your tongue?'

'Hello, Auntie Wendy,' Rosie said.

'How's Angel?'

'Very well, thank you.'

'Mama!' said Angel, as if in confirmation.

'Now sit down and make yourself comfortable,' Granny Byfield ordered. 'I'll make the tea, and David can bring it in.'

The little tea party went on as it had begun. It would have been a difficult meeting at the best of times. But with Granny Byfield there we had no chance of success whatsoever. She could have blighted a field of potatoes just by looking at it.

I tried to talk to Rosie, but on that occasion I didn't get very far. She answered in monosyllables except when I asked if she was looking forward to going to school.

'No,' she said. 'I want to go home.'

'I expect you and Daddy will soon have a new home, and then you –'

'I want the home we had before.' She stared at the top of the doll's head. 'I want *everything* to be like before.'

We stayed less than an hour. David came downstairs with us, pulling out a packet of cigarettes as we reached the communal front door of the flats. We left Rosie helping her grandmother clear the tea table, a small, blonde slave poised on the verge of mutiny.

Henry accepted a cigarette and produced his lighter. 'Any news about a job?'

David shook his head.

'Is it because of Janet?' I asked.

His face didn't change at the name but I felt as if I'd kicked him. 'I don't think it helps. But really it's simply that the right sort of job hasn't come along yet.'

'A university chaplaincy, perhaps?' Henry suggested. 'You'll want to carry on with your book and so on, I expect.'

'I thought I might go into parish work. I'm helping out here.'

I was surprised but didn't say anything.

'I did a lot of thinking in Yorkshire,' David went on, answering our unspoken questions. 'And praying. I came to the conclusion it was time for a change of direction.'

Henry said, 'Wendy and I thought – well, if you ever want a job in a prep school, you've only got to ask.'

'I don't think I'd be very good at teaching small boys. Or small girls, come to that.'

'But you'll come and stay, won't you?' I said. 'Come now, if you like. And Rosie. There's bags of room.'

'Thank you. I'll bear that in mind.'

He turned away from me as he spoke because gratitude never came easily to David. I glanced up at the window of the flat and saw Rosie looking down at us.

'It would be nice for Rosie, of course,' Henry said. 'And I expect she'd be a civilizing influence on our little barbarians.'

'Is she all right?' I asked. 'She seemed rather quiet.'

'She wants her mother.' David stared at the tip of his cigarette. 'I think she'd like to be four years old again and stay that way for ever. Of course, there's not much for her to do here, and that doesn't help.' He moistened his lips. 'It's not been easy for her. Or for my mother, come to that.'

'Your mother must seem quite – quite formidable to a small child,' I said.

'Mother has very firm ideas about children and how they should behave.' He glanced at me, and I thought I saw desperation in his face. 'She thinks Rosie's very babyish, for example. So she tries to encourage her to be more grown up. Once she took that doll away from her, and there was a terrific fuss.'

'Rosie told me she wanted to go back home.'

'She still finds it hard to accept what's happened.'

'To accept that it can't be changed?' I thought of the Hairy Widow. 'To know that it's something she'll never escape from, for the rest of her life?'

Henry cleared his throat. 'Poor little kid, eh? Still, time's a great healer.'

David was still looking at me. 'Mother's right, in a way. Rosie *is* being babyish at present. But that's only because on some level she thinks it might somehow cancel out what's happened. You see?'

'Like a sort of magic?'

'Yes. But she can't go on doing that for the rest of her life.'

'What about clothes?' I said.

'What?'

'I couldn't help noticing that dress was rather small for her. Getting some new clothes might help her start making a break with the past.'

'When in doubt, go shopping,' Henry said. 'It's every woman's motto, young and old.'

David rubbed his forehead. 'I don't think Rosie's had anything new since we left Rosington.'

'Then why don't I take her up to town? I'm sure she'd enjoy that – it would take her out of herself, give her something new to think about. We could make a day of it.'

'I couldn't possibly –'

'Why not? I'd enjoy it too. It would be nice if we could do it this week. We'll be pretty busy after that.'

'I must admit it would be very useful. Mother's not as mobile as she was. She doesn't really like shopping. And perhaps you're right – perhaps it would help Rosie come to terms with things.'

'That's settled then.' I took out my diary. 'What about Thursday?'

'Fine, I think. I'll ring to confirm, shall I?' He turned to Henry. 'Are you sure this won't cause problems? When does term start?'

'Next week. I'm as nervous as hell, actually.'

'Teaching's like riding a bicycle,' David said. 'Once learned, never forgotten. Mother's the same with people. Never forgets a face.'

It wasn't the teaching that worried Henry. It was the responsibility.

David looked at me. 'Which reminds me – my mother remembered whom she saw in Rosington.'

I looked at him blankly for a moment, and then nodded as the memories flooded back. I'd just driven Granny Byfield up from the station and she'd seen a woman whose face was familiar going into the Close by the Sacristan's Gate. Henry and I had seen her lunching at the Crossed Keys a few hours earlier. Also, according to Henry, later that afternoon she'd driven up Rosington High Street in a big black car with Harold Munro beside her.

All this on the last day of Janet's life. And at this moment I didn't give a damn who the woman was. The only thing that mattered at present was David, who was trying to mention the day of Janet's death as if it had been any other day. I wished I could hug him as I'd hugged Rosie.

'My mother met her last month at a charity lunch in Richmond. It's Lady Youlgreave.'

'What on earth was she doing in Rosington?' Henry said. 'Did your mother find out?'

'Oh yes. They had quite a chat once they discovered they had something in common. She'd been on a motoring holiday in East Anglia and she stopped for lunch in Rosington. Apparently Francis Youlgreave was her husband's uncle.'

I dared not look at Henry. An idea slipped into my mind, as unwelcome as a thief in the night. If Harold Munro had been in Lady Youlgreave's car, then didn't that suggest that Simon Martlesham wasn't Munro's employer? Didn't it make it much more likely that Martlesham was Munro's quarry?

45

The Old Manor House at Roth smelt to high heaven of old money. Quite a lot of it. I pulled over to the side of the road and we sat and admired the view.

It was a long, low house a few hundred yards away from the Queen's Head, where Henry had stayed. The windows were large and the walls had recently been painted a soft bluey-green that shimmered like water. Between the house and the road was a circular lawn with a raked gravel drive running round it and meeting at the front door. An offshoot of the drive ran down the side of the house to the back. The leaves of the copper beech were changing colour in the garden behind. Outside the front door was a large car, its paintwork like a black mirror.

'Is that the same car?' I asked. 'It looks as if it might be.'

Henry grunted. He was grumpy because he hadn't wanted to come. 'It's a black R Type Bentley Continental, and so was the one we saw in the High Street. You don't see many of them around.'

I took the keys from the Ford's ignition and felt for the door handle. 'OK. Let's go and see if the owner's at home.'

'Wendy – can't we leave it?'

I turned to face him. 'I'd like to know what she was up to. And why.'

'She was curious about her uncle. What's so strange about that?'

'If she's only a Youlgreave by marriage, then he wasn't her uncle.'

'That's hair-splitting. You know what I mean. You don't think perhaps that because you're pregnant, you're –'

'Making too much of things? All right, tell me why she was being so mysterious about it? She could have come to Rosington and asked all those things herself. Instead she hired that nasty little man. If it's nothing more than simple family curiosity, it just doesn't make sense.'

Henry shrugged. I knew what he was thinking – that I was behaving no less oddly than Lady Youlgreave. I knew I could never begin to tell him the muddled reasons why Francis was so important to me, and why he would never quite be able to understand me even if I tried. The answers were tied up with him, as well, and with the Hairy Widow and David Byfield and above all with Janet. I'd failed with Janet. I didn't want to fail with this.

'Wendy –'

I didn't wait to hear what he had to say. I pushed open the door and swung my legs out of the car. A moment later I was walking down the drive towards the front door. Behind me I heard the slam of Henry's door and his footsteps hurrying after me. I rang the doorbell. The front of the house was in shadow and the air on my bare forearms was suddenly cool. Henry came up beside me. When I glanced at him he grinned.

'Just be polite, darling,' he murmured. 'That's all I ask.'

I rang the doorbell again. 'If she's in.'

'Remember – she might have grandsons who could come to Veedon Hall.'

There was a pattering on the gravel behind us, and suddenly Henry was dancing up and down while something brown and hostile snapped at his ankles.

'Beast!' said a voice behind us.

Henry swore in a way unlikely to impress the average grandmother. I kicked the dog in the ribs.

'Beast! Come here!'

The dog, a dachshund, reluctantly abandoned Henry and sidled back to its mistress by a roundabout route. For the first time I got a good look at Lady Youlgreave. She was a small, stooping woman with dark dyed hair. Her face was lined like a monkey's and in no way beautiful, but expertly and expensively made up. She was wearing well-cut slacks and a silk blouse. Once upon a time, men had probably found her attractive. I thought she could have been any age between fifty-five and seventy-five.

A large Alsatian strained at the leash held in her right hand. Pulled by the dog, Lady Youlgreave moved towards us in a series of darting movements like a bird's. The dachshund kept between us and his mistress, ready to intervene again if things grew nasty.

'And what can I do for you?'

The voice had the calm assurance of someone who has always had money, who has always told other people what to do. There was no warmth in it, no friendliness.

'I'm Wendy Appleyard,' I said. 'This is my husband, Henry.'

I watched the name register on her face. It was like watching someone respond to a mild electric shock. The Alsatian sniffed the toe of my shoe, the one that had kicked the dachshund.

'Is this Beauty?' I asked.

Lady Youlgreave nodded and waved the dog away from me with a hand whose fingernails were thickly encrusted with purple varnish.

'Are we right in thinking you're Lady Youlgreave?'

She nodded, looking faintly surprised I'd had to ask. Then she waited, leaving me to say why we were here.

'You know Mrs Byfield, I understand?'

'Slightly, yes.'

'We've just been having tea with her and her son and granddaughter.'

She stared up at me with large, dark-brown eyes like muddy ponds. 'It was a sad business at Rosington,' she announced.

'Yes, it was.'

'I think Mrs Byfield mentioned you were living in the house at the time?'

'I think you already knew that. Harold Munro would have told you.'

For an instant the monkey face was blank. Then the wrinkles rearranged themselves into an expression that could have been a grimace or a grin. 'I want to take the weight off my feet. Let's sit in the garden, shall we?'

She led us down the side of the house to a formal rose garden. We passed under an archway of greenery and on to a large square lawn bisected by a stone-flagged path. Round the enclosure ran an old brick wall lined with trees and shrubs. Beyond the wall were the roofs of a sea of box-like houses. The garden was a green island, embattled and existing on sufferance, like Rosington surrounded by the Fens, and the Close surrounded by Rosington.

Lady Youlgreave made a beeline for a cluster of garden furniture – four wicker armchairs with cushioned seats and a table with splayed bamboo legs. She perched in the largest chair, which had a tall back like a throne, and waved at us to sit down as well.

'I can only spare a few minutes.'

'Then I'll keep this brief,' I said. 'Munro was working for you.'

Her shoulders lifted. 'Was he?'

'Would you mind telling us what you wanted him to do?'

'I don't think it's any business of yours, Mrs Appleyard.'

'I don't agree. You see, he was watching me some of the time. That makes it my business. He tried to talk to all sorts of people in Rosington. Did you know he almost frightened one old lady to death?'

The dogs had settled down on the grass by Lady Youlgreave's feet. But something in my tone made them both raise their heads. She scratched the Alsatian between its ears and then examined her hands, which wore more rings than I'd ever owned in my life.

'I hired Mr Munro to make some enquiries on my behalf about one of my husband's relations.' She looked up at me. 'That's the long and the short of it. By the way, what was the name of the old lady you mentioned?'

'Mrs Gotobed.'

There was no mistaking the pleasure in Lady Youlgreave's face. 'But she recovered?'

'For a short time. She died a few weeks later.'

Henry drew in his breath sharply. 'Of course, my wife isn't actually implying that Mr Munro caused Mrs Gotobed's death. Just that –'

'He certainly gave her a bad fright,' I said. 'I saw her just after it had happened. She thought Munro was trying to break in.'

Lady Youlgreave nodded, not committing herself.

'He traced Simon Martlesham,' I went on. 'Why would you want him to do that?'

'To trace Martlesham? Because as a boy he'd known Francis Youlgreave.'

'I think what really interested you was why Francis Youlgreave left Rosington. There was a scandal, wasn't there?'

'That's common knowledge.' She raised plucked eyebrows, black as ink. 'Women priests – I wonder where he got that one from. I don't think he even liked women very much. Frightened of them, probably. A lot of men of that generation were. But there's no great secret about that, Mrs Appleyard. Mr Munro even found me a report in *The Times*.'

'He also ripped out everything about it from the backfile of the *Rosington Observer*. Straightforward theft, was it, or was he trying to muddy the trail for anyone who came after him?'

'Mr Munro did have a tendency to cut corners, I give you that.'

'Did?'

'I'm no longer employing him. He finished the job I wanted him to do.'

'But your uncle was involved in another scandal, Lady Youlgreave, and this one wasn't ecclesiastical. I think they just used that sermon about women priests as an excuse to get rid of him.'

'How very melodramatic.'

'It was to do with Simon Martlesham and his family.'

She leant forward, and her fingers stopped scratching the Alsatian's scalp. 'Go on.'

'Mrs Gotobed was Simon Martlesham's aunt. The Martleshams were very poor. They came from a part of Rosington called

Swan Alley, a slum by the river – it no longer exists. Simon cleaned the boots in the Bishop's Palace. And he had a little sister called Nancy. But you know all this, don't you?'

'I know a lot of things, Mrs Appleyard.'

'Then the mother died, and the children became the responsibility of their aunt. She was working in a haberdasher's shop then – she hadn't married Mr Gotobed. The children were a burden to the aunt, partly because she wanted to get married. Mr Gotobed was the head verger, and he had a house in the Close. He didn't like the idea of children who came from Swan Alley. Perhaps he wanted his own children. Is this making sense to you?'

Lady Youlgreave nodded in a way that suggested she didn't much care whether it made sense or not. Henry stirred in the chair beside me and the wicker creaked.

'Luckily a solution was at hand,' I went on. 'Canon Youlgreave knew the Martlesham children. Simon had helped him when he fell over in the Close. And Canon Youlgreave had taken an interest in the boy, given him books to read and so on. And he'd done the same for Nancy, the sister, as well. I expect all that increased his reputation for eccentricity.'

'I don't want to hurry you, Mrs Appleyard, but I do have another engagement.'

I nodded. 'This won't take long. Mrs Gotobed said that people in the Close thought he was being over-friendly with children from Swan Alley. Anyway, he came to the rescue as far as the Martleshams were concerned. He paid for Simon to emigrate to Canada, and learn a trade there. But this is where it gets confusing. When I first talked to Simon, he said that Francis Youlgreave had also paid for Nancy to emigrate with him. But then we found a photograph that proved that Nancy had stayed in Rosington. So Simon changed the story. He said Canon Youlgreave had arranged for Nancy to be adopted by wealthy friends. But as far as I can see, there's no evidence that he actually did that. After the summer of 1904, Nancy Martlesham simply vanished.'

Henry wriggled and cleared his throat. 'Nothing necessarily sinister in that, of course.'

'Do go on,' drawled Lady Youlgreave. 'It's so interesting to have another perspective on Uncle Francis.'

'I've talked to people who knew him,' I said. 'I've read his poetry. Did Mr Munro tell you that he was in the habit of cutting up animals? Or did you know that already from something you'd found here?'

I paused. But she said nothing. She stared at me with those opaque brown eyes.

'I think he believed that eating a child might make him stay young.'

Lady Youlgreave hooted briefly with laughter, a surprisingly loud sound in that quiet garden. 'Uncle Francis was eccentric, I grant you that. It's common knowledge. Unbalanced, even. Did you know he was addicted to opium? But I doubt if he had the strength to kill a fly. Just think about it, Mrs Appleyard. Think about the practicalities of killing something, even a cat.'

'How did you know there was a cat?' I asked sharply.

She dismissed the question with a wave of her hand. 'Munro turned up something.'

'So he *was* strong enough.'

'More likely the animal was already dead.'

'He was strong enough to kill himself, by all accounts.'

She glanced pointedly at her watch. 'Aren't we getting rather hypothetical, Mrs Appleyard?'

'You're interested in the Martleshams as much as Francis Youlgreave. I think you were trying to trace them. And in particular you were looking for Nancy. Because something you'd found or heard made you think that Francis had killed her.'

This time Lady Youlgreave laughed properly. It was one of those well-bred laughs that don't express mirth. When she'd had enough, she sat up in her chair and smiled at me. It unsettled me, that smile, because it didn't belong on this face at this time. I could have sworn it was a smile of relief.

'How imaginative you are, Mrs Appleyard. But I'm afraid I have to disappoint you. I've never for a moment thought that Uncle Francis killed her. And for a very good reason. I'm Nancy Martlesham.'

46

Veedon Hall was a place with aspirations, a tall, ugly house built by a nineteenth-century manufacturer of corsets. It had a large garden which the school prospectus referred to as the Park, a pond known as the Lake and a ditch called the Ha-Ha. One of the bedrooms was said to be haunted by the ghost of an aristocratic girl abandoned by her lover.

The reality was kinder than the aspirations and almost cosily suburban, despite the fact we were in the depths of rural Hampshire. The rooms were large, airy and well-lit. Generations of small boys had humanized the place. I liked Veedon Hall very much, which was just as well because I now owned twenty per cent of it.

The previous owners, the Cuthbertsons, had invited us to stay the week after Janet's death. When Henry told me, I assumed there had been an element of calculation in the invitation, that they wanted to safeguard the sale they had agreed with Henry. It's always easier to believe the worst about human nature than the best. But when I met them, I soon realized they simply wanted to help.

Henry and I had spent much of the summer term at Veedon Hall, gradually growing used to the place and to each other. I was surprised to discover that as far as the school was concerned I was one of Henry's advantages. His new partner was what we used to call a confirmed bachelor and, as Mrs Cuthbertson told me, the mothers liked to think there was a woman about the place. As for Henry, he slotted into the rhythms of the school as though he'd never been away.

'The boys actually work for him,' Mr Cuthbertson said.

'Lord knows why, but there's not many of us you can say *that* about.'

I was fond of Veedon Hall for what it was and what it could be. Best of all, it wasn't the Close at Rosington. It was another miniature world, but this one was dominated by a hundred and seventeen fairly healthy little savages. The boys had to learn about the subjunctive of *Amo* and simultaneous equations, which fortunately was not my province, but they also had to be fed and watered, looked after when they were ill and comforted when they were sad. One of the junior matrons left suddenly when her mother fell ill and I took on some of her duties.

It made me feel as if I was someone else now, knowing that I was not only pregnant but owned part of the school. Henry had put both our names in the contract. So far I'd enjoyed the school more than the pregnancy. Henry and his partner might be wonderful teachers but neither of them had the slightest idea how to organize the place or control the money. Gradually I began to take over the administration. I had come a long way from 93, Harewood Drive, Bradford, but part of me was still the daughter of a Yorkshire shopkeeper.

So I was busy. During the summer term and afterwards, I didn't have much time to brood or to grieve about Janet. I didn't have much time to think about what had happened. That suited me very well. But I could run away from Rosington for the rest of my life. I could never run away from Janet.

Janet. However busy I was, she was always there in the back of my memory, waiting patiently. I'd kept cuttings about the case in a large manila envelope because I knew sooner or later I would have to read them again.

One of the newspapers carried the headline THE WOMAN WHO DIED FOR LOVE. The *News of the World* said Janet was an Angel of Mercy who had killed to save suffering. She had done the wrong thing for the right reason, and had made herself pay the price. The general verdict was that she was kind-hearted but fatally weak. It was taken for granted that suicide was a coward's way out. I didn't understand that,

313

and still don't. Killing yourself must take more courage than I ever had.

None of the accounts mentioned David's lost job or indeed David's failings as a husband. He and Rosie were confined to the margins of the drama. Janet would have been glad of that. She wasn't vindictive, and she cherished her privacy. At some point before swallowing the rest of her father's sleeping tablets, she wrote three letters and put them under her pillow.

The coroner's letter was read out at the inquest. Janet said she was sorry to be such a trouble to everyone. She'd decided to take an overdose and kill herself because she'd killed her father. She had not been able to bear him going senile, and she knew how desperately unhappy he was, and how much more unhappy he would be when he went to the nursing home. He had begged her to kill him, she wrote. She added that she couldn't stand living with the knowledge of what she had done, and that in any case she was very depressed after losing a baby. The coroner saw the letters to David and me but did not think it necessary to read them out in open court.

I never knew what was in Janet's letter to David. Mine was short and to the point, and more than forty years later I can recite it word for word.

There's nothing anyone can do, even you. The police know I killed Daddy and I think it's only a matter of hours before they arrest me. You've always been a sort of guardian angel to me, but please don't think this is your fault.

This way it's better for everyone, especially David and Rosie. I want so much for them to be free to make a fresh start and they can't do that if I'm here. I know you'll help them if you can. Thank you for everything.

Do you know how much Henry needs you? Give him my love and to you, as always, my special love.

Janet

The coroner was scrupulously fair and even sympathetic.

314

The evidence presented by the police left no doubt that Mr Treevor had been killed. A number of witnesses, including David and myself, had testified that Mr Treevor was very unhappy and had on several occasions asked to be killed. Dr Flaxman had told the court that Mrs Byfield was seriously depressed after losing her baby and that he was worried about her mental health.

Then came the clinching piece of evidence. The police had visited the council dump. A few hours after Mr Treevor's death, early on Tuesday morning, the dustmen had done their round. So detectives painstakingly picked their way through a mound of rubbish until they had found items from the Dark Hostelry.

Inspector Humphries testified that these included envelopes addressed to the Byfields and to me, and an empty Worcestershire sauce bottle with Janet's fingerprints on it. A few inches away they found a damp bundle of newspaper, the *Church Times*, as it happened, containing potato peelings and a quantity of wet rags. Under examination, the rags had proved to be part of a cotton winceyette nightdress, Inspector Humphries said, originally cream-coloured and with a pattern of small pink bows.

Much of the fabric was stained with what forensic tests established was blood identical to Mr Treevor's blood type. The police believed that Janet had tried to wash the nightdress and herself after killing her father, and had then decided to cut up the nightdress with scissors and put it out with the rubbish. On the hem of the nightdress was a laundry label which had been traced back to the Dark Hostelry. David himself confirmed that his wife had owned such a nightdress. Neither he nor the police had been able to find it in the house. He was almost sure that his wife had been wearing it on the evening before her father's death.

So she hadn't put on the pale-blue nylon nightdress to make herself look pretty for David after all. I wished I believed in God so I could at least pray for Janet's soul. I'd failed her, you see, because I was so tied up with my own affairs, with Henry and Francis Youlgreave. I hadn't noticed that my best friend was driving herself into a corner.

The coroner said it was a tragedy, which I suppose it was, and that Janet had loved not wisely but too well. I wondered if there had been hatred mixed up with the love. Nowadays the psychologists would say that Mr Treevor had behaved 'inappropriately' with Rosie on several occasions, perhaps many. Had he also behaved 'inappropriately' with Janet when she was a child? I couldn't imagine her hating anyone enough to kill them. Except of course herself, the person she always hated most of all.

But what about David? I'd seen the way he had looked at Mr Treevor when he had found him in Rosie's bed, heard the tone of his voice. Hatred turned David into someone else. If hatred alone could kill, then Mr Treevor would have died long before he bled to death.

Janet loved David. In a sense she'd lived for him. When I stopped feeling numb, and when I stopped trying to distract myself with the doings of a hundred and seventeen small boys, I started to think again. It was then that it occurred to me that Janet might have done more than live for David. She might have died for him as well.

47

On that Sunday we didn't talk much as we drove back from Roth to Veedon Hall. When we turned into our drive relief dropped over me like an eiderdown. I must have sighed.

'What is it?' Henry said.

'Do you know, this is the first proper home we've ever had?'

'Better late than never.'

After supper we went for a gentle walk in what we had taken to calling the Parklet. Mist was already creeping up the lawn towards the terrace. When I glanced back at Veedon Hall, for once it looked beautiful, a house from a fairy tale.

I slipped my arm into Henry's. 'It's so quiet.'

'Wait till the little hooligans get back. Then we'll know what noise means.'

Because of my pregnancy Henry insisted on strolling at a pace suitable for a funeral procession. He was also smoking his pipe, a messy habit which at least kept away the midges. The pipe was a recent innovation designed to make him look solid and dependable in front of parents. Henry hadn't quite mastered the art so he was practising in private with me.

'After all,' he said, 'you'll soon be a parent.'

There was a stone bench beside what we naturally called the Lakelet, and we sat here for a while, despite the fact the midges were worse near the water. Henry was convinced I needed a rest. It was still light but now the sun had gone the air was rapidly cooling. Ducks sent ripples swirling across the silver water. I thought of the mallards I'd fed with Rosie near the place where Swan Alley had once been, and wondered if Nancy Martlesham had fed their ancestors when she was a child growing up by the river.

'She hasn't any,' Henry was saying. 'That's one consolation.'

I'd missed something. 'Who hasn't? And hasn't any what?'

'Grandsons. Lady Youlgreave's got no children at all. So we don't have to be nice to her on that account.'

'You *asked* her?'

'No, it was when you went to the lavatory. I happened to mention you were pregnant, you see. And she said she was glad she'd never had children because looking after herself was a full-time job as it was.'

'Do you think she's happy?'

Henry shrugged and sent a wavering plume of smoke across the water. I suspect he was trying to blow smoke rings.

I said, '*I* don't think she lets herself think whether she's happy or not.'

Henry sucked on the pipe, which made a gurgling sound. 'I don't see what she's got to complain about. She's obviously not short of a bob or three.'

Lady Youlgreave told us that Uncle Francis had never lived in the Old Manor House. In his day the family's home was Roth Park, a redbrick mansion whose chimneys were visible over the roofs of the newer houses. He died at Roth Park, too, jumping from the sill of his bedroom window to the gravel beneath. In his way he had been very kind to her, Lady Youlgreave said, and she used to call him Uncle Francis.

It wasn't Francis she'd hated. It was the people who had sold her to him. Her mother's sister Aunt Em and her brother Simon Martlesham. She didn't use the word hate, but that's what I thought I saw in her sallow little face as she sat on her white wicker throne in the garden of the Old Manor House.

'Uncle Francis thought he was acting for the best. But it's never nice for a child to be torn away from her family.' Lady Youlgreave smothered a little yawn, as though either we or the subject bored her, possibly both. 'Especially if your mother has just died. At first he sent me to live with a dreadful woman in Hampstead. She'd been a governess to the Youlgreave children when he was a boy. She taught me how to mind my p's and q's. She bought me clothes.' Her lips curled. 'She gave me elocution lessons.'

'How long were you there?'

'A couple of months. It seemed like centuries. But Uncle Francis was being cruel to be kind. He didn't want me to come as too much of a shock to the couple who'd agreed to adopt me. And I didn't. I settled in very well. Father' – she gave the last word a faint ironical inflection – 'was a solicitor in Henley. We had a house by the river. I had my own governess. My father's aunt had married a man named Carter who owned land in Roth. That's how Francis knew him. I rather think Francis had been in some sort of legal trouble and Father helped him out.'

'Why?' I'd said. 'Why this business with Harold Munro?'

'After all these years – is that what you mean? You'll understand when you're my age, Mrs Appleyard. When you're young you've no time to look back. But when you're old there's little else to do. Besides, I wanted to know what had happened to my brother.'

'And your aunt.'

She laughed. 'That was a bonus. I'd assumed she was dead. She must have been over ninety.'

'But all the secrecy –'

'Why should I have made a song and dance about it? Tell me, Mrs Appleyard, if you'd been brought up in Swan Alley, if you'd been bought and sold as a child, would you like the world to know? Of course you wouldn't. That's why I chose a private investigator. A journalist would probably have ferreted out the information more efficiently, but I couldn't have relied on him to be confidential. The only obvious alternative would have been a lawyer. But that would have been much more expensive.' She stared haughtily at us down her nose, which was small and pitted. 'I'm not made of money, you know.'

All the while she was talking, I had the feeling she was laughing at us.

'When I first talked to your brother, he said you'd gone to Canada with him.'

'That's Simon all over. Wouldn't want to put himself in a bad light, the one who'd abandoned his little sister. He always was a dreadfully *smarmy* boy. You should have seen him with Uncle Francis. He'd have said black was white if Uncle Francis wanted him to. At least Aunt Em was quite open about it. She didn't want children wrecking her last chance of marriage, especially not children from Swan Alley with a mother like ours and no father worth mentioning. To hear her talk about Sammy Gotobed, you'd have thought he was the Archbishop of Canterbury.' She twisted her features into a pop-eyed, hollow-cheeked mask and intoned in a deep voice, 'The acme of respectability.'

'You've read the poems, of course?'

Her head dipped. 'Of course. Munro sent me a copy of *The Tongues of Angels* he found in Rosington Library. But there was no point. I already have it.'

'Do you have *The Voice of Angels*?'

'It's the same thing. A privately printed edition of *Tongues*. For some reason he changed the title slightly.'

'He also added another poem.'

She stared without expression across the white table. 'So? Perhaps his publishers wouldn't let him include it in the edition they produced.'

'It's rather an odd poem.'

'You could say that of almost all of them.'

I was the first to drop my eyes. What she said was reasonable by its own lights. It was probably the truth.

Henry murmured that perhaps we had taken up too much of Lady Youlgreave's time. He had been very patient with me. I found that was one of the few advantages of being pregnant. People tended to humour you when you had whims. You were almost expected to behave irrationally.

It was then that I asked to use the lavatory. Lady Youlgreave took me into the house by a side door. Shaky bladder control was one of the many things I didn't like about being pregnant. But I admit I was nosy too. The part of the house I saw was full of battered furniture and paintings in tarnished frames. Nevertheless it smelled of money, just like the car, the sort of money that has been part of your life for so long that you no longer notice it.

As she walked down the hall with me, Lady Youlgreave said, 'I hope you won't mind treating this as confidential, Mrs Appleyard.'

'I suppose so,' I said.

'I'm sure you understand that it's not very pleasant to have one's family secrets displayed in public. As poor Mr Byfield has found out.' She waved towards a door. 'It's in there.'

'Don't think I'm prying – well, I am, I suppose – but how did you come to marry into the family?'

'It's not so very strange. My parents' – once again that ironic inflection – 'used to visit my great-aunt's house here. The Carters. Most of their land is under the Jubilee Reservoir now, and the house too. They had a dance for their daughter's twenty-first and that's where I met my future husband.' She looked at the door of the lavatory, barely trying to conceal her impatience. 'So you see – it's all quite simple.'

The lavatory had rich mahogany woodwork, brass taps and blue-and-white tiles. The pan was raised on a dais and I felt like a queen as I sat there hoping to squeeze out more than the usual two teaspoons'-worth so I wouldn't need a lavatory again before we got home.

But I found it hard to concentrate. I felt uneasy, a sensation that was almost physical, like a mild form of morning sickness. Perhaps I was wrong, and certainly I had only first impressions to go on, but Lady Youlgreave seemed an arrogant, self-sufficient woman with so much money and so few ties that she had no reason to worry about the opinions of others. She had no reason to talk so frankly to a strange woman who turned up with her husband out of the blue on Sunday afternoon.

So why had she answered my questions so frankly?

Another perk of pregnancy was early-morning tea. You need perks when your body has been invaded by a demanding little stranger, your hormones are behaving like disruptive toddlers, and your digestive system is in the throes of a revolution.

Henry was so convinced of my infinite fragility that he

would get up early to make the tea. In the back of both of our minds was the memory of what had happened to Janet and the baby she had thought was a boy.

On Monday morning he put the tray by the bed and kissed me. Being together had become a routine, though not I think one we would ever take for granted. He poured the tea and wandered over to the window, twirling the cord of his dressing gown.

'Lovely morning.' He sat down in the chair by the window and fumbled in his pocket for cigarettes. 'There's a letter for you on the tray.' He paused just long enough to alert me. 'A Rosington postmark.'

I sipped my tea and then picked up the envelope. The handwriting was familiar but I couldn't put a name to it. I slit the envelope with the handle of a spoon, pulled out the letter and glanced at the signature. It was from Peter Hudson.

My dear Wendy

I imagine you're both very busy, on the verge of the new term. I am writing partly so June and I can wish you and Henry the best of luck with your new venture.

The cataloguing of the Cathedral Library has at last been finished! James Heber (a friend of Mrs Forbury's nephew) spent the summer finishing what you so ably began. He has just completed the History Tripos at Cambridge and is going on to do his MA at Durham. He found no more surprises, thank heaven! No decision has yet been made about what we shall do with the books, nor with those in the Theological College Library.

The dean's exhibition in the Chapter House has been a success, you will be glad to hear – so much so that there are plans to expand it and make it permanent. So the dean asked young Heber to have a look at the Rosington Archive in Cambridge University Library to see if there was anything worth including. It's a collection of records and other material, some monastic but most Post-Reformation, relating to the Cathedral and the diocese. It was lodged in the University Library by Canon Youlgreave. Someone catalogued it in a rather perfunctory way in the 1920s, but only in part.

Heber turned up several possible exhibits. He also came across a reference in the Sacrist's Accounts for 1402 to the cost of fuel and other expenses relating to the burning of heretics. There was some debate about who should be ultimately responsible for meeting these expenses – the Abbey felt it was the King's responsibility, not theirs. The interesting point is that those burned were named – two of them came from the village of Mudgley, and one of those was called Isabella. So perhaps that poem of Youlgreave's had some foundation in fact after all. Unfortunately there was no mention of the precise charges.

There's one other thing. I had a letter last week, addressed to me as Cathedral Librarian, from a man named Simon Martlesham. He said he had been trying to get in touch with you at the Dark Hostelry, had found out you had moved, and wondered if I had a forwarding address. He said you knew how to contact him so I've dropped him a line saying that I've passed his request on to you.

We hope to see David and Rosie in October if all goes well. I know you have been in touch too. Remember us to them when you see them.

June sends her affectionate good wishes to you both, as do I,

Peter

I passed the letter to Henry and watched him read it as I finished my tea. I saw the frown shooting up between his eyebrows as he neared the end.

'I think we should call it a day,' he said after he'd finished.

'Call what a day?'

'All this Youlgreave-Martlesham stuff. You're not going to get in touch with Martlesham, are you?'

'I don't know.'

'It's all in the past. You have to put it behind you.'

Some things I would never put behind me, among them Janet and the Hairy Widow. 'I'll see,' I said.

'Let it be,' Henry advised. 'Please.'

'Is there anything more to know?' I peered into my cup, looking for my fortune among the leaves. 'And is there any more tea in the pot?'

48

Three days later, on Thursday, I met David, Rosie and Angel under the clock at Waterloo Station. Henry had offered to come with me, but I persuaded him to stay at school. I didn't want a fractious husband in tow. Henry didn't enjoy buying clothes, even for himself.

'You won't overdo it,' he had said when he drove me to the station. 'Promise.'

'I promise.'

David looked relieved to see me. He had a briefcase under his arm and dark smudges under bloodshot eyes. I wondered whether his God was being much help to him now. Rosie was wearing another dress I recognized, navy-blue needlecord dotted with pale pink horses, with puffed sleeves and a Peter Pan collar. It was the one Janet had given her for her fifth birthday. Someone had plaited her hair rather badly. In one hand she carried Angel. In the other she clutched a miniature handbag made of plastic and intended to look like patent leather.

'Are you sure this won't be too much trouble?' David asked.

'Not at all. I shall enjoy it.'

'You must let me pay for your lunch as well.' He took out a worn wallet. 'And you'll need something for taxis. How much do you think one should budget for the clothes? About ten pounds?'

'There's no need,' I said. 'This is my treat.'

'I can't allow that.'

Rosie stared up at us, her eyes moving from David's face

325

to mine. Her expression was intent, as though the fate of the world rested upon the result of the conversation. The fingers holding the handbag strap whitened. For a moment I said nothing because there was no need for me to say the words aloud.

Let me do this for Janet's sake.

'Where and when would you like to meet?' David asked.

He had capitulated and we both knew it. As soon as we had arranged a rendezvous, he couldn't wait to get away. He was going to have a day of unbridled fun working on his book on Thomas Aquinas in a library. I think he was so relieved to escape from Granny Byfield that he would have enjoyed anything, even shopping for clothes with Rosie and me.

Later, when David had left and Rosie and I were queuing for a taxi, she slipped her hand into mine, which wasn't something she often did voluntarily. She tugged my arm as though pulling a bellrope for service in an old-fashioned hotel.

She turned her perfect face up to mine. 'Auntie Wendy? Do you think I could have a dress with a *belt*?'

'I should think so.'

We went to Oxford Street and spent most of the morning shopping. I spent a small fortune – I was reasonably confident that neither David nor his mother would have an accurate idea of the cost of children's clothes in the West End. Angel was never far from Rosie, and before we bought anything Rosie went through the ritual of asking the doll's opinion.

After Selfridge's, we were both exhausted so we found a restaurant and had lunch.

'It looks as if Angel could do with a few new clothes as well,' I said as we were waiting for our pudding. 'What do you think?'

'Yes, please. Angel would *love* that, wouldn't you?'

'Mama!' squawked the doll, because Rosie had pushed her chest.

I studied Angel. The fabric of her dress had shrunk and in places the pink had run.

'Granny washed her clothes,' Rosie said. 'It didn't do much good.'

'We'll see what we can do.'

She nodded and bestowed a small, prim smile on me. She was a well-brought-up child, and had done this whenever I had offered to buy her something. I would have preferred it if she'd thrown her arms around me and kissed me. Or better still, said she loved me, though in my heart of hearts I knew even then it could only be cupboard love. But Rosie was such a pretty little girl, and my best friend's daughter. I wanted to hear her say she loved me. I wanted to believe it, too, and I still hoped that one day she might mean it.

I realize now that Rosie disliked me. No, it was worse than that, much worse, though it hurts me to admit it. She *hated* me. They'd been a happy little family at the Dark Hostelry until I turned up, or Rosie thought they had. Then I'd taken her mother away from her for ever and ever, and there was nothing anyone could do to bring her back. So here I was, trying to make up for an absence, trying to compete with a ghost.

'We can go to Hamley's after we've finished here,' I said, still playing the game I was doomed to lose. 'Have you been there before?'

She shook her head.

'It's a very big toy shop. I'm sure they'll have something.'

'I want some more angel clothes for her. The dress you made got messed up.'

'That's a pity. But never mind. Perhaps we'll find something better.'

Limpid eyes stared across the table. 'Mummy soaked it in cold water but it was no use.'

Then the waitress arrived with our ice-creams coated with chocolate sauce and decorated with two wafers in the shape of fans. Rosie picked up her spoon and dug it into the ice-cream. I sat there staring across the table at her. I searched my memory, trying to remember what Angel had been wearing, and when. Especially when.

'Rosie, what was on the angel dress? What made it messy?'

She had just put a spoonful of ice-cream in her mouth.

She ate it very slowly, looking at me all the while through her lashes. She was not the sort of child who talked with her mouth full. Finally she dabbed the corners of her mouth with her napkin.

'Mummy said it was a secret.'

A stain you soak in cold water?

'Mummy's not here now,' I said, suddenly ruthless. 'Only you and me.'

Rosie considered this for a moment. 'But Mummy *said*.'

'How would it be if I just made a suggestion? You could nod your head. Or shake it. So you wouldn't be actually *saying* anything.' Another spoonful of ice-cream. Then she swallowed and nodded her head.

I ignored the faint clamour of my conscience, pushed the bowl away and reached for my cigarettes. 'Was it something like – like tomato ketchup?'

Another nod.

'I wonder if it was Grandpa's?'

A third nod.

I shook a cigarette out of the packet. My hand trembled as I put it in my mouth and at first I couldn't make the lighter work. I was conscious of Rosie watching me, of her continuing to eat ice-cream. I felt simultaneously hot and cold and in dire need of a dry martini. I inhaled fiercely, and the smoke scorched my lungs.

'How did it get on the dress?'

She swallowed. 'Angel fell into it. But Mummy said I mustn't tell. Never ever.'

'It's all right.'

'She cut up the dress and put it down the lav.'

'And Grandpa?'

'Grandpa? It's what he *wanted*.'

Her spoon scraped round the bowl, greedy for the last crumb of wafer, the last smear of cream and sauce. What was *implied* was important, not what was said. I remembered Mr Treevor wishing he was dead, the last words I heard him say, and Rosie had heard him too. And afterwards she'd asked me about dying. I'd confirmed that dead people go to heaven, and that heaven was very nice.

'You knew where he kept the knife?'

Rosie nodded. 'It was one of our secrets.' She wriggled in her chair, a flirt's twitch. 'We hid it at the back of the fireplace in his room. He was going to get me some more wings for Angel. Can I have your ice-cream if you don't want it?'

I pushed the bowl across the table to her. 'Mummy found you? Afterwards?'

'She came in just after I'd done it. He moved when I put it in and he knocked Angel out of my hand. Angel was all messy.'

'What did Mummy do?'

'She tried to wake Grandpa but he was asleep. Then she said we'd have to tidy ourselves up.' Suddenly the face crumpled – the beauty vanished and all I could see was a frightened child. 'I wish Mummy was here.'

'So do I, darling.'

At last it made sense. First Janet hoped that the death of her father would be taken as suicide. When that had failed, she valued herself so little that taking the blame on herself seemed the best thing to do from everyone's point of view. Perhaps she'd welcomed the chance. I don't think she wanted to live any more. She must have thought that by killing herself, and by taking the blame for her father's death, she was sparing David something even worse. She was preventing Rosie being labelled as a murderer for the rest of her life.

Later on I found in a bookshop one of those formidable blue Pelican paperbacks that used to march across the shelves in David's study at the Dark Hostelry. This one was about criminal law. As I turned to the chapter about juveniles, my fingers left damp smudges on the pages. The author quoted the precise wording of Section 50 of the Children and Young Persons Act of 1933.

It shall be conclusively presumed that no child under the age of eight years' can be guilty of any offence.

'The presumption,' Mr Giles commented, 'is irrebuttable.'

In other words Rosie could never have been tried because by law she could not commit a crime. So she could not have been labelled as a murderer. Had Janet known that? Even if she had known, would it have mattered? Janet must have wanted to do what was best, or rather least bad, for Rosie and David. If she had told the truth to David and me, to Dr Flaxman and Inspector Humphries, the law would have said Rosie could not commit a crime – but people weren't so scrupulous.

You can never hide from malicious curiosity. Even if the Byfields had changed their names and gone to live in Australia, someone would have found out.

I don't know. Perhaps I'm making it too complicated. Sometimes things are heart-breakingly simple and not at all rational. Perhaps Janet didn't want to live very much. Perhaps she was looking for death and her daughter showed her how to find it.

I said to Rosie, 'Have you told anyone else?'

She shook her head and spooned the last of my ice-cream from the bowl.

'If I were you, Rosie, I wouldn't. Will you promise?'

She touched her mouth with the napkin. 'All right.'

I did it for Janet, I swear. It spared David even more pain, and Granny Byfield and Rosie herself. Would it have helped anyone if I'd told David the truth, if I'd rung up Inspector Humphries and informed him that my best friend had pulled the wool over his eyes and mine? Above all I wonder, would it have saved other lives later?

If I shut my eyes I see Rosie with the knife in one hand and Angel in the other. I see Janet bending over her father and the blood pulsing slowly out of his neck. But you can never know what would have happened if you'd made another choice. I hold on to that.

The waitress was hovering and I asked for the bill.

'Will we ride in a taxi to Hamley's?' Rosie asked.

'It's not very far.' I saw her face fall. 'Would you like to?'

'Yes, *please*.'

The taxi question was a welcome diversion. We had enough parcels to justify the extravagance to myself, and Henry would be pleased because I would be taking his advice and not overdoing it. A short journey meant a small fare. I wanted to give Rosie a treat. It sounds odd that I was thinking of things like that when my world had been shaken so violently to its foundations. But I did. We are odd, all of us. We distract ourselves with details. It's a way of coping.

At Hamley's we struck lucky, or rather Rosie did. We found an assistant who was willing to take the question of dolls' clothing very seriously indeed. After much discussion we bought two outfits for Angel. The first was a short multi-coloured cocktail dress in synthetic taffeta with a wide off-the-shoulder wrapover neckline and a fitted bodice. The skirt was bell-shaped and had a special petticoat to go under it. The outfit included a pair of high-heeled shoes.

'She'll look so lovely at parties,' the assistant said. 'Won't she?'

Rosie pressed Angel's chest. 'Mama,' the doll said.

Fifteen minutes later, we decided on the second outfit. Angel could now dress casually in a sleeveless cream blouse with a low square neckline, and a pair of fitted navy-blue linen shorts. The assistant persuaded us that Angel would be underdressed on holidays without a pair of blue leather mules and a straw hat with a ribbon round the brim.

'After all,' she said, 'you wouldn't want her to wear high-heeled shoes when she's yachting or on the beach. She'd look silly.'

Finally, we managed to find a plain white nightdress which fitted. It was trimmed with lace at the neck and cuffs and perhaps rather low-cut for an angel, but Rosie did not mind.

While the assistant was wrapping our purchases, Rosie wandered round the department examining other dolls, their clothes, their houses and their furniture. She sidled over to me as I was writing the cheque.

'Auntie Wendy?'

'Yes?' I tore out the cheque and looked down at Rosie. Despite everything, I found myself envying her. She was so beautiful, you see, then and later, and so self-contained, which armoured her against suffering.

She towed me over to a display of baby dolls and the equipment which went with them. 'Do angels have babies?'

'No, dear. I don't think they do. They don't bother with that sort of thing.'

'Are you sure?'

'Pretty sure. You can ask Daddy, though.'

'Angels don't have babies,' Rosie said, 'because angels don't *need* babies.'

Her tone of voice made it clear she was advancing this as a possibility rather than stating it as fact.

'I'm sure you're right.' I didn't want to have to buy a baby doll as well, and of course a baby doll would need a pram and a cot and a complete wardrobe. 'But Daddy will know.'

She nodded. 'I don't want to have babies.'

'Why?'

'They're too much trouble. They make too much mess. I expect that's why angels don't have them.'

She slipped away from me and went to smile at the assistant, who was all too ready to be smiled at. I sat down heavily on a chair in front of a counter.

Babies are too much trouble. They make too much mess . . .

Rosie's words went round and round in my mind, speeding up like a merry-go-round, and the faster they went the worse I felt. I remembered something that Simon Martlesham had said and linked it for the first time to one of Mrs Gotobed's remarks, or rather to its implication.

All the dolls on the displays were staring at me, their painted faces masks of horror, their perfect eyebrows arched in shocked surprise like Lady Youlgreave's. I needed someone to say it wasn't true, I'd made a mistake.

'Madam? Madam?'

I looked up at the assistant stooping over me.

'Are you all right, madam?'

'I'm fine, thanks. Just a little faint.'

'It's rather hot in here. They find it so hard to get the temperature right.'

'Let's get a taxi,' Rosie suggested. 'Then you won't have to walk anywhere.'

I breathed deeply. The baby inside me needed air. *Concentrate on the baby. My baby.*

'A taxi?' I said. 'Good idea. But I'd like to make a phone call first.'

'Where are we going?' Rosie asked.

'What would you say to another ice-cream?'

49

I damned the expense and told the taxi driver to wait. Rosie and I went inside the Blue Dahlia Café. The sad-faced woman was behind the counter polishing an already gleaming urn. When she saw Rosie, she brightened as if inside her a candle had burst into flame.

'I've come to see Mr Martlesham,' I said. 'He's expecting me.'

'Just a moment, miss. I see if he's ready.'

'I wonder if you could look after Rosie while I'm talking to him.'

'Oh, yes.' The woman smiled down at Rosie, who smiled back, scenting an easy conquest. 'That's a pretty dolly. What's her name?'

'Angel.'

'What a pretty name. Does Angel like ice-cream?'

Rosie nodded and stared at her feet.

'When Mummy talks to Mr Martlesham, I make you an ice-cream and her an ice-cream. You can help me.'

Rosie said nothing and nor did I, but Angel squawked, 'Mama.' The woman went through the archway and for a moment the multi-coloured strips of nylon ribbon fluttered like a broken rainbow.

Rosie squeezed my hand as if ringing a bell for service. When I looked down, she said, 'Will the lady let me eat Angel's ice-cream?'

'I expect so.'

A moment later the woman came back. 'He see you now.'

'You be good, Rosie. I shan't be long.'

'We make ice-creams,' the woman said. 'Lovely ice-creams for little angels.'

She swept Rosie round the counter, ignoring a customer at the table in the window who was trying to attract her attention.

I went through the archway and tapped on the door to the left. Martlesham told me to come in.

At first sight he was unchanged, as dapper as ever. He sat behind the big desk, the chair angled so I saw only the right side of his face, the side undamaged by the stroke. Today he was wearing a blazer and a loosely knotted cravat. Gold gleamed in the folds of the cravat, the tiepin with the horse's head inlaid with enamel. He extended his hand over the desk to me.

'Forgive me if I don't get up.' He wrenched the words out of himself. 'Not too fit at present.'

'I'm sorry.'

We shook hands. His skin was dry and cold, like a snake's.

'Someone in Rosington passed on my message?'

'Yes.'

'Good of you to come in person, Mrs Appleyard. I thought you might write or phone. Have you come far?'

'Hampshire. My husband and I are living there now.'

Everything about Simon Martlesham was as immaculate as ever. What had changed was something inside. He wasn't fighting any more.

'I was ill during the summer.' He wasn't asking for sympathy, merely stating a fact. 'I would have written to you sooner. I was sorry to hear about your friends. What was their name?'

'Byfield.'

'I saw it in the papers.'

'Their daughter's in the café now. She's having a lovely time and lots of ice-cream.'

'Claudia likes children. Now Franco's grown up, what she needs is grandchildren. Do you want anything, Mrs Appleyard? Tea or coffee?'

'No, thank you.'

'I don't like loose ends,' he said. 'It wasn't me who hired that private detective. I think I've seen him once or twice, watching the café. Claudia noticed him too . . . They're very good to me, in their way, her and Franco. But I didn't hire the man, I promise you that.'

'I know.'

'But I want to know who did. It's a worry, you see.'

'I got it the wrong way round, Mr Martlesham. It wasn't you trying to find your sister. It was your sister trying to find you.'

In his shock he turned to face me. The left-hand side of his face was worse than it had been before. I guessed he'd had another stroke over the summer. He licked his lips and leant across the desk, cupping his ear with his hand.

'Who?'

'Your sister Nancy.'

He sat back in his chair. Breathing heavily, he pulled a handkerchief from his trouser pocket, dabbed his forehead and blew his nose. 'Tell me, please. What happened?'

So I explained that Francis Youlgreave had kept his promise and that Nancy was indeed a lady, and in more senses than one. I said I'd talked to her, and tried to describe the Old Manor House. He listened, nodding his head slowly.

'Do you want her address?' I said.

'No.'

For a moment neither of us spoke. The old man's mouth worked, as though he was chewing words. I thought of him as old, though he was only sixty-seven.

'He was a good man,' Martlesham said at last. 'Canon Youlgreave. I always said he was.'

'I know you did.'

Now I had the opportunity. Now I had a chance to ask the question. Perhaps the last chance. And I didn't want to do it. Because Martlesham was dying and none of us can face too much undiluted truth, whether about other people or ourselves. I looked around the room with its battered ex-War Department furniture. I wanted to go home, back to Veedon Hall and Henry.

'Do you think he was a good man?' Martlesham barked, making me jump. 'Do you, do you?'

The colour had risen in his face. His right hand, the one unaffected by the stroke, was trembling on the blotter. I thought he might be on the verge of another stroke.

'I think he did some good things,' I said. 'And he did some bad things too. Like most of us. But perhaps he went to extremes, and in both directions.'

'What do you mean?'

'Your sister, Lady Youlgreave – she hired Munro to trace you and to find out what people knew about Francis Youlgreave. Why do you think she did that?'

He shrugged one shoulder. 'How do I know?'

'I think perhaps you could guess. Why don't you want to see her now?'

'I told you why.'

'You said that in the past, when you came back to England, you would have been an embarrassment to her, and that she thought you'd sold her. Maybe both those things were true, but there was something else, wasn't there?'

His right hand raised itself on its fingers and scuttled slowly across the blotter. He stared at his hand, not me.

'Did you know your aunt was alive until very recently, until June?'

He raised his eyes. Slowly he nodded.

'And did you know you've got a cousin, too – Wilfred Gotobed?'

'You talked to them?'

'Yes.'

'*Aunt Em* talked to you?'

'She was careful what she said, of course, she had to be. For the same reason you had to be, and Lady Youlgreave. Lady Youlgreave most of all.'

His nails scraped the blotter, as though trying to scratch out something. 'I'm tired. I must ask you to leave.'

'I will.' I stood up, smoothed down my skirt and picked up my handbag. 'But before I go, Mr Martlesham, I'll tell you what I think happened. Mrs Gotobed said that when she wanted to get married, the children were a problem, her sister's children, because Sammy Gotobed didn't want them. At the time I thought she meant you and Nancy. But that didn't make sense, because you were more or less off her hands. You were working at the Bishop's Palace before your mother died, and living there too. Then Canon Youlgreave sent you off to Canada. Either way, you wouldn't have been much of a burden on your aunt.'

'She was an old woman. She got confused about how old I was.'

'And then you told me, the last time I saw you, that your mother had died in childbirth. Mrs Gotobed said that before she married her verger, she lived in lodgings and your mother's children came to live with her. The landlady complained about the trouble and the mess they made. "I'm not a nursemaid," that's what she said.'

The hands were completely still now.

'Even if you *had* been living with them, a thirteen-year-old boy with a job of his own wouldn't have needed a nursemaid.'

Martlesham had old man's eyes surrounded by crumpled skin and swimming with moisture. I watched a tear gathering on the lower lid of the right eye.

'*Children*,' I said. 'More than one.'

He said nothing. He blinked, and the tear vanished.

'What happened to the baby?'

He didn't answer, would never answer. Nor would any of them. Francis Youlgreave had given the three of them a future, Simon, Nancy and Aunt Em, and in return he took the baby. It had been simple. All that remained were a few fragments of the crime.

'I could find out,' I said. 'I could go to Somerset House and look for the birth certificate.'

Martlesham's head twitched and something like a smile crept across the ruined face.

I knew then it was no use. The birth hadn't been registered. This was a slum baby, an orphan, unwanted by the living and expected to die. So even the victim had been legally non-existent, just as Rosie legally could not be a murderer.

A new-born baby is so small. Not very different in size

from a cat or a chicken, and much less able to defend itself. Simon and Mrs Gotobed might not have known what would happen, though perhaps they had guessed. But Nancy?

Simon Martlesham wouldn't meet my eyes. I left the room, closing the door quietly behind me. I wiped my eyes and blew my nose. On the far side of the ribbons, Rosie was sitting in state at one of the tables surrounded by an audience of admiring women and finishing a bowl of ice-cream daubed with chocolate sauce. It took me a while to drag her away. The sad-faced woman would not let me pay the bill.

The taxi driver looked up from his *Post* as we came out of the café. I shook my head and pointed at the telephone box on the corner of Fetter Passage. I took Rosie's hot, sticky hand and tugged her towards it. I opened the door of the box and a warm waft of urine and vinegar swept out.

'It's smelly,' Rosie said. 'Who are you ringing?'

'Just someone I know. You can wait outside.'

She stood by the box and talked to Angel while I phoned directory enquiries. I was lucky – I had been afraid the Old Manor House number might be ex-directory, and I knew that if I didn't try now, I never would. *Consume the better part, No more. For therein lies the deepest art* . . . Pregnant women have odd fancies and sudden, overwhelming fears. That's what Henry would think when I told him about this.

If I told him.

The voice of a woman I didn't recognize crackled in my ear. I pressed the button, gave my name and asked for Lady Youlgreave.

'Tell her it's about Uncle Francis,' I said.

I waited, my left hand resting on my stomach, my baby.

A moment later, Lady Youlgreave came on the line. 'Mrs Appleyard. What can I do for you?'

'I've just seen Simon.'

'Who?'

'Your brother.'

'I hope you didn't give him my address.'

'He doesn't want to see you.'

'Why have you been pestering him now?'

I was bobbing on a great tide of emotion, anger and fear,

revulsion and pity, rising higher and higher. 'I know what happened. I know about the baby.'

'Do you indeed. Which baby might that be?'

'Your little brother or sister. The one that Francis Youlgreave bought. What sex was it? Did you even give it a name?'

'I beg your pardon?'

'Did you help him kill it?'

'What a vivid imagination you have,' Lady Youlgreave said, and put down the phone.

'Why are you crying?' Rosie said as we walked down Fetter Passage towards our taxi.

I couldn't be bothered to pretend. 'Because people are such a terrible mixture of good and bad.'

Rosie tossed her head as though I'd said something so childish it was beneath contempt.

'Nobody's perfect,' she said. 'Except Angel.'